PRAISE FOR
THE MURDER HOLE

"...there's time to savor the complexities of the story and take in the scent and sense of Scotland. The author has a wonderful sense of humor and a gives us a story that moves right along and a heroine who doesn't take herself too seriously."

—Diana Vickery, *Cozy Library*

"Carl creates vivid images of the Scottish scenery and her characters ring true. There is an element of woo-woo involved in figuring out the mystery, but it seems appropriate to the setting. This is a thoroughly enjoyable addition to the series."

—Shirley H. Wetzel for Over My Dead Body.com

"The legend of Loch Ness has been around for a long time. Will it finally be put to rest? Will the mystery of what lies beneath the deep finally be solved? These are intriguing questions that you will just have to read the book to find out."

— Penny at *Lovesromancesandmore.com*

THE MURDER HOLE

LILLIAN STEWART CARL

WILDSIDE PRESS

To the Antipodean wise woman, Sylvia Kelso.

THE MURDER HOLE

This edition published in 2009 by Wildside Press.
www.wildsidepress.com

ONE

When Jean Fairbairn picked up the newspaper from her desk and turned to the friends melting into her couch, she felt as though she were picking up a gauntlet and choosing her seconds. "Did you see today's *Scotsman?*" she asked, and read aloud:

> Inverness — American scientist Roger Dempsey arrives at Loch Ness today to launch his Water Horse Expedition. He intends to prove once and for all whether Nessie is an actual animal or merely the sort of beastie one sees on the way home from the pub. "The carvings on the Pitclachie Stone," he says, "are incontrovertible evidence that the ancient Picts were familiar with the race of creatures we now call Loch Ness monsters. They clearly show the creature's head emerging from the water."
>
> Experts at the Museum of Scotland who've studied the Pitclachie Stone say that it's an incomplete class I Pictish carved stone, dating from almost 2000 years ago, and that the symbols are typical of its time period.
>
> The Stone is situated on Pitclachie Farm above Loch Ness, the home of environmental activist Iris Mackintosh. Miss Mackintosh declined an interview, saying only that Dr. Dempsey is not the first amateur scientist to see what he wants to see.
>
> Dempsey dismisses the anonymous letter warning him off the expedition as the work of a crackpot, and will open the Midsummer Monster Madness Festival as scheduled. The Northern Constabulary is making inquiries.

Jean shoved her glasses up the damp bridge of her nose and sent a significant look toward her guests. While she theorized that most married couples grew to resemble each other, this thirty-something couple had probably looked alike from the beginning, their faces sculpted by intelligence, humor, and the refusal to suffer fools gladly. Although who was the fool now — Dempsey, Mackintosh, or Jean herself — remained to be seen.

"And you're away to interview the pair of them?" Michael Campbell-Reid asked. "Nothing like a bit of controversy and a threat or two for increasing the circulation. Yours and the magazine's as well, I reckon."

"Yes, Iris agreed to an interview with no problem, but then, she's never met me. Roger has, and he won't be so eager to please. Neither might the person who sent the anonymous letter to him."

Michael's wife, Rebecca, said, "Good luck," but either her tone added a silent *you're going to need it* or Jean's strolling paranoia added it in.

That Jean was taking the high road to Loch Ness tomorrow was one reason she was sweating. Not with heat-sweat, with flop-sweat. Luck? Never underestimate the power of luck, for good and for bad. Or was it luck alone that had turned her last trip out of town for an interview into a case of murder, which in turn had introduced her to a certain Northern Constabulary detective? Maybe it had been the variety of luck called fate.

Through the nearby window the Princes Street gardens and the rooftops of Edinburgh shimmered in a haze of heat, light, and water vapor. Jean felt as though she were looking into deep water through a glass-bottomed boat. But water in this part of the world more often hid than revealed. Especially the haunted waters of Loch Ness, its abyssal depths dark with peat and cold with snow-melt. Loch Ness never gave up its dead — or so the story went.

Her business was checking out stories. Some held water, some didn't, and some were about much more than H_2O.

She set the newspaper on the desk, next to the Kelly-green stuffed Nessie toy that had arrived with Dempsey's press kit, and opened the window to its miserly limit. A warm breath of diesel, damp, and the sea filtered into the room. Ladies might glow, not sweat, but right now a runnel of glow trickled down her back beneath her T-shirt like the ectoplasmic tingle of a ghost along her senses. Stifling the sensation, she sat down next to her guests. "This is the first time since I moved here I've been hot. Of course, back in Texas we'd be wearing sweaters because of the air-conditioning."

"Hot? Speak for yourself. I'm toting around a little furnace, a.k.a baby Linda." Rebecca patted the globe of her abdomen, which strained against her *Scottish: The Next Generation* hatching T-shirt.

With a glance at his wife's stomach like that of a farmer inspecting his crops, Michael uttered a string of diphthongs and glottal stops that Jean interpreted as, "That's as may be, hen. Just now it's time to be off. Some of us are working for a living."

"No need to be stroppy just because I'm on leave." Rebecca might be the American part of the Campbell-Reid equation, but her accent was catching up fast with her husband's. She heaved herself toward the edge of the couch. Michael took her hands and hauled her to her feet, where she swayed a moment, orienting her center of gravity.

Jean stood up with considerably less physical effort — it was her psychic center of gravity that had been wobbling lately — and picked up the brown envelope lying on the coffee table. "May I take this with me?"

"Oh aye," said Michael. "The Museum has copies aplenty."

Jean pulled the large black and white photograph from the envelope. She'd already inspected it over tea and fortune cookies, but it was worth several more looks.

Judging by the meter stick propped against the fine-grained rock, the Pitclachie Stone stood about four feet tall and tapered smoothly upward to a jagged rim. The photographer's raking light, light that would have made a human face resemble a bleached skull, here cast the carved symbols into razor-sharp relief. A decorated crescent crossed by a right-angled line was paired with a horse's head that looked like the knight from a chess seat. A line beneath the horse's head could represent anything from the sculptor trying out his stroke to, as Dempsey claimed, the surface of Loch Ness.

Just above the crescent, a small hole pierced the rock. A figure eight-shaped symbol called a double disc barely fit between that and the broken edge, implying that a fourth symbol, the other half of a second pair, had been carved on the lost piece.

The stone conjured times past. It evoked human hands long gone to dust and thoughts lost beyond memory. If it had a voice, it would be calling Jean to its side. Even if none of her interviews produced anything to write about in her history-and-travel magazine, her journey would be worthwhile just to see this stone. "What a shame it's broken. I guess some old farmer thought a symbol stone was no more than pagan rubbish. At least he re-used part of it as a doorstep — face downward, thankfully."

"Oh aye," said Michael. "Save the Stone was broken a bit too recently for comfort. That edge isna weathered at all, not like the hole, so smooth it's dished out. Neither's the surface of the stone itself."

"Oh. I see." Jean turned the photo this way and that, and had to agree that the serrations along the broken rim were sharp as teeth, so long as the teeth were molars, not incisors. That was an even bigger shame, that someone would use a steel chisel on the stone . . . A chisel? Wouldn't ordinary vandals use a sledgehammer? "Do you think Ambrose Mackintosh did it?"

"He said he found the Stone there at Pitclachie Farm when he renovated an old cottage," Rebecca said. "But he didn't write about it in his *Pictish Antiquities*. He barely wrote about his amateur excavating at all, more shame to him. Or where he found that hoard of bronze and silver artifacts. To his generation archaeology meant collecting antiquities, not mapping out postholes."

"Maybe he thought he could get twice the money if he sold two stones instead of one," said Jean.

"Even in the nineteen-twenties, he'd know a Class I Pictish stone was more valuable in one piece. Besides, he didn't try to sell it. He didn't even tell anyone he had it. It was Iris who reported it to the Museum, just last year."

"We were hoping you'd be asking her for the details," added Michael, "considering the Museum's not got the resources for a proper excavation at Pitclachie. And the site's on private land, not endangered by construction or the like. Whatever's beneath the sod is better off there, considering an archaeologist murders his witnesses."

While Jean appreciated that excavating a site destroyed it, and agreed that not publishing your results was the equivalent of burning and pillaging, she would have shied away from that particular metaphor. More sweat trickled down her back. She should consider trying out for an anti-perspirant commercial.

Rebecca's roll of her eyes toward Michael — no, diplomacy was not his forte — footnoted her cheery, "Good luck."

Well, Jean told herself in as chipper an internal voice she could muster, since the Campbell-Reids had not one but two murder cases in their past, the fact that Michael didn't shy away might mean that the raw scabs of memory could eventually turn into scars. She slipped the photo back into its envelope and said, "Yeah, right, that's a great way to start the interview. Hey, Iris, did your dad indulge in a bit of archaeological vandalism along with Nessie-spotting and wizard-watching?"

"Wizard-watching, eh?" Michael repeated, undaunted by Rebecca's wifely disapproval. "You're covering — or uncovering, rather — Ambrose's old scandal, are you?"

"I'm afraid so. That's Miranda's idea. She runs *Great Scot*, you know, I'm just the silent partner. I can't blame her for trying to get more bang for the bucks — the pounds — she's spending to set me up in Iris's B&B." Jean put the photo on her desk, picked up a plastic Waterstone's bag, and pulled a paperback book from inside. Its cover was decorated with black and white drawings of symbols as enigmatic as those on any Pictish stone. In lurid red letters across the top was written, *Loch Ness: the Realm of the Beast. By Ambrose Mackintosh.* "No, this isn't about Nessie. It's a reprint of Ambrose's biography of his guru, Aleister Crowley."

"That nut case back in the early twentieth century who claimed to be a magician?" Rebecca took the book and flipped through it.

"He was an egotistical maniac," said Michael. "So mad for attention he named himself the Beast from Revelations, created his own religion, and made a meal of the scandals. Went through women like loo paper, drove more than one to suicide."

Rebecca considered a chapter heading. "He had a house at Loch Ness, didn't he?"

"Oh aye," Michael said. "I was raised in Inverness, mind. Folk thereabouts are right affectionate toward Nessie, with her turning a few bob for the community and all. Never saw so much as an air bubble myself, but there are those who swear something's there. Crowley, now, they're squeamish about Crowley. His estate at Boleskine has an eerie air even today."

"Any ghosts?" asked Rebecca with refreshing matter-of-factness.

"Never hung about long enough to notice. And I canna speak for Pitclachie, either. Still, my granny was dead certain Ambrose murdered his wife in some sort of occult ceremony."

"The verdict at his trial was Not Proven. The prosecutors had no body and no real evidence, police procedure being a lot more casual in nineteen-thirty-three than it is now." *As I know only too well,* Jean added to herself, anything but chipper. She took the book from Rebecca's hand and fanned its pages, casting a wisp of cool breeze on her face. "Not that evidence is Ambrose's strong point — he says here that Crowley was really able to work magic. Exhibit A being Nessie, which he called from another reality."

Rebecca grinned. "That theory is as good as the one that says Nessie is the escaped pet of aliens who dropped by the loch in their UFO for a picnic."

"And just as likely," said Michael. "Strange how no one said a verifiable word about Nessie until Ambrose Mackintosh reported that first spate of sightings in nineteen-thirty-three. Not even C rowley, who'd have taken credit if there'd been credit to take."

"It's the strange that's going to make this story — these stories — ones that will sell magazines. That's the idea, at least." Jean set the book down on the desk beside the photo and the Nessie toy. "Speaking of pets. Not to mention aliens . . ."

Her cat, Dougie, lay along the windowsill, his paws extended like a miniature gray sphinx, his ears rotated toward her. When she walked over and picked him up, he lay as limp in her arms as a fur stole, his half-open amber eyes saying: *The shrine isn't open just now, formal services are at mealtime.*

"You're going to visit Riccio for a few days," Jean informed him. She carried Dougie into the bedroom and thrust him into the pet carrier hidden behind the bed so swiftly he didn't have time to transform into a feline caltrop and jam himself in the opening. Only when the gate clicked behind him did he realize what was up, and Jean felt his baleful gaze through the air holes.

She dumped his creature comforts into the empty Waterstone's bag, added Dempsey's toy Nessie, and handed the bag to Michael. "Thanks for taking the little guy in. Usually Hugh next door looks after him, but he and his band are finishing their tour at the Festival this weekend. It's actually been quiet around here — I love folk-rock, but not through the wall at two a.m."

Michael, himself a piper, grinned. "Eh, what's that you say?"

Rebecca laughed. "If you don't mind carrying Dougie, Jean, we'll walk up to the High Street and hail a taxi there. I need to keep moving."

"Sure." Hoisting the cat carrier, Jean followed the others outside and shut the door.

"Mind your step, hen." Michael's hand hovered solicitously at Rebecca's elbow as she started picking her way across the cobblestone courtyard of Ramsay Garden.

From here, the tall brightly painted buildings with their whimsical cupolas and balconies seemed merely an idiosyncratic collection of apartments. It was only from Princes Street that you could see the full picture, the fanciful structures wedged in between the medieval threat of the Castle and the Victorian sanctimony of the University School of Divinity. But then, the street plan of Edinburgh was only one exercise in perspective.

Rebecca's rosy complexion ripened to crimson and her steps faltered. Michael put his arm around her, propelling her up the steep slope of Ramsay Lane. Jean dragged along behind. Dougie was gaining weight at every step — on purpose, she was sure.

They emerged onto the High Street and stood panting next to the door of the Camera Obscura. The shadow cast by the tall medieval buildings only partly relieved the hot, acrid air trapped in the tunnel of the street. To the right the Castle loomed beyond thickets of pipes and braces. Already the bleachers for the yearly Festival were under construction. Statues of various historical worthies looked as though they were playing hide and seek in the scaffolding.

Scaffolds of death and dismemberment had once stood on the castle esplanade. If Aleister Crowley or Ambrose Mackintosh had lived several hundred years ago, they'd have met those scaffolds up close and personally. But now sudden death was shocking, not just one more encounter on your way to dinner. Thank goodness, Jean thought, for changing human perspective.

Michael gestured. A taxi that had just dropped off a couple at the posh Witchery Restaurant made a U-turn and pulled up to the curb. Jean opened the rear door and stowed the pet carrier inside. "Dougie, remember you're Riccio's guest and behave accordingly." Behind the grating, Dougie's bright eyes closed, resigned to his fate.

"Thanks for dinner." Rebecca managed a sideways hug. "Have a good trip, okay? Don't worry, nothing's going to sneak up on you."

"Nope, I'll be glancing over my shoulder so often I'll see it coming." Jean returned the hug. "You know me. I'm evidence that worry works — ninety-five per cent of what I worry about never happens."

With an encouraging wink at Jean, Michael piloted Rebecca into the interior of the taxi and clambered in after her, leaving Jean to admire not only his denim-clad posterior, but also how he could protect his wife without patronizing her. "Give us a shout if you find the rest of the Pitclachie Stone or anything else Ambrose left lying about in his shrubbery. Or if Dempsey turns up Nessie, though I'm not holding my breath for that."

"Oh he'll turn up something. He always does." Jean stood waving as the taxi moved off.

In the distance a siren wailed. A tourist bus lumbered off down the High Street, known more evocatively as the Royal Mile, strewing myth like pixie dust among the shops, pubs, and offices of real life. But then, myth — personal, national, and everywhere in between — was real life.

And right now real life demanded that Jean go home and pack. She might not be entirely resigned to her fate, but at least she could meet it wearing clean underwear. She made a firm about-face and found herself confronting the window of the Tartan Weaving Mill.

On it was taped a poster: Midsummer Monster Madness, sponsored by Starr Beverages PLC and the NEW! Cameron Arms Hotel. Drumnadrochit, Loch Ness, June 21-23. Beneath the words a green cartoon dragon wearing a Glengarry bonnet held a pint of beer in one hand — not flipper, hand — and a set of bagpipes in the other. The conceit was innocuous to the point of banality, the cold depths of the loch notwithstanding.

With a wry shrug, Jean headed back to Ramsay Garden. She was just skirting a shiny red sports car that was now parked next to and repeating the color of her potted geraniums when she realized her front door was standing open. What with Dougie, she hadn't locked it. But she could have sworn she'd shut it.

Oh boy. And then there was the myth that your own doorstep was free of danger. Clenching her fists at her sides, she climbed the steps and paused on the threshold. "Hello?"

Two

From inside came Miranda Capaldi's melodious voice. "It's only me."

"Oh, hi!" Feeling vaguely indignant — she'd earned her paranoia the hard way, darn it — Jean shut the door. She should have recognized the car. It belonged to Miranda's — well, Duncan wasn't a boyfriend, with the soda-shop implications of that word. And "lover" was a bit bald for such a civilized relationship.

"Sorry!" Like a cuckoo clock, Miranda glanced out of the kitchen doorway and then vanished back inside. "I came round with the papers for your hire car and chapped at the door like a proper guest, and then I thought I'd just try the knob, and I was inside before I quite knew what I was about. I've just missed your friends from the Museum, have I?"

"Afraid so." Jean found her friend and business partner spooning leftover Szechuan tofu and rice onto a clean plate.

"May I?" Miranda asked. "Your meal smells delicious. And fortune cookies as well! Super!" Her manicured fingertips played a solo on the microwave, the tiny diamonds on her tennis bracelet winking. Today her crest of hair was chestnut red. Fashionable high-water pants and a pastel cotton sweater accentuated a figure that was almost as slender at forty as it had been at twenty, when she and Jean were college roommates. The brilliant silk scarf draped around her shoulders probably revealed the designer's name to anyone sophisticated enough to recognize the symbols, or logos, as they were now called. The symbols on the Pitclachie Stone must have carried similar meaning.

Self-consciously Jean brushed crumbs off her size medium T-shirt with its decorative dribble of soy sauce — her chopsticks, like the plans of mice and men, had gone oft agley. She'd long ago given up on fashion just as she'd given up on calculus, and was fond of saying she couldn't tell the difference between Armani and Old Navy. Which, Miranda was fond of retorting, was snobbery of its own. That Jean had just recently started coloring the strands of gray infiltrating her mop of brown hair she attributed to Miranda's influence, not self-consciousness, no, not at all.

"You're away first thing the morn, then," Miranda stated. "No need to go writing up the Festival, though you'll be asking Iris her opinion of it. She'll say it's all for the tourists, I expect."

"I'm not much more than a glorified tourist myself."

"Ah, no, like Dorothy in the Emerald City, you've seen behind the screen."

"That's my job, writing about what's behind the screen."

The microwave beeped. Miranda extracted her plate and set it on the cabinet. Rejecting chopsticks in favor of a knife and fork, she assessed a small bite. "Mmmm. Nice burn. You've got a dab hand with a chili pepper, Jean."

"I was weaned on a jalapeno." Jean started filing the plates and glasses in the dishwasher. "Michael and Rebecca told me a bit about Ambrose Macintosh. But what can I expect from Iris?"

"She's a bit of an eccentric, but not so much as her father, not by a long chalk. Mind you, I don't know her well. We cross paths at meetings of Scotland the Green, when they're sharing out the grants for deer fences, re-forestation, mountain path repair, and such."

"She's a board member, isn't she?"

"Oh aye. And you're not invited to sit on the board unless you've donated a packet to the cause, as I'm knowing all too well. The B&B must be quite the success. Could be Iris inherited from her mum, the American heiress, or is selling off her father's collections. I'll ask about, shall I?"

What financial and social blips on the contemporary Scottish radar Miranda didn't know weren't worth knowing. "Please don't. I'll be prying into her personal affairs quite enough as it is." Jean shooed a fly away from the pots and pans piled in the sink, turned on the hot water, and added a squirt of Fairy Liquid. Steam billowed. Soap bubbles went floating upward, each one a tiny prism.

Rebecca had volunteered Michael to help clean the kitchen, but cleaning was Jean's guilty pleasure. She could achieve the same sort of Zen contemplative state washing, drying, mopping, and sweeping as she could knitting, with the bonus that she then had a tidy environment. Her ex-husband Brad used to say her zeal for tidiness was a control issue. She hadn't argued with that. She hadn't argued with much at all. That was one reason for the divorce. Love hadn't turned to hate, but to apathy.

Jean realized Miranda had gone ominously silent. "What?" she asked.

"You're having a problem asking Iris about Ambrose, then."

"Sort of," Jean admitted. "Whether Ambrose was mistaken about seeing Nessie or whether he was committing a fraud is the question, and not one Iris may want to answer — assuming she knows the answer — especially now that the story has taken on a life of its own. Although, to give Ambrose the benefit of the doubt, weird things do happen."

"Weird things happen to you," Miranda stated, knowing that

nothing weird would dare sully her own well-organized life, and mashed the last of the rice onto the back of her fork.

"I used to think weird things happened only to me. Brad had me convinced of it, at least."

"He was wrong."

"No, he was playing it safe." Jean rinsed off Miranda's empty plate and placed it in the dishwasher.

"If everyone played safely we'd have no stories to write, would we now? Look at Iris's mother's disappearance and all. There's a grand mystery for you to solve. Me, I'm thinking post-partum depression and suicide by loch, but then, Ambrose was tried for murder." Miranda leaned over and stirred the fortune cookies in their bowl. She looked like an oracle searching for an omen rather than simply making sure she chose one whose cellophane wrapper hadn't come open.

"Miranda, when you spoke with Iris, what did you tell her I was going to ask?"

"I didn't speak with Iris. I spoke with Kirsty-something, who booked the room and said she'd set up an interview."

"Aha! Iris will assume I'll be asking about her work, not ambushing her about her parents' personal lives."

Miranda chose a cookie and looked around. "If you're afraid of asking tough questions, then you're in the wrong profession."

"If you want me to be an investigative reporter, then you took on the wrong partner. There are questions, and there's digging through dirty laundry. I bought into *Great Scot* because I wanted to drag historical skeletons out of closets, not air contemporary scandals. No one appreciates privacy issues more than I do."

"Privacy? Or secrecy? There's a difference. You've not lost your nerve, have you now . . ." Miranda bit her sentence short. Her eyes softened. "Ah, Jean, I'm sorry. If you're not remembering your own scandal, then you're remembering what happened when you went asking questions last month. You're quite right. *Great Scot* is no tabloid rag."

"Don't apologize. Someone's got to rouse the rabble here. It's just that I've realized what a hypocrite I can be — show me yours, but I won't show you mine. I've seen how curiosity can kill, and not just kill me, either." Jean swished her dishcloth through the suds, her grimace suddenly buffered by a chuckle. In her old life she had been accused of asking too many questions. Making a new life out of asking questions had seemed like vindication. Discovering that not all the answers were ones she wanted to hear was poetic justice. Since justice was a rare enough event, she could live with that. Or so she intended. "What do you want to bet that my curiosity is only hiding under the bed, like Dougie does when he thinks he's completely concealed but his tail is sticking out in plain sight?"

"There you are," said Miranda, with one of her wise expressions. She tore the cellophane away from the cookie and wadded it crinkling into a ball. "I'll not be telling you that history doesn't repeat itself. You and I both know better than that. And we're knowing that it can catch you up no matter where you are or what you're doing."

"Well, yes."

"And aye, I'm after being a bit cavalier with Iris's feelings, but then, I don't know what her feelings are, do I? Could be she'd fancy a chance to tell her story."

True enough. "In other words, when I fall off my professional horse into a murder investigation, I should climb right back on?"

"Oh aye. Just that." Case closed, Miranda cracked her cookie. She read, "'A man's good name is his finest possession.'"

"No kidding. And a woman's good name is hers."

"You made your point about that, right enough, when you sued the university for unlawful termination and won. Well done, Jean." Crunching, Miranda reached for a dishtowel.

It was done, whether well or not. Feeling like Lady Macbeth washing her hands, Jean pulled the stopper out of the sink. With a gurgle the water spiraled down the drain.

Miranda polished the large platter, made a face at her reflection, and said with lead-footed nonchalance, "I suppose the Monster Madness folk will be laying on extra policemen for the weekend. For the odd drunken brawl and the like. Not to mention the odd anonymous letter threatening the paying customers."

"Probably," Jean returned. Rats. She'd been doing a great job of suppressing her queasiness over Dempsey's threatening letter.

"Drumnadrochit's on the Northern Constabulary's patch, isn't it? Your chum D.C.I. Cameron might be there."

She hadn't been doing so well suppressing her squeamishness over Alasdair Cameron. Her nonchalance just as heavy, she said, "He's not my chum. He's just a business acquaintance. An acquaintance made during a bad business."

"Right."

"Besides, he's a detective. They'll only have the uniformed cops there. The plods."

"You've not heard from Cameron, then? Or worse, you've not contacted him?"

"No, why should I? Maybe we'll run into each other — eventually I'll have to testify about the murder last month . . ." And how would she react then? Jean imagined the formal handshake and the sort of polite, "Hello, how are you?" that didn't require a truthful answer. Not that that would fool either of them.

"And this Cameron Arms Hotel in Drumnadrochit, the name's only a coincidence, is it?"

"Of course it is. Cameron's a common name. It's not a sign of any . . . Oh."

Miranda was grinning, the tease. Still, her keen perception was sandpaper against Jean's rationalizations. Fine-grained sandpaper, like a jeweler would use to polish precious metal, but any sandpaper scraped harshly against a scab. "Damn it, now you're ambushing me!"

"You were telling me you moved house to Scotland because you were tired of playing it safe."

"Yes, I did. And I am." Jean rinsed out the sink, splashing so vigorously a wave leaped onto her T-shirt. "Oh, for the love of . . ."

Her grin going lopsided, bracketing sympathy and amusement, Miranda handed over the dishtowel and wandered discreetly away.

The air in the kitchen was no longer scented with garlic and soy but with Fairy Liquid and a whiff of Miranda's perfume, a clean, fresh scent like the intoxicating smell of the Highlands. With a smile, one a lot dryer than her shirt, Jean threw in the towel.

From the television in the living room came a reporter's oh-so-sincere voice. ". . . Madness, sponsored by Starr Beverage PLC here at Loch Ness."

THREE

Jean found Miranda sitting on the couch, waving the television remote like a wand. "ITN's reporting on the Festival just now."

The screen was filled by the image of a large pavilion set up in a field beside several buildings, all silhouetted against a green hillside. Flags, both national and decorative, rippled in the wind while people bustled around with speakers, coils of wire, and chairs. Another shot filled the screen, the familiar picture postcard of Urquhart Castle on the shores of the loch. The ruinous red stone walls cut a ragged edge against a mirage-like shimmer of water, reminding Jean of the mutilated symbol stone.

"This ancient castle," said the reporter's voice-over, "dates back to Pictish times. It was visited by Saint Columba. Here he saved one of his followers from the monster. The famous Shiels photograph of the monster was taken from here. Dr. Shiels said he called the monster from the loch with his telepathic powers."

There was the photo, of an open-mouthed serpent's head rising from the waves. The picture could just as well have been, and probably was, of a plastic dinosaur in a farm pond. Jean laughed. "Are they going for the record amount of misinformation or what?"

"Ah, but the consumers make a meal of it," Miranda pointed out.

Back to the reporter, who held up a rubber Nessie probably made in Hong Kong, and squeezed a squeak from it. His smirk said as clearly as words, *what a joke.* "A new Nessie-hunting expedition is launching this weekend. Operation Water Horse is directed by Dr. Roger Dempsey, from the Omnium Technology Organization in Chicago, America."

"His degree is in business administration," Jean told Miranda, "and his doctorate is honorary. He's a dilettante like Ambrose Mackintosh, except he's using electronic devices that Ambrose would have thought were magic."

Dempsey's image appeared on the screen. It had been seven or eight years since they'd met, although she'd seen a recent photo in the press kit he'd sent *Great Scot* — and no doubt every other media outlet in the UK. Animated, his scrub brush of a beard framing a grin too knowing to be childlike, the bill of his baseball cap bobbing and weaving, Dempsey seemed more like a teenager on a joy ride than a businessman testing the company product. The wrinkles framing his eyes and the gray streaks in his facial hair looked like aging make-up troweled onto a youth performing in a high school play.

"Dr. Dempsey," asked the television reporter, "has the arrival of a second threatening letter discouraged you in any way?"

"Second?" Jean asked. "There's been another one?"

"Well, well, well." If Miranda had been a cat, her whiskers would have gone on alert.

Or maybe ill, ill, ill, Jean thought, but held her tongue.

"Those letters are too wishy-washy to be threats," answered Dempsey. "We're not going to give up our quest for the truth because some yellow-bellied yahoo who's afraid to face me sends a few letters saying that Loch Ness never gives up its dead, that sort of pure-D crap."

True, Jean thought, people who sent anonymous letters weren't automatically confrontational. But false, people drowned quickly and easily in the cold, dark waters of the loch, if drowning could be considered an easy death, and their corpses were seldom recovered. Loch Ness was one of the deepest bodies of water in Britain, given to odd winds and waves, as dangerous as it was beautiful. Long before Ambrose or anyone else spotted Nessie, the loch itself had been a tourist destination. There was a reason Nessie was sometimes equated with the water horse, the *each uisge* of Celtic legend, a creature that bore unwary riders down into the depths.

The reporter asked Dempsey, "Do you have any idea who's sending the letters?"

"The scientific establishment doesn't want us to find any trace of the creatures that live in the loch because that might upset their preconceptions. The tourist industry doesn't want us to prove there is no monster because that would close down all the souvenir shops."

"Not bloody likely," said Miranda.

Jean said, "All the electronics in the world can't prove a negative."

"Scientists or tourist officials are trying to frighten you away?" the reporter persisted.

Dempsey waved his hand — devil take the hindmost. "Whoever it is, we're not taking their games seriously. We're not letting them disrupt our work."

"Still, you've handed the letters in to the police."

"Far be it from me to deprive the Northern Constabulary of work."

"D.C.I. Alasdair Cameron of the Northern Constabulary told us this morning that his technicians are examining the letters," the reporter intoned in an aside.

"Aha," Miranda stage-whispered. "Kismet."

The prickle of gooseflesh across Jean's shoulders — like the nettle shirt of a fairy tale — was not entirely unpleasant. But this was no time to start analyzing her feelings yet again, when, as Alasdair himself would be the first to say, there was a threat to analyze. She said, "A nut threatened and then fire-bombed an expedition back in the eighties. But two anonymous letters don't have to mean anything like that. The reporter's trying to build up his story. So is Dempsey, for that matter."

"Public relations make the world go round," said Miranda.

On the television, Dempsey plunged onward, parading his dogs and ponies. "Our expedition is using state-of-the-art remote sensing devices manufactured by Omnium. It will prove once and for all whether the Loch Ness monster exists, or has existed in the past."

"Some of your funding is from Starr Beverages, as well as your own Omnium."

"Let's face it. The Loch Ness monster is quite a draw. A real star, you might say." Dempsey's grin emphasized his pun.

The camera drew back, revealing Dempsey's T-shirt. It was emblazoned with Celtic-style letters reading, "Operation Water Horse," as well as with a design that Pictish scholars called a swimming elephant — not that Jean had ever seen elephants with trunks sprouting from their foreheads. The same symbol was also called a gripping beast, although it had neither talons nor even hands to grip with. But since Jean believed imagination was one of the most important human faculties, she couldn't fault either Picts or scholars for displaying it.

The camera panned to the side, taking in several bystanders. A woman dressed in another Water Horse T-shirt stood with her arms crossed. A broad-brimmed hat and sunglasses concealed the top half of her face, but the diamond studs in her ears winked with all the subtlety of a stop light. Mrs. Dempsey, probably. The lower half of her face was fixed in the smile of the politician's wife, appearing to hang on every word while actually thinking of England. Or Chicago, as the case may be.

Two young men, both wearing Water Horse logos, and a young woman who was not stood a few steps away. The square-shouldered and square-jawed man offered the camera a matinee-idol smile. The one whose bulbous brow indicated either intellect or Klingon ancestry, looked blank. The woman ducked out of the shot, leaving Jean with an impression of long silky brown hair veiling a delicate face out of a pre-Raphaelite painting of Ophelia. Drowned Ophelia . . Imagination, Jean reminded herself, was a wonderful servant but a poor master.

"Not everyone is pleased to have the controversial Dr. Dempsey here," the reporter's voice went on. "Earlier we interviewed Iris Mackintosh, the well-known eco-warrior."

Iris appeared on the screen. She looked like the sort of elderly lady Jean intended to become in the far distant future — an iron-gray-haired ramrod-straight gadfly wearing an old cardigan and a no-nonsense expression. She didn't appear to be chained to a tree, which rather undercut the reporter's *eco-warrior.*

Her gray eyes, so icy they looked silver, targeted the camera. She delivered her statement in the accent of the class and generation of Scots who'd been taught "proper English". "It has been clearly demonstrated that nothing larger than salmon lives in the loch. Sightings of the so-called monster can be attributed to natural phenomena or fraud. Dr. Dempsey is using the legend to further his own business interests, and in the process is trivializing important environmental issues such as logging run-off."

Back to Dempsey. "Hey, if there's a monster in the loch, it's part of the ecology, isn't it? My assistants and I would be glad to include Miss Mackintosh on our Saturday morning cruise for the press. She can check us out — no logging, I promise."

"And there you are," said the reporter with another nudge-nudge-wink-wink arch of his eyebrows. "The Starr Beverages PLC Midsummer Monster Madness Festival gets under way tomorrow night with fireworks and a pipe band. Be there!"

A musical interlude and a sequence of dissolving images of clouds, deserts, and monsoons, led into the weather report. It predicted a generally sunny and warm Friday for Inverness-shire, gathering clouds and cooler temperatures for Saturday, and a deluge on Sunday. That figured, Jean thought. Still, a little typical Scottish weather wasn't going to stop her curiosity from creeping out from under the bed. "You don't suppose Iris sent the letters?"

Miranda turned off the television. "I can't see her wasting her time on something like that, no. This Dempsey chap, now, he looks to be a bit of a nutter. Could be he sent them himself, for the publicity."

"It's possible, I guess. He's a no-guts no-glory type of guy. An engineer like Brad, except unlike Brad, Dempsey's mostly a businessman and a heck of a promoter. I met him once, at a conference in Colonial Williamsburg on the archaeology of standing buildings. He came sweeping through the meet-and-greet handing out copies of an article he wrote for *The Journal of Field Archaeology* that wasn't much more than a commercial for a remote sensor that can see through walls. Set my teeth on edge, I'm afraid."

"You shot him down, did you?" asked Miranda.

"I couldn't help myself. He was making some generality about the structure of medieval abbeys that was just flat wrong. I corrected him. He stared at me, turned around, and stalked off. I spent the rest of the weekend angling for a chance to — well, not apologize. To smooth things over. But he avoided me. Maybe he still is avoiding me. He never answered my e-mail confirming the interview you set up. I'll tackle him when I get to the loch."

"He'd not be avoiding you if he'd been the one to correct you," Miranda pointed out.

"You think?" replied Jean. "It's a shame Brad was out playing tourist during the conference. He would have loved to have picked Dempsey's brains."

"At least he attended the conference with you."

"That was the last one. He finally gave up trying to explain even his consulting work to me, let alone the academic stuff, just about the same time I gave up trying to explain mine to him. It was like speaking different languages, he's going on about submersibles and electro-magnetic radiation and I'm going on about the Casket Letters and the Red Book of Westmarch . . ." There was an echo in here, Jean thought. She'd told Rebecca and Michael the same anecdote, in almost the same words.

"Thinking about Brad quite a bit, are you?" asked Miranda.

"That's the first lesson in being Scottish, nursing old grudges and rehearsing old glories."

Miranda nodded, understanding Jean's sentiments if not her examples. "The Casket Letters have to do with Mary Queen of Scots, but the Red Book . . ."

"The Lord of the Rings."

"Oh aye." Miranda said politely. Her reading and movie-viewing leaned toward book-club weepies. Standing up, she reached for her handbag and produced a folder bearing a yellow Hertz label. "Here you are. A Focus. Not so posh as Duncan's Maserati, but reliable."

"That's all I ask. Thanks." Jean strolled beside Miranda toward the front door. "So are you off with Duncan, or just with his car?"

"With Duncan, of course. We thought of popping across to New York, but I'm thinking a quiet weekend — golf, dinner at the club — would go down a treat."

And sex more aesthetic than athletic, Jean thought. Not that she lusted after Duncan, a silver-haired and silver-tongued lawyer so polished Miranda must use suction cups to keep from sliding off him. He was Miranda's type, not hers. Like Miranda, Duncan wanted his champagne dry, his facts straight, and his lovers uncommitted. Although Jean had manifestly never figured out just what her own type was, she had the awful suspicion that commitment was too near her center of gravity to encourage a tidy affair like Miranda's with Duncan.

Jean watched Miranda and the Maserati disappear into the

sultry twilight, then locked the door. Just as she returned to the living room the phone rang. She hurried to the desk. "Hello?"

A hale and hearty male voice with an accent like her own, ranging between a bleat and a quack, boomed into her ear. She'd heard that voice emanating from the speaker on her television only minutes earlier. Speak of the devil. "Jean! Roger Dempsey! Long time no see!"

And the devil was speaking to her. *Go figure.* "Oh, hello, Dr. Demps . . ."

"It's Roger, it's Roger. My go-to guy, Brendan, tells me we've got an interview lined up. Tomorrow afternoon at five, on the boat at the pier in the loch, tra la!"

"Yes, that's what my colleague Mir . . ."

"So you've gone over to the enemy, you're a reporter now! Using your maiden name, huh? Glad to hear you're out of the publish and perish rat race, girl! What's Brad up to here in the Auld Country? Engineering connectors and breakers in Silicon Glen? It'll be great to see you again, hope he can come along too, we can lift a glass to old times and old friends, right?"

Wrong, on several counts, not least of which was that she was no girl. But Jean didn't owe Roger or anyone else an account of her divorce and relocation-cum-escape. "Wel . . ."

"See you tomorrow afternoon at five, okay? Cheers!"

"And cheers to you, too," Jean said, even though he'd already hung up. Switching off her phone, she eyed Ambrose's book accusingly, as though it were responsible for the holes in Dempsey's story.

In her request for an interview she'd skipped the inconvenient details, saying merely that she'd met Dempsey at the Williamsburg conference and signing her name as "Jean Fairbairn (Inglis)". Maybe he did remember her, and his remark about publish and perish was meant as a joke at his own expense.

Whatever, there were no old times to lift a glass to. Dempsey was claiming a closer and more cordial acquaintance than they'd really had. And not because of her sparkling personality. Because he wanted her to hype his expedition. Crass, yes, but hardly surprising. Although you'd think Dempsey would have learned by now to lose the egregious "girl."

However, unless she'd mentioned Brad in conference small-talk before things heated up, Dempsey had no reason to have even heard of the man . . . *Oh boy.* Jean spun away from the desk with a two-fisted gesture of frustration. Dempsey was so eager to ingratiate himself that he'd researched *her.* Once past the *Great Scot* masthead, the first items in an Internet search on her name were the headlines about her lawsuit against the university, to say nothing — and heaven only knew she'd like to say nothing — of the scandal behind it. And then there was the murder case last month, generating more headlines. His remark about going over to the enemy gave Dempsey away. It was Jean who had occasionally found the media to be her adversary. To Dempsey, reporters were the tools of his trade.

Jean stopped beside the window, considering the ghostly shape of her own reflection. If her divorce from Brad Inglis was mentioned on the net at all, it was buried so deeply that Dempsey even with his remote-sensing devices hadn't found it, and so added gaffe to presumption. Typically over-the-top, to claim Brad, too, as a friend. And odd, too, not that Jean could claim immunity from oddness.

Outside, the raking light of late evening glared off the western faces of the buildings but sank their eastern sides in blackness. Even as she watched, the light faded into a fragile gloom. Her damp T-shirt lay chill against her breast and stomach. The water horse, she thought. You get up on it, and it takes you down into the dark depths of your own soul.

If she had wanted comfort, she could have stayed in Texas, bunkered in an air-conditioned office while the sun beat on the parched earth outside. She could never have asked Alasdair Cameron to dinner, last month, as the gentle rain softened the green hills of — well, it was home now.

It was time, she told herself, for her voyage of self-discovery to include a trip down the loch with all the other tourists who hoped to see the head of something rich and strange emerge from the waters. When you know fate is lying in wait for you, you could do a lot worse than get up on your horse, water or otherwise, and ride out to meet it.

Four

Jean peered around the tour bus clogging the road ahead of her and spotted a sign reading *Pitclachie House*. At last! She two-wheeled her rented Focus into an asphalt drive before the harried paterfamilias in the car hugging her bumper got a squeaky Nessie in the ear and rear-ended her.

The big blank spot to the southeast of Loch Ness on a Scottish road map said as much about the terrain as a topographical survey. Jean had had two ways to get to Drumnadrochit from Edinburgh, neither of them remotely related to flying crows. She'd chosen the northern route, through Inverness. That way she could stop at Culloden, the 1746 battlefield, to pay her respects to Bonnie Prince Charlie's lost cause, scour the visitor center bookstore, and eat lunch. Her cup of tea and sandwich had been spiced by the presence at the next table of three re-enactors, a Highlander, a redcoat, and a woman wearing an apron splattered with red. Jean had driven away thinking that here time didn't heal, it only numbed.

The main road ran along the northwestern bank of Loch Ness, the most scenic of scenic routes, especially on a sunny day. To her left, the water had glowed an opaque indigo below the green banks and braes of its far shore. To her right, steep hills patched with yellow fields had climbed toward craggy heights skimmed by clouds. But except for quick glances, all Jean had seen was the tailpipe of a bus and its back window stacked with knapsacks.

Now she sighed in appreciation of a gust of fresh air and followed the long driveway as it wound up the hill, toward several trees from which sprouted a square tower and the peak of a roof. The former displayed a satellite dish and the latter a set of intricate Tudor-twist brick chimneys. Parking her car, Jean collected her things, turned toward the house, and thought, *Cool!*

Pitclachie House might have been built in the nineteenth-century neo-Gothic style beloved of horror movies, but in the afternoon sunshine Jean found the place enchanting, every mullioned window, half-timbered gable, and decorative spire of it. The same reddish stone as that of Urquhart Castle peered cheerily from between swags of ivy. The castellations of the tower were so crisply defined, Jean suspected it wasn't part of the original 1830's house, but was part of the renovations and improvements program Ambrose had put into effect after marrying his heiress.

A path led across the corner of a lawn smooth enough for the genteel arts of lawn bowling and croquet, and skirted a slate terrace edged by rose bushes thick with large blooms and broom thick with small blossoms. Jean made a point of stopping to smell a rose, which was blood-red, of course . . . Something rustled in the underbrush. She spun around. A cat was watching her, its fur so aggressively calico it looked as though it had been painted by Picasso. "Hello there," she said, and grinned as much at herself as at the cat.

It whisked away, like most of its species unimpressed by mere humanity. Jean walked across a courtyard, past a cottage whose door was set into a circular turret, and up to an arched porch hollowed into the facade of the main house. The door inside was equipped with a knocker shaped like a dragon dangling a brass ring from its teeth. Tapping the ring against the door, she produced a sound that was less a sepulchral thud than a comedian's rim shot. Jean's grin widened.

The door opened silently, on oiled hinges, to reveal a young woman. Her silky brown hair was swept in an Art Nouveau swirl back from a delicate face. White jeans and a lime-green blouse suggested rather than revealed a lissome figure. She gulped, probably less in awe of Jean than in swallowing her chewing gum, and smiled a well-rehearsed smile, just dignified enough to set the tone of the establishment, just friendly enough to be welcoming. "Good afternoon."

"Hello. I'm Jean Fairbairn. Miranda Capaldi booked a room for me for four nights. And she set up an interview with Miss Mackintosh."

"Oh aye. Kirsty Wotherspoon here. Please come through." The girl — she could hardly be twenty — waved Jean and her baggage into the house.

In the moment it took her eyes to adjust from sunlight to shadow, Jean saw the after-image of the scene on her TV screen last night, the young woman standing with Dempsey's assistants and then ducking aside when the camera turned in her direction. "Did I see you on television, Kirsty? The ITN piece on Operation Water Horse last night?"

Jean's vision cleared in time for her to see Kirsty's peaches-and-cream complexion redden into a strawberries-and-cream hue. Her stance went from formal to stiff, and she darted a quick glance toward a slightly open door marked *Private*. "I was having a squint at the Festival is all," she said, more loudly than was necessary.

Uh oh. The girl doth protest too much. And in a Glasgow accent that was two glottal stops short of incomprehensible. She'd probably wandered down to the Water Horse interview and then remembered that Iris, her employer, wasn't on the best of terms with Dempsey and company. Was Iris sitting behind that door, listening as Jean made a meal of her own foot? An apology would only compound her misdemeanor. She tried a diversion. "Hugh Munro and his band will be playing at the Festival. I really like his new album, don't you?"

"That I do," Kirsty returned, picking up her cue. But this time Jean was the object of the quick glance, one that barely concealed resentment.

Checking out the entrance hall gave her an excuse to break eye contact. The vaulted ceiling and stenciled arcades were exquisitely detailed. A staircase edged by intricate banisters curved upwards. Beyond it, a doorway opened onto a library. The gilded letters on the spines of leather-bound books sparkled in the light streaming through tall windows. Not the faintest breath of mold or mildew reached Jean's nostrils, only the odor of books, potpourri, and baking bread. Miranda could keep her French perfume. Jean would rather dab bits of this heady mixture behind her ears.

". . . change in plans," Kirsty was saying. "Mr. and Mrs. Bouchard booked The Lodge, our self-catering cottage, for their honeymoon. But now they're after finishing out their holiday in the main house. Aunt Iris went and transferred your booking to the cottage. At no extra charge. You're welcome to take breakfast here in the dining room and to sit in the library as well."

Aunt Iris? Well, well, well. "The Lodge is the cottage with the turret?"

"Oh aye, that. Right posh. No extra charge."

"It sounds great, no problem."

Kirsty turned toward a small table. A rack held not only the usual sightseeing brochures but also a collection of environmentalist pamphlets. Next to a wicker basket labeled "Letters" lay an iron key so large it was surely intended for a dungeon. She handed it to Jean.

The key was heavy, and so cold Jean wondered whether they'd been keeping it refrigerated. "When will Miss Mackintosh be free to talk to me?"

"She'll show you round the garden after breakfast the morn. She's mad keen to discuss her work." Kirsty's brittle voice, not to mention the upward flicker of her dark eyes, indicated that she did not share either Iris's keenness or her point of view.

From behind the private door came the sudden rattle of an old-fashioned typewriter, the clicks syncopated, as though whoever was hitting the keys was only doing so perfunctorily. Like any good Gothic house, Pitclachie's walls did have ears. Jean, too, pitched her voice a bit louder. "I want to write about her work, of course, but I was also hoping to discuss her father's work and life story as well."

"Uncle Ambrose, is it?" This time Kirsty's complexion reddened to a cherry tinge. "The Lodge — it was a farm cottage, by the road. He had it shifted up here and fitted out as his study. All gentlemen had studies then, didn't they? Places they could go shutting themselves away?"

She was still protesting too much, Jean noted. "Yes, of course they did. You're related to the Mackintoshes?"

"That I am, my great-grandmother was Ambrose's sister . . ." Making a quick sidestep toward the still-open front door, an evasive maneuver if Jean had ever seen one, Kirsty called, "Hello there! Miss Fairbairn, Charles and Sophie Bouchard."

The Bouchards, a handsome young couple dressed like fashion models, minced their way in as though avoiding stepping in dog doo. "*Bonjour*," said the woman, and the man added in French-accented English, "How do you do."

"Hello," Jean said. The couple glided on up the stairs, leaning together like twining vines. Ah. Honeymooners. Emitting a sigh more pensive than reminiscent, Jean turned back to Kirsty.

She was holding the door open, her stance so stiff she looked like a taxidermist's sample. "Thank you, Miss Fairbairn."

"It's just Jean. And thank you." Feeling like Eve turned out of Paradise even though she'd barely begun nibbling at the apple, Jean trundled her suitcase out into the courtyard. Behind her, the front door shut with a small but solid snick.

The key opened the Lodge's heavy wooden door, this one with decorative iron hinges. Jean stepped through the circular vestibule and past a burgundy velvet curtain shoved to one side, where it could stay. She wouldn't need to keep out any drafts, not this time of year.

She had half-expected the cottage to be full of quaint and curious volumes of forgotten lore, but no, Iris had done a thorough renovation to her father's study. The Lodge owed more to Martha Stewart than to Edgar Allan Poe. A fringed carpet softened the flagstone floor, and bright printed fabrics covered the furniture and the windows. A vase of flowers stood on a small dining table. Shelves held ranks of books and magazines, and a television and DVD player occupied a discreet corner.

Was that a hint of pipe tobacco below the pervading flower-and-polish aroma? She wouldn't have expected Ambrose's years in this room to be dismissed with only bleach and paint. Whether Iris had cleaned away any negative feelings or bad vibes or whatever pop culture was calling paranormal manifestations these days, Jean couldn't say. Not yet, anyway. When she was pulling away from the house on her way back home, then she'd say.

She nodded approval at the cleanliness of the kitchenette and smiled at the old photos of Nessie hanging on the walls, most of them now proved to be either fakes or mistakes. Then, leaving her canvas carryall beside the table, she dragged her suitcase up a narrow flight of stairs to a short hallway. The floor creaked expressively beneath each step.

The first of three doors was locked. A second opened into a bathroom. Through the third door she found a bedroom with a four-poster bed and a dressing table set into the bulge of the turret. The Bouchards' loss was very much her gain, although even someone who was curiosity-impaired would wonder why a honeymooning couple had retreated to the not so private house.

Curiosity-ridden Jean had no clever theories about the Bouchards, so she turned her inquisitiveness to Kirsty. Her — well, "aunt" was more respectful than cousin — Iris had obviously schooled her in upstairs manners, but her anxiety about Pitclachie's downstairs issues kept breaking through. The question was, were Kristy's issues Dempsey and his assistants, Ambrose's dubious reputation, Iris's activism, all of the above, or none of the above?

Jean hoped her remark hadn't gotten the girl into trouble, but then, if Iris had watched her interview she knew about Kirsty's visit to the expedition. Jean indulged herself while she unpacked by speculating whether the anonymous letters had been written on a typewriter.

She was contemplating her own renovations when she heard voices. Through the windows behind the dressing table she saw the courtyard and a good portion of the terrace lying before her like a stage set, with the five ivy-covered stories of the tower at dead center, ready for Rapunzel — or Kirsty — to appear at the topmost window and let down her hair.

Toward the house walked a tall thin man who looked so much like a stork Jean was surprised his legs didn't bend backwards — he had rounded shoulders, a long neck, and a sharp nose supporting thick glasses. A tow-headed little boy bounded along beside him. Behind them trudged a short, plump woman with a lank dishwater-blond ponytail and the posture of a pigeon destined for a pie.

The boy chattered away in the pluperfect accent of a child who's not yet watched enough television to corrupt his native dialect, which in this case was mid-class English. ". . . sonar readings. . . Nessie . . . dead brilliant . . . must I have a nap, Mummy?"

It was Daddy who answered. "Yes you must, Elvis, if you mean to stay awake for the fireworks. It's midsummer, won't be dark enough for fireworks 'til well past your bedtime."

"Fireworks!" Elvis's enthusiasm made his voice leap upward an octave. Oh, for the innocent enthusiasm of a child, Jean thought. He wasn't saddled by the knowledge that tonight's fireworks were the equivalent of the ancient midsummer bonfires, which were as much fertility rite as celebration.

Mother and child disappeared into the house. Father peered at the dragon knocker and scraped at it with his fingernail before following them. The red numerals on the clock radio by Jean's bed rearranged themselves to read 4:25.

Almost show time. She cleaned her glasses, applied lipstick, and ran a comb through her mop of naturally surly hair, which wouldn't be achieving any Art Nouveau effects. She added a light jacket over her shirt and pants combo, signaling that she was now on duty.

Locking the door, Jean dumped its key into her mini-backpack and checked out the exterior of the Lodge. A small skylight opened above the staircase. The window of the locked room was neatly shuttered beneath the gingerbread-carved eaves. Well, any self-respecting Gothic household needed a locked room, although this one was more likely to hold cleaning supplies than the body of Ambrose's murdered wife. Who hadn't necessarily been murdered.

Jean didn't see the harshly truncated pillar of the Pitclachie Stone rising from the stretch of lawn below the main house. It wasn't propped up in the herbaceous border along the terrace, either. She'd look for it later. Right now, on this lovely afternoon, she was going to deny that either she or this personable house had ever known death and destruction.

To her right lay the white-painted houses of Drumnadrochit. Before her lay Urquhart Bay, a deep scoop in the side of the loch. Boats large and small rode the slow waves, rubber dinghies darting like insects between them and the shore. On the far side of the bay, from a neck of land separating it from the main body of the loch, rose the tower and walls of Urquhart Castle, built in the days when travel down the Great Glen was by boat. Boats in the water, towers overlooking the water — surely, Jean thought, someone would have seen a large creature, one so unusual its presence would have made waves both literal and metaphorical.

Slinging her backpack over a shoulder, she strode off down the drive. A brisk walk would not only wake up the corpuscles in her brain, she'd earn a few extra calories at dinner time. The bay and the castle disappeared behind trees as she descended to the road, but Jean never lost sight of her goal — Roger Dempsey, who like Ambrose Mackintosh, proclaimed himself a True Believer.

FIVE

Jean had to walk only a short distance back towards Inverness before she reached the road that led down to Temple Pier, two docks jutting into Urquhart Bay. She stepped aside as a van paused at the intersection, then eased itself into the traffic. Its front door wore a sign reading *Omnium Technologies Organization*. Dempsey's public, apparently, leaving an audience.

Several exclamation-pointed brochures in Jean's press release lauded Omnium, a multi-national corporation devoted to inventing and manufacturing tools that increased man's dominion over and profit from every living thing that moved upon the earth, not to mention those things that grew from it, could be dug out of it, or swam in its waters.

While the looking-through-walls scanner Dempsey had been touting at the conference would work just as well for a SWAT team — or so he had insisted — Jean suspected that the medical and scientific devices were his first love. Through them he could dabble in archaeology and paleontology. Omnium super sonar was finding sunken ships from Ireland to Indonesia. Their remote-scanning equipment set the standard at excavations both scientific and commercial.

A sports car was parked by the private pier. Both a Stars and Stripes and a Union Jack waved from the stern of the clunky barge-like boat tied up there. A youthful male figure moved purposefully around canvas-shrouded bundles on the boat. A second sorted through boxes stacked on the dock. A police constable stood watch, his hands folded at parade rest and his poker face turning back and forth like a radar dish. "Good afternoon," he said to Jean, but didn't challenge her further.

"Good afternoon," she returned. So the Northern Constabulary — read, D.C.I. Cameron — was taking those letters seriously. Not that one policeman could stop a frontal attack. His presence was the equivalent of a video camera mounted behind the cash register at a convenience store. Wondering whether he was the local plod or a reinforcement from Inverness, Jean started along the pier.

The man in the black diving suit slipped over the edge of the boat and into the water like a seal. The other, wearing a thin red and black life preserver vest, straightened up from his box and targeted Jean with beadlike eyes. "Eh! Have you got an appointment?"

"Yes I do. I'm Jean Fairbairn from *Great Scot*." She pulled a business card out of the side pocket of her bag and handed it over.

From the water came a slightly muffled American voice. "I set it up, Jonathan. Geez, relax already. You're as jumpy as a guy tap-dancing in a minefield."

Jonathan tucked the card into the pocket of his shorts without looking at it and with one last myopic glare at Jean, turned back to his box.

Roger Dempsey ducked out of the main cabin of the boat, a small metallic object in each hand. Jean assumed they were not both cell phones. One might be a PDA and the other a GPS unit — not that she knew anything about electronics. She felt about devices such as computers and DVD players the same way she felt about a car, wanting only to turn them on and make them go. She knew even less about boats, except that they figured prominently in the large bodies of water she found compelling.

Dempsey looked up from beneath the bill of his Omnium cap and essayed an ingratiating smile, a flash of long carnivorous teeth in his facial shrubbery. He put down his doodads, wiped his hand on his dirty and sagging jeans, and extended it toward her. "Jean! Welcome aboard!"

"Hello, Dr. Dempsey." His hand was as soft and damp as a sponge, but it steadied her sensible shoes across the washboard-like gangplank and onto the deck, which was rising and falling to the swell. Her stomach was more likely to react to the faint odors of bilge, fish, and gasoline than to the motion, but fortunately the wind blew the smell away.

Dempsey was taller than she remembered, but then, she was short enough that most people seemed tall. He squeezed her hand, approximating a handshake, and let it go. "It's just Roger. The PhD is honorary, recognition from the old alma mater for my work, they said, but we both know it was actually for my building them a state-of-the-art science lab."

Jean smiled appreciatively at that. "Roger. How's it going?"

"Great," he returned. "Sit down, sit down."

A large wave, probably reflected off the tourist cruiser just putting out from the public dock down the way, slapped up against the boat. Jean dropped into a canvas chair. Roger perched on a stool surrounded by tentacles of wire, control panels, screens, and, for all Jean knew, the remnants of Skylab. He bellowed toward the cabin, "Tracy! How about some tea!"

"A cuppa will have to do, we've got no biscuits at all," returned a female voice

"That's okay!" Roger muted his bellow to a confidential rumble. "The first time I was in Scotland, right out of college and wet behind the ears, a waitress asked if I'd like an egg with my tea. I figured it would be a hard-boiled egg floating in the cup like those buoys in the water there, but hey, if that's the custom of the country, go for it."

"And what you got was a full supper, right?"

"Oh yeah. My wife's from England, she's been teasing me about that ever since we met. Which was right out of college, too. She's done a real good job of drying out my ears."

He was another American soul seduced by Britain. Jean identified with that.

"Yo, Brendan," Roger called to the diving-suited man as he flopped back onto the boat. Consulting one of several monitors, Roger delivered instructions in electronic Esperanto.

"Sure thing," Brendan replied, and back over the side he went.

So he was the "go-to guy" Roger had referred to on the phone, the assistant with the broad shoulders, square jaw, and cleft chin. If Brendan peeled off his hood, would he have a curl in the middle of his forehead, like Superman?

Judging by his accent, the other assistant, Jonathan, was a Brit. His domed brow made his head look too heavy for his body. His arms and legs were positively spindly beside and below his padded chest. Jean told herself that he probably had a very nice personality, his belligerent greeting to the contrary.

Carrying a coil of wire, Jonathan picked his way across the gangplank and then the deck. He leaned over the gunwale and called, "Mind you don't mess the flex about, Sunshine. It's not pasta."

"Give me a break," Brendan's muffled voice replied.

"And it's not five minutes you were asking me to take your place this evening." Jonathan handed down the wire.

"What? That gives you the right to insult me? You'd better be sure you don't fall in the water. With that giant chip on your shoulder you'd sink like a rock, life-jacket or no life-jacket." A splash like that of a sounding whale cut off Jonathan's reply. With a quick, wary glance toward Roger, Jonathan retreated back to the dock.

Roger ignored the static. Turning to Jean, he radiated sincerity. Either he didn't remember her putting him in his place, or was willing to let it go. She appreciated someone capable of letting go, no matter what his ulterior motive was. "Are your assistants both electronics experts, like you?" She fished her notebook and pen out of her bag and jotted, *June 20. Loch Ness. Roger Dempsey.*

"I'm no expert, just a hobbyist. Jonathan — Jonathan Paisley — he's a geek, could hack into NORAD, I bet. Brendan Gilstrap's a marine biology student, just got back from a tour of the Great Barrier Reef."

"And why are you here, searching for a legend?"

"Because it's there!" Roger replied, with an expansive gesture toward the loch and the hills beyond. "Even if Nessie's not obviously there, no one can prove she doesn't exist, just like no one can prove there's no such thing as a UFO. Absence of evidence isn't evidence of absence."

Absence of evidence didn't prove a thing, but Jean gathered that was Roger's point. "Are you into ufology as well as cryptozoology?"

"Hell, no. That's just people letting their imaginations run away with them."

"Imagination is the explanation for most of the Nessie sightings. Wind, waves, birds, otters, deer — the loch creates illusions, especially when you're looking for a mysterious creature."

"Just because people jump to conclusions, and just because there have been outright frauds, doesn't mean the creature doesn't exist. There's just too much eyewitness evidence."

"Any policeman will tell you that eyewitnesses are notoriously unreliable," Jean stated, knowing what she was talking about. "We have photos of snow leopards in the Himalayas, but not one of Nessie, who lives over the river and through the woods from millions of people. Scientists of all stripes have spent decades exploring the loch, and haven't proved any creature exists."

"They've come up with such bizarre explanations it would be easier to believe all those eyewitnesses are lying. Animals acting in ways completely atypical of their species. Logs propelled by decaying gasses. Yeah, right! There have been sightings of mysterious water beasts going back centuries, not just in Loch Ness."

"The sources before nineteen-thirty-three are references to references to other references," Jean said. "By the time you track them down, they turn out to have been taken out of context or are simply wrong. This scenery has been a tourist attraction for over two hundred years. Before then the loch was a major thoroughfare. No one ever reported a creature in the water until Ambrose Mackintosh did, unless you count the story of St. Columba,"

"And you don't, I take it."

"In context it's a typical saintly miracle tale. And if it happened at all it was in the river up near Inverness, not here in the loch."

Roger leaned forward. Beneath the bill of the cap his eyes danced. They were an odd color, an indeterminate gray-blue-green, as though he'd spent so many hours in sunlight reflected off water they'd bleached out. "Let me guess. You're playing devil's advocate."

Not exactly, no, but she replied mildly, "You think?"

"I do think, yes I do," he said with a chuckle.

How about that? His wiry shoulders covered by the Water

Horse T-shirt appeared to be one hundred percent chip-free.

"Up to a point," he went on, "Ambrose Mackintosh was a fine scientist, the first one to seriously research the creature. The point comes with the crap about Aleister Crowley — that makes rotting logs and stuff look reasonable. Ambrose ignores any evidence from before his own time because it violates his thesis about Crowley."

"That's not good science," Jean murmured.

"It sure as hell isn't good science. Ambrose should have mentioned the old legends. Shape-changing animals like water bulls and water horses and kelpies were the local people's way of explaining heads, humps, snaky coils — a variety of sightings. I talked to one old guy who grew up in Foyers in the thirties, says his grandmother told him to stay away from the loch because there were nasty creatures in it. They take their myths seriously here."

Yes they did, realizing that myth didn't have to be true to be real. And yet taking legends *too* seriously could be as big a mistake as not taking them at all — or so Alasdair maintained, and, as usual, he had a point. Jean suggested, "What better way to keep a little kid from drowning than to scare him so badly that he doesn't go near the water?"

"Listen," Roger insisted, blithely disregarding that that's exactly what she was doing, "just a few years ago the skipper of a sport-fishing boat wanted to sneak through the Caledonian Canal during the night because his customers had caught over their limit. But the crew absolutely refused to sail up Loch Ness after dark."

"Where did you hear that?"

"From a guy who knew the skipper himself."

"Roger, that's urban legend territory. For one thing, how was the boat planning to get through the canal when all the locks close down and their operators go home for the night?"

He stared at her for a long moment, then grinned. So he'd learned since the conference that when painting your way into corners, charm got you out again much faster than combativeness. "Well, okay, so much for eyewitness evidence, huh? Don't believe everything you hear."

"I don't." Jean couldn't help but return his grin and remind herself that she had not come here to praise, bury, or even debate him, simply to report on his point of view.

Dempsey raised his hands in surrender. "Granted, if the sightings were just a matter of opinion, of hearsay, that wouldn't be good science. Even if you count psychology as a science, which I don't. Where I come in is crossing quantifiable science — you know, the bit about repeatable results, that sort of thing — with something that makes academically-trained scientists uncomfortable.

"Every science needs dedicated amateurs," he continued, "Archaeology had Schliemann uncovering Troy and Ventris deciphering Linear B and, well, me. You saw the article in the press kit — I plotted a Roman city in Turkey that was being flooded by a new dam. Nessie had Mackintosh and Dinsdale and Edgerton and all, and now she has me, too. Nothing against academics. Some of my best friends are academics."

"Mine too. And a more hidebound group it would be hard to find. Fundamentalists, maybe, but I'm not going to go there."

"Then we're on the same side."

Jean wouldn't go that far, but she said only, "Tell me about your equipment. Your flyers talk about submersibles . . ."

"No, no, no. Old hat." He shooed that concept away as though it were a mosquito. "We've got state of the art ROVs. Remote operating vehicles. You control the whole shebang from the boat, safe and sound. No risk to the operator. We've got cameras, sonar, hydrophones that can hear an underwater fart at three hundred meters. And that's just for the water part of the mission. On land we have a magnetometer, a new ground-penetrating radar, an electromagnetic ground conductivity meter — all manufactured by Omnium, top of the line. We're going to work from the boat while the Festival crowds are milling around, then look for evidence on land when it's over."

"On land?" Jean repeated. "It would be even harder for Nessie to hide on the land than in the water."

"There have been sightings on land, and not just by people on their way home from the pub." He paused while she laughed, then indicated the boat, the pier, the water, and the distant hillsides, like an evangelist beseeching the Almighty for a sign. "Jean, people have been laughing at me for years. They said I'd never make a living buying used lab equipment, fixing it up, and selling it. Wrong! Rebuilt lab equipment, computers, sensors, some tweaks of the existing technology, and the next thing you know, I was starting Omnium. They said it would never get off the ground. Wrong again. So here I am, re-paying my debt to the scientific community. Like Thomas Edison moving on from inventing the light bulb to doing research in physics."

Unlike Edison, Roger hired other people to invent his light bulbs. But like Roger, Edison had also been a businessman with a good opinion of himself. No one built empires on either light bulbs or used microscopes, Jean allowed to herself, without nerve as well as brain.

Brendan heaved himself back over the gunwale and splashed onto the deck. That water was forty-two degrees. Even with the diving suit he must be cold.

"There you are! What took you so long?" said Roger, not to Brendan but to a woman who emerged from the hatchway carrying a tray lined with several mugs.

"That cooker's a beast itself," she said. "I'm resigning as galley slave. With people tramping about here all day long I could do with a sundowner." Like flicking a switch, she turned a neon smile on the tramp of the moment. "Hello! Jean, isn't it? I'm Tracy."

Jean politely accepted a mug. "Jean Fairbairn with *Great Scot*. So you're the woman behind the great man?"

"That I am, yes," said Tracy, without the least hint of sarcasm. "Is your husband here with you, Jean? I'm looking forward to meeting him."

So both Dempseys had checked Jean out. Well, she, too, believed in being prepared, and answered coolly, "Brad and I are no longer married."

"I, uh, I'm sorry to hear that." Roger's caterpillar-like eyebrows crawled toward his hat, then toward each other.

Tracy shot him a sharp glance Jean could not interpret. To Jean she said, "Ah. That's why you've gone back to your maiden name, I expect, not the change of career. Quite right — mustn't cling to the past."

Jean smiled politely, sipped her tea, and offered no more details, since the details had nothing to do with the case in hand, Roger's false intimacy and genuine charm be damned.

Roger took off his cap, revealing shaggy salt-and-pepper hair, and tilted the mug into his beard.

For a moment Jean thought she detected the scent of Earl Grey tea, but no, hers was plain black tea, brewed so strong that even with milk and sugar it was stiff enough to scrub the deck. Sipping, she watched as Jonathan and Brendan claimed their mugs and retreated toward the front deck of the boat. They sat there, either chatting or exchanging barbs, short English vowels dueling with long American ones.

Then there was Tracy, who posed gazing off over the loch. Now here was a woman who was not aging gracefully, but was fighting every step of the way. Jean could sympathize with that. She herself felt as though she were being frog-marched into middle age.

Still, didn't Tracy realize that her linen pants and cotton sweater were so tight they gave the impression she was plump when she was merely woman-shaped, like Jean, not girl-shaped like, say, Kirsty? And while her designer-cut hair showed not one gray strand, the bronze color didn't look natural next to her fair skin. Assuming "fair" was her actual skin tone — her complexion was smooth as porcelain, and as liable to crack at any moment beneath its layers of foundation, blusher, and shadow. Jean had never been able to wear foundation without feeling as though she'd dipped her face in Crisco. But to each her own.

According to Dempsey's biography, he and Tracy were both in their late forties and had been married for twenty-five years, with no issue except a corporation. They gave the lie to Jean's theory that after a while man and wife would start to resemble each other. If Tracy was trying out for *Vogue*, Roger was ready for the special *Popular Mechanics* issue of *National Geographic*.

Tracy turned to Roger. Her thin, miserly lips, meticulously lined to make them seem full — and therefore making them seem hard — kept on smiling, while a flatness in her eyes informed Jean that the woman was not. "I'm off to the hotel. You'll want a wash and brush up before the Tourist Authority dinner, won't you, dear? And we're opening the Festival."

"I'll get there, I'll get there, give me a chance." Roger replaced his cap, leaving several tufts of hair sticking out at odd angles, like horns.

"Where are you staying?" Jean asked Tracy.

"The Cameron Arms Hotel, the new one working with Starr to sponsor the Festival. And to sponsor us as well."

"So it's not exactly a blinding coincidence that y'all happened on the scene just in time for the hotel opening and the Festival?"

"Marketing and promotion. It's all part of protecting one's investment."

"And the anonymous letters haven't discouraged your work?"

The corners of Tracy's mouth dropped abruptly and her lips tightened to a red slit. Her smile may not have been reflected in her eyes, but her anger certainly was. "Iris sent them, mark my words. She may think Loch Ness is her private preserve, but she won't interfere with Operation Water Horse. You won't keep Roger much longer, will you now, Jean?" Without waiting for an answer, let alone adding, "There's a good girl," Tracy headed toward dry land. The high heels of her impractical but handsome strappy sandals tiptoed across the gangway and tapped up the pier. A moment later the deep-throated roar of the sports car rolled across the water and faded toward town.

Okay, Jean told herself. Roger might dismiss the letters, but Tracy, spousal minder and manager, didn't. Did she know about the Nessie-hunting expedition that had been fire-bombed in the eighties? Did Roger? If not, it wasn't Jean's place to fan the flames — so to speak.

With a jaunty wave after Tracy, Roger turned back to Jean. "I'll get Brendan to set up another interview once we start the land part of the expedition."

"Where on shore are you going to look?" Jean set her half-empty mug down beside her chair — she'd reached the day's complement of caffeine — and picked up her pen.

"Pitclachie Farm, to begin with. 'Pit' is an old Pictish prefix, and 'clachie' is probably the Celtic 'clach' or stone. In other words, the place was named after the Stone."

Oh yeah. Roger's theory about the Stone. He was digging at Pitclachie?

"Pictish animal carvings are perfectly recognizable as eagles, bulls, boars, whatever. Except for the 'beast'." Roger indicated the logo on his T-shirt. "Maybe this symbol is from the life, too, huh? What if the horse's head on the Stone is Nessie's head sticking out of the water? Some witnesses say the Loch Ness monster looks like a horse. You know, water horse?"

Jean, expressing no opinions, kept on writing.

"And maybe the broken part had a gripping beast on it, which is a representation of the creature out of the water, on land!" Beaming, Roger saluted the loch with his mug and then took another gulp.

Jean kept her opinion of that flight of fancy to herself. She was going to be the combative one if she wasn't careful. She had yet to learn the art — the trick — of just letting her interview subject run on and on until he'd revealed more than he'd intended.

She realized she wasn't smelling Earl Grey tea, she was smelling whiskey. No wonder Roger's tea was the dark brown of the water surrounding the boat, not caramel-colored like hers. She remembered how he had been the first in line at the conference cash bar. When it came to alcohol consumption, he was no amateur. But then, he was no drunk, either. Or hadn't been, then.

"Pitclachie Farm?" Jean asked. "Iris Mackintosh isn't a big fan of yours, whether or not she sent the letters."

"Iris is kind of a nut, yeah, but in ways she's the opposite of Ambrose. She isn't imaginative enough to think of sending anonymous letters, and too straight-arrow to do it."

That was pretty much Miranda's assessment. "But she gave you permission to search her farm, even though she doesn't believe in what you're doing?"

"Yes, she did." Roger swirled the liquid in his mug, his cap hiding his eyes, contemplating the drink, or the deck, or a coil of wire at his feet — anything that was not Jean's face.

Her own personal remote-sensors blipped, although she didn't know why. If he didn't have permission from Iris to search Pitclachie, he wouldn't be announcing to all and sundry — Jean being the sundry — that he did. But it seemed a bit Quixotic, even for Dempsey, to search for Nessie on land. She tried, "Maybe Iris intends for you not to turn anything up, then she can say she was right all along."

"Let her. It's no skin off my nose if she won't see what's right beneath hers."

"And if Iris didn't send the letters," Jean persisted, "who did? Who doesn't want you here? Who's harassing you?"

"How could searching for Nessie threaten anyone? Some dork's just playing a stupid joke." Roger picked up one of his electronic gadgets and inspected its tiny screen. "Nessie can run, or swim, whatever, but she can't hide. We'll find her, or evidence that she exists."

End of interview. "Well, you have places to go and things to do," Jean said to the button on the top of Roger's cap. "I'll leave you with it. When's the press junket — er — cruise tomorrow?"

"Ten a.m. I'll save you a seat." He offered her another ingratiating grin, this one from under his brows, warily.

"Thanks. I'm looking forward to it." Jean stowed her notebook and pen and stepped across to the pier. The gangplank disappeared from behind her heels the moment she gained terra almost firma.

Roger dropped the gangplank onto the deck with a crash. "Brendan! Jonathan! Let's get the boat anchored in the bay. We don't want the local fuzz to give us a parking ticket."

The two young men jostled each other like brothers confined to the back seat of the family car. A moment later the throb of the engines made the dock vibrate beneath Jean's feet and filled the air with exhaust. Water churned and splashed, and a cold droplet landed on her hand. She turned toward the shore with a friendly nod at the local fuzz. He glanced at his watch. Time for him to close down the sentry post and proceed to happy hour at the pub. Once the boat was anchored in the bay, it would be protected by a natural moat.

Funny, she thought as she strolled up the drive, how she found herself not just tolerating Roger's ego, but actually liking his goofy charm and shameless enthusiasm. Exactly as he'd intended. Several times he'd delivered himself of a statement and then paused, like a stand-up comic revising his routine to suit the audience's reaction.

Well, if so, then so what? She was probably the twentieth reporter today to ask him the same questions. Even if she'd been the first to challenge his assumptions about Nessie, he'd handled himself well. His agenda was open for inspection. Nothing shady about Roger and Tracy building on his previous acquaintance with her. Nothing shady about them sucking up to her. She'd come here to tell Roger's story. To promulgate his myth. Because doing so would entice readers to *Great Scot*. Scratch my back, I scratch yours. Right?

Jean paused at the top of the road, frowning. So why was her curiosity about the Dempseys and their agenda leavened with so much skepticism it expanded into suspicion? Because Roger seemed to have a history with Iris? Because he and Tracy had checked up on Jean herself? Because of the threatening letters?

She looked back, past the pier, to Dempsey's boat cutting a white furrow in the surface of Urquhart Bay. Beyond it, the open water of the loch glimmered like a great teasing eye, in on the joke . . . No, Jean told herself. She wasn't going to assume anything — not Roger Dempsey, not the letters, not Nessie herself — was only a joke.

SIX

By the time Jean had eaten dinner and whiled away several hours in the town and at the Festival, the sun had sunk far enough to cast Pitclachie House and the bay below into delicate shadow, although light still gleamed on the mountains to the east, across the loch. The waves close to the far shore emitted a furtive gleam or two, although not, so far as Jean could see, any flippers, prehensile necks, or proboscis-sprouting horse heads. She was disappointed. Considering the power of suggestion, she'd fully expected to see a corps of Nessies performing water ballet.

Inside the Lodge, there was enough light to find the switches without having to grope for them. Who knew what she might touch, feeling around in the dark? She stowed the food she'd bought in the village, freshened up, and glanced inquisitively at the locked door.

Jean strolled back outside and around the corner of the main house, brushing at a tickle along her hairline. Ah, good, the wind on the terrace side was strong enough to keep the midges at bay. The infuriating biting gnats played a much larger and less benign part in the Highland psyche than Nessie did, and there was no controversy at all about their existence.

The expanse of the terrace was deserted. No Kirsty, no Iris, no Bouchards. Jean imagined the honeymooners sitting on a window seat, draped in dressing gowns and Gallic insouciance, pretending they weren't looking forward to the fireworks.

In a window on the ground floor sat the calico cat, grooming itself, its eyes glinting eerily. Faint lights glowed in the tower, shining not only through the arched windows but also through each of the mock murder holes spaced beneath the overhang of the topmost story, so that they looked like a string of tawny diamonds. Was Iris up there, watching over her domain? She was hardly boiling up oil — or less evocatively but more probably, water — to repel invaders. These murder holes, like the spires and arcades and ginger breaded gables, were all for show, part of the nostalgia game. At least, thought Jean, one of the re-enactors taking tea at Culloden was stained with the red of blood.

A rolling cart was parked just outside the French doors of what Jean assumed was the dining room, its array of bottles and glasses twinkling with all the glamour of a jeweler's window. A small, neatly-printed sign read, "Please help yourself." Not one to turn down a formal invitation, Jean poured herself a wee dram of the wine of the country and took the most comfortable chair.

Her dinner of venison casserole redolent with herbs had scoured her mouth of the taste of bilge, while the crème brulée and unleaded coffee had cleared out the flavor of diesel exhaust, leaving her palate available for further stimulation . . . Ah, yes. The malt whiskey conjured the tea-colored water of the River Spey and its surrounding hills with their fields of sun-ripened grain.

Rolling the stinging fragrance around her mouth, she tried to situate herself in the present, to be there now. But a relaxed and meditative state was about as easy for her to attain as sainthood. She realized she was tapping her foot, stopped herself, and a moment later was tapping again. No, she wasn't nervous. She was just very, very alert.

On the surface of the bay below, the different boats rose and fell. The windows of the Water Horse barge were fitfully illuminated, as though by a firefly. Were the intermittent lights reflections, or was someone was still on board, one of Roger's assistants detailed to burn the midnight oil in the never-ending quest for truth, justice, and the technological way — or however those sentiments had been expressed in the Omnium brochure.

Jean had nothing against technology, within reason. But she couldn't help but think that while Roger's technology might extend the ordinary five senses, it was useless when it came to the odd — very odd — unquantifiable, unrepeatable, sixth sense, like her own ability to perceive the emotional emanations called ghosts.

Maybe Nessie was a ghost. Maybe that's why some people sensed her but couldn't get photos of her. Jean could imagine Miranda's reaction to her starting her series of articles with that sentiment. Better a straightforward, "Two great mysteries meet at Loch Ness. The Picts are the greatest puzzle of Scottish archaeology, like Nessie is the greatest puzzle of Scottish . . ." What? Biology? Psychology?

The sound of a door opening and shutting derailed her train of thought. Two people came walking down the terrace. This couple did look alike, round of cheek and hip, considerably more comfortable with middle age than Jean was. But then, they'd had more time to get used to it. They wore plastic-rimmed glasses, jeans, loose shirts, and thick-soled, white athletic shoes that proclaimed them to be Jean's fellow Americans. The massive shoes seemed to be the only things keeping them from floating away like helium balloons.

"Hi!" said the woman. "We saw you from our window when you checked in."

Yes, Jean informed herself, windows were two-way. "Hello. I'm Jean Fairbairn."

"Dave and Patti Duckett," said the man, "from Moline, Illinois. I work for John Deere and Patti runs a day care center. This is our first time across the pond. Where are you from?"

"Originally Dallas, but I live in Edinburgh now. I work for *Great Scot* Magazine. History and travel and . . ." she insisted, ". . . innocuous stuff like that. I'm here to interview Iris Mackintosh and Roger Dempsey. Not at the same time, though."

Patti glanced at Dave, then back at Jean. "We saw that TV show last night. No love lost between those two, is there? Although we don't know Dr. Dempsey personally."

"I only know his public face. And I haven't met Iris at all yet. It was Kirsty who let me in."

"Isn't she a pretty little thing?" asked Dave.

"So nice to see a young girl without a ring in her nose or a tattoo," Patti added.

Beneath her clothes, thought Jean, Kirsty could well be tattooed with the map of Scotland, with a navel ring marking the site of Glasgow. If so, that was her own business.

Dave went on, "She's off with her boyfriend tonight. I saw them walking down the driveway."

"Cute couple," said Patti. "He's one of the boys from the boat, you know, Dempsey's assistant."

"Oh?" Jean asked, but before she could get any more gossip, let alone pole-vault to any conclusions, the child Elvis shot around the corner of the house, careened across the terrace, and stopped dead in front of the three adults.

"Hello there, sonny," said Dave. "How old are you?"

Elvis peered up at his inquisitors from beneath his sheaf of flaxen hair. "Six," he allowed cautiously, like a witness wondering whether his testimony would be used against him.

The cadaverous form of his father materialized from the twilight, Dracula-like, and ambled down the terrace. "Oh, hullo. Martin Hall. The lad's Elvis. Ah, drinks." Martin's amble sped up fractionally, to a mosey. He picked up a bottle, then asked over his shoulder, "Here, have you seen a corkscrew?"

"No, sorry," Jean answered, although it was the darned elusive Iris who should be apologizing.

Thwarted, Martin set down that bottle and chose another, a creamy liqueur with a screw-off top. He filled a small glass with it and a large one with what the locals called lemonade — citric-acid soda — adding, extravagantly, one ice cube from the bucket provided.

"Ta!" Elvis clasped the fizzing glass with both hands and gulped. A moment later he produced a loud belch. Martin muttered some reprimand. Jean pretended she hadn't heard. The Ducketts laughed.

Elvis set his glass on the edge of the cart and ran off across the terrace. Martin sat down to nurse his liqueur. His thick glasses and distracted air confirmed Jean's impression that he'd been forcibly removed from a library or lab and was going through withdrawal. She could have initiated a conversation by asking where Elvis's mum was, but Martin, if not obviously strong, seemed to be the silent type. She commiserated with the need for silence, even though its corollary was sometimes loneliness.

Dave and Patti, though, did not. After various dithers — "Is that Drambuie? How sweet it that? Is Lagavullin one of those smoky ones?" — they chose their respective poisons. Settling down between Martin and Jean, they started chatting about their travels, the loch, and how they'd picked up some Omnium brochures from the Water Horse boat and wasn't underwater exploration the wave of the future — wave, get it, wave?

Jean returned the conversational birdie with a few remarks about Dempsey's theories and technical prowess. Martin offered that he, Elvis, and Noreen-the-wife had toured the Water Horse boat. While the lad had been right chuffed, Noreen, he added in tones so weary they approached contempt, had developed a migraine and was now having a lie-down.

Tracy had been right about people tramping through all day long, Jean thought. Maybe Jonathan's belligerence was evidence that he hadn't appreciated being on show. Was he out with Kirsty tonight, or had she gone with Brendan?

The sound of bagpipes, part swagger, part lament, drifted up from the Festival field. That was why armies marched with pipers — the sound carried for miles. Jean's nervous system quivered with awe and delight and regret.

Then the fine hair on the back of her neck stirred, ever so slightly, as though a chill breeze had blown across her skin. Her irritating hypersensitivity to the paranormal was picking up an allergen — a ghost, walking the gardens of Pitclachie House . . . No. The subliminal tickle was gone. It hadn't been sweat. It hadn't been the wind. It hadn't even been a probing insect. Something perpendicular to reality — however she defined reality — had come within range of her senses and now was gone.

She hadn't realized how the sounds of music and voices had faded until they returned, harsh against her ears. No one on the terrace had skipped a beat any more than the drummers at the Festival. No one here shared her sensitivity to ghosts.

Goosed to her feet, Jean stood up and paced down the flagstones into the twilight. She sensed nothing except the wind stirring the bushes clustered along the outer rim of the terrace. Leaves dipped, flowers nodded, tiny yellow broom petals whirled away and vanished.

There might be a ghost here, but ghosts weren't dangerous. Living people, they were dangerous.

Beyond the grounds the dusk — the gloaming — lingered on, the light growing thinner and more delicate and, in that alchemy peculiar to these northern climates, more polished. The opposite bank of the loch drew a black horizontal line between the faint obsidian glow of the water and the Prussian blue of the sky, clear and taut as a membrane . . . A solitary spark shot up from the field above the castle.

"Look!" Elvis leaped up on the low wall surrounding the terrace. Martin followed, steadying him with a firm paternal hand.

The spark burst into bright red and gold blossoms. Another spark, and another. Red and green and gold sprays of light reflected in the water of the loch. In the village, the band reached a crescendo, the high, clear skreel of the pipes punctuated twice by the muffled booms of the explosives, once as they went off and again when the crump echoed from the opposite shore. Nessie probably thought she was being depth-charged.

Grinning, Jean ordered herself to turn down her emotional thermostat and enjoy her bit of a holiday. After all, if she'd been a set of pipes, her drone would be anxiety, but her melody would be anticipation.

The adults oohed and aahed appreciatively, and Elvis laughed and clapped his hands. "Look at that one! Look at that!"

Sparks drifted slowly down toward the bay, faint trails of luminescence, like fireflies. Then a sudden spurt of flame roiled up and out, larger and brighter than any spark. Jean's heart lurched against her ribs. "What the . . ?"

"Brilliant!" Elvis shouted.

Dave Duckett exclaimed, voice shaking, "Oh my God!"

A detonation rolled into the night, rattling the windows of the house. Bits of fire fell back to the surface of the bay, some winking out, others bobbing up and down. A flurry of movement came from the other boats, and a cry went up from the shore. Patti's wail of dismay was much louder. The music squealed and, raggedly, stopped, but the shouts did not. A siren began to whine.

"Oh," said Elvis, his small face crumpling. "That wasn't right." Martin picked him up and carried him inside.

Jean gasped for air. She shut her eyes and opened them. But still she could see that where the expedition boat had been anchored was now only black water, surrounded by burning debris. An accident. The explosion was an accident . . .

Roger had received anonymous letters reminding him that the loch was dangerous, that men died there.

Jean sank down on the wall and slumped forward, dully, heavily, as the dark, cold, peat-stained water seemed to close over her head and suck her down toward nightmare.

SEVEN

Without exchanging more than a polite murmur with the Ducketts, who looked shell-shocked — much like she did, no doubt — Jean slunk back to the cottage. Slowly, methodically, she prepared for bed, and slipped between the chilly duvet and a bed as hard and cold as a marble slab.

And lay there. Behind her eyelids the boat exploded again and again, in real-time, in slow-motion, in animation. Each spark that extinguished itself in the unforgiving waters of the loch left a trail of questions like bright after-images across vision and memory alike. She knew she couldn't answer any questions now. She knew she couldn't even ask any. And yet the sparks swirled on and on . . .

The noise of a shutting door jerked her out of a merciful doze.

Had she forgotten, under the circumstances, to lock the outer door? And if so, who had just come into the house? Jean put slippers on her sock-clad feet and a robe over her flannel nightgown and listened at the bedroom door. Nothing. She called, "Hello?" Nothing. Turning on the hall lights, she stepped cautiously down the stairs. The front door was locked. Several yellow broom blossoms lay on the floor of the vestibule. She'd tracked those in herself, right?

She'd been half-asleep when she heard the sound. She'd probably misinterpreted the slam of a car door or traffic noise from the road below.

She trudged back upstairs and checked the bathroom and the mystery room across the hall from the bedroom, bracing herself in case its door flew open when she turned the knob. It, too, was still locked. Less puzzled than resentful, Jean left the hall light on, locked the bedroom door, and lay down on the bed. By sheer force of will she at last slipped into stupor . . .

Again she spasmed into alertness. This time she heard not only a door shutting, but also footsteps and the creaking of the hall floor. Slowly she swiveled her head toward the bedroom door. The light-slit beneath it wavered and steadied, as though someone — something — had come out of the locked room and walked down the hall. The fine hairs on the back of her neck prickled like feelers on the pillowcase, and the air condensed around her shoulders, pressing her against the mattress. *Resistance is futile.*

She lay quietly, every sense extended and shrinking at once. The rich aromas of coffee and pipe tobacco filled her nostrils and then dissipated. The steps stopped. Voices murmured, a man's voice and a woman's, rising and falling simultaneously, like dissonant chords.

Then the woman screamed.

Jean jerked in horror, then reminded herself: They're ghosts. It's a memory-video. I can't do anything to change it.

The scream either ended abruptly or attained such a high note Jean could no longer hear it. But she could feel it, a raw, chill bite in the air and along her nerves. What she heard was the crashing and thudding of a body falling down the stairs. And then silence, a silence so deep that her own breath, her own heartbeat, seemed to reverberate in the night.

Nothing else happened. After a while she managed a long exhalation. She pulled the duvet up to her chin, thinking that if she lived to be a hundred and fifty, she would never get used to sensing ghosts. And now she'd sensed two at Pitclachie House. The first one, the one outside in the shrubbery, had been only a wisp of feeling, a trace of dismay and dread. This one, though, had real power, searing emotion, behind it. There had been if not a murder here, then a sudden and unexpected death.

To say that Ambrose had spent so many years shut up in his study that even death couldn't pry him out was to evade the real issue. His spirit was lingering here in the Lodge because it had some unsolved business. Was it too great a leap of extrapolation to think that business was the death of his wife?

Had Eileen fallen down the stairs? By accident? On purpose? Had Ambrose hidden her body? Or had this particular scene happened long before her death? Who knew?

Those questions found space on the already crowded carousel in Jean's mind, and spun round and round until at last, in exhausted self-defense, she fell into a doze and stayed that way, drifting in and out of a restless sleep, until she woke suddenly to a ray of sun streaming through an inch-wide gap between the curtains.

Birds were caroling. The clock showed eight a.m., hours past dawn. Groaning, Jean crawled from the bed and padded across the icy floorboards, her skin prickling with natural, not paranormal, goose-flesh.

That must be why the Bouchards had moved into the main house. Not that they'd necessarily sensed or even scented the ghost. She'd met few other people cursed with an allergy as strong as hers, one of whom, through fate's fiendish sense of humor, happened to be Alasdair Cameron. But the Bouchards could have felt uneasy. Plenty of people could feel a tickle in the nostrils without ever succumbing to the full explosive whiplash of a sneeze.

Blowing a raspberry at the blank facade of the still-locked door, she went downstairs and straight to the kitchen, where she fired up the coffeepot and assembled cheese toast. Miranda was paying for her to eat breakfast in the main house, but neither fretful speculation nor greasy bacon would sit too well on her stomach just now.

Hmmm. Her rear echelon. Miranda. Michael and Rebecca. Hugh Munro, who should have gotten into Drumnadrochit last night. Not that she needed to make any phone calls just yet. It wasn't as though she'd had anything to do with the explosion.

She imagined Roger standing on the dock and tearing at his hair, and Tracy saying "I told you so," and Jonathan and Brendan . . . No one had been on the boat when it exploded, right? Those lights in the windows had been only reflections, hadn't they?

Please, Jean prayed to her thoroughly tarnished guardian angel, *please let no one have been on that boat.*

The coffee pot hissed and steamed, emitting its delectable aroma. Instead of standing over it with her tongue hanging out, Jean shoved her toast into the toaster oven and turned toward the television set. And saw that the velvet curtain was drawn across the vestibule, where she had most emphatically not left it after her middle-of-the-night lock inspection.

In three swift steps she crossed the room and threw the curtain open, revealing no more than sunlight shining through the transom over the door and the scattering of broom blossoms on the floor. Not that she'd expected to see anything. Ambrose's ghost was repeating his actions in life, drawing the curtain not only to keep out drafts, but also to secure his inner sanctum, where he wrote his arcane books . . . The books. Something nagged at the corner of her eye. She turned slowly around.

The DVDs were piled on the floor. Some of the tourist guides and popular histories were jammed tightly together, while gaps opened between others. Some were shoved all the way back into the shelf, others stuck out as far as its edge. A well-worn copy of Ambrose's *Pictish Antiquities* was laid crosswise atop the other books, along with an equally worn copy of *The Water-Horse of Loch Ness,* the book that collected all his newspaper and magazine articles about the monster, but never mentioned his theory about Aleister Crowley's role in its, er, creation.

Last night Jean had gone straight upstairs. She hadn't noticed, either then or when she came down to check the door, whether the shelves had been disarranged.

Now she ran her fingertip along the uneven row of books, releasing not one mote of dust, then picked up Ambrose's *Antiquities* and opened it to the photo inside the back flap. The man's long lantern jaw and partly befuddled, partly lugubrious expression reminded her of classic horror writer H.P. Lovecraft — an appropriate resemblance, considering. Ambrose's round spectacles, like two tiny magnifying glasses, and his severely parted and slicked-down hair also evoked in Jean's mind implications of plutocrats as well as scholars. Well, he had both inherited and married wealth, although how long he'd kept it was up for discussion.

As Michael Campbell-Reid had pointed out so graphically, *Pictish Antiquities* was Ambrose's only archaeological publication, despite years of amateur digging. Or plundering, as the case may be. Its sober historical account was colored by off-the-wall theorizing. That the Picts re-used ancient Neolithic sites had been borne out by recent excavations. That they were performing magical ceremonies in them could never be proved — even though archaeologists' routine explanation for any puzzling object or setting was "ritual use." At least Ambrose was weirdly consistent, segueing from magical Picts to water monsters to *Loch Ness: the Realm of the Beast,* a title conspicuous by its absence. No surprise there.

The surprise, quickly ratcheting up into alarm, was that yesterday Jean had noted how tidy the bookshelf was, and yet today it was a mess. What? Had the ghost of the old man been making sure guests in his premises noticed his work? Repeating his routines from life was one thing, deliberately trying to get her attention was another, one that strained credibility.

What unfortunately didn't strain credibility was that someone living had searched the cottage. Jean inspected the rest of the room, but nothing else was disarranged. The flowers still stood on the table next to her canvas carryall . . .

The smell of burning toast turned her lunge toward the table into a lunge toward the kitchen. Easing the toast onto a plate, she poured herself a cup of coffee and carried both to the table. While they cooled she inventoried everything in her bag. The large envelope with the photo of the Pitclachie Stone. A couple of file folders with copies and clippings. The biography of Crowley and several Nessieology books. Roger's press release, the Omnium brochures tucked inside. She'd left her paper notebook sitting on the table last night, and it was still there, if not exactly where she'd left it at least not obviously elsewhere. Beside it sat her laptop, cold and silent.

Okay. Jean munched her toast, washed it down with coffee, and pondered the possibilities. Maybe someone had come into the Lodge while she was gone yesterday and ransacked the shelves. Kirsty and Iris had to have a key, but why would one of them leave the shelves disarranged?

Someone else with a key might have looked through the shelves, even taken something from them, but Jean couldn't tell if anything were missing. Besides, the logical place to look for — whatever — would be in the locked room, which would argue either a second key or the sort of frustrated violence that would leave telltale marks on the door or the knob.

Or, she thought with a chill that cooled the coffee on its way down her throat, had someone come into the house last night? The first sound to wake her had been that of a door shutting. Maybe she'd been more deeply asleep than she'd thought, and while she'd heard an intruder leave the cottage, she hadn't heard him or her come in. Her sixth sense had responded only to the second round of noise, when the click of a door had been accompanied by footsteps and the creak of the floor. And yet there was no reason to assume the first sound hadn't been the ghost, too. Maybe he'd just been warming up for the full manifestation.

Besides, why would someone sneak into the cottage while it was occupied and run the risk of being caught? That was pretty bold, even if he or she knew that Jean had no better weapon than her toothbrush.

She informed herself sternly that she had no evidence the mysterious searcher was after her things, let alone her person. In fact, she had no evidence there was a mysterious searcher at all. She might just as well throttle the galloping paranoia back to walking caution. That took a lot less energy.

A second cup of life-affirming caffeine in one hand, Jean used the other to turn on the television. Only BBC Scotland was showing news, and that was the morning Gaelic broadcast. A shot of two yellow-jacketed policemen standing beside Temple Pier, the loch behind them smeared into watercolor by early morning haze, switched to a shot of a clean-cut young man wearing a suit and tie. His eyes, as large as those of a Japanese anime character, gazed into the camera as though expecting it to bite him. Whatever he was saying was drowned out by a voice translating it into soft but incomprehensible Gaelic syllables. Jean got the message, though, loud and clear.

That was Detective Constable Gunn. He had to have a first name, but she'd never learned it during her brief contact with him and his superiors back in May. Those same superiors had sent him out today to hand the news people the standard line: The Northern Constabulary is making inquiries into the matter. Move along, move along, there's nothing to see here.

Had D.C.I. Cameron been dispatched from headquarters to deal with the matter of an exploding boat? Prying her gritted teeth far enough apart to fit in the rim of her coffee cup, Jean remembered the moment Alasdair Cameron had dragged her out of danger, his arm strong and solid around her waist. And the last time she'd seen him, over an Indian meal in Fort William, when she'd mentioned the Casket Letters and the Red Books of Westmarch. He'd not only recognized both references, he'd smiled his dry, reserved smile, and said, "The wardens of Westmarch were named Fairbairn. Ancestors of yours, I reckon."

Like Michael and Rebecca, she and Alasdair Cameron would have been a lot alike to begin with, wounded by duty and commitment, had there been a beginning. But that same evening he'd warned her off. *Don't go breaking my shell, woman. You might not like what's inside.* And they'd walked away from each other. Once burned, Jean thought, you tended to leap back hyper-ventilating from a sudden spurt of flame.

More than once she'd told students complaining about a difficult assignment, *let it be a challenge to you.* More than once in the last few weeks she'd wondered if Alasdair's words had been just that, not a warning but a challenge. Maybe she would soon find out.

Jean switched off the TV and rinsed off her dishes. Then she typed the notes from her interview with Roger into her laptop, even though the story he'd told her yesterday had been overrun by events. As for today, Kirsty had said Iris would show Jean around the garden "after breakfast." Glancing at the kitchen clock, she decided that nine-thirty had to be after breakfast — and that Dempsey's ten a.m. press junket had been cancelled.

Just in case her paranoia was justified, she tucked her laptop into its case and the case into the carryall, and locked them both in the wardrobe in her bedroom after she dressed. *Here we go again . . .* Except, she reminded herself very firmly, this time she really was just an innocent bystander.

On her way out, Jean tried the front door key in the lock of the locked room. But it was too big, and left a gleaming scratch on the age-darkened metal plate. Great, she thought, she'd been driven to vandalism. Even though there were other scratches around the keyhole, too, some quite recent. Had someone picked the lock? Leaning over, she peered through the keyhole to see nothing but darkness. Short of finding a ladder and dragging it around to the window, she wasn't going to find out what was in that room.

Forward momentum, then, as one of her favorite fictional characters was fond of saying. To which she could only add, *and don't look back, something might be gaining on you.*

EIGHT

With a sound between a snort and a sigh, Jean shut the door of the Lodge and locked it. Maybe she should title her next article *Locking Doors for Fun and Profit*.

The birds were singing, the sun was shining, a boat trailed a foaming white wake like the train of a bridal gown across the surface of the loch. You'd think there were no cares to be had in the world. You'd think there were no secret agendas, ones that impelled the bloody-minded not only to make threats but to also carry them out. Making long, purposeful strides across the courtyard, Jean imagined herself taller, stronger, a more formidable opponent . . . Dempsey had enemies, she told herself. All she had were irritants.

The front door of the main house opened and decanted the Bouchards, dressed in Abercrombie and Fitch's latest hiking-up-Fifth-Avenue gear. "Good morning," Charles said with a gracious inclination of his head. Sophie adjusted the zipper on her jacket and said, "Pretty sunshine day. Good to walk."

"Yes, it's a lovely morning." Jean replied, not without a suspicious glance at the so-far innocent white clouds swanning overhead.

The Bouchards went on down the terrace. Jean lingered to pet the calico cat, who was sunning itself on the low wall where Elvis had stood last night to watch the show — both acts of it. This beastie wasn't in the mood to be elusive, but emitted a comfortable and comforting purr.

All right! The slate flagstones rimming the terrace were carved with Pictish symbols, among them the gripping beast, Dempsey's logo. The stylized shapes of bull, boar, eagle, and serpent reminded Jean of the drawings in the Book of Kells and other old Celtic Bibles. Which led her back around to beasts from Revelations or from the loch or both. Brushing away a scattering of broom petals like a drift of gold flakes, she crouched down for a better look.

A tattoo of footsteps announced Kirsty, walking around the base of the tower with her maiden — well, if Iris was not a maiden, at least permanently unmarried — aunt at her side. Iris was not only the taller of the two, her posture made a regimental sergeant major look slouched. Kirsty was sidling along with her head tilted up, speaking in a voice that made up in vehemence what it lacked in volume. Today her hair was pulled tightly back from her face, sharpening its curves into angles. Iris's face was already angular. Her expression was the same as it had been on the television screen two nights ago, dealing sternly with the facts, thank you, not with anything as disreputable as fancy.

The two women stopped in the corner where the tower met the house, beside a small arched doorway. Kirsty's voice rose. "Roger's is just another expedition!"

"It wasn't that even before he got his boat blown up last night. Good riddance, I'm thinking."

"How can you go saying that? Jonathan Paisley has been missing since the explosion!"

Jean winced. So it was too late for angelic intervention. Poor Jonathan. Talk about being in the wrong place at the wrong time.

"Not to speak ill of — of him." Iris made a gesture that came close to patting Kirsty's head. "But it just goes to show how Roger Dempsey will do anything, will sacrifice anyone, to further his ambitions. The other lad, the American, his back wants watching, I should think. If Roger had the least bit of respect, he would take his circus and go away home."

"He's not after going home, he's making plans to get on with the ground survey."

"How did . . . Ah. I see. That phone call. That was the American lad, was it?"

"His name is Brendan Gilstrap," said Kirsty, her chin taking on that stubborn tilt Jean had seen all too often in her students. "And aye, I went walking down to hear the music with him last night. Dinna go tarring him with the brush you're using on Roger."

"Roger's tarred himself. He needs no help from me. As for this Brendan, I promised your mum I'd look after you, considering what happened in Glasgow and all. Hanging about with Dempsey and his sort — no, I don't think you'll be doing that. I don't think so at all."

Silence, except for the wind in the shrubbery and Jean's shoes making stealthy tracks away from the scene before the women realized they hadn't been alone. There you go, she thought. The classic story of a young woman with an unsuitable boyfriend. Or unsuitable by Iris's standards. Her own mother had been an American — surely that wasn't the issue. Did Iris disapprove of monster-hunters in general or of Roger in particular, especially now that he had attracted violence?

And, parenthetically, what had happened with Kirsty in Glasgow that she had been more or less exiled here? Jean stopped at the far end of the terrace, straightened from her crouch, and spared a thought for youth, death, and solitude.

Then she focused on the vista before her. Plants and flowers of every color and description spilled up the hillside behind the house, bulged out across gravel paths, and strained against a fence. Drops of dew glinted like jewels tucked away in the foliage. Beyond a gate lay open pasture, grass short as a putting green, dotted with the gray of — oh, those lumps weren't rocks, they were sheep. That explained the well-manicured lawn. Further up the hill the open fields were splotched with the dark green of heather and the pink-purple of foxgloves.

At the crest of the hill several Scots pines stood in solitary splendor, their limbs calligraphy against the mountainside beyond. The fence encircling them was fringed by what looked like large, lush Boston ferns but were actually bracken, fronds rippling in the wind. The Bouchards stood there scrutinizing a piece of paper.

"Good morning, Miss Fairbairn," called Iris's deep voice from behind Jean's back.

She probably realized Jean had overheard her conversation with Kirsty, but courtesy consisted of mutual denial. Assuming a guileless smile, Jean turned around. "Good morning, Miss Mackintosh."

Iris's khaki and wool-clad form marched on past, over the edge of the terrace and onto the gravel garden path. "I hope the Lodge is all right for you."

"I'm enjoying the space," said Jean, scurrying to catch up. "I'm curious, though — why is one of the upper rooms locked?"

"Oh that. It's too small for a bedroom so I use it as a lumber room for the occasional old family possession."

Possession was the right word, thought Jean. But she'd only alienate her subject by pointing out that most B&B owners were happy to rent out rooms barely large enough for a bed. "Were you or Kirsty looking for a book in the Lodge yesterday afternoon? I found the shelves disarranged this morning."

Iris stopped dead in the path. Jean skidded to a halt behind her. Her nose was so close to the much taller Iris's knitted cardigan that she caught a whiff of bacon, revealing who had cooked the breakfast she'd skipped.

"I'll have Kirsty set them to rights." Iris's t's were honed to sharp points.

"No problem, I just wondered . . ."

Iris started off again, leaving Jean to sidle along the way Kirsty had, head cocked upward. Iris hadn't answered the question, had she? Jean went on, "I'd like to ask you about . . ."

"My garden," stated Iris. She stopped at the gate, made an about-face, and launched into a botanical litany. Jean barely had time to whip out her notebook.

Meadow sweet. Thyme. Flag iris, origin of the *fleur de lis* of France and its Auld Alliance with Scotland. St. John's wort, almost a weed in Jean's garden in Texas. Soapwort, woundwort, ragwort —

known as Stinking Willy after the infamous William, Duke of Cumberland, the victor at Culloden. Prickly purple thistles, the symbol of Scotland. Wild roses, woodruff, silverweed, vetch, eyebright. More broom. *The Bonny, Bonny Broom* was one of Hugh's folk songs.

Iris's face softened with both affection and pride, as though she talked about grandchildren. She pointed out the boxwood hedges, box being the clan badge of the Mackintoshes, and indicated the elder trees rising at the back of the house and the rowans at the front, that particular arrangement guarding against witches. Jean wanted to comment that it had apparently not guarded against Crowley, but thought better of it — Iris had already segued into plant dyes, wool, spinning and knitting.

A knitter herself, Jean asked, "Do you use the wool from your own sheep?"

Iris gazed out at the fuzzy gray blobs that dotted the field. "Yes, I do. And I conduct classes. Cottage industries, mind you, make more ecological sense than these giant factories. Do you fancy a look at the Pitclachie Stone?"

"Yes, please." Jean's head was spinning. She thrust her notebook into her bag and followed.

Iris headed through the gate and up a muddy path, her boots splashing through the puddles. With her not-so-sturdy but thankfully flat shoes, Jean played hopscotch with the dryer patches. She waited next to the corrugated prints of the Bouchards' hiking boots while Iris unlatched the gate in the deer fence and pushed it open. An inquisitive branch of the bracken brushed against Jean's ankle, sending a creeping sensation up her leg.

Stepping into the pine glade was like stepping into a remote, mysterious place out of another century, or even another world. Even the song of the birds seemed muted. No one else was there — the French couple had either not gone into the enclosure at all or had walked through it and out the gate on the far side.

The trees murmured in the wind and their shadows rippled over the shape that stood beneath them, as though shadow itself could erode like water. But the slab of stone had been deliberately broken, not eroded. It rose from a pile of smooth silver rocks stained by whorls of gold and gray lichen, lonely and yet dignified. Jean stepped toward it reverently.

The Stone was taller than she'd thought from its photo, as high as her chest. There was no way of knowing how high it had stood when complete, but the stump was solid enough to have supported several more feet of stone. She traced the carved horse's head with her forefinger, set her fingertips into the shallower line beneath, then laid her hand flat on the unmarked surface to the side. The rock harbored a chill that was deeper than mere cold, sending a frisson up her arm, and felt like fine-grained sandpaper against her skin. The small hole looked like a mouth shaped in an O of sorrow.

Without quite realizing what she was doing, Jean stooped and peered through the hole, just as she'd peeped through the keyhole of the locked door. She saw merely the green and gold rush of light and shadow, no glimpses of ancient times or other dimensions. Her sixth sense remained dormant. Whatever flicker of ghostly energy she'd felt last night didn't seem to have emanated from here. She was almost disappointed.

Straightening, she brushed her fingertips across the broken edge, gingerly, but it wasn't sharp enough to cut. Only then did she remember Iris was standing behind her. "How did the Stone get broken?" she asked in a voice that was almost a whisper.

"I don't know. This piece of it was lying here amidst the bracken when I was a child. When I returned to Pitclachie in the seventies, after my father's death, I had it erected. Seemed the least I could do to honor the ancient people who once lived here." Iris's drill-sergeant voice softened, as though she, too, sensed the weight of time in this place. "Nomenclature can be a bit dodgy as evidence, I know, but the word 'Pit-clachie' does suggest that the Stone was a local landmark many centuries ago. As a boundary marker of the old kingdom of Fidach, perhaps."

"Do you know where the rest of the Stone is?"

"Vandalized and destroyed long since, I daresay."

"Your father found this part being used as the doorstep of the same cottage that's now the Lodge? Why didn't he set it up himself?"

When Iris didn't answer, Jean looked around. The woman stood with her hands on her hips, gazing between the tree trunks down the hillside past the island of house and garden — of modernity — toward the distant glint of water. Was that a certain queasiness in her expression? No. Her face was stern and cold, enigmatic as that of the Stone.

"My father was the local representative of the Office of Works during the nineteen-twenties," she finally replied. "He helped excavate Urquhart Castle. He was quite the scholar when it came to the archaeology and folklore of the area."

Instead of saying, *I know*, Jean waited.

"He wrote that he found the Stone when he shifted and repaired a seventeenth-century cottage, yes. He believed these small stones . . ." Iris nudged one with her foot. ". . . are all that remains of an ancient cairn, which is why he left it here, I suppose. The Pictish cemetery of Garbeg is further up the hill. This might be related to it."

"I know he wrote about Garbeg," Jean said, without adding, *at least he only excavated one grave and left the rest to archaeological posterity.* "I didn't know he wrote about finding the Stone. Where? Not in *Pictish Antiquities.*"

"No, not at all. In some of his personal papers." Iris's emphasis on the word "personal" was unmistakable.

That Ambrose had personal papers was news to Jean, although she was hardly going to faint in amazement. "Have you ever thought of publishing some of his papers? His field notes would interest historians and archaeologists. The Museum of Scotland would love to know where he found that silver hoard, whether here at Pitclachie or at Urquhart or on the south side of the Loch. I'm sure my partner at *Great Scot* would make you an offer."

Iris took a hasty step away, no doubt realizing she'd said too much. "Very kind of her, but no."

"Perhaps I could just read a few of the papers while I'm here, then, and take notes."

"No," said Iris again, biting off the word, and then, with a half-smile that could be interpreted as apology, "He was a much-maligned figure in these parts, Miss Fairbairn. Most unfairly. He had his eccentricities, yes, but was at heart a good man with no vices — he neither smoked nor drank to excess, for example. Feel free to look over the library in the house. Much of his collection of books and antiquities is there."

But not those intriguing personal papers. Was that what Iris meant by "the occasional old family possession" stored in the locked room in the cottage? The room that smelled of pipe tobacco — well, he could have given up smoking when his daughter was born.

Feeling an itch in her palms, Jean murmured, "Thank you, I'll do that." She told herself to get a grip. By "papers," Iris could mean anything from laundry lists to bank statements. A diary reading, "February 4, 1933. Today my daughter Iris was born" was possible. One reading "March 29, 1933. Today I killed my wife by pushing her down the stairs" or "May 2, 1933. Today I invented the Loch Ness monster" was much less likely.

Whatever, Iris did not want those papers read, let alone published. Ambrose might be a historical figure of sorts, but not far enough in the past for family feelings to have dried up and blown away. In a country that ran to ghosties and ghoulies dating back millennia, seventy years or so was a mere blink of the eye. Jean had known all along she'd be reluctant to grill Iris about her father's — personal, private, secret — matters. What she'd suspected all along was that once she reached the scene, curiosity would win out over reluctance.

Iris walked to the gate and opened it, her extended hand directing

Jean down the path toward the house. Obligingly, Jean moved out, but not without one last breath of the tang of pine and one last look at the Stone. How Roger intended to prove his theory that the symbols carved on it represented an early Nessie even her imagination couldn't fathom.

From the house came the gleeful shriek of a child, answered by a shouted maternal directive. Car doors slammed. "I'm sure the B&B is very popular, right here on the main tourist route," said Jean.

"That it is," Iris replied, her steps steady on Jean's heels. "Tourists can be a bane as well as a blessing, mind. We're caught in a vicious circle. The visitors come, therefore need facilities, and the facilities then change for the worse the very thing the visitors have come to see. To say nothing of attracting even more visitors."

Alasdair Cameron had muttered about selling your own heritage. If not for tourists, though, Scotland would be in serious financial trouble. Jean asked, "Like the new Historic Scotland visitor center at the Castle?"

"Hysterical Scotland." Iris didn't smile when she said that, so Jean suppressed her own. "Not wishing to be burdened by the facts, it ignored my environmental impact statements and destroyed the site in order to 'improve' it. The traffic has gone from bad to worse. Human beings can't leave well alone, can they?"

No, Jean thought, leaving well enough alone was harder for your average human being than losing that last five pounds. And she didn't exclude herself from either. "I guess you're not too happy with this Monster Madness stuff, then."

"This area has a great deal to offer the visitor without going on and on about chimerical creatures in the loch. Why, some pseudo-scientist or another has actually introduced American flatworms to the eco-system, brought in on their equipment. Shocking!"

"Surely the flatworms were introduced by accident."

Muttering something about common sense preventing accidents, Iris opened the garden gate, ushered Jean through, then shut it with a resounding clang.

"Maybe the explosion last night wasn't an accident," suggested Jean. "I hear Roger Dempsey received some threatening letters. Do you have any idea who could have sent them?"

"Someone who wanted to stop his expedition, I expect. Considering Roger's reputation, it could have been almost anyone. Although blowing up his boat does seem a bit — drastic." Iris walked on toward the house, trailing her hand through the leaves and flowers crowding the path, leaving Jean to play catch-up yet again.

"I hear one of his assistants is missing," she said to Iris's back.

"A shame, that. But then, Roger has never hesitated to put others at risk in order to serve his own ambitions. I have nothing against educated amateurs, mind — I'm one myself — but the ones who don't realize their limitations can do far more harm than good."

"He told me he's going to search here at Pitclachie. I guess he means some sort of geophysical survey, not actually digging, not unless he finds something."

Iris made a sound that Jean interpreted as a thin, taut laugh, the sort of laugh that teetered uneasily between humor and a harsher emotion, although she couldn't tell what that emotion was. Annoyance? Embarrassment? Perhaps even grief? Jean was beginning to suspect that something more than academic disagreement had soured Iris's feelings toward Roger.

Iris stepped up onto the terrace and spun around. Her pale gray eyes didn't look at Jean so much as through her. "Please go back out to the Stone any time you wish. Just make sure the gate shuts properly, so that the sheep don't get into the garden."

"Thank you." It was time to slip gracefully out of the interview before she was forcibly ejected. "Can we talk again soon, perhaps this evening? I'd like to hear about your work with Scotland the Green. And your father's archaeological work as well — I'm hoping to do something about the spirit of scientific inquiry running in the family."

Iris nodded at that. "Well then, yes, there are important matters that should be brought to the attention of the public, such as ATV damage in mountain passes. And some of my earlier work might be of interest — deforestation in Brazil, water conservation in India and the like. "

"Great!" Jean heard another set of car doors slam. That must have been the Ducketts taking off for the day, unless Kirsty was running some errands.

No, here came Kirsty around the corner of the house, her arms waving. "Aunt Iris!"

Without another word to Jean, Iris strode away across the flagstones, bent her head close to Kirsty's urgent murmur, and then vanished around the corner. Kirsty skipped briskly after her.

Wondering what that was all about, Jean pulled out her notebook and jotted down first what Iris had said, and second what she had implied.

No one would admit faster than Jean that there was a fine line, a very tense line, like quivering piano wire, between privacy and secrecy. She reminded herself that she was not an investigative reporter but a mild-mannered journalist after mild-mannered stories for a history and travel magazine. Still, she could try to make friends with Iris, hoping she'd talk about Ambrose and the Stone and, if she was lucky,

Eileen's disappearance.

Which was what Roger was doing with Jean. If there was a line between secrecy and privacy, there was also one between being friendly and exploiting that friendship. Iris's chill cordiality seemed like a refreshing breeze after Roger's — well, he hadn't quite sunk to the level of smarm. Jean would rather go without a story than smarm Iris or anyone else.

So far, though, she hadn't learned much about Ambrose she didn't already know. He'd been a teenager when he fell under Crowley's spell, metaphorically speaking, just before Crowley left Scotland around 1900. Soon afterwards, Ambrose went up to Oxford and read history and archaeology, then shared his time between family in Britain and Crowley on the Continent. In 1914, unlike the blatantly anti-war Crowley, he went off to do his duty on the western front.

After the war, Ambrose helped excavate Urquhart Castle, wrote florid prose about area antiquities and legends for various newspapers and magazines, married, and remodeled the family estate. While rarely or never seeing Crowley, Ambrose remained an admirer. By the 1930s, the old wizard had devolved from evildoer to laughing-stock. Ambrose probably wrote the justificative biography for just that reason — if your guru's a joke, then so are you. Jean understood. One of the reasons she'd followed through with the lawsuit against the university was to protect her students' reputations as well as her own.

She tucked away her notebook, thinking that she could sure empathize — boy, could she empathize — with a policeman growing frustrated at not getting the whole story. Except that a policeman was usually justified in demanding the whole story and nothing but, and Jean wasn't.

An all-too-familiar male voice echoed harshly in the courtyard, a loud sarcastic voice that demanded rather than asked. Jean's hackles bristled. *Shit!* The minute she saw D.C. Gunn on television, she should have known that the Northern Constabulary's token troll, Detective Sergeant Andy Sawyer, was skulking around the area, too.

It might have been amusing to hang around and see how long it took Iris to turn him into stone, except Jean had never found anything amusing in D.S. Sawyer. In a thoroughly undignified scuttle, she whisked around the far side of the cottage and gained her car without being accosted. But not without telling herself that if Sawyer and Gunn were on the scene, D.C.I. Cameron couldn't be far behind.

NINE

Failing at her attempt to ignore the knot in her stomach — when it came to Alasdair Cameron, denial was growing increasingly futile — Jean stopped her car at the end of the drive. She'd have to make a right turn across both lanes, but traffic was moving slowly. Each car in turn came almost to a stop as rubberneckers looked at the blue-and-white police tape closing off the road down to the pier.

There. She made it safely into the left-hand lane. Not that she had anywhere to go, other than away from Sawyer. She'd have to run Roger Dempsey down eventually, to get his view of what had happened and to ask him again about Iris, but. . . She'd check out the new Urquhart Castle visitor center. Hysterical Scotland aside, it deserved a few lines in any article about the area.

She drove through the village at walking speed, easing her car past the bumpers of the media vans parked haphazardly along the road. Several people stood outside the police station, a small office annexed to the local constable's home. More people thronged the souvenir shops, restaurants, and Tourist Information Center, where cars circled the jam-packed parking lot like sharks scenting gasoline in the water.

Once past the road-clot, it took Jean only minutes to drive to the point of land crowned by the ruined castle. Its new parking lot was several times larger than the one she remembered, but was almost full. Iris had been right about the increased traffic, although surely some of these people had been lured in by the Festival . . . A camper with a German license plate was just pulling out. She nipped into the space.

The moment she emerged from the car, her bag erupted in Mozart's *Rondo*. Quelling her start, she dug out her cell phone and flipped it open. The screen read, *Miranda Capaldi*. Jean smiled. "You're slow off the mark. The boat blew up last night."

"I didn't hear 'til now, did I?" returned Miranda. Her smooth voice was muffled by the wind blowing past Jean's ear.

She assumed the cell phone crouch, head tucked, her free hand covering her free ear. "Before you ask, I haven't the foggiest notion what happened. I'm just an innocent bystander."

"Oh aye, that you are," said Miranda consolingly. "How are the articles getting on? Any joy from either Roger or Iris?"

"Only their party lines. Iris says Roger uses people to further his ambitions."

"That's not shocking news. Either her saying it or it being true."

"Yeah, but still, she's letting him do a ground survey of Pitclachie

Farm. I hear he's going on with it, boat or no boat. And did you hear that one of his assistants is missing?"

"Aye, that was on the telly as well. Your old chum D.C. Gunn . . . No, don't say it, he's naught but a business acquaintance."

On the one hand, Jean thought, it was helpful that Miranda knew her so well. She didn't have to dissimulate. On the other hand, it was annoying that Miranda knew her so well, because then she couldn't even rationalize, let alone deny. "Iris is impossible to read. She's like one of those books in her library, hide-bound."

"Ah, but you're a grand researcher."

"Hah," Jean returned. "She did tell me that Ambrose wrote about the Pitclachie Stone in his personal papers, but when I told her that *Great Scot* might consider a publishing deal, she turned me down. In fact, when I asked if I could just see them, she said that the papers are, well, personal. No dice."

"Ooh," said Miranda. "You'd almost think she was hiding something."

"Just because she doesn't want to fling open her family cup-board for public inspection doesn't mean there's a skeleton in it — literal or not. But you do get the impression she's trying to protect Ambrose's reputation, don't you? Were they close? She said something about returning to Pitclachie at his death that made me wonder."

"She spent a good many years traveling and working in other parts of the world, aye, but I suppose they got on well enough. Mind the turning."

"What?"

"I'm speaking to Duncan, sorry. We're just arriving at the club-house, have a round scheduled for eleven."

"Have a good game, then. When I know anything else, I'll let you know."

"I'm sure you will. Cheerio." Miranda's words were punctuated by background voices, probably all the caddies flocking forward. Duncan and Miranda had long ago noticed that good tips meant good service.

Jean shut her phone, stowed it away, and blinked. For a moment she'd seen the manicured fairways of — where were they? Muir-field? Gleneagles? She, however, was at Loch Ness, if not up to her neck at least up to her waist in another set of mysterious circum-stances, and not exactly struggling to break free.

Below a low wall edged with shrubs, the ground fell away, rose again slightly to support the shattered walls of the castle, and then plunged to the murky gray-blue water of the loch. Which was starting to get choppy, making even a passing barge rock and roll.

The wind was freshening, its cool gusts tugging at Jean's hair and jacket, and those big white fluffy clouds were now being jostled from the sky by darker, more serious ones.

She made her way through the traffic to the mock turret that was the entrance to the Visitor Center. Paying a not-inconsiderable fee admitted her to its interior, where staircases led down to an educational display and movie, a gift shop, and a restaurant teeming with humankind — Scandinavians, Africans, Moslem women in their head scarves. While Jean wasn't going to suggest joining hands and singing "Kumbaya," she had to smile at how the myth mongers had succeeded in giving the ruined building universal appeal. An appeal that might have gone unnoticed if the castle hadn't been situated on a major road, next to a loch with a vivid myth of its own.

The Visitor Center was as much following the crowds as enticing them. The last time Jean had visited, she'd waited in line to use a spartan Portakabin toilet with a group of Japanese women, each of them ready with her antiseptic wipe. Still, Iris had a point about people destroying what they came to see. Historic Scotland had dug out the side of the hill to build this structure, demolishing God only knew what in the process. Some of the authenticity, for one thing. At least they hadn't Disneyed the place up with audio-animatronic clansmen and a Nessie running back and forth on an underwater track.

Mulling over issues of Theme Park Scotland, Jean exited past a terrace equipped with tables and chairs. The construction scars were covered with lush greenery, cut only by a path that slanted steeply downward. She took small steps, hoping she wouldn't be swept away by a sudden avalanche of humanity, and punched a number on her phone.

"Hello," said Rebecca's voice.

"Hi. It's Jean, calling from the bonny banks of Loch Ness. Literally. I'm walking down to the castle right now."

"I told you she'd be calling," Rebecca said faintly, and then, into the phone, "We saw the news this morning. What happened? Was the explosion an accident or sabotage?"

"I don't know any more than you do right now."

A couple of clunks signaled Michael switching on the extension. "Well then, Jean. You've put the boot in again. That is, a reporter's after being where the action is and all."

"Nice try, Michael." Jean went on, "Iris showed me the Pitclachie Stone this morning, and said something about Ambrose writing about it in his personal papers. I don't suppose the Museum has any of those?"

"No, but telling me he had private writings is like telling me it's

Saturday. No surprise."

"How do we know, then, that Ambrose really did find the Stone in the door of the cottage? There are some pictographs carved in the terrace of the house . . ."

"Oh," said Rebecca. "You think he carved the Stone himself."

"Not necessarily. I'm just exploring possibilities."

Michael answered, "We've got possibilities aplenty when it comes to Ambrose, but that one's right out. It was a mason working on the cottage who turned up the Stone, and who went on record about it. Ambrose could have paid the man to say he found it, but why?"

"Good question. Ambrose didn't try to profit from the Stone — he dumped it into a grove of trees behind the house. You'd expect an antiquarian to set it up. But it was Iris who did that."

"It was Iris who reported it to us. Mopping up after her father, I'm thinking."

"Sounds like it." Jean stopped at the bottom of the slope, next to the medieval siege engine that had recently been constructed for a television show. With its swinging beam removed, it looked like a wooden rocket on a timber launch pad. An American was saying to his wife, "This was used to defend the castle. Pretty well preserved for being so old, isn't it?"

And so was myth generated, Jean thought. "Was the Stone broken when the mason found it?"

"Good question," Michael replied. "I'll look out the man's statement on the Monday, shall I?"

"Please. Not that Ambrose has anything to do with Roger's boat blowing up."

"Does Iris?" Rebecca asked.

"I can't imagine what Iris might have to do with it. Well, I can imagine any number of things, but whether any of them are even logical, let alone the truth . . ." Jean shook her head, trying to shake away the frustration but only tangling herself further up in it. "I don't suppose Iris ever tried to sell you the Stone. I mean, renovating an old house and fitting it out as a B&B takes a lot of money."

"Don't believe so, no, though we were offered a fine Pictish silver chain from that area just last year, if I'm remembering aright. A bit unusual to find Pictish silver there, but Ambrose's hoard might could be evidence of an alliance."

"How about an arranged marriage?" Rebecca suggested. "And the Stone is like the wedding license."

"Linecrescent Horsehead marries Doubledisc-something, carrying a bouquet of foxgloves and meadowsweet, wearing a becoming gown of blue paint? Maybe the stone was broken to signify a divorce . . . No, that's right, it was broken recently." Jean shrugged. "The chain was one of those heavy-duty numbers with the big links and a cuff holding the ends together?"

"Oh aye, just that. I'll suss out the provenance. Could be from Ambrose's mysterious hoard, right enough. However . . ."

"Iris would get more money for Ambrose's artifacts if she took them straight to the antiquities market," Rebecca chimed in. "Anything from an old family collection like that wouldn't fall under the laws of treasure trove. She wouldn't be obliged to offer it to the Museum first."

Jean stopped on the drawbridge spanning the now-dry moat. "Miranda said something about an old family collection, too. And they are an old family, right?"

"Oh aye," said Michael. "Mackintosh of Pitclachie is an old landed family, right enough. Bar the one who became a Red Indian chief in your part of the world, they were a right colorless family as well, 'til Ambrose appeared."

"On top of his other eccentricities," said Rebecca, "when he finally got married, it was to an American. Although her wealth cancelled out her nationality, society-wise."

"I know about that. Eileen was half his age, only eighteen."

"Oh aye," said Michael. "Not that that was scandalous, mind."

Rebecca snorted. "Never has been. Now if it had been the other way around . . ."

Jean nodded agreement, even though they couldn't see her. A group of schoolchildren rushed past her and into the castle like cheerful lemmings, the wood of the drawbridge shivering to the soft pounding of their sneakers. "So was it a love match, do you think? Or another kind of alliance, new American money — her family got rich selling mustard gas and tinned food during the war — for the prestige of an old if not exactly wealthy family name?"

"Who knows?" said Rebecca. "People were more discreet with their private lives then."

"My granny says Eileen used to be quite the lady of the manor," Michael went on, "but what with Ambrose's building projects they might could have got through all her money. They'd sacked most of the servants by the time Iris was born, and by all accounts the marriage itself was falling apart."

"So they had a baby," Rebecca said. "When will people learn?"

"Never, probably. If they did, Miranda and I would go out of business." Jean straightened up and turned toward the castle. "A psychologist could have had a field day with Ambrose. No surprise Iris is so matter-of-fact. I bet she wants to make the world safe for rationality."

"Ah, but the world isn't rational," Rebecca said. "At least, not the human part of it."

"Amen," Jean said. "And thanks. I'll keep you posted. If you'll let me know what you find out about the chain, I'd sure appreciate it. Pet Dougie for me, will you?"

"He and Riccio are having a nap just now," Michael said. "They've been playing with the wee Nessie — thank you kindly for sending it along."

"Only Roger Dempsey would think of sending Nessies out with his press kits."

"You take care, Jean," said Rebecca, showing her friend enough respect not to repeat her *nothing's going to sneak up on you.*

"You do, too, you and little Linda. And don't worry about me — this time I'm an innocent bystander." And if she repeated that often enough, it might turn out to be true.

Jean switched off the phone and stowed it away, telling herself that discretion might be the better part of valor, yet discretion didn't answer questions or discharge responsibilities.

Bracing her shoulders back, she walked into the entrance tunnel of the castle and peered warily upward. The passageway had once had a wooden ceiling. The upper side of that ceiling had been a floor pierced with openings called murder holes, handy for ambushing attackers with boiling water, arrows, rocks — whatever was convenient. Now, though, the stone vault of the passageway was no more than a blank arch, stained dark and exuding the musty scent of age.

Jean emerged from the corridor's shadow into another sort of shadow, a gray cloud drifting past the sun. The oldest part of the castle, a few Pictish stones fused together by fire, sat atop the higher ground to her right. The fortress had been built, and had fallen, and more structures had been built on top, only to be themselves modified over the centuries by the exigencies of war and clan raids and the weather, a formidable foe itself. Now even the "new" tower perched above the loch had partly collapsed, exposing the floor levels inside like an architectural model.

Tourists walked up and down and children played hide-and-seek along battlements that had once run with blood, but the castle itself remained aloof, listening to the music of another time. Or today, as the case might be. A piper in full kilt and bonnet outfit was tuning his pipes in the courtyard of the tower, emitting sounds that combined the squeal of a frightened pig with the squawk of a stepped-on cat. Funny, how the actual music was glorious. Anticipating glory, Jean tossed a pound coin into the piper's carrying case and went inside.

A spiral stairway led upwards. She placed each foot carefully on the narrow, hollowed treads, thinking that medieval people must have had prehensile toes. Just as she emerged onto the small landing at the top of the tower, she was greeted by a burst of sunlight from above and a burst of music from below. *Scotland the Brave!* All right!

Her grin petrified. Like a downpour of burning oil through some psychic murder hole, recognition seared every nerve in her body. That man, his sturdy hands bracing his compact body against the railing as though preparing to repel raiders — that man, his cropped hair rippling in the wind like a field of wheat touched by frost — that man, wearing his dark business suit like armor. His back was turned, but she knew him. Alasdair Cameron.

TEN

Alasdair hadn't seen her. She could creep back down the stairway. . .
No. Even if she wanted to turn tail and run, here came a family clogging the escape route, parents cajoling the children in Italian.

He didn't look around at the sound of their voices, just as he
hadn't looked around at the sound of her steps. But Jean knew that
his stillness was deceptive. He was very much aware of how many
people were gathered behind him, and yet, intent on the expanse of
water before him, he saw no need to take notice of them.

This encounter was part serendipity, part Murphy's Law. Here
she was and here he was and what kind of adolescent game would
she be playing to pretend she hadn't wanted to see him again? She
realized she was holding her breath and let it out in a long sigh of
acceptance.

He spun around as though answering a peal of alarm bells. As
though he'd felt her breath on the back of his neck. His slate blue,
sleet blue, eyes brightened. His lips with their elegant curve expanded into a grin as bright as lightning and as quickly gone.
"Jean." Just the one word, falling like a rock down a well and
landing with a resounding thump deep in her abdomen.

She blinked, thinking she'd imagined that grin, knowing she
hadn't. She inhaled, tried a wobbly smile, and groped through several greetings: *We have to stop meeting like this*, or *Seen any ghosts
lately?* and settled on a simple, "Hello, Alasdair."

He made no effort to bridge the arm's length gap between them
with a handshake. Instead his patented expressionless gaze roamed
up the mountain crags behind Pitclachie Farm to where minute
reddish dots might be deer, to the official vehicles gathered at the
pier across the bay, to the family washing around him and Jean like a
stream around the stones in its course. Then his gaze re-connected
with hers, and his quiet voice said, "Here you are, then. You found
me."

Whatever she'd expected him to say, it wasn't that. She emitted
a lame, "What?"

"You didn't come looking me out, after asking questions about
the explosion?"

"No. Sawyer turned up at Pitclachie House so I thought I'd
make myself scarce. I just came down here to look around the castle
. . ." She stopped herself before her tongue ran off at the end with,
nothing personal.

"Ah. Well then. Good show, Andy's temper has hardly

improved. You'll not be getting shut of us quite so easily as that, though. Dempsey handed in a list of the people visiting the boat — the ones he knew, at the least. Half the folk in Inverness-shire, it sounds like, and your name amongst the rest. Gave me a bit of a turn, that."

I bet it did. Nothing was personal. Yeah, right. At least she hadn't ambushed him quite as badly as she'd first thought. "I was the last . . ."

His elevated forefinger counseled caution. The Italian family edged past and trooped back down the staircase, leaving Jean and Alasdair alone atop the tower. Below, the piper began to play "Amazing Grace," another of the old standards likely to earn him tips.

Feeling less than graceful and not at all amazing, Jean tried again. "They pulled the boat out into the bay right after I left, so I was the last visitor."

"You came here to interview Roger Dempsey, then."

"And Iris Mackintosh. I'm hoping to do an article about her father Ambrose, the antiquarian and part-time nut case. I had nothing to do with the boat explosion, but as long as I'm here . . ."

"You might could write a story about it," he said.

"I don't want to write about it, no — I'm trying to avoid being the ambulance-chasing kind of reporter. It's just that I can't help but wonder what the story is. What the stories are. You know me, I can't leave well enough alone."

An oscillation at the corners of his mouth made her suspect that he was curbing a laugh, a rueful laugh not at her but with her.

Jean looked down at her feet, avoiding his intense — intensely curious — gaze. *Why,* a small voice in the back of her mind whined, *why was it that Alasdair never saw her at her best?* Right now she probably looked like Rip van Winkle wandering back into town after his "nap," creased and confused . . . *Damn.* She was concerned about how she looked to him.

She peered warily into his face. The line of concentration between his eyebrows was deeper than she remembered and his eyes more guarded. It wasn't so much that his upper lip was stiff, as that it was stiff all the way to his hairline. If her contents were under pressure, his were doubly so. She doubted if anything she could say would help, let alone anything she could ask. But she had to ask, just as she had to breathe. "Have you found Jonathan Paisley yet?

"No. He's not been seen since the boat went up. We're thinking he was aboard at the time, and went into the water. "

"Yeah, I saw lights on the boat right before the fireworks started," Jean said, and added before he could ask, "I saw it go up from the terrace of Pitclachie House."

Alasdair nodded, deadpan.

"Poor Jonathan," Jean said. "He was — and I guess the word is 'was' — just a kid. His family must be devastated. And I bet Roger's plenty upset."

"He is that. Kept repeating, 'I don't believe it', as though believing it makes some sort of difference."

Poor Roger, too. "Was the explosion an accident?"

"We don't know as yet. The forensics chaps are having a go at the debris, though most of that's on the bottom of the loch. I daresay Paisley's there as well. In water this cold, it takes some time for decomposition to bring a body to the surface. If it ever does at all."

"So I hear. Loch Ness never gives up its dead." She firmly rejected the imagery that went along with his statement.

"Did you have your interview with Roger, then?"

"Yes. He's doing both water and land surveys looking for Nessie. I assume he's sucking up to the other reporters as blatantly as he is to me, except with me he's acting like we're old friends because we once met. To no good purpose, but we met."

"He's presuming on the acquaintance, is he?"

"Yes, and that makes me . . . Okay, okay, I've only been a journalist for a few months and already I'm firmly convinced that everyone has a secret agenda. He wants publicity, that's all."

Alasdair said nothing, expressing no skepticism about Dempsey's agendas, Jean's convictions, or even Nessie's existence. Unlike her, he was very good at that old journalist's trick, to keep so quiet the subject runs on and on. She might be a subject and not a suspect, but she didn't have much to run on about. "There was a lot of electronic equipment on board the boat, like you'd expect, although I couldn't tell you anything about it. It's just as well I didn't stay very long, that boat aroma, you know, bilge and gasoline, got to me . . ."

"Gasoline?" asked Alasdair. "You're saying that you smelled petrol?"

"I've got kind of a sensitive nose, I notice smells . . ."

"The Water Horse boat was powered by diesel."

Her brain screeched around a sharp curve, only two wheels in contact with coherence. Gasoline. Diesel. That's right, she'd smelled the diesel fumes when the boat pulled away from the pier. "They could have had gasoline for a generator or — or . . . You don't mean the smell could have come from a Molotov cocktail!"

"A petrol bomb. Oh aye."

Good God. She'd been sitting on a bomb. She filed that thought in her denial basket and plunged on, "Someone threw a petrol bomb at an expedition camping along the shore about twenty years ago. No one was hurt, and no one was ever charged. The nut they suspected left the area and that was that. Or it was that, until now."

"Oh aye?" Alasdair said again. His left eyebrow arched upward, infinitesimally.

"That bomb was thrown from a passing boat. This one must have already been on board. Someone had to have been there to light the fuse or start the timer or something."

"Perhaps Jonathan himself, but he didn't escape before it went up."

"Why would he want to blow up the boat he was working on?" She frowned out over the water. Below the tower, a tourist boat wallowed in the waves while its passengers took photos. Since her picture was going to be in several vacation albums, maybe she should wave or even curtsey.

She swiveled back around without doing either. "When I first got there and Jonathan demanded my bona fides, Brendan shouted, 'You're as jumpy as a guy tap-dancing in a minefield.' Then, later on, Jonathan said to Brendan, 'And it's not five minutes you were asking me to take your place this evening.' Take his place working on the boat that evening, or somewhere else? Why was he so nervous? And Brendan said that Jonathan should be careful about going into the water, he'd sink like a rock from the weight of the chip on his shoulder. They weren't getting along well, in other words, although that bit about going into the water could just be a badly-timed turn of phrase."

"Or it might could have been a threat. Anything else?" Alasdair's other eyebrow arched upward to join the first.

Whoa, Jean thought, she was on a roll. To what, she didn't know, but she was rolling. "Haven't you got anything from the threatening letters?"

"I'll not be saying that." His hint of a smile partly apologized for not confiding in her, partly reminded her that he was the interrogator here. "Whoever sent the letters was after stopping the expedition, aye, but that's not necessarily the same person who blew up the boat."

"Good point. Iris said that considering Roger's reputation, just about anyone could have wanted to stop the expedition, although blowing up the boat did seem a bit drastic."

"Iris said that, did she? What else was she saying about Dempsey?"

Nothing that would make Jean feel as though telling Alasdair was betraying a confidence. "That Roger puts people at risk in order to serve his ambitions and that amateurs like him can do more harm than good. I got the impression Iris feels some sort of personal betrayal. Roger hinted he'd already gone several rounds with her. But that's only a marginally stronger impression than my feeling Roger's up to something behind the scenes."

"The expedition might could have been the set-up for an insurance scam."

There was a thought, but not one she was comfortable with. "Roger loves his gadgets. I can't see him destroying them on purpose."

"Who was with you when the boat exploded?"

"Some of the guests at Pitclachie House, the Ducketts and Martin Hall and his little boy."

"No one else? Not Iris herself?"

Back to Iris. The only reason Jean could keep up with Alasdair's acrobatic thought processes was because hers tended to leap and twirl, too. "No, Iris wasn't there — I didn't meet her until this morning. Kirsty, her niece, wasn't there, either. She went out with Brendan last night. Iris isn't too happy about that. She thinks he's been contaminated by Roger, I guess."

"Who else is stopping at the B&B?"

"The Hall family, the Ducketts, and a French couple, the Bouchards. Iris and Kirsty put me in the Lodge, a separate cottage, because the Bouchards didn't want to stay . . ." Oh hell, if she could tell anyone, she could tell Alasdair. That moment they'd each realized the other had the same ghostly allergy was not one she'd soon, if ever, forget.

She leaned in a bit closer. Her nerve endings stirred in that energy field she remembered all too well. Like a tickle, it was neither entirely pleasant nor entirely irritating. "There's a ghost in the Lodge. Ambrose, I bet — it used to be his study. I heard the door of a locked room open and shut, footsteps, the smell of coffee and tobacco. I also heard a man and a woman arguing, and what might have been Eileen Mackintosh scream and fall down the stairs. I didn't get up and look. There's a ghost in the garden, too, not as strong a one, though."

"Eh?" Alasdair tilted his head toward hers. He wasn't that much taller than she was, so he didn't have far to tilt. "Ambrose was tried for murder, wasn't he?"

She tried not to shrink away like some sweet young thing on her first date — she wasn't sweet, she wasn't young, she wasn't a thing, and this sure as heck wasn't a date. "He was, yes. But that's over and done with. What isn't over and done is that before I heard the ghost, I heard another door shut, maybe the outside one. Which was also locked."

"You're thinking that was a living person. Had anything gone missing this morning?"

"Nothing of mine. I can't speak for everything in the house. A bookshelf was disarranged is all. Oh, and a curtain was drawn, but

I'm sure that, at least, was Ambrose."

"And you're on your own in this cottage at night, are you?"

"Somebody could have been searching for something there, but they'd have no motive to come after me!"

"You don't know that for certain, do you now?"

She smiled tightly. "Thanks, Alasdair."

"You're welcome, Jean," he returned, almost sober, but a similar smile lurked in the depths of his eyes. He turned his gaze to the blue-tinted mountains that dwindled away to the south.

No, he couldn't explain the small mystery of the doors either, but he wasn't about to reject anything as irrelevant to his investigation. Damn, Jean thought, she was still able to read him. That was not a skill she'd meant to cultivate. And damn him, while she was at it, not only for pointing out that she just might could maybe be in danger, but for that knowing if subtle smile that got under her skin every time.

Voices and the scramble of footsteps echoed up the stairs. Down below, the piper struck up *Auld Lang Syne*. Alasdair stepped away from her the instant she stepped away from him, his expression locking itself down. "We're needing a statement."

"I know the drill," she returned, and glanced at her watch. "I'm supposed to catch up with Hugh Munro — my neighbor, you remember, the musician — at the Festival, but then I can stop by the station."

"I bought one of Munro's albums, since you spoke so well of him. Fine music."

Surprised, not to mention pleased, Jean was inhaling to respond when five or six people clambered out of the stairwell and crowded the top of the tower.

Alasdair motioned toward the stairs with a curt, "Right."

"Right." Jean expelled her breath and took a step.

"Look!" The shout sparked a general rush to the side of the tower. Cameras leaped to attention and started clicking. "It's Nessie!" someone else said, and the word passed from voice to voice like a hot potato from hand to hand. "Nessie! Nessie!"

Jean almost tripped over her own feet, she spun around so fast, and was pulled along in Alasdair's wake as he cut through the group. She bumped up against the railing between him and a plump woman, and followed the trajectory set by the multiple pointing fingers.

A mottled dark hump bobbed up and down in the waves just below the castle. Around it floated what looked like appendages, mere suggestions just below the surface of the opaque water. This time Jean's brain ran smack up against a wall and stopped. *Nessie? No way!*

The piper stopped playing. In the sudden quivering silence Jean could hear more excited voices drifting up from below. A brush against her arm was Alasdair reaching into his jacket and pulling out a cell phone. Stepping away from the parapet, he punched buttons then put the phone to his ear.

Oh. It was all in the perspective, wasn't it? An explosion, a fire, might singe the red of a life preserver into mottled black. But it would still be buoyant. Jonathan hadn't sunk at all.

Jean mouthed the words as Alasdair said them, his voice flat, dull, professional: "We've found Jonathan Paisley."

ELEVEN

In the rush of police cars and media vans along the road toward the castle, Jean felt like a salmon swimming upstream. She presumed boats were on the way, too, but she couldn't see the bay from the town. So that's why intelligent and imaginative Alasdair had been loitering with intent at the top of the tower. Because he hoped that Jonathan's body would eventually drift by.

Poor Jonathan, she thought again, those two words wearing a rut in her mind. There he'd been, cautiously wearing that life preserver, and all it had preserved was his body, an exhibit in a crime scene. Some life preservers were made with blocky extensions around the neck to keep an unconscious person's head above the water. Not the kind Jonathan had been wearing. He'd chosen a light sports model that wouldn't limit his flexibility while he worked with Roger and Brendan. But he'd gone into the water alone, in the fiery darkness. Into cold water that would have sapped first consciousness, then life.

Shuddering, Jean drove up to Pitclachie House and parked next to a second police car. Was Iris so formidable that Sawyer had called for back-up? Jean wouldn't have minded witnessing the confrontation, but not if it meant getting caught in the line of fire.

Was Jonathan an innocent bystander who had been caught in the line of fire? Or had the mad bomber intended to kill him? Had he intended to kill Brendan or Roger — especially Roger? Unless Roger himself was the mad bomber as Alasdair had theorized, Alasdair being a man who always considered his options.

When she told Miranda she was tired of playing it safe, Jean hadn't necessarily meant she wanted to put herself at risk, either physically or emotionally. And yet she had. Now she wasn't sure which part of D.C.I. Cameron's concern she found more disturbing, that he thought she might be in danger or that he cared about her safety. He was only doing his job, she rationalized.

Rationality had its limits. Nessie was only one of the creatures that frolicked in the blank spaces at the edge of the map. She'd been rooting for Nessie yesterday afternoon. Before the explosion.

Just as Jean turned away from the house and her own thoughts, the Water Horse van careened off the road and up the drive, Roger at the wheel with Brendan riding shotgun. He skidded to a stop beside her and leaned out of his window. "Hey, Jean."

"Hello," she replied, suppressing the impulse to add, *you look terrible.*

He must know he looked terrible, with bags hanging slackly from his bloodshot eyes. Although, judging by the trace of egg clinging to his beard, he hadn't looked in a mirror for quite some time. Even the bill of his cap drooped dispiritedly, and his voice was dull. "We're going on with the survey. Jonathan would have wanted us to. He was a real supportive guy, Jonathan — was."

"In other words, the police told us not to leave," said Brendan. He was leaning away from Roger, against the opposite door, giving Jean the impression the two men had been arguing.

Roger focused on Jean. "We had the ground-penetrating radar and magnetometers stored at the hotel, along with some of the computers we weren't using on the boat. We didn't lose as much as we might have."

One if by land, two if by sea, Jean thought irreverently and irrelevantly, and asked. "Do you have any idea what caused the boat to explode?"

"It was an accident. No other option."

"But the threaten . . ."

"The stove in the galley," Roger stated. "Tracy says it's been playing up. Acting up. She even mentioned it to the guy who owns the boat. He ignored her, and now look what happened."

"Wasn't it a propane stove?"

Roger stared at her as though she'd just spoken in Elvish. "Yeah, that's just the point. Leaking propane, a spark from the equipment, boom."

Either he hadn't noticed the gasoline smell or . . . Or what? She knew better than to trespass on Cameron's theories or his witnesses. If Roger wanted to indulge in denial, prevarication, or both, all she could do was take note. She tried an innocuous, "Maybe you can show me your remote-sensing equipment some time."

"Yeah, great. We'll do that." He tried to grin and produced a ghastly grimace instead.

Brendan's face was soberly downcast, his cubical jaw tucked into his jacket collar like a box wrapped in gift paper. Still, his eyes glinted warily as they looked from Jean to the police car waiting at the top of the drive and back again. She wondered if he was feeling guilty over — well, maybe no more than his hasty words to Jonathan, or trading places . . . *Oh.* He and Roger didn't know Jonathan's body had just turned up. She could try telling them, and seeing what their reaction was. But Alasdair would prefer doing that himself. He kept as tight a control of his variables as his emotions.

"See you later," Roger said, and accelerated toward the house.

Jean inhaled the damp wind scented with the slightly musty smell of the loch. What she had thought was some emanation from the neighboring fields she now realized had been Roger's breath. Knocking back a few drinks was the time-honored response to disaster, she told herself. He was entitled.

She walked briskly down the length of the drive and onto the sidewalk that ran beside the main road. Since it was also the shoulder of the road, she stayed as close to the fence-lined side as she could — taking into account that some of the leafy wonders filling the gully between asphalt and fence were stinging nettles. This country was filled with an amazing variety of prickly things. And people. *Go figure.*

The festival occupied a bumpy open field that lay between the old hotel housing the Official Loch Ness Exhibition — distinct from the Original Loch Ness Exhibition down the road — and the new Cameron Arms Hotel. Jean paused a moment to admire the contemporary building's slate roof, stuccoed walls, and crow-stepped gables, a design that recognized Scottish traditional architecture without becoming the sort of "authenticity" that was actually mockery.

A sudden pricking of her thumbs made her first frown, then look quickly around and up. What the . . ? Ah, Tracy Dempsey was framed in a large bay window on the second floor of the hotel. She was staring down at Jean, her face set in something between a scowl and a sob, like Medusa catching a glimpse of herself in a mirror.

Tracy had every reason to be grief-stricken, frustrated, angry — or all of the above. Just as Jean lifted her hand in a sympathetic wave, a thin, tall silhouette wavered in the window behind Tracy and she vanished as abruptly as though she'd been jerked back by a rubber band.

Jean stood with her hand upraised. Had she seen a second person in the room or had she been deceived by Tracy's reflection on the glass? If someone were there, it sure wasn't Roger, not unless during his explorations along the edge of science he'd learned how to be in two places at once. As for who was there — the body shape was Martin Hall's — it was none of her business.

Like that was going to stop her, Jean thought.

She picked her way across the muddy patch inside the gate of the Festival Field and up the hill. Flags strained against their moorings, her hair whipped around her face, and the fabric of the large central tent ran a swell like the water of the loch. Technicians used lengths of cable to knit together microphones, amplifiers, and mixer boards on the stage, while vendors of food and souvenirs around the periphery were already making sales to the gathering multitude. A wide selection of Starr beverages was available, Jean noted, from water with caffeine or vitamins, to beer and whiskey served up with warm scones, meat pies, and other high-carb, high-grease selections. Festival food, in other words.

A sensual fiddle melody rose and fell on the wind, luring Jean to a smaller tent. She peeked through the flap. Aha, this was the green room, furnished with chairs and provender for the performers. Hugh Munro was sitting there dreamily sawing away at a ballad, not that "sawing" was the right word for the motion of his bow across the strings of his fiddle. It danced, tracing arabesques in the air. Or, Jean thought in spite of herself, it made love to the fiddle — connecting, receding, connecting again. If words could barely describe the action of making music, they failed utterly when it came to describing music itself, emotion in sound. And like emotion, some music was uplifting and some was painful.

Jean suspected Hugh wasn't so much rehearsing as — no, not amusing himself. He was breathing. For a musician, business was pleasure and pleasure was business. Even historians couldn't quite say that.

Most of the time Hugh looked like Santa Claus, polished bald head fringed by neatly-trimmed white hair, apple cheeks fringed by a neatly-trimmed white beard, stomach shaking with humor. Other times he morphed into Karl Marx, his stomach shaking with indignation and his eyes flashing fiercely. His protest songs were so stirring they would drive the most rabid reactionary onto the barricades.

Now Hugh's clear blue eyes beamed with goodwill to man — and woman. He brought the song to a close and said, "Here you are, then," echoing Cameron's statement.

"Here I am," Jean returned, "in the thick of it."

Carefully Hugh tucked his fiddle into its well-worn case and the case beneath his arm. "Your story's blown up on you again, has it? And aye, I'm intending the pun."

"I don't do these things on purpose," she told him with a sickly smile.

He bowed her out of the tent, patting her shoulder reassuringly as she passed. "No, I'm not thinking you do. I hear there's a lad gone missing."

"Not any longer. We — er — they found him just a few minutes ago, floating in the loch."

"I'm sorry," said Hugh.

"Me, too," Jean stated. "So where were you when the boat went up?"

"The lads and I were unloading the bus. Bloody thing broke down twice on the road from Dundee, we were hours late arriving here. That flack from Starr looked to be having a coronary."

"Flack from Starr? A public relations guy?"

"Oh aye, name of Peter Kettering. A right ponce, scunnered I'd missed some sort of posh dinner with the Tourist Authority folk.

Carted me away for a drink with the VIPs, including the American scientific chap and his wife. Mutton dressed as lamb, she was, low-cut frock, ankle-breaking high heels. If that's not too unkind a cut."

Jean thought, there but for the grace of common sense . . . "I used to wear high heels all the time — when you're only five-three people don't always take you seriously. Tracy would be about that tall without her shoes, I bet. And she wants to be taken seriously."

"Don't we all?" said Hugh. "Dempsey now, he seems couthy enough, if a bit cracked. They were serving good whiskey, thank the gods for small favors, but the conversation was hopeless. Kettering and My Lady Dempsey were making talk so small it was microscopic, all the while sniffing each other like dogs. And Dempsey himself drank and looked about like an alien suddenly set down on the earth."

Jean grinned. She could see the entire scene.

"A handsome young couple was there too," he went on. "Didn't say much, though — never caught their names."

"Did you catch their nationality?" Jean asked, wondering if the Bouchards had attended the dinner.

"He was a Yank, whilst she had a Glasgow accent, I'm thinking. Bonny lass, she was, and clever enough not to go ruining her looks by painting her face."

"Ah, that was Kirsty, Iris Mackintosh's niece. And Brendan, one of Dempsey's assistants. The surviving assistant, although Jonathan was still alive if this was before the boat blew up." Unless someone killed him and staged the boat explosion to cover up the murder, whispered the insistent voice in the back of Jean's mind. Some people had muses, she had Miss Marple.

"It was before the boat blew up," Hugh said. "Kettering marched us all away to hear the pipe band and view the fireworks, and I escaped back to the bus in good time to see the explosion. Bad business. No accident, I take it?"

"It might not be, no," Jean said.

They stopped at the side of the pavilion, Hugh looking over the proceedings with a critical eye that belied his cherubic smile. "This Roger Dempsey chap, he's ex-university like yourself?"

"No, not really, although I first met him at an academic conference. Basically he's a businessman and engineer with a yen for exploration. His companies build all sorts of remote-sensing equipment."

"Radar, sonar, and the like? It's all a mystery to me."

"Me too, although I learned a little bit about it when I was married to Brad. He was — well, he still is, funny how you say was — a professor of mechanical engineering. Every now and then he'd do some outside consulting, design work and such. Once he actually paid good money to go down in a submersible and see the *Titanic*. Me, I'd have stayed on the ship and watched everything on a computer screen, via remote sensing equipment. But that's Brad, he has a taste for scientific inquiry as strong as Roger's, just a lot more . . ." She was wondering whether "conventional" or "dull" was the right word, or whether she should just drop the subject — the man was her private version of Marley's ghost — when she was interrupted by a male voice speaking in a mouthful-of-marbles English accent.

"How are we getting on, then, Hugh?"

Jean looked around and up — the man was a head taller than she was. His lean body wore a three-piece suit and striped tie that might just as well have included a neon sign flashing *I am important.* His hair was slicked back in stiff, gelled strands, and his smile was broad, over-whitened teeth seeming to melt together into a crescent of glare like oncoming headlights.

"Hullo," he said to Jean. "Peter Kettering, Starr PLC."

"Jean Fairbairn, *Great Scot.*"

"Ah, *Great Scot*, is it? I sent along a press release about our new products, vitamin-enriched spring water and low-carbohydrate beer."

Hugh winced. As far as he was concerned, beer was one of the basic food groups, not to be improved upon by marketing departments. "Ah yes," Jean said noncommittally. "Thank you."

"If you'll excuse us, Jean," Kettering went on, "I'm needing a bit of a chin-wag with Hugh here."

"Cheers," said Hugh, and patiently suffered Kettering's hand on his arm steering him through the crowd toward the stage.

Jean was beginning to miss how Alasdair had called her "Miss Fairbairn" not only when they first met, but well beyond. They'd gone through multiple alarms and excursions together before they began using first names. Which, she thought, meant that they were either out of touch with contemporary usage or wary of even the most superficial intimacy.

Alasdair. She could dawdle around all day, but eventually she was going to have to go to the police station and make her statement. The longer she stalled, the more likely Sawyer would be there, too. On the other hand, the police people would be dealing with Jonathan's body for a while yet. After lunch, she'd go after lunch.

She turned around and bounced off something large and pleasantly soft. "Oops," said Patti Duckett. "Sorry, I was in your way."

"No problem," Jean replied. "I wasn't watching where I was going."

Behind Patti, Dave was returning his wallet to his pocket. "Great stuff they've got here."

"Look what we found for the grandkids." Patti opened one of

several plastic bags so that Jean could see inside. It was filled with toys, from squeaky rubber Nessies to plush stuffed ones, a long-haired Highland cow and a black-faced sheep keeping them company.

Somewhere in China, Jean thought, a factory was working overtime. "How many grandchildren do you have?" she asked.

"Three," said Patti, "Two boys and a girl."

"Do they live in Illinois, too?"

"They do now, yes. They were born in Florida but they came back last year after they lost their father . . ."

"Look," Dave said, gazing toward the main tent, "there are some guys in kilts. You'll never get me in one of those things. A bit breezy for my taste."

Since Dave understandably didn't want to dwell on what might have been anything from a divorce to a tragedy, Jean answered him, not Patti. "Scots are tough. Still, it's not surprising they go to Florida for winter vacations."

Patti closed her bag of toys and peered into another bag, this one holding a bright tartan blanket, but she didn't seem to be actually seeing it. "Have you heard anything more about the boat blowing up? How about the boy who's missing? A real shame about him being caught in the explosion and everything."

Might as well spread the word. "They found his body in the loch."

"That's a real shame," Patti said once more, her voice cracking.

"It sure is. Accidents happen, but sometimes people can be damned careless . . ." Dave still stared into the distance, the light reflecting off his glasses making them seem opaque. "I guess no one knows what happened yet?"

"No," said Jean. She turned one way and the Ducketts turned the other, making their way toward the chairs set up in front of the stage.

The Ducketts seemed to be nice salt-of-the-earth people. How sad that crime and mortality had scratched the glossy coat of their holiday. And how funny an American accent sounded now. It was flat, almost whiny. Jean's ears had adapted to the variety of local lilts. Before long she'd be talking like Rebecca, the plateaus of her native voice broken by the hills and valleys of Scotland.

Speaking of the Campbell-Reids, little Linda provided a dandy excuse to buy a stuffed animal or two. So did Jean's nieces and nephews back in the States.

She toured the tables and booths, acquiring a plush Nessie wearing a tiny tartan tam and a couple of the appealing woolly sheep. The ratio of quality goods to dreck, she discovered, was a good one. For every plastic doll dressed in Day-Glo tartan was a hand knit Aran sweater. For every Nessie refrigerator magnet was a piece of Rennie Mackintosh design jewelry or cut-glass whiskey decanter. And one vendor had — oh happy day! — piles and piles of books.

Hitching her bag of toys up her arm, she assessed the display. A stack of *Great Scot* magazines sat beside a selection of history and travel guides, including Ambrose's *Pictish Antiquities*. She picked up a book titled *Hidden Treasures of Scotland* and leafed through it, pausing to admire photos of the Traprain Law hoard. A picture of Bonnie Prince Charlie headed up a chapter about his missing gold coins. Been there, done that, worn the T-shirt so many times the logo had washed away. Jean turned several pages at once.

A photo of Tobermory Bay on Mull illustrated a chapter about the Armada ship that sank there in 1588. Except for a cannon, its contents had never been recovered, although not without repeated efforts. Maybe if and when Roger admitted defeat at Loch Ness he'd take on the Tobermory galleon. The actual identification of the sunken ship — which had also mysteriously blown up — was still a question, and whether there was any treasure to be found on it was an even bigger one, but there was no doubt it actually existed.

She put the book back on the table, thinking that while, traditionally, dragons guarded treasures, here at Loch Ness the dragon was the treasure. No surprise that most of the books on offer were Nessie books, ranging from Ambrose's *The Water-Horse of Loch Ness* through Whyte's *More Than a Legend* to Binns' *The Loch Ness Mystery Solved*, which if it didn't solve anything to the high standards of, say, Alasdair, at least debunked quite a lot.

An old copy of Ambrose's biography of Crowley was wedged between two travelogues. She pulled it out and fanned the pages, catching a faint whiff of mildew and something else, something sweet. The flyleaf was autographed in flowing script: *To my dear E., remembering the good times, Ambrose Mackintosh*. The trailing end of the faded sepia "h" coiled into a serpentine flourish on the yellowed paper. E for Eileen, Jean supposed, but what an ambiguous sentiment to inscribe to one's wife.

The dealer, an elderly man as tall and straight as a Doric column, scented a live one and came strolling over. He saw what she held and recoiled, his seamed face registering distaste verging on disgust. "Och, where did you turn that up?"

"It was right here," she told him.

"My assistant brought it along, then. Tis of local interest, make no mistake, but Crowley, he was a nasty piece of work. Lived just across the loch, there." He gestured toward the southwest, where the clouds were building into gray ramparts. "Mind you, he raised demons. People would go round, miles and miles, to avoid passing by his house at Boleskine, and even so, terrible things happened. His lodge keeper went mad, his butcher accidentally sliced open an artery and died . . . Well, no need to go on. Two pound and that book is yours."

Terrible things happened a long way away from Crowley, too, but most people didn't revel in them, like he had done. Even Ambrose had allowed that the man, while more sham than evil, was not a healthy influence. Ambrose, though, rationalized that Crowley had been driven to his excesses by the taunts of an unappreciative public.

Jean dropped two pound coins into the dealer's huge, callused hand. In his youth, he could have picked up a tree — and probably had, in the Highland sport of caber-tossing. And she thought Alasdair had large hands. "I see you have Ambrose Mackintosh's other books here."

"Ah well, Ambrose was a fine scholar. Daft, mind you, and perhaps wicked, but Scripture tells us to judge not, lest we ourselves be judged. In any event, folk hereabouts didna trust him. Keeping bad company disna help your reputation, does it?"

"No, it doesn't." Jean tucked the book into her bag beside the toys. Maybe they would sap some of what the dealer obviously felt was its evil aura. "I bet the disappearance of Ambrose's wife didn't help his reputation any, either."

"No, that it didna. Too much like Crowley he was, with the women and all. Poor wee Iris, my mum always said, no mother and her father off his head, perhaps a murderer forbye. No wonder she's a bit of a loony herself."

"How much do you want for this?" asked a man at the end of the table. Jean recognized the scrawny form of Martin Hall, without child, and smiled a greeting, which Martin returned distantly, as if he wasn't quite sure who she was. Or as if he'd seen her looking up at Tracy's bedroom window a little while earlier. Although, now that Jean thought about it, it could just as well have been Peter Kettering in that room, discussing promotional fees, perhaps.

The dealer turned toward Martin. Jean, scenting a source, picked up a business card from the pile on the table. It read *Gordon Fraser, Highland Books and Maps, Fort Augustus.*

An arm like a side of beef landed around her shoulders. She jerked away and spun around, ready to do battle.

D.S. Andy Sawyer was looking down at her with small squinting eyes set close together beneath a forehead like a cinder block wall. Broad lips smirked at her below a lank blond moustache. So he'd shaved off his beard since last month. Bad move. His receding chin was now exposed to innocent eyes. "Well then, lassie," he said, his sarcastic voice relishing the diminutive, "avoiding us, are you now? Strange, how you keep turning up, like a bad penny, eh? Cut along now, D.C.I. Cameron's waiting on your pleasure."

Oh, for the love of . . . And she thought she'd been able to read Alasdair. She'd thought they were on the same side. But he'd sent his henchman to get her. And she hadn't had time to fortify herself with a sandwich, or a lousy cup of tea, even, although straight whiskey might have improved her own temper. Or loosened her tongue, which wouldn't have helped a bit.

She spun away from Sawyer, stumbling and adding embarrassment to anger. *Damn!* He had a police car waiting at the edge of the field. People were staring. At least it was D.C. Gunn who was holding open the door of the back seat for her, his mouth set in a wobbly line a la Charlie Brown, chagrin and nausea combined.

Head up, back straight, Jean walked over to the car, offered Gunn a version of his own expression, and climbed inside.

TWELVE

In the five minutes it took to drive to Drumnadrochit's miniature police station and ease through the scrum of reporters outside its gate, Jean's head of steam began to dissipate. Her encounter with Alasdair on top of the tower had been cordial. Comradely. They'd understood each other, albeit in a duck-and-cover sort of way. He hadn't sent Sawyer to get her.

Sawyer, unimproved temper and all, sat beside her, not twirling the ends of his moustache. And not razzing her any more, either, which meant he had some minimal level of perception.

When the car stopped. Jean piled out and beat Sawyer to the door of the office — if he opened it for her, he'd imply she was a prisoner, not a free agent. She stepped into the tiny room with its informational posters, filing cabinets, and computer-topped desk, and looked around, poised for action. But no one, least of all Alasdair, was there.

A door on the far side of the room stood open on a narrow slice of domesticity, now filled with all the computerized paraphernalia of an incident room. Even as she headed toward it, propelled by Sawyer's battering-ram entrance, Alasdair stepped through the opening and shut the door behind him. In his left hand a plastic tray held one complete half of a tomato and cheese sandwich and a bite of the other half. Turning toward Jean, he scooped that up and inserted it between his elegantly curved lips.

"Here I am to make that statement," Jean said, and, with a glance behind her, "The sergeant decided he just couldn't wait to see me again."

Cameron chewed. His gaze moved from Jean's truculent expression to Sawyer's scowl. He swallowed. His eyebrows lifted and then tightened, minimally. His lips thinned. Without having blinked once, he looked back at Jean.

He might be at his most inscrutable, but she knew that he was irritated with Sawyer's presumption. He wasn't going to show it in front of anyone, though, least of all her. She went on. "I was going to have lunch and then come in, you know, blood sugar and stuff like that."

Alasdair extended his remaining sandwich half toward her.

No way was she going to do something as personal as share his food in front of — well, in front of anyone. "No, no thank you. I'm okay." She'd told the teacher on the bully. It was time to shut up before she sounded so lame they sent out for crutches. Jean plopped down in the hard wooden chair beside the desk and tucked her shopping bag beneath it, hoping no one would notice the cutesy stuffed animals.

Sawyer leaned against the outside door, ostentatiously blocking her escape. Gunn settled across the room, hunched defensively over his notebook. That was odd. Jean remembered him being deferential to his superiors, not afraid of them.

"Right," Alasdair said, although his frosty glance at Sawyer suggested otherwise. He sat down behind the desk, wiped his hands on a napkin, then pulled a small plastic bag from inside his jacket and held it out to Jean. "This is yours, I reckon."

With a queasy feeling of deja vu, Jean took the bag. It contained one of her business cards, the cardboard puffy and the ink blurred but legible. She felt its cold dampness through the plastic. "Where did you . . ? Oh. It was in Jonathan's pocket, wasn't it?"

"Got it in one," said Sawyer from the door.

So that was why he'd taken it upon himself to come after her. Reasonable enough, on the surface. It was what was below the surface, some sort of strain not in the plot but in the cast of characters, that made her feel there wasn't enough oxygen in the room. And it wasn't just the tension she always felt in Alasdair's presence, either.

Jean handed the card back to him. "I gave this to Jonathan when I arrived at the Water Horse boat and he challenged me. I had an appointment for an interview."

"You're a chum of Dempsey's, then," said Sawyer.

"No, I'm not," she told him over her shoulder. "We met briefly several years ago is all. I hadn't heard from him until his press release landed on my desk last week, and he must have sent one, little Nessie and all, to every reporter in the UK."

"Nessie?" Alasdair asked.

"The toy Nessie that came with the press release."

"None of the other reporters we've interviewed said anything about a toy."

"Why should they? They — we — get that sort of promotional gimmick all the time."

"Aye." Alasdair laid the plastic bag out on the desk blotter, his sturdy fingertips smoothing it down as delicately as a fortune teller laying out Tarot cards. "The preliminary report is that Paisley has no wounds other than cuts, bruises, and burns from the explosion, and that he drowned. Just now we're thinking that he was killed by accident. Even so, we're looking into his background."

Jean didn't want to know whether Jonathan had been conscious when he went into the water. Setting her jaw, she met Alasdair's cool, correct expression with one of her own.

"The bomber might could have meant to kill Dempsey," he continued. "Mrs. Dempsey tells us he has a habit of working late and losing track of time. This is assuming the explosion was meant to kill anyone at all, not merely to stop the expedition. Just now we've got no evidence the one way or the other."

"Tracy was insisting he get to that dinner on time," Jean agreed. "What about Brendan and Jonathan trading places? Could someone have wanted to kill Brendan?"

"It's possible."

"Hugh Munro said he saw Brendan with Iris's niece Kirsty at the Tourist Authority dinner last night." A snort from behind her back wasn't exactly that of a bull, but still she felt like a matador. She didn't turn around. "Maybe what Jonathan traded with Brendan was his place at the dinner. Brendan could have thought he'd make points with Kirsty by taking her to a posh function."

"That's likely." Alasdair allowed her reasoning a slow nod. "Or he might could have been setting himself up an alibi."

"Using Kirsty. Yes."

"You overheard Iris telling Kirsty she shouldn't be seeing any more of Brendan, did you?"

"More or less, yes. There's a real Romeo and Juliet scenario going on, with Iris playing the old money, the Capulets, and Roger playing the brash new Montagues."

Another snort indicated Sawyer's impatience with literary similes. Alasdair didn't rise to the bait. If anything, a blizzard blew across his expression. "You were asking about the anonymous letters. Despite fingerprint and saliva evidence being inconclusive, we may have found the person who sent them."

"May have?" demanded Sawyer. "We've got her dead to rights."

"Her?" Jean asked. "You mean Iris?"

In three steps, Sawyer was across the room and looming over Jean. "What do you know about it, then?"

Alasdair said nothing. Jean turned her face upward to meet Sawyer's glare. His eyebrows were so pale they were almost invisible. No wonder he didn't seem quite human. Even cartoon animals had eyebrows, to show emotion. "Who doesn't suspect Iris, with her attitude toward Dempsey? When I heard her typing on an old typewriter yesterday afternoon, even I wondered if the letters were typewrit . . ."

Sawyer's already narrowed eyes became slits.

"You're kidding me." Jean swung back around to Alasdair. "You mean those letters *were* typewritten? On Iris's typewriter?"

"Not typed, no," he said. "Computer-generated and printed, the both of them. But Iris has a computer as well."

"That makes sense. Why would Iris or anyone else incriminate herself by using a typewriter?"

"Or by printing those letters on paper and posting them in envelopes provided to the guests at her own B&B?" Alasdair asked.

"Say what?" replied Jean.

"Oh aye." Sawyer said. "Thanks to reporters like yourself, everyone knows his way round the forensics. You've made our job that much more difficult."

"Don't look at me, I only write about cases long over and done with," Jean retorted, and added before he could, "As for the case in May, all I wrote was a series of historical articles. Period. And they haven't been published yet."

Alasdair re-called the meeting to order by clearing his throat. "You've got no more reason than Iris's dislike of Dempsey to suspect her of sending the letters, have you, Miss Fairbairn?"

"No. She seems to be way too smart to stoop to anonymous letters, to say nothing of incriminating herself up one side and down the other."

"You're handing Iris too much credit, las —" Sawyer thought better of one diminutive but defaulted to another "— Jean. She's telling us she used her own paper and envelopes, and posted the letters in Inverness to Dempsey's office in Chicago, the first on May five, just after he announced his plans, and the second on June twelve, so it would reach him just before he came away from the US."

"She's confessed?" demanded Jean, not of Sawyer but of Alasdair.

"Aye," his lips stated, but his eyes were far from convinced.

Jean could only shake her head. That did not compute.

Beside her, Sawyer went smugly on. "If you smelled petrol on the boat, then the bomb was hidden there before you arrived. Iris was seen pottering about the bay in her boat on the Thursday evening, whilst Dempsey and the others were interviewing with ITN at the castle."

"She's researching the ecology of the loch," said Jean. "Did anyone actually see her on the Water Horse boat?"

"She climbed on board from the side facing away from the shore."

"But the bomb didn't go off until Friday evening."

Alasdair said, "You were telling me she wasn't at the B&B just then."

"I said I didn't see her at the B&B. She could have been there. Besides, why not take the bomb out to the boat at the same time you intend to set it off? Sounds to me like there was some kind of timing mechanism. Or that Jonathan set it off himself, which doesn't make sense. Or doesn't make sense with the evidence we have now."

Judging by the roll of Sawyer's eyes, he resented her imperial "we."

Jean didn't correct herself. "Even if Iris did send the letters, that doesn't mean she blew up the boat."

"She's not confessed to that, no," said Alasdair. "Still, the dive teams found a corkscrew from the B&B amidst the debris."

"A corkscrew?" This time it was her brows that went up. "Well, yeah, Martin Hall was looking for one last night, but corkscrews all look alike, don't they?"

"This one was a bit of an antique, with Ambrose's monogram. Miss Wotherspoon identified it."

Sawyer darted Gunn a sneer and said, "Kirsty the crumpet. Didn't realize she was grassing up Aunt Iris, did she?"

What? Jean wondered. Had Gunn flirted with Kirsty? Inappropriate, maybe, but hardly the hanging offense Sawyer's scorn made it out to be. Or else, more likely, Sawyer had been ogling Kirsty and Gunn had been offended enough to call him on it.

"That's Miss Wotherspoon to you, Andy," said Alasdair, in the quiet but menacing voice Jean remembered only too well.

A shiver trickled down her spine, and not one of fear. The voice drew no reaction from Sawyer except another roll of his eyes. She said, "I'm impressed you can find anything identifiable in the debris."

"It's a matter of noting the objects you're not expecting to find. We expected quite a few bits of electronic equipment, pieces of Dempsey's submersible, and the like. What we weren't expecting were the broken wine and liquor bottles."

"Well, that would explain the corkscrew, sort of. Roger's a pretty hard drinker. Although how he got the corkscrew from the B&B . . ."

Alasdair spelled it out for her. "As luck would have it, one bottle wasn't broken. It contained petrol. The bomb was made of several bottles partially filled with petrol and fitted up with fuses. Amongst the electronic debris might could be the remains of a timing mechanism. Perhaps Paisley was having a go at defusing the bomb when it exploded."

"Oh." Jean visualized a young man trying frantically to — to what? Cut the blue wire? Had he thought he didn't have enough time to call the authorities, or had he thought he could handle it? Her knowledge of bombs and timing devices was on a par with her knowledge of nuclear physics. "Rigging up a timing mechanism would indicate some expertise, wouldn't it? Could Iris have done it?"

"She worked with the electric flex whilst renovating the house," said Sawyer. "She makes the repairs to the appliances. Kirst — Miss Wotherspoon was telling us that, as well."

Jean didn't think the one translated to the other, but didn't waste her breath saying so. "I ran into Roger a little while ago. He thinks the explosion was caused by the propane stove, said it had been acting up."

"He was telling us that, aye," Alasdair said. "The chap who owns the boat says that's nonsense, he'd vetted every item on board. Including a small generator that runs on petrol."

"That could explain the smell, someone was being careless with the petrol. The gasoline. That could explain the explosion, for that matter. Except," Jean said, sinking down in the chair so that her spine rattled across the hard ribs of the back, "except you found a bottle filled with petrol, something the boat owner would keep in a proper container. But . . ."

"We're not asking your opinion." Sawyer said, ignoring the fact that Alasdair *was* asking her opinion.

The door to the other room opened and a constable beckoned to Sawyer. With never a by-your-leave he stepped across to the door and slammed it behind him.

Whoa, there was oxygen in the room again. Jean was about to make some snide remark about Sawyer, then decided that someone had to take the high road.

Alasdair's face was, if anything, even more cold and quiet than usual. She already knew that he could exercise admirable restraint, but still, she was impressed.

He frowned at the door, shedding an iceberg or two in the process, and shot an impenetrable look at Gunn. She glanced around to see the young officer huddled in his chair as though he was trying to vanish into the woodwork like an insect. Even as she watched he relaxed, straightened, and sent a bashful half-smile toward her and Alasdair, either separately or together.

So what was going on? She'd learned the dynamics of the investigative trio the last time around — Sawyer butting his head against Cameron's chill shell, with Gunn playing both ingénue and straight man. But something had changed, like an already tart fruit gone rancid. "Well," she said to Gunn, "at least you still have all the paperwork from last time. You know, my name, rank, serial number."

"That we do, Miss Fairbairn."

Jean looked back to see one side of Alasdair's mouth tucking itself up in a suppressed smile, although whether it was at her or Gunn she had no way of deciphering. "What else was Dempsey telling you just now?" he asked.

"Not much, just that the remote-sensing equipment he brought along for the land part of the expedition was stored at the hotel, reasonably enough. He must have lost some of his computers, though, not to mention the sonar and the ROVs, the remote operating vehicles. That's what you meant by submersible. Not quite the same thing, a submersible is a mini-sub and has a person inside. An ROV doesn't."

Alasdair nodded, filing that away in the infinite recesses of his mind.

"It's a tough break for him. That sort of equipment is so expensive an expedition will rent it — like Roger did with the boat — although I guess he didn't have to rent or buy anything manufactured by Omnium." She told herself that if anyone was resilient, it was Dempsey. Or would be, tomorrow. As for Iris — well, even though Alasdair hadn't formally arrested her, he wasn't satisfied with her story. "If Iris hadn't confessed, I'd say that someone was trying to frame her. It wouldn't be that hard to pick up some paper and envelopes matching the ones from the B&B."

"Or to pinch some from the B&B itself. Along with the odd corkscrew, come to that."

"I figured you'd come to that all-too-obvious corkscrew."

"Someone might could be trying to stitch Iris up for the explosion," Alasdair went on, "but the letters, now, the letters are a bit of a problem. Iris isn't telling us all she knows."

"Or she's telling Sawyer what he wants to hear, to get him off her back."

"I reckon the immovable object's meeting the irresistible force." This time it was the other side of Alasdair's mouth that almost smiled, and directly at Jean.

"You don't seriously think she sent the letters."

"You're telling me my business again, Jean."

She caught the glint in his eye, like a lamp glowing behind an ice-covered windowpane and thawing a peephole. *Here we go again.* This time, though, the thought wasn't heavy and dull. There was an odd sort of sparkle to it. With all due respect to Jonathan, of course. And Dempsey, and Iris. She said over her shoulder, "D.C. Gunn, I'd sure like a cup of tea. Do you think you could rustle one up for me?"

Her idiom made him smile. "Oh aye, no problem." Gunn put his notebook down and vanished into the main part of the building.

He had a nice smile when he let it escape, bright and open. No matter if he was a bit gawky, Sawyer had no right to bully him.

Jean turned back to Alasdair. With him sitting behind the desk she felt like a supplicant or a client, not an equal. But then, she wasn't an equal, not when it came to police work. "What's repeating itself here is you letting me in on the case. If all you want to know is what Iris or Roger has to say for public consumption, you could ask anyone. What is it you're trying to lure me into doing for you?"

"Is it that hard to guess?" he asked, leaning forward.

There was the energy field again, tightening her follicles. It was like sensing a ghost, except it wasn't like sensing a ghost. Alasdair was no disembodied flash of emotion. Clearing her throat, she held her ground. "I can play devil's advocate for you, no problem. But there's more to it than that. The letters seem to have come from the B&B. I'm staying there. I'm a reporter, I have an excuse to ask questions. I'm a nice person, so maybe I can offer to help Kirsty while Iris is gone. In other words, you expect me to spy for you."

"I'm expecting you to conduct yourself as a public-spirited citizen and help the police with their inquiries. Without putting yourself in danger, mind. We've got a criminal here who's either determined or careless. I'm hoping for the former, as that would make him predictable. Program your mobile with my number and Gunn's. Here you are." He scribbled two numbers on a bit of notepaper and shoved it across the desk.

She tucked the paper into her pocket. "I'm here because I'm curious — because curiosity is my job — but I'm only a member of the audience, not part of the play. There's no evidence I'm in danger."

"Someone's roaming about your wee house in the night. There's less proper evidence than that for Nessie, and she's supporting an entire industry."

"Nessie being a 'she' because of her stubborn and uncooperative temperament?"

He grinned at that, a little less briefly than he had grinned at seeing her atop the castle.

The effect made Jean slide back into her chair. *Oh my.* No, this was not a debate. She might as well save her energy for an argument she wanted to win. "Okay. I'll help you with the case without putting myself in danger. And without putting myself forward, either. I get it."

"You were already planning to suss out the story of Iris's father, weren't you now?"

"Yes I was, although I don't see . . ." Jean caught herself in midphrase. "You don't know yet what's relevant to the case, so you're looking into everyone's background. Besides, Eileen Mackintosh's disappearance was never really solved, and you're curious about it."

"There's a bit of residual feeling about that in the area, or so I hear."

"From whom?"

"Hamish Cameron, who owns the Cameron Arms Hotel."

"A relative of yours?"

"Second cousin twice removed."

Jean laughed. Once she had thought Alasdair had sprung full-blown from the brow of the Chief Constable, solitary as a hermit.

But no. He was a Cameron, with all that implied. The last clan raid in this area had been perpetrated by Camerons in 1545. They had taken everything not nailed down, including women, and pried up a few things that were. Alasdair's shell, thick as armor, was probably suppressing centuries of passion for good and bad.

He leaned on the desk, his eyes fixed on hers, knowing why she was laughing but refusing to acknowledge it with anything more than a surreptitious twinkle that approached but didn't quite achieve a conspiratorial wink. *This is just between the two of us, mind.*

She plunged on. "Ambrose's association with Crowley damaged his reputation, that's for sure. People around here think he got away with murder. I've only seen the story in some newspaper files, but the way I understand it, Ambrose and Eileen were having problems, it was the servants' day out, so he was alone with her when she disappeared — well, except for baby Iris, who doesn't count. He was a shady character to begin with, and when a wife disappears, often the husband *is* at fault. And vice versa."

"Was that the only evidence against him? Their ghosts hardly count as evidence."

"Hardly," she agreed. "There were one or two little things, but the casual attitude of the detectives would curl your hair. Like the officer in charge not wanting to upset Eileen's family by going through her belongings."

Alasdair winced. "Well then, I'll have our archivist find the original reports and transcripts. If she makes copies for you as well, will that pay you back for your spying, as you put it? I'd rather have you working with me than against me."

"I wouldn't be working against you," she assured him.

"I'm remembering a bit of a competition." His voice softened into a register that tended more toward velvet than gravel.

Jean realized she was leaning forward, closer to the crinkles that shaped the corners of his eyes and mouth like subtle punctuation marks. "The only competition, Alasdair . . ."

The door opened. Jean lurched back. This time it was she who winced, as her vertebrae slammed against the chair. Alasdair retreated more slowly, the smile that had been playing along his lips evaporating before it reached fruition, his gaze dropping to the desktop.

Gunn set a steaming mug and three plump oatmeal cookies down in front of Jean. "I'm thinking the biscuits would go down a treat, since you've had no lunch."

"Thank you," she told him, as grateful for his entrance as for the food. What had she been about to say? *The only competition, Alasdair, was between our heads and our hearts?*

Alasdair picked up his sandwich, bit off a portion of the remaining half, and with a glance that made up in intensity what it lacked in length, slipped soundlessly through the doorway. Jean exhaled, feeling as though she'd been holding her breath the entire time she'd been talking with him — and not because his agendas were at all hidden. Ambiguous maybe, but not hidden.

He pulled the door shut but it didn't catch, and drifted back open an inch or two. Through the aperture she heard Sawyer's bray. "I'm away to collect the old witch at Pitclachie and carry her to Inverness. Keep her overnight in stir, that will take her down a peg or two. Unless she's already spilled her guts to W.P.C. Boyd over a cuppa and a biscuit, all nice and cozy. Hah."

"She's Miss Mackintosh," Alasdair told him. "You will treat her — and everyone else involved in this case — with courtesy."

"Are you after solving the case or are you after winning a Girl Guides award? There's no making an omelet without breaking an egg or two."

"Don't go wasting my time or yours with that sort of rubbish."

"Ah, that's the way of it, then. It's rubbish when I'm doing my job, and heroics when you're doing yours. If arresting your own partner isn't breaking an egg, then what is?"

Jean's lips tightened in righteous anger. That was ugly, reminding Alasdair of the scandal — and its consequences — in his own past. Last month he'd said he felt Sawyer's breath on the back of his neck. Now she realized what he meant. Alasdair had climbed the ladder of rank because of his competence and honesty, painful though the latter might have been. But Sawyer was one of those men who climbed by stepping on the fallen bodies of others.

Alasdair enunciated so clearly each word fell like a pellet of hail. "That's a low blow even from you, Detective Sergeant Sawyer. In the future you will keep your tongue behind your teeth."

A long pause, prickling with frost. Then Sawyer, lacking a devastating riposte, said in a tone so light it was mocking, "Oh aye, never you worry, Chief Inspector Cameron."

Jean visualized Alasdair's face, cold, pale, impassive, and his body, upright and very still, seeming taller than Sawyer even though he was actually two inches shorter. She imagined Sawyer, his face red and overblown and his arms swinging loosely from his shoulders, knuckles dragging the floor. Menace for menace, she'd back Alasdair any day. But then, she was partial.

Gunn tiptoed toward the door and pushed it shut, slowly and silently. He was very good at moving silently. He must have found that a useful survival skill.

Taking Alasdair's place at the desk, he drew forward a tape recorder and looked at Jean, his own face pale and set. She looked at him. No, neither one of them had heard a word.

"Right," said Gunn. "I've got most everything here, if you'd not mind repeating a bittie or two."

She minded, but there was no point in saying so. Nibbling at one of the cookies, she began, "I came here to interview Roger Dempsey and Iris Mackintosh."

THIRTEEN

Standing beside the Water Horse van, Jean watched the police car turn onto the main road. Gunn had chauffeured her back to Pitclachie House. With no one else in the car, she'd sat up front and eyed reporters and passersby alike from her height of importance, although she'd restrained herself from a making any regal waves.

Now she rolled her eyes as much at herself as at the situation. The details of this case weren't like the last, she thought — as though criminal investigations came her way on a regular basis — but the broad picture was disturbingly so, right down to that undeniable tug of attraction between her and Alasdair. A tug that neither of them could bring themselves to acknowledge, which is why they flirted with it and not with each other. No surprise there. They were both wounded by broken marriages. They were both struggling to find a compromise between personal space and loneliness. Neither of them needed a reclamation project for a relationship.

Which begged the question, just what *did* either of them need for a relationship?

Jean unlocked the door of the Lodge, telling herself she could be misinterpreting his just-between-us intimate moment, let alone that last searching glance. She didn't want to make a fool of herself by responding to a signal he hadn't sent. And that thought alone told her there was nothing foolish about this situation, either criminal or personal.

In spite of Sawyer's visit, let alone Iris's enforced departure, the Lodge had been cleaned and tidied. The bookshelves were neatly arranged, the dishes were washed and stacked, the bed had been made and the towels folded in a bathroom smelling of pine cleanser. The locked door, Jean ascertained with a twist of the knob and a push, was still locked.

So was the door of the wardrobe. She stowed the toys and the old book, liberated her laptop, and pulled her cell phone out of her bag. A moment later she was talking to Miranda. "Yep, it's me again. I have news and a request."

"I doubt your news is more reliable than the sort off the telly," said Miranda.

That wasn't a dig, that was a compliment, "doubt" meaning "expect" in Scots. *I'm going native*, Jean said to herself, and to Miranda, "First of all, Iris has confessed to writing the threatening letters to Roger."

"She never! Where did you hear that?"

"From D.C.I. Cameron, in person."

"He's there, is he? What luck!"

Lucky for the case? Or lucky for her personally? "I agree that she never, but why she said so is another matter. Not to mention who really did send the letters, and whether they were trying to frame Iris or whether they were just careless."

"As yet you've got more questions than answers, then."

"So what else is new? And speaking of questions . . ."

"Oh, good shot," said Miranda, and to Jean, "Duncan's holed a putt long as my front hall."

"Good for him." The appeal of golf escaped Jean, but then, so did the appeal of hitting herself in the head with a hammer. Her phone to her ear, her laptop beneath her arm, she stepped carefully down the stairs and waited to be recognized again.

"Well then, what is it you're wanting me to do?"

"Find out just what Roger's position with Omnium is. I mean, I know he's the founder, and he runs a lot of the research and development, but he's not actually chairman of the board, is he?"

"Ah, you're asking who's lost the greenback dollars lying at the bottom of Loch Ness."

"Sort of. Just wondering about the state of the Dempsey's finances — now that sort of question is relevant." Jean pretended she didn't hear Miranda's whiskey-flavored chuckle.

"Right. I'll make further inquiries. And now my ball's teed up and ready to go flying."

And fly it would, Jean was sure. "Enjoy your game. Thanks."

She switched off the phone and stood staring at the dining table. It had a drawer. She pulled it open. Yes, sheets of plain white writing paper lay next to plain white envelopes and a pen. Was this the same kind of paper the letters had been printed on? If so, the writer was as likely to have stolen it from the Lodge as from the house.

Jean nibbled a protein bar from her emergency stash while she typed in whatever notes about the case and its cast of characters she was able to brainstorm. No patterns suddenly emerged. Neither did any way in which she could be in danger, Alasdair to the contrary, although the problem with danger is that it usually didn't walk up and introduce itself before it pounced. Since running back to Edinburgh and hiding beneath her bed was not an option — a temptation, but not an option — she dug Alasdair's note out of her pocket and dutifully programmed the numbers into her cell phone. Even though she'd like for him to be wrong, she wasn't going to cut off her nose to spite her face. He was only concerned about her because he didn't want anyone hurt on his watch. That was all.

Right. Jean tucked everything away again and locked the door of the Lodge behind her. As she crossed the courtyard, a raindrop plunked down on her head. She looked up to see the sky almost as opaque as the look Alasdair had sent toward Gunn, although his eyes were blue with a sheen of gray, and the sky was gray with a sheen of blue.

Was the dragon-shaped knocker on the front door going to take on the shape not of Marley's ghost but of Jonathan Paisley's? No. Pitclachie's ghosts were more subtle than that. Jean stepped into the house, inhaling its delectable odor yet again. A soothing odor, she decided, even if its bread component made her stomach growl. She eyed the closed door of Iris's office and the staircase leading upwards into terra incognita. A police team would be along presently to search the premises, Gunn had said, which meant Jean did not have permission for overt snooping. The library, now. The library was open season.

She walked through the arched doorway and stopped dead. *Oh my! Paradise!*

Bookshelves almost completely encircled the room. Arched moldings rimmed the ceiling. An ornate Gothic mantelpiece shaded the fireplace. Even though the hearth was cold, the calico cat lay before it like a supplicant before an altar. He opened an eye, then closed it again with that typical feline expression that blended nonchalance with haughtiness.

Today not enough sunlight filtered through the tall windows to pick the older books with their gilded lettering out from the newer, paper-covered books. Still, the array was inspiring. And the glass-topped display case beside the right-hand window attracted Jean like a magnet an iron filing. She had taken several paces across the Persian carpet when a voice behind her said, "Hello."

Innocuous enough, but that didn't keep her from jumping and then pretending she hadn't. *Nervous? Moi?* She looked around to see Kirsty sitting in a wingback chair next to a closed roll-top desk, knitting. The light of a lamp made the half-completed scarf glow crimson and the aluminum needles glint, but hooded Kirsty's downcast face in shadow. With her hair piled on the back of her head, she looked like a proper Victorian miss at her needlework.

"Oh, hello," said Jean, with as sympathetic a tone as she could summon — and she'd be sympathetic even without Alasdair's programming. "This is a very handsome room. Was it designed by Ambrose?"

"That it was."

"Did he add the tower onto the house, too?"

"Aye, so he might could watch for the creature in the loch."

"And what's your opinion on the creature? Do you think it

exists?"

"You don't expect me to go denying the local religion, do you now?"

Smiling, Jean moved on to a topic that was, if no less interesting, also less peripheral to her brief as nosy journalist and police henchwoman. "This room doesn't look as though it's been changed from Ambrose's day. I guess Iris felt she couldn't improve on it. Except to add books, of course."

"The furnishings are the same, Aunt Iris says. Except for this desk, it was shifted from the Lodge when Iris did the place up."

"So that was where Ambrose wrote his books? Amazing, isn't it, how people wrote entire books in longhand? Or did he use something as newfangled as a typewriter?"

"He had a typewriter. Iris still uses it."

"But I bet she can use a computer, too."

Did Kirsty grimace at that, or simply frown in concentration as each stitch moved with a brisk stab and an abrupt tug from the first needle to the second. "Oh aye, Aunt Iris has a computer. Canna run the business without one, I'm thinking."

Yes, Iris *could* have sent the letters to Roger. But Jean still bet she hadn't. Irritating, to have to contradict the woman's own confession. "Was it you who tidied up the Lodge today?"

"I dinna usually, but Aunt Iris was obliged to go away to Inverness."

That was a delicate way of putting it. But some games Jean just wouldn't play. "I know. D.C.I. Cameron told me Iris was helping the police with their inquiries."

Kirsty's hands stopped moving on the stitches, but she didn't look up. Maybe she was wondering not so much whose side Jean was on as whether there were sides to be taken.

Having run her standard up the flagpole, Jean went on, "It's nice of you and Iris to let me have so much space. You could put several people in the Lodge. Or you could if you opened that room with the locked door. Is that another bedroom?"

"It's a lumber room is all. Bits of furniture and the like." Kirsty started knitting again, reached the end of the row, and turned the scarf around.

An old sepia-tinted photograph stood on the desk. It showed a summerhouse, the intricately-carved barge boards looking as though they'd been designed by William Morris and executed by elves. A man and a woman sat in the wide doorway, on either side of a tea table. The man Jean recognized as Ambrose, holding his cup and saucer like rare artifacts. The woman was dressed in the shapeless dress and thick stockings of circa 1930. The top of her head barely came to his shoulder, although whether this meant she was small or he was tall Jean couldn't say. A certain fox-like sharpness to the woman's face reminded Jean of Iris. "Is that Ambrose and Eileen?" she asked.

"Oh aye. Having tea in the summerhouse."

"Here? There's no summerhouse in the garden now, not that that one looks sturdy enough to survive seventy years or so of Scottish weather."

"Iris had it torn down. I saw it once, years ago. It was overgrown, dark, with a bad smell and a bad feel."

"A bad feel?" Had Kirsty sensed the garden ghost? "You mean it felt spooky? Eerie?"

"Uncanny, aye, but I was no more than six or eight, mind, and right fanciful." The young woman's head bent even further, concealing her face, and her shoulders hunched as defensively as Gunn's. Who had criticized her for being imaginative? Iris?

Taking the hint, Jean finished her trek across the room and peered into the glass case. *Oh my, yes.* By today's standards Ambrose had been little more than a grave robber, ignoring occupation layers in his quest for ancient artifacts, and then failing to record those artifacts' exact provenance. But their lure was undeniable. A small bronze pot lay with its hanger-chain wrapped around it like a dragon's tail. Several silver-gilt crescents that could have been anything from scabbard tips to brooches were etched with knot work designs and ended in stylized animal heads. They weren't quite the homogenized interlace that signaled Celtic art to today's consumers — they had an angularity, an edge, a nervous energy.

What particularly caught her eye were two matching diamond-shaped silver plaques, only a few inches long, engraved with the same crescent and line design as the Stone. Another plaque, somewhat larger, displayed the Stone's figure eight symbol, the double disc. Holes at the top of all three told Jean she was looking at two earrings and a necklace.

If the symbols on the Stone were the names of a local magnate and his wife, then this might have been the bride's wedding attire. Maybe the groom had worn the chain with the thick silver links, an engraved cuff holding the ends together, that lay next to the earrings. Such chains were so heavy and so rare, they must have been symbols of power.

Hmmm. Several areas of the burgundy velvet background cloth were more deeply-colored than the rest, and defined in the shapes of several artifacts. The objects in the case had been rearranged, exposing areas that had been protected from the light for, perhaps, decades. Jean counted first the objects, then the patches. Yes, there were now three fewer artifacts.

Michael had said that the Museum was recently offered a similar silver chain. Maybe it had spent the last sixty years or so in this exact display case. "Did Ambrose find these when he excavated in the area?"

"Who knows? Aunt Iris was telling me of an old cemetery atop the hill. Don't know why he'd spend time and effort digging round old bones, but digging up artifacts, now, there's motivation for you."

"Very definitely." Jean leaned over the case toward the window. There, beyond the garden, in the field beside the grove of pines, Brendan trundled along a large box on wheels while Roger guided the wires extending from it. That had to be some sort of geophysical implement that showed cavities beneath the ground.

Again Jean thought how eccentric it was for Dempsey to look for Nessie, alive or dead, on land. Or at least on land so high above the water. And suddenly, like the tumblers of a lock falling into place at the insertion of the correct key, her thoughts formed a pattern. What if Roger wasn't looking for the Loch Ness monster? What if he was searching for more Pictish artifacts, ones that fit the definition of treasure? What if Nessie were no more than scaly-hided, protective coloring?

FOURTEEN

For a moment Jean basked in the dazzling light of her bright idea. Then she told herself that that idea sure opened a can of worms — or miniature Nessies, as the case might be. Not least being the question of why, of all the ancient and possibly treasure-bearing sites in Scotland, had Dempsey come here to Pitclachie, where he was not welcome? Because of the cryptic message on the Stone, which he chose to interpret as proof of an ancient Nessie tradition? But how did that tie in with treasure of the silver and bronze variety? Because Ambrose had written about ancient Pictish ceremonies and had also turned up an ancient Pictish hoard?

What her idea didn't open was any insight into who blew up the boat and caused Jonathan's death, not to mention who wrote the anonymous letters. But still she needed to tell Alasdair. He wouldn't laugh at her for free-associating. He knew that evidence could be more slippery than the Loch Ness monster, and as likely to be caught between the rock and the hard place of seeing and believing.

Exhaling through pursed lips, Jean looked on suspiciously as Roger and Brendan trudged across the field, much as ancient Picts must have done with oxen dragging a wooden plow. Beyond them the pines swayed, concealing the Stone, and clouds spilled like wisps of smoke over the mountaintop.

And here came the Bouchards out of the glade, closing the gate behind them. Charles strolled over to Roger and Brendan. Roger stopped in his tracks, forcing Brendan to stop too. The younger man stood flexing his arms and hands while Charles and Roger gesticulated so broadly they might have been mimes, communicating in symbols rather than words. Digging, Jean interpreted. Structures. People walking. Caverns — or graves, maybe? The creature dog-paddling through the loch. Sophie waited on the path, glancing at her watch.

Then, with a tally-ho gesture, Charles led his wife on toward the house and clean clothes, food, and drink. The day had grown so dark the lighted window of the library probably beckoned invitingly . . . Sophie looked right at Jean and waved. She waved back, less at Sophie than at her own ghostly reflection in the glass.

The front door opened and shut. Footsteps climbed the staircase. Another door slammed and floorboards squeaked. Jean turned to Kirsty. "What are Roger and Brendan looking for?"

"Herself. Nessie, or so Brendan's telling me." Kirsty frowned down at her knitting. "Bones, I reckon."

"Funny," Jean said, "that Iris would let Roger search here at Pitclachie. There doesn't seem to be much love lost between them. She objects to his methods, I gather. Or is there more to it than that?"

"There's something from the past."

"His past or her past?"

Kirsty's lips moved, counting her stitches. Maybe she'd said all she was going to say to a presumptuous stranger. Maybe she had nothing else to offer.

Jean drifted toward one of the shelves. Tilting her head to read the titles, she inspected the books with all the delectation of a gourmet at a wine-tasting. She had learned long ago how to separate the sheep from the goats among her house-guests. There were the people who abandoned conversation and went through her bookcases, and there were the people who seemed to regard them as so much wallpaper. So far she'd had the good taste, or the good luck, to never host anyone who asked accusingly, "Have you read all of those?" as though reading was the sort of private function you had to wash your hands after doing.

Lining the shelves were books ranging from leather-bound classics to academic tomes to a vast collection of Nessie-ology to popular novels of all eras down to the present . . . Good heavens! That looked like a 1937 first edition of *The Hobbit*, a very valuable book indeed.

"A librarian stopped here in May," said Kirsty.

Jean looked up. That's right, she was pumping the girl for information. "Yes?"

"She worked at the Library of Congress in Washington D. C. Name of Sirikanya — isn't that pretty? Originally from Thailand, she was saying. You should have seen her the day she came running in to read the Nessie books, over the moon, sure she'd seen the monster in the loch! She was telling Aunt Iris she had some right valuable books and should be finding herself a proper expert."

Scanning the shelves again, this time critically rather than curiously, Jean noted not the books themselves but the gaps where ones had been removed. "I doubt, er, suspect that Iris knows exactly what she has here. Has she ever done business with the rare-book dealer from Fort Augustus, the one who's at the Festival?"

"Gordon Fraser, is it? Now there's a pillock. We were at the shops in Fort Augustus not a month since when Aunt Iris saw a cookbook in his window and stopped in to buy it, and here's him taking her money like it's cursed and showing us both the door before we could so much as look about."

Jean's ears perked up like the cat's. "I was talking to Fraser at the Festival. He seemed uneasy about Ambrose's relationship with Aleister Crowley. And, I assume, the, er, mystery about Ambrose and Eileen."

"Oh aye," Kirsty said with a bored sigh and beseeching look upward. "That verdict of Not Proven went down right badly in these parts. My folk were away to Glasgow, putting the past behind them and all."

And convincing you that imagination was a bad thing, thought Jean, people having a tendency to throw babies out with tubs of bathwater. She pointed toward three books tucked away in the darkest corner of the room. Two of their spines displayed the names Lawrence and Boccaccio, the third . . . "I see Iris has a copy of Crowley's own *Moonchild*. Plus a couple of other popularly unpalatable books from Mandrake Press. There's a really obscure and short-lived publisher."

Kirsty looked up. "Mandrake Press, is it? That's the cat's name, Mandrake. Here's me, thinking he was named for the screaming plants in *Harry Potter*. Not that Aunt Iris has time for fanciful stories such as that."

The calico cat opened an eye, partly acknowledging the name, mostly not caring less.

"The press was named for the plant, I bet, which has all sorts of magical properties and is toxic to boot. If that's the cat's name, it sounds like Iris has some sense of humor about her past." The elephant of "the past" had been lying in the middle of the room all this time. It was time to goad its massive rump. "The question, and I'm sure the police asked you this, is whether Iris has enemies from her past. Or present, for that matter. Someone who could have sent those anonymous letters, trying to . . ."

"Bloody hell," said Kirsty. "I dropped a stitch two rows back. They'll want unraveling."

"I'll show you how to pick it up." Jean hurried across the room and took the needles with their pendant scarf from Kirsty's hands. While the interruption might have occurred conveniently before she finished her question, Jean saw that the dropped stitch was only too real. "Do you have a crochet hook? Or a bobby pin — a hair clip — would do."

Kirsty reached to the hair piled on her head and pulled out a pin. Sitting down in the desk chair, Jean used the pin to pick up and interlock each errant stitch in turn. She added the last loop of yarn to the row of stitches already on the needles and handed everything back to Kirsty. "See? Like most things, it's not hard once you know how to do it."

"Thank you kindly."

"Glad to help. Did Iris teach you to knit?"

"That she did. Told me if I kept my hands busy I'd not be biting my nails." Kirsty waggled her pristine fingertips. "Knitting's not so naff a business as it was a few years back, now it's right trendy."

"I've been knitting since I was a girl. I'm glad to see it's respectable again. It's a metaphor for life, really. Stitches can be too tight, too loose, or just right. Patterns can be plain or intricate. You can use up all your yarn and not be able to find the same color or texture. You can tie yourself into a knot and have to start over. You can notice that you made a mistake several rows earlier, but it's not a simple dropped stitch — if you, like, cable front to back instead of back to front, you have to cut or unravel, but either way it's a nuisance and you can dump a bunch of stitches before you're done."

Kirsty was staring, the needles stationary in her hands, her expression compounded of confusion and caution.

Yes, it was a rare mind that appreciated free-association. Jean glanced again at the photo, where Eileen looked as though she was a bit out of her depth and resentful of finding herself there. Jean couldn't help Eileen, but she could take pity on Kirsty and cut to the chase already. "If you need help with anything else, just ask. With the explosion and the police taking Iris away, your schedule's really been disrupted."

"What I'm needing is Aunt Iris back." Taking a deep breath, Kirsty set her chin and sat up straighter. "You say you're chums with this Cameron chap. Can you tell me, then, why they took Aunt Iris away? What was she telling them, that they'd suspect her of blowing up boats?"

It was Jean's turn to stare, jaw slack, possible responses doing a Keystone Kops routine in her mind. Would she be exceeding her brief if she told Kirsty about Iris's confession? *No.* "Iris was seen puttering about the bay Thursday evening, during Roger's ITN interview."

"She's after doing that every few days, checking her flatworm traps. Keeps a power boat at the pier."

"That's as may be," Jean began, and realized she sounded like Alasdair. "Maybe so, but she also confessed to sending the anonymous letters to Roger Dempsey. I know she doesn't care for him, but does threatening him seem any more likely to you than it does to me?"

"She confessed to . . ?" A flush started in Kirsty's cheeks and bloomed outward. With deliberate if jerky movements she finished the row of stitches and dropped her knitting into her lap, so that the scarf and the ball of yarn made a puddle the same color as her face. Then the sudden flow of crimson ebbed so completely from her complexion that even in the lamplight she seemed ghostly pale and cold. A strand of hair dangled beside her face, limp as seaweed.

Once again, Jean thought of drowned Ophelia, a pawn in the designs of others. More steps clumped slowly, almost stealthily, across the ceiling, accompanied by the sound of trickling water. Mandrake stretched and began to groom his already sleek fur. Finally Jean asked gently, "Kirsty, what's going on here? Do you think Iris sent the letters?"

"No, she couldna have done, it's not like her. But I dinna know, do I? She's come over all strange since the Water Horse folk arrived. She's always been one to get on with what needs doing, but now, no, she's sitting up the tower instead of washing dishes and the like."

"What's at the top of the tower?"

"A room. All dust and cobwebs. Iris locks it up, disna allow the guests there, but then, there's nothing there worth doing."

"Except looking out at the loch?" Jean hazarded. "And, the last few days, at the Water Horse boat?"

This time it was Kirsty's gaze that strayed to the framed photo and then back to Jean's face, where it clung. Any port in a storm, it seemed. "She used to tell you straight out what she's thinking, but not now, no, she's after keeping something back"

"She's pretty straightforward about her feelings for Roger. And she didn't mince words about not wanting you to see Brendan any more. Sorry," Jean added to the flash in Kirsty's eyes, "I was on the terrace this morning and overheard you talking to her."

"So did half the town, I'm thinking. Oh aye, she's dead set against Brendan, for no more reason than that he's working with Roger, so far as I can tell. As for why she's taken against Roger, that's a question she'll not be answering."

"The answer lies in the past," Jean said half to herself, and, louder, "As for the present, I heard you identified a corkscrew the police found in the wreckage of the boat. It must have been taken from here recently — there wasn't one on the drinks table last night."

"Iris forgot it when she made up the table, did she? Like I was saying, she's not herself." Kirsty shook her head. "The corkscrew the polis showed me, now, that was never on the drinks table. It went missing from the desk here a couple of months ago."

That was interesting. "Do you think someone's trying to frame Iris for blowing up the Water Horse boat, not to mention for writing those letters?"

"So it seems." Kirsty turned the knitting over and over in her lap, inspecting it carefully but not actually making any stitches. The twin spikes of the needles chimed together.

Funny, Jean thought, every time the subject of the letters came up, Kirsty ducked and covered. That might be something worth exploring, but then, there was a lot else to explore, too. "What about Brendan? You went to the Tourist Authority dinner with him last night. You were with him when the boat exploded."

"Oh aye, that I was."

"I know how Iris felt about your going with him. But how did Roger and Tracy feel?"

"The trout, Tracy, asked right sharpish where Jonathan was, why Brendan was there instead. She never took any notice of me. Roger now, he seemed right pleased to see me. Thought he was putting one over on Iris, most likely."

Jean's ears pricked again. "So Jonathan was supposed to be at the dinner."

"He was that, aye. Tracy, she wanted the Brits front and center for the Brit press, didn't she? But Jonathan told Brendan he couldn't be bothered with a posh dinner. Brendan swapped with him so as to take me out." Some of the color seeped back into Kirsty's face at that.

"Was Brendan supposed to have stayed on the boat?"

"No, he'd been told to drive to Inverness. The post needed collecting."

"But Jonathan wasn't driving to Inverness, he was on the boat. Why?"

"If he'd told anyone you'd not be asking me, would you?" Kirsty returned, cutting Jean no slack for a rhetorical question. "Brendan, now, he reckons Jonathan was a spy. Industrial espionage. He sneaked onto the boat to take photos of the submersible he might could sell to another company."

Jean sat up straight, wondering if she was hearing more tumblers falling into place or simply the clatter of scattershots, taken at random. "Photos of one of the ROVs, you mean?"

"Brendan said submersible. Close to being the same thing, isn't it?"

"Close, yes. Why does he think Jonathan was a spy?"

"He was asking too many questions and prying about in areas that weren't his affair."

"If asking questions and prying is enough to make someone suspicious of you, then I should have been carried off by the police long ago!"

A dry, almost sarcastic laugh escaped Kirsty's lips. "But you're a reporter, and you're working with the polis, aren't you now? Jonathan wasn't a reporter, he was a computer . . ."

A sudden thudding sound cut Kirsty off in mid-sentence and made both women sit back abruptly, like conspirators interrupted at their plotting.

Fifteen

The sound, Jean realized, was coming from the business end of the dragon knocker. The front door opened and a male voice called, "Miss Wotherspoon?"

"In here!" Kirsty returned, and shrank down in her chair, her face curdling into a scowl. "That Sawyer chap, he said he'd be sending a forensics team."

Jean clenched her jaw. *Good timing.* In another few minutes Kirsty might have shared a confidence or two. Typical Sawyer, a Scottish bull in a pottery shop.

The thunder of footsteps in the hall sounded like the running of the bulls at Pamplona. Jean hauled herself to her feet. "Well, you can always hope they have D.C. Gunn with them."

"Who?" Kirsty asked,

"D.C. Gunn. The cute young guy about your age."

Kirsty looked blank. If he'd been flirting with her, she hadn't noticed.

A constable peered through the doorway. "Miss Wotherspoon?"

"Hang in there," Jean told Kirsty, and received an impatient but not actively hostile snort in acknowledgment.

Jean pushed her way through the front hall and away, telling herself, *if you can fake sincerity, you've got it made.* But she wasn't faking her wish to reassure Kirsty. Or her need to know. It was only after she had spurted out into a fine, misty rain and was halfway across the courtyard that she registered neither Gunn nor Sawyer in the official group milling around the front hall. That made her feel a bit better about abandoning Kirsty, not that she wouldn't have been requested to remove herself from the area anyway. And if Kirsty didn't know how to take care of herself, she needed to learn that particular life lesson ASAP.

The Lodge was so silent Jean could hear the ticking of the kitchen clock. She skimmed up the stairs, and with another glare at the locked room — no, she hadn't suddenly developed x-ray vision — she grabbed her notebook and folding umbrella. Back outside, Jean keyed Michael and Rebecca's number into her phone. A series of chirps and clicks hinted the call was being forwarded, and Michael's voice said, "Hello?"

"Hi, it's Jean. Sorry to bug you again, but the questions are coming faster and faster."

"No problem, though you'll have to be going on with one set of answers. I came away to the Museum to work so's Rebecca could have a good rest."

"Well, it's a Museum question. Is there any evidence Ambrose found that hoard in the Pictish cemetery up the hill from Pitclachie?"

"Like excavating King Tut's tomb? Not likely. The Picts didna believe in grave goods. And Ambrose only excavated the one grave."

"So he said."

"Oh aye. He might could have turned over the entire hillside and no one's the wiser. Come to that . . ." His pause was as pregnant as his wife. "The silver chain we were talking about earlier the day, the one offered the Museum last year. It came from the Great Glen all right, but not from Iris. She sold one to the Museum twenty years since, though."

"When she started fixing up the house." Maybe the marks on the velvet backing from that one had faded. Maybe it had never been in the cabinet. Fantasizing about treasure chests in Pitclachie's dungeons, Jean said, "She's sold some old books too, I bet, but she's still got three from Mandrake Press, including Aleister Crowley's *Moonchild*. You think they might be valuable?"

"Most likely, aye, depending on whether you're after collecting or burning them." Computer keys clicked. "Oh aye. Mandrake was started up by two of Crowley's admirers in nineteen-twenty-nine. Almost failed the next year, but was re-organized by a consortium led by Crowley himself — and here you are, Ambrose Mackintosh had a financial interest. They published a small load of obscure and controversial items, but went bankrupt after eighteen months."

"Ambrose invested in a publisher? He'd have gotten a better return betting on horse races. Thanks, Michael. I'll check with you on Monday about Ambrose's stone mason. And see what else you can find about that silver chain from last year while you're at it, please."

"My powers are limited, but I'll do my best. Take care, now."

"That's the idea. Cheers." Thrusting her phone into her purse, Jean contemplated the plants and trees alongside the terrace, wondering where the summerhouse had once stood. Leaves rustled and flowers bobbed up and down in the wind. Or against the wind, actually. A faint prickle oozed through her body, raising gooseflesh, and then passed on. The mysterious ghost in the garden or just the breeze, not so much the physical one as the chilly breath of the past.

A shape in a nearby window became Mandrake the cat, his sleek body distorted by the old glass, his eyes hard and steady, focused on the same patch of greenery that had attracted Jean's extra-sensory attention. His tail curled back and forth, making question marks. Jean had heard that animals could sense ghosts. Probably, like people, some did and some didn't. But if Pitclachie's pet had been immune to the paranormal, she'd have been disappointed.

Frowning up at the tower — there was another mysterious if not necessarily locked room — Jean walked around the corner of the house.

In the parking area, Roger was clambering into the driver's seat of the Water Horse van while Brendan slammed the back door. Their jeans were muddy and their hair slicked down, wet with rain. Back to headquarters to crunch the data, Jean supposed. She waved as Brendan vaulted into the van, but Roger had already started the engine and neither somber face turned toward her as they drove away.

A short sharp shower of rain made her hoist her umbrella. She contracted herself into its meager shelter, seeing not the gray waves of rain rumpling the water of the loch but Jonathan Paisley's floating body, hearing not the spatter of the raindrops but Kirsty's voice: *Jonathan wasn't a reporter, he was a computer* . . . Nerd or geek, Jean finished for her.

But what if he *had* been a reporter of some sort? Computer and journalistic skills weren't mutually exclusive. And if he had been a reporter, maybe he'd been after a story Roger didn't want revealed, the secret agenda Jean had already suspected.

She was just starting off down the driveway — wet shoes wouldn't kill her — when the Bouchards hurried around the corner of the house, sheltering beneath a big black umbrella that was hardly fashionably Parisian but was much more practical.

"You go to town?" asked Sophie.

Charles unlocked the doors of their pale gold Renault. "Here. Come to ride with us. Not so wet."

"Why thank you!" Jean flattened her umbrella and tumbled awkwardly into the back seat.

Sophie glided swan-like into the front seat and adjusted her scarf around her shoulders. "The gendarmes, they tell us to go. They will search our room, they say. Very unpleasant."

The police would search the Lodge, too, Jean thought, and with a stab of regret realized she wouldn't be there when they asked Kirsty to open the locked door.

Charles started the car. A cold gust from the defrost parted Jean's hair. She propped her umbrella next to the door, where it could drip on the carpet and not on the books lying on the seat: a Michelin Guide, an Automobile Association map of the UK, two *Art and Antiquities* magazines, and the same paperback edition of Ambrose's biography of Crowley as Jean's own. "What do y'all do?" she asked, and modified the idiom into, "What is your work?"

"Ah," Sophie said with a flutter of her hands, "it is a shop for *objets antiques.* La Bagatelle d'Or."

Jean did a mental double-take. Sophie could wave her hands all she liked — she wasn't driving. The steering wheel was on the left, not the right. *Duh.* The car had a French license plate, already. "It's brave of you to bring your own car. I'd be really nervous driving on the left side of the road with my steering wheel on the outside. Isn't it hard to see when you can pass?"

"Sophie helps to see," said Charles, and took a right onto the main road without even stopping, let alone looking left, sublimely assured that even if Sophie couldn't see a thing, their guardian angel was playing traffic cop.

Jean winced, and in a voice that sounded like a Mickey Mouse impression, asked, "Are you enjoying your holiday?"

"Yes," replied Sophie.

"What did you think of the Pitclachie Stone?"

"Very amusing."

"Where do you go?" Charles asked. "The Festival? Beyond?"

"To the Festival, although if you could just drop me off at . . ." Having been spared being struck by a car, Jean was now struck with an inspiration. ". . . the Cameron Arms hotel. It's tea-time, more or less."

"Ah. Tea and cakes," said Sophie. "Very amusing."

"We," Charles added, "have later dinner at the Glengarry Castle Hotel."

"Nice place," Jean said. Although she'd never been there, she knew from the reviews in *Great Scot* that it was both exclusive and expensive. The couple was not honeymooning on the cheap. She wondered if Miranda had ever visited chez Bouchard, trolling for just the right knickknack. Funny, how one era's *tchotchke* became a later era's antique.

Charles guided the car into the parking lot of the Cameron Arms. The rain slackened into a few spits and splats, and the freshly-painted white sides of the building gleamed in an uncertain ray of sun. The Water Horse van sat skewed across two parking places, as though Roger and Brendan couldn't wait to abandon it. On the far side of the Atlantic this wouldn't be tea-time but happy hour. Maybe Roger and his acolyte had gone to ground in the hotel bar.

Jean slid across the supple leather seat to the door. "Did y'all see the boat blow up last night?"

"Yes," said Sophie, darting a glance at Charles. "We saw from the village. Very bad."

"Very sad, the man who dies," Charles went on. "He was not so pleasant when we visited the boat, but that is not important, is it?"

Jean paused with her hand on the door handle. "Y'all toured the boat?"

"We were walking, and the boat was there, and the lady — Madame Dempsey — she says to come to look, it is open to all."

Sophie indicated an Omnium brochure tucked into the console, good as a ticket stub. "See here?"

"I see," said Jean, and opened the door. The car had become so warm in just a few minutes that the outside air felt like a cool compress on her fevered brow. "Thank you very much for the ride."

"*De rien*," Charles responded. The moment Jean slammed the door, he took off with yet another right-hand turn that was more quick than dead, thank goodness for the slow traffic, and disappeared down the highway to the south.

So the Bouchards had not been holed up at Pitclachie when the boat exploded. And they had an antiques shop. Had they ever bought items from Iris? Or were they simply at the loch on a busman's holiday, er, honeymoon? *Busman's Honeymoon*, Jean thought, the classic detective novel with the newlyweds doing their thing upstairs while the murder victim lay undiscovered in the basement. . . . Damn! She should have thought of some way of asking Sophie and Charles why they'd moved from the Lodge to the house. Too late now.

The interior of the hotel revealed Cousin Hamish's good taste. He had designed his establishment simply, neither going overboard with tartan tushery nor veering too far into the streamlined European style that to Jean signaled not sophistication but sterility. The lobby smelled faintly of paint, although the more palatable odor of frying and baking grew stronger as she advanced past the reception desk.

She paused in the door of the bar long enough to ascertain that neither Brendan nor Roger was holed up drowning his sorrows. Good. She wasn't up to a probing conversation right now. She went on into the dining room and within minutes was sitting at a small table covered by a dazzling white table cloth, a blazing hot pot of tea set ceremonially before her. She poured, doctored, and drank. *Ahhh.* Hot tea, the universal panacea.

Through the nearby window Jean could see the Festival field with its one big tent and several smaller ones, and beyond it cars jockeying for parking places from hotel lots to gravel terraces far up the hillside. A stronger ray of sun illuminated the scene, then winked out.

By the time her food arrived she'd filled a page of her notebook with notes and flow charts — Kirsty, Roger, the Bouchards, Pictish antiquities, Nessies large and small — which made her feel she was accomplishing something. What, she didn't know, but something. Putting her notes aside with a sigh of frustration, she dug into her omelet and chips, and eyeballed the other people in the room. Tourists, she decided, fortifying themselves for the evening's music, monsters, and madness.

Well, well, well. Staking out the water hole was paying off. Here came Roger and Tracy, ushered by a white-shirted waiter to a table on the far side of the room. He had changed out of his wilted, muddy clothes into nondescript khaki slacks and a sweater. Tracy wore a smashing tweed outfit, accented by a vintage brooch glittering with what were probably not rhinestones. Jean shifted her chair just a bit, hoping she'd blend into the beige wall with its collection of watercolors and prints, all for sale, of course, but neither Dempsey so much as glanced in her direction. They did not, then, see themselves as prey.

Roger ordered and swiftly consumed a pint of dark ale. Tracy fell as though parched onto a pot of tea. They both stared so glumly at glass and cup, respectively, they could have been seated at separate tables. Then Tracy's lips moved in a murmur. Roger's head went up. Their eyes connected, then shied away, as though looking each other in the face was the equivalent of touching a hot iron.

Well, yes, Jean thought, who wouldn't be upset? But a crisis usually made a couple close ranks. Not that she was any expert on couple behavior. She looked down at her own plate long enough to smear strawberry jam on the second half of her scone. Sugar meant calories, and calories meant energy, right?

When she looked up again, Tracy was leaning across the table toward Roger, gesturing with her fork as though it were a dagger she held before her. Jean couldn't quite see her face, but the woman's jaw was stiff and the sinews in her neck were corded with tension. With anger.

Roger, on the other hand, was doing that typical male vanishing act, face averted, eyes glazed, lower lip almost as pendulous as the bags under his eyes, as though resenting his wife's intrusion into a more absorbing train of thought. Logarithms, maybe. The newest Microsoft security patch. He might just as well be holding his hands over his ears and humming.

At last Tracy thumped her hand, fork and all, against the table. Crockery jangled and several other diners looked around. Jean could read her body language as surely as though she were holding up cue cards: *Listen to me! This is important!* Was this their usual M.O. when more or less in private, when the public masks of courageous independent scientist and adoring wife walking three steps behind slipped away, and the woman behind the great man took center stage?

Roger focused, his face no longer blank but resentful, perhaps even angry. When the waiter brought his fish and chips, Roger looked at it as though the fish were still raw and wriggling. Tracy used her fork to stab viciously into a salmon salad.

Jean decided she'd gleaned all she was going to glean — not much. She finished her meal and signaled for the bill. "Roger-Tracy in dining room," she wrote in her notebook. "Stunned. Angry. Big surprise." Replacing the cap on her pen, she stowed everything, including her umbrella, in her bag and slipped away as furtively as a rat, around the edges of the room and out into the hall.

A glance back showed Roger pushing bits of potato and fish around his plate, liberally doused with blood-red catsup, and Tracy squinting into a small mirror, equally red lipstick ready to fill in the maroon outline of her lips. . . . She looked up and saw Jean.

The two women stared at each other, Tracy hostile, Jean trying to put together a polite smile and failing. Then, like wrestlers told to break a hold, Tracy raised her mirror and Jean did a swift about-face.

She paid her bill at the reception desk and hurried out of the building, reassuring herself that Tracy's hostility wasn't personal. Maybe the Dempseys had courted *Great Scot* before the explosion, just as they'd courted all the media, but now reporters equaled bad publicity. If marketing was a way of protecting your investment, right now Tracy was seeing her and Roger's investment sinking like that boat.

Jean could almost side with the Dempseys, not against them, except Jonathan was dead, and the ripples of his death were spreading outward like those in the famous photo of Nessie. Alasdair was just about the only person here she could trust. She needed to talk to Alasdair.

Sixteen

Jean realized she was almost running, whether toward or away from she couldn't say, and forced herself to slow down before she slipped in one of the puddles dotting the asphalt sidewalk hugging the road. Never mind Kirsty learning to take care of herself. One hostile stare and Jean was acting like a veteran with post-traumatic stress syndrome. She was a big girl. She could put off the moment of truth with Alasdair — or the moment of inconsequence, whatever — a little while longer.

The sun was shining again, its rays focused between mounds of white and gray clouds and illuminating the hillsides into a green so intense it was like a platonic ideal. The wind had grown colder, teasing the hem of Jean's skirt and sending sneaky little drafts up her legs. The muddy patch inside the gate to the Festival Field was now a muddy quilt. Undeterred by the chill and the mud, people of all ages and races were milling around and through the tents. Two constables paced around the periphery, and a camper-van marked with the logo of the Northern Constabulary sat discreetly to one side. A couple of men bearing TV mini-cams wandered about like inquisitive aardvarks. At least print reporters could be a little more subtle.

Alerted by the sound of amplified voices, Jean looked toward the big top. Several roadies were fussing around with cords and amplifiers, not unlike the way Brendan and Jonathan had been fussing around with cords and gadgets on the boat. Peter Kettering stood to one side, consulting a clipboard, a cell phone, and his watch simultaneously. In his three-piece suit he looked like a waiter, compared to the be-kilted figures that stood at the front of the stage extolling the virtues of Starr Beverages.

A kilt was a surpassingly attractive garment, Jean thought with a smile. It complemented almost any male shape and dressed up any number of professions. Including police detectives.

She reconnoitered the outer ring of tents and booths as though clues would be laid out on tables at markdown prices. Gordon Fraser was doing good business, although presumably not in books about Aleister Crowley, Ambrose's or any other. How sad that despite his "poor wee Iris," he was visiting Ambrose's — well, maybe not sins, eccentricities — upon the daughters. Memories did go back a long way in this part of the world.

So did appetites. A food vendor's booth emitted the full-bodied scent of fried meat and pastry. Brendan and Kirsty stood nearby, munching on meat pies. She was snapping bites out of hers, he was nibbling, with wary sideways glances at Kirsty.

Jean walked on. More than once she had to turn sideways and ease past chattering knots of people. Someone would occasionally react to her murmured apology, but more often than not no one took any notice of her, leaving her feeling invisible. Or maybe covert, as in covert operator.

At last she worked her way back around to the road and strolled further toward the town. A hundred yards along, in a garden area near the entrance of the Official Loch Ness Exhibition, she spotted another familiar face. Little Elvis Hall, a plastic Nessie clutched in his hand, squatted beside a pond eyeing a fiberglass Nessie the size of a huge swan that floated in the water teasingly out of reach.

The plump blond woman standing over him was Noreen, his mum. Every curve of her face sagged in defeat, as though she had lost not a skirmish but an entire campaign.

"Hello," said Jean. "I'm Jean Fairbairn. I'm staying at the B&B, and was talking to Martin and Elvis last night."

"Oh," said Noreen. "Bad business that, the fireworks and all. Or the boat blowing up rather, not the fireworks themselves, they didn't cause that, did they now? I didn't mean to say they did. That boat could have gone up at any time, and there's us, having a tour. Dreadful smelly place, never so nice as the B&B, and Elvis after pushing every bloody button. I knackered myself chasing him about."

"Wasn't Martin with you?"

Noreen glanced over her shoulder. Martin stood just outside the courtyard made by one side of the old stone hotel that housed the Exhibition and the series of shops attached to it, shops that formed a gauntlet of souvenirs that everyone exiting from the otherwise quite sober Exhibition had to run. Martin was smoking a cigarette and not so much chatting with Dave and Patti Duckett as standing there silent while they chatted at him.

"He was there, right enough," Noreen said, "but he was having himself a natter with Mrs. Dempsey, being in a similar field and all. Biology. He's doing ever so important research for Bristol University, on eels."

"There's the theory that Nessie is a giant eel," offered Jean, skipping past the fact that while Roger was as much a biologist as Jean herself was a hard-hitting investigative reporter, Tracy wasn't a biologist at all . . . Maybe the shape in Tracy's window had been Martin's, after all.

"I've heard tell of that eel idea, oh yes. And all the others as well."

"Is Martin a Nessie enthusiast like Elvis?"

The child was making his plastic creature swim through the weedy, murky water. "That he is. Like father like son," Noreen said with a sigh, quickly suppressed, and another glance toward her husband.

"Has Elvis seen the Exhibition?"

"Martin took him in when we was here in April. Me, I had me one look at the price of the ticket and said no thanks, I'll wait. That's me, always waiting, waiting tables in the motorway caff, waiting on . . ." She cut herself off. This time she didn't look at Martin, but by the set of her shoulders Jean deduced that took a deliberate effort. "I mean, his work's ever so important, it's the least I can do, isn't it, to help pay the bills and all?"

The first words that sprang to Jean's mind were about the relatively high prices at Pitclachie House. She tried, "The B&B is very nice. Iris sets a high standard. A good thing she has Kirsty to help her."

"Yeh, nothing like a bit of slave labor, is there? All Kirsty gets is her room and board and a few quid for spending money, in return for working like a navvy and sucking down loads of advice from Iris."

"Kirsty doesn't seem particularly resentful," Jean ventured.

"It's not like she has a choice, is it? I mean, we was having us a nice natter back in April, Kirsty and me, and she told me about the aggro in Glasgow and all. Bloody shame the lad pushed her into sending those letters and then told the polis. He should be the one paying the price, not her. But no, her family sends her up here even though she gave him the elbow quick smart."

Jean's ears pricked up so far they sprouted points. "Letters?"

"Well, that's not what we was talking about, was it? We was talking about choosing the wrong man — it's always the woman who pays." This time Noreen did look over at Martin, her resentment so heavy it sagged into despair.

Jean tried to think of something positive to say, but all that came to her mind was the counsel that staying together for the kids was a much over-rated reason to stick out a bad relationship. And she was no counselor. Funny how neither Roger nor Tracy, who had reason to assume someone was waiting to pounce on them, were acting like prey, and yet here was Noreen behaving like an antelope downwind of a lion. Marriage could do that to a woman, Jean told herself with prejudice aforethought. And if Kirsty had had a manipulative boyfriend back in Glasgow, that would explain Iris's attitude toward Brendan . . .

A splash and a cry jerked her around. Noreen lunged. Elvis, predictably, had leaned too far and was now standing in the water, his face as bewildered as though the fiberglass monster had reached up and pulled him in.

Throwing down his cigarette, Martin loped to the pool, plucked the boy from the pond, and set him down on the grassy bank. "Have a care there, lad."

"My shoes," said Elvis, his face crumpling. Balancing on one foot, he extended one of his small athletic shoes. A rivulet of water poured from its heel.

"Hush," said Martin. "They'll dry themselves. No harm done."

With a heavy sigh, not suppressed, Noreen sat down on a rock, pulled Elvis onto her lap, and began to untie his shoelaces. "Those shoes, they cost a packet."

"Well then, you should have been minding him properly." Martin's Adam's apple bobbed up and down in his stalk of a throat, a judge's gavel rising and falling. "Leave off your fussing. Take him back to the B&B before he catches a chill."

Noreen didn't respond. She didn't keep working with Elvis's shoes, either.

Jean looked up at Martin, a foot taller and half as wide as she was, but he took no notice of her. She looked down at Noreen, who even when standing up was two inches shorter and twice as broad. Compared to this couple, the Dempseys resembled twins.

She wandered diplomatically away, to where the Ducketts were diplomatically gazing off toward the mountains. Martin's cigarette lay smoking on the cement. Jean ground it under her shoe, harder than was necessary.

"We waved at you earlier," Dave said. "You were getting out of the French couple's car at the Cameron Arms. We'd just had an early supper and were heading over here to the Exhibition."

"I didn't see you, sorry." If she'd been an antelope she'd be dismembered and half-digested by now, she added to herself. A lively fiddle tune echoed from the Festival, signaling an end to the Starr Beverages PLC commercial break. "That's Hugh Munro. If you haven't heard him before, he's worth a listen and a few CDs, too."

"Sounds nice and cheerful. Let's go listen to the music, hon." Patti hoisted her shopping bag, brimming with yet more toys and tiny garments. Jean was reminded of one of her cousins, lavishing gifts on her grandchildren after her son's divorce, trying to stay a part of their lives. But Patti had said something about the kids moving back to Illinois, hadn't she?

Dave took the bag, and Patti's arm, and escorted her toward the music. The Halls, too, walked away, Elvis wriggling like a marionette at the end of Martin's long arm. Noreen made nervous gestures over him and shot nervous glances at her husband. Her dishwater blonde head bending over Elvis's golden one looked like after and before photos in a hair color ad.

Shuddering, Jean took a step and caromed off a kilted man the size and coloring of a grizzly bear. With mutual apologies they danced around each other, and she hurried back to the Festival field chiding herself yet again. Too much input. That was it.

The swing and sway of the music, the rhythm of a kilt around a man's knees, summoned her to the main tent. Hugh and his back-up lads — Billy on pipes, Jamie on guitar, Donnie on keyboard — were playing a bravura reel that might not actually wake the dead but would certainly rouse the comatose. Shuffling her feet, Jean joined in the clapping and hooching. At least she hoped her cries of enthusiasm were proper Scottish hooching, the secular cousin of the gospel audience's occasional outburst of prayer: *Amen, brother!* If music was like prayer, then Hugh's fiddle was the next best thing to a holy relic.

And the bagpipes! Pipe music was an acquired taste for the non-Celt, or even for the odd reconstructed Celt. It was in-your-face and up-your-spine. It was wildly romantic. In other words, it was dangerous.

Jean saw Noreen and Elvis, now alone, trudging along the sidewalk toward Pitclachie. And here came Tracy striding toward the Festival. Noreen pulled Elvis out of the way and all but curtseyed. Tracy brushed by without acknowledging them, picked her way through the gate into the field, and disappeared into the crowd. Noreen jerked Elvis, collateral damage, into a fast trot.

At the edge of the tent, several couples began performing the intricate sets of Scottish country dancing, the ancestor of the American square dance. One red-headed man's short-sleeved shirt revealed arms covered with tattoos. All he needed was a tunic instead of jeans — or nothing but blue vegetable dye — and he'd be a painted Pict from Roman legend. Unless the Picts had been blue from the cold.

Some experts postulated that the designs carved on the stones began as tattoos, which led Jean back to her musings on Pictish treasures, whether "treasure" could be defined as artifacts valuable to collectors or potsherds of interest to no one but scientists. Or the bones of a mythical beast. Whether the Bouchards with their shop and Ambrose with his collection and Roger with his scientific interests were simply on different parts of the same spectrum. Whether the fact that people often killed for treasure meant anyone was intent on killing for it now.

Time to download some data before her brain exploded. Kirsty and something about letters, for one thing. That would surprise and gratify Alasdair, or she'd eat her junior detective's magnifying glass and deerstalker hat. Pulling out her cell phone, she told herself that with her luck, he'd gone back to Inverness and she'd have to wait until tomorrow for a face-to-face meeting. Not that there was anything wrong with that.

Whoa. Here came a bulky shape casting a grotesquely long shadow in the evening sun. D.S. Sawyer was cruising the crowd, so heavy-footed Jean could almost feel each step reverberating in the earth. She imagined tiny biplanes circling his head while he drummed on his chest and swatted at them, and she started looking for an escape route. But Sawyer was after fresher meat.

D.C. Gunn was chatting to Kirsty and Brendan, one hand in his pocket, the other holding a soft drink. Brendan and Kirsty looked less woebegone than they had earlier, if far from cheerful. Gunn said something that was accompanied with a shrug. That they hadn't made any progress on the case? Brendan opened his mouth to reply just as Kirsty saw Sawyer bearing down on them and quailed so quickly she bounced off Brendan's nicely filled-out chest.

Shutting his mouth with a snap, Brendan put his arm around Kirsty and pulled her close. For a second she stood stiffly against him, then leaned into his embrace. Gunn stood his ground, his face set with icy courtesy — a copy of one of Alasdair's repertory of expressions. Gunn chose his role models well.

Sawyer bore down on the trio. His forefinger targeted Kirsty and Brendan. His recessed chin split with a humorless smirk like the smile on the snout of a crocodile. He slowed down just long enough to hiss something into Gunn's ear.

Gunn made a face like that of the offendee in a mouthwash ad. His left hand came out of his pocket and hung clenched at his trouser seam. Jean could almost hear the creak of the soft drink can as his other hand tightened on it. And yet he said nothing, only stood his ground as Sawyer stomped on by.

Kirsty blinked and Brendan frowned. Sawyer, having counted coup against Gunn, continued his circuit of the tent. He was headed directly for Jean. She spun around and pushed through the crowd, propelled by righteous anger and frustration — at what, she wasn't sure, but she'd back Gunn over Sawyer any day. Heck, she'd back Kirsty and Brendan over Sawyer, and for all she knew they were hip-deep in conspiracy.

Jean bounced off the soft body of a woman, ricocheted off the skinny body of a man, and thudded straight into a third body. This one was hard, rock-steady. Large, firm hands grasped her upper arms and both pushed her away and held her upright. She knew who it was before she tilted her face up to his.

"Well now," said Alasdair's brushed-velvet voice, the warmth of his breath bathing her cool cheeks. "What's all this then?"

SEVENTEEN

One corner of his mouth was tucked in and his eyes were twinkling . . . No, that was heresy. Alasdair's eyes didn't twinkle. They might scintillate gravely, or elude Jean's gaze like a will o' the wisp, or glow like twin blue flames.

He wasn't eluding Jean's gaze. He was staring back, his brows drifting downward and his lips tightening, no doubt thinking his policeman-as-cliché joke had thudded down like another cliché, the infamous lead balloon. If she'd laughed he might have come back with a smile and a *Move along, nothing to see here.* But it was too late now for a light moment, drat it all anyway.

"It's been a long day," Jean said neutrally, hoping to excuse her lack of appreciation. Hoping to excuse her blindly playing human pinball, for that matter, without dragging Alasdair back to humorless reality by mentioning Sawyer.

"Oh aye," said Alasdair, also neutral.

She liked the feel of his hands on her arms, and had to resist the temptation to flatten her own hands on the lapels of his coat. Or open the lapels of his coat and press her palms against the starched white front of his shirt. And yet, at the same time, she also had to resist the temptation to flinch and flounce away with a feminist mutter. She did neither, which was a compromise like most compromises, less than satisfactory to both sides. "You can let me go now."

"Ah." Releasing her, he raised his hands in front of his chest, palms out, making simultaneously a warding motion and the universal gesture of *I'm unarmed.*

She would have sagged had she not been holding herself alertly upright. Funny how her arms seemed cold and weak without the pressure of his hands. Dropping her gaze, she noticed a few scone crumbs clinging to the breast of her less than posh tweed jacket and quickly brushed them away.

"You've had your tea, then," said Alasdair, following her gesture.

"At the new hotel," Jean replied. "Nice place. Good food. Kudos to your cousin Hamish."

Alasdair nodded approval of either Hamish's designer or his chef.

"I hope you've had more than that sandwich you were eating earlier," she said.

"Oh aye, Hamish sent along several meals by way of having the exploding boat sorted and swept away as soon as possible. I'm thinking the case is bringing in more business, not less, but then, there's more than money to consider."

"Like safety? Yes, there is that."

Alasdair gestured toward a nearby booth stocked with an array of whiskey bottles. They glinted every shade of amber as one last ray of sun squeezed between the western mountains and thickening gray cloud. "I could do with a wee dram just now. Fancy joining me?"

"Sure, as long as you don't mind my doing a data-dump at the same time."

"Eh?"

"Telling you what I learned in my afternoon's snooping," Jean amended.

"That goes without saying. I'd not be sharing a whiskey with just anyone." He turned toward the booth.

She told herself not to waste time assaying that remark.

"A Lagavullin and . . ." He glanced toward Jean.

Of course he'd like a dry malt flavored with sea spray and smoke. The Speyside malt she'd drunk last night — five years ago, it seemed now — had been almost sweet. "The same," she said, and reached for her bag.

"It's my shout. You paid for the dinner in May." Alasdair produced suitable coin of the realm before she could unzip her bag.

Except her bag was already unzipped. *Rats!* She must have been in such a hurry to escape Tracy at the hotel she hadn't closed it after paying for her tea . . . *Whew.* There was her billfold, safe and sound. She zipped up the bag and made sure the tab of the zipper was tucked into its down and locked position.

Alasdair was holding a plastic glass toward her. "They're just out of the Waterford crystal."

"Thank you," she said with a smile, and managed to take the glass from his hand without actually touching him.

Alasdair tapped his glass against hers. "As my sainted granny used to say, preserve us from a disorder whiskey canna cure."

"Hear, hear." Jean inhaled more than sipped the bright, brisk fragrance of the whisky, soothing and invigorating at once. "First a cousin and now a grandmother. I thought you were the lone ranger."

"Chance would be a fine thing," he replied sarcastically, and drank. The elegant curve of his lips thinned in a smile.

Dazzled, she went along quietly as he escorted her to one of several folding chairs grouped beneath a canvas canopy, a small no man's land neither below the big top nor right next to the police van. Hugh and his band were playing one of their part folk, part rock specialties, Jean noted with pleasure, even though this position closer to one set of speakers than the other distorted the sound just a bit. But it also meant the volume wasn't as high.

Alasdair didn't pull out his handkerchief and wipe off the seat of her chair. Jean almost wished he had — the damp seat sent an icy shock wave up her body. Well, that was why the Scots had invented whiskey to begin with. She drank deeply. *Aaaah.* Liquid fire burst in her mouth and sent rivulets of flame first into her stomach, then out through each limb like sap coursing through a tree. Fire and ice met in her gut, and she shivered with a strange alloy of pain and delight.

Alasdair sat down and gazed expressionlessly out over the field. Jean gazed at him. What a shame he was wearing his police uniform of suit and tie — the latter knotted against his throat, even at the end of day — when so many of the other men were wearing kilts.

But wee dram or no wee dram, joke or no joke, tonight he was On Business, his shoulders taut if not exactly tense, his face still if not exactly stern. "What are you after telling me, then?"

"I talked to Kirsty, and to everybody else at the B&B, more or less. And I saw Roger at Pitclachie and later with Tracy. . . You can tell I'm an academic, can't you? I start out by giving you the abstract. Whether it all adds up to an actual paper or is just random noise is the question."

She expected him to respond, "That's for me to decide, isn't it?" But he merely tilted his head toward her, the better to hear.

No need to get out her notebook, it was all fresh in her mind. Jean summed up her conversation with Kirsty — Iris and Roger and the tower, Ambrose's corkscrew, books, Gordon Fraser, Jonathan, Brendan. Even the bad feel in the summerhouse and the knitting.

Alasdair listened, his eyebrows making sine waves of comprehension and intelligence. Then they furrowed. "Knitting?"

"Well, the knitting itself isn't important. It just gave me a chance to read Kirsty's body language. Obviously she's upset about Jonathan and about Iris being taken away for questioning. But it was when I told her that Iris had confessed to the letters that she really cringed. And . . ."

"You told her that?"

"Did you want to keep that quiet?"

"No, no. Kirsty didn't already know about the confession?"

"Why should she? All she knew was that Iris had gone off to Inverness."

The crease between his brows deepened. "Iris and Kirsty are both playing silly beggars with us, like as not. Have you gone and asked yourself why Iris confessed?"

"I can make a guess . . ." A spark in his eye tipped her off — she was just about to take a big bite out of her deerstalker. "Okay, Alasdair. What do you know that I don't know?"

"We've checked the backgrounds of everyone at all associated with the Water Horse Expedition, as per routine. Only one is known to the police. Kirsty Wotherspoon."

Jean felt her jaw drop. Retrieving it, she said, "Really?"

"Oh aye. Two years since, she was one of several students harassing a teacher by making it appear the school had a poltergeist."

"You mean they threw things around when the teacher's back was turned and then claimed it was a poltergeist?"

"Oh aye. Most poltergeist cases involve adolescents. It's hard to say how many are genuine. Like ghosts," he added in a soft growl.

Jean wondered whether Alasdair had been able to sense the paranormal all his life, as she had been all of hers, and whether his friends and relations had given him as much grief about it in his youth. Before he, like her, had learned to keep his uncanny light — his will o' the wisp of perception — under a bushel. Traditionally, the Highlanders were more open to the paranormal, but then, Kirsty's family hadn't been, unless that was a result of Ambrose's aversion therapy. "If Kirsty has a sixth sense, perhaps acting out as a poltergeist wasn't that far-fetched for her."

"That's as may be, but the affair in Glasgow was admitted to be a hoax and sorted by the juvenile authorities. What's interesting is that the scheme fell apart when Kirsty wrote a poison-pen letter to the teacher, gilding the lily, so to speak. Or perhaps deliberately giving the game away. It was then the teacher called in the police."

"Aha! I knew that!" Jean exclaimed.

Alasdair didn't leap out of his chair in surprise, but he did tilt forward in interest.

"Noreen Hall said something about a boyfriend getting Kirsty into trouble over some letters. He must have been one of the other students involved, maybe even the driving force."

"A boyfriend, eh?"

Ah, something he didn't know. "I bet that's why her family sent her here, to get her away from not only the school, but also the exploitive boyfriend. And now Iris thinks Kirsty sent the letters to Roger. She confessed to protect her. And Kirsty cringed the way she did because she knows that's what Iris is doing, and she's blaming herself."

"Great minds think alike, Jean." Alasdair raised his glass in a salute. There was that spark again, and another, not enough to be fireworks and yet not unlike the lit fuses of fireworks.

Focusing on the case, Jean said, "But Kirsty didn't send the letters, did she? It makes even less sense for her to have done it than for Iris. Unless she thought she was helping Iris for some reason. And here I was picturing Kirsty as Ophelia. I guess you don't have many of these contemporary girls doing the Ophelia bit."

"Make up your mind. Earlier you were comparing her to Juliet."

"Yeah, well." Not so long ago, that sort of remark would have yanked her hackles out by the roots. Now Jean sat back and sipped again at her whiskey, barely prickling.

Hugh's voice emanated from the speakers riffing on the more absurd aspects of Scottish history, wry humor being the stick that kept the jaws of tragedy from snapping shut. Overhead the clouds coagulated into a blanket of gray, so that beyond the bright lights of festival and town, Midsummer's day failed of its promise and darkened to a murky twilight.

"What's irritating," Jean said, "is that Iris's confession is obscuring the real issue."

"And just what is the real issue, are you thinking?"

"Roger's expedition, surely."

"Your guess is as good as mine, Jean."

"No, it's not," she told him. "You talked to every single person who visited the boat yesterday, didn't you? That's quite a job."

"I didn't interview them personally, mind. I have my resources."

"Whereas we reporters have to take what scraps we can. Maybe some of my investigative cousins several times removed would have gone ahead and searched the house themselves, but me, I sit here and politely ask you if your team found anything."

"And if I wasn't letting you in on the case, would you be waiting to ask?"

"That sounds like the old saying, keep your friends close and your enemies closer."

"Are we enemies?" he asked, with a sideways glance that also mingled fire and ice, to the same disquieting effect on her stomach. He sure was saying *we* easily these days.

"No, we're not enemies." As for what they were . . . She let the implications blow away in the wind that flapped the edge of the canvas and ran its cold fingers through her hair. "So did you find anything in the main house? How about the Lodge? There's a locked door upstairs that's driving me nuts. Both Kirsty and Iris say it's only a lumber room."

"That's what my team is saying it is, as well. Furniture, boxes, two paintings, a right mixtie-maxtie of bits and pieces. The Mackintosh family collection of mathoms, to use Tolkien's word."

"Rats. No boxes of Ambrose's private papers?"

"Not a one, or so they say."

"How about the room in the tower, then? Iris's lair?"

The corner of Alasdair's mouth quirked. "Nothing helpful in the tower room, either. Bar turning over the place myself — and I'm not discounting that — I've got no new evidence about the letters, let alone the explosion. As you say, rats."

"So what about your interviews? Kirsty's previous track aside, did you find anyone who isn't who they say they are? Brendan? Anyone from the B&B?"

"Not a one. They're a right difficult lot, helpful to a fault. Brendan's saying he and Jonathan hadn't been getting on, no — two young stags trying their antlers, I'm thinking — but he made the remark about Jonathan going into the water by chance."

"No surprise there. If he were planning to eliminate a rival or whatever, he'd hardly signal his intentions that baldly."

"Not with you listening, no," Alasdair said. "Some of the witnesses, now, some are more sensitive than others. I mind you saying you smelled petrol on the boat."

"We'll skip past my sensitivities, thank you. But yeah, that's a good point. Let me guess — Noreen Hall smelled it, too. Martin said last night she had a migraine."

"Oh aye. Mrs. Hall seems a bit nervy, I'm thinking, but . . ."

"Who doesn't?" Jean finished for him. "Did she tell you they were here in April? Martin has a thing for Nessie, too. And I thought I saw him in Tracy's hotel room, although, to be fair, it could have been the guy from Starr, Kettering. Still, Noreen said Martin was talking to Tracy on the boat."

"Ah," said Alasdair with a nod. "That might could be important."

"Or not even accurate."

"Oh aye." Alasdair tilted his glass so that the last drop of whiskey ran down into his mouth, then licked his lips in a gesture that in anyone else would be sensuous.

And why wouldn't it be sensuous in Alasdair? Because in him sensuality was only a brief glimpse, like a distant flicker of lightning? Or because knowing Alasdair harbored any sensuality at all beneath his carapace made her uncomfortable? Jean had wondered what it would be like seeing him again, talking to him again. Now she knew. Being with him wasn't a state, it was a continuum, and multiple answers applied. Sipping her own whiskey — ah, her cheeks were starting to burn, a sure sign of alcohol intake — she looked at the stage.

Hugh wasn't making sensuous music but was leading the crowd in a rousing chorus of "The John Mclean March." He was a breath of fresh air, even if at times it was the sort of fresh air that turned your umbrella inside out.

Tracy Dempsey came shouldering her way through the multitude, dragging Roger along like a mother dragging her child off to the woodshed. Jean leaned over toward Alasdair to point them out just as he leaned over to her, so that they were each encompassed by the other's warm whiskey breaths.

"And is Mrs. Dempsey playing Lady Macbeth?" he murmured.

"If you're asking me if she ordered someone — like Jonathan — killed, I can't imagine anyone doing that. But then, killers are your specialty, not mine."

"You spotted the killer last month."

"I owed you that much."

"Oh aye, that you did." His face turned toward Tracy. Jean followed his gaze.

Roger wrenched his arm away from Tracy's grasp and shouted, "Haven't you done enough already?" His words sliced cleanly into Hugh's brief fiddle solo between verses of the song. Several people faltered in their clapping and looked around.

Tracy rose in her shoes, into Roger's truculent face. Her red lips hissed "investment." Jean could fill in the rest — *in for a penny in for a pound* or some similar sentiment.

Roger's right arm was still extended. His hand clenched, and for a second Jean thought he was going to commit wife abuse right in front of her. Alasdair stiffened, probably wondering if he should intervene. Then the song started up again, Roger dropped his hand to his side, and those people who'd been attracted by his shout turned away — except for the Ducketts, Jean saw, who watched from the rim of the crowd with every appearance of horrified fascination.

Peter Kettering appeared just beyond them, twisted like an Egyptian wall-painting, both standing still and retreating. Tracy spotted him. Shooting a commanding glance at Roger, she marched up to Kettering. Roger's fierce scowl at her back deepened the creases on his face to trenches. With an intake of breath so deep his entire body heaved, he moderated his expression, flexed his hands, and followed.

Kettering smiled politely, even as his gaze darted back and forth, scanning the throng. It lit upon Alasdair and Jean and leaped away again, press plus police equaling doubly negative publicity.

Roger said his piece to Kettering, punctuated with the same digging motions he'd used to Charles Bouchard. Kettering replied, his gestures both soothing and dismissive. Tracy stood with her hands on her hips, shoulders back, looking first at one man, then at the other. Her smile had a feral quality to it, as though she were both the lady and the tiger.

Roger didn't look at her at all. He offered his hand. Kettering took it. They shook, then turned abruptly away from each other. Kettering's cell phone leaped into his hand and he was in full conversation before he had walked two paces. Roger strode purposefully, even grimly, toward the whiskey booth. The Ducketts subtracted themselves from the scene.

Left alone, Tracy sagged, one manicured hand pressed to her face. Then Jean caught the gleam of eyes through Tracy's fingers. If she hadn't noticed the peanut gallery of police and press before, she did now.

She snapped back upright and whipped around too fast for Jean to register her expression — a snarl, a grimace of determination, the bared teeth of a cornered animal? — and walked off after Kettering, moving amazingly fast in her high heels. Then she, too, was gone, like the others no more than a figment of a fever dream.

EIGHTEEN

Jean really was feeling a bit feverish. She could blame that on the whiskey, on the Dempsey drama, on the friction — physical, emotional, and intellectual — between her and Alasdair. She looked at him.

He looked at her, great minds still thinking alike. "They're seeing their funding from Starr run through their fingers, I reckon, though I doubt there's more to it than that."

"Roger looks more decisive than he did at the hotel. Then he was punch-drunk. I would have said it was impossible to faze him, but having someone killed on his watch would do it."

"You saw them just after we told them we turned up Paisley's body, then."

"How'd they react to the news?"

"As you'd expect."

"So in the restaurant she was telling him they had to pull their socks up and get on with it. 'Onward, onward, half a league onward . . .'"

"'. . . into the valley of death,'" Alasdair concluded dourly.

Thanks. "If Roger's expedition is the issue — and he was getting on with it just fine earlier today, Tracy or no Tracy — then Roger himself is the epicenter. I'd like to know why Iris gave him permission to search Pitclachie. Why they put together a truce of some sort."

"Because of a common enemy?"

"Spoken like a policeman. How about a common interest? You know, capitalism at work. United in greed we stand."

Alasdair's right eyebrow arched upward, Spock-like. "We've not counted out an insurance scam, if that's what you're thinking. I'm not seeing how that would involve Iris, though."

"No, that's not what I'm thinking. I was looking at the display case of Ambrose's artifacts at Pitclachie, and at Roger and Brendan doing some sort of survey of the hillside, and it hit me — what if the Nessie search is only part of the story? Maybe even a full-fledged diversion? What if Roger is really after more valuable artifacts? There's an almost undisturbed Pictish cemetery uphill from the Stone. The Picts aren't known for their grave goods, but still, most of Ambrose's collection was found in one hoard somewhere around here." She waved her hand toward the hillside, although she could just as well have waved it toward the loch.

"Or so he said." Alasdair's eyebrow drifted back down and assumed a contemplative curl.

"The Bouchards have a shop in Paris, maybe they're working with Roger. Or with Iris. Maybe all the hissing and spitting between Iris and Roger is just for show. Maybe it's a vast conspiracy."

His eyebrows tightened. He wasn't buying it, and now that she'd articulated it, she wasn't either. She started again. "The bottom line is, why, out of all the ancient sites in Scotland, did Roger come to Pitclachie? Yeah, supposedly Nessie's been spotted crossing the road — to get to the other side, I know, I know — but she's an aquatic beast, already. Unless you elaborate some Pictish Nessie-cult from the pictographs on the Pitclachie Stone, and then factor in Ambrose's treasure, there's no reason for even a nut like Roger to be looking for her on land."

Jean knew that Alasdair knew how she could extrapolate from zero to sixty in five seconds. When she finally stopped for breath, she could hear the gears grinding in his brain. Catching up with her, he said, "More than a little depends on whether Roger or any other folk believe Nessie exists."

"Do you believe she exists?"

"Do you?"

"If seeing is believing, then believing is seeing," she replied. "'A triumph of hope over experience,' as Samuel Johnson said."

"That's his definition of a second marriage," said Alasdair, so dry dust eddied around him. "As for Nessie, I'm after keeping my fantasy compartmented."

And his memories, too. Jean leaned back, if not deflated at least down some pressure. They'd had similar discussions before, conducted with less cordiality but also with fewer undercurrents. Feel as she might about Brad, the one time Alasdair had spoken of his marriage his bitterness had been sharp enough to acid-etch the subject of relationships with *No Trespassing*.

Damn it, she was parsing his every word. "It's all your fault. You're making me look for double and triple meanings in everything. Pretty soon I'll start analyzing a baked potato for means and motives."

"Right," he said, with a ghost of smile that perhaps acknowledged those undercurrents, that perhaps didn't. "If Roger's motive is to find something on land, he's gone a bit overboard — no pun intended there, either — stocking the boat with equipment."

"True. I'm not saying that's the entire picture. Or any of it, for that matter."

"You were saying Kirsty thinks Jonathan was a reporter. Or a spy of some sort." Alasdair didn't add, *but that's redundant.* "There is one thing. Everyone's background has checked out, aye, but Jonathan told his mum he was working for someone else as well as for

Roger. Someone here, at Loch Ness. Not surprising, he was a bit of a hired gun, electronically-speaking — though I'm never speaking electronics — but there was something a bit hush-hush about this job. We've not yet found a soul who's owned up to hiring him, let alone what he was doing. Our opposite numbers in England are speaking with his bank manager."

"Tracking down any paychecks not from Omnium." Jean nodded approval, not that Alasdair needed her approval — it kept her from thinking about Jonathan's mother. "If he was into, say, industrial espionage, that might explain his nervousness. So would his being on to something Roger wanted kept quiet, a treasure hunt or anything else."

"Either might could be a motive for murder."

"Yeah, but it would have to be a heck of an either, to drive you to murder."

"To drive *you* to murder, aye."

She shrugged understanding. "If Roger wanted to kill Jonathan, it would have been easier to just bash him over the head or poison his tea or something, not rig up an elaborate plot with anonymous letters and a bomb that would blow up his boat and all his equipment. At a time Jonathan wasn't even supposed to be there."

"I see we'll be having another go at Roger," said Alasdair, with a set to his mouth that made Jean glad she wouldn't be the one he would be going at. "Brendan, now, he's not changed his story, told us everything he told Kirsty and is dead certain there was a submersible on board. He's had experience of marine biology, mind, he knows the difference. Roger keeps going on about his ROVs, but judging by the bits we've been bringing up from the loch, a small sub went up and then down with the boat."

"And you knew all this before I lectured you on submersibles and ROVs at the police station this afternoon, right?"

"Right."

"Alasdair," Jean said, "you'd make a great poker player."

"Well now, there's a valuable skill for a detective." He almost managed a poker face at that, but a crinkle at the corners of mouth and eyes gave him away.

Either he was giving a lot away this evening, or she had learned to read him too damned well. But then, she was someone he could trust, wasn't he? Maybe he was running, too.

Jean skipped around that thought. "Roger told me submersibles were old-hat. If Jonathan was a spy, wouldn't he be after the newest technology? Maybe some hush-hush project of Roger's that just resembles a submersible?"

"We're looking out an expert, but being Saturday and all, we've not found one yet."

"Oh." Jean's glow, strained to its utmost, burst. The damp chill of the evening closed in around her. The lights were ringed with haloes, mist choking the air the way unshed tears choked the throat. But she couldn't back off from her inspiration, not when circumstances transcended her own sensitivities. "I know a mechanical engineer you could probably get hold of right away. My ex-husband, Brad Inglis."

Alasdair didn't move a muscle, but still Jean could sense him withdrawing, mind and body, from the demilitarized zone where they'd been parlaying. She hadn't realized how warm his voice had become until it chilled back into cool, correct formality. "He's back in the States, is he?"

"He should be, not that I keep track of his movements. It's afternoon there. I'll give him a call. I mean, no time like the present. If nothing else maybe you could e-mail him some photos of the debris or something . . ." Clamping her teeth on her babbling, she reached for her bag and pulled her cell phone from its pocket.

Damn it, she was trying so hard to satisfy both her curiosity and Alasdair's directive she'd just hoisted herself with her own petard. She hadn't really wanted to know that she felt uncomfortable talking to Alasdair about Brad.

"I'll just have a word with the constable on duty, shall I?" Alasdair picked up her empty glass and his and walked determinedly toward the police van, leaving Jean in her own little island of solitude. Not that any woman was an island.

With similar determination, she scrolled down her phone's menu. She and Brad had had to touch bases a time or two about the sale of the house. Investing in a cell phone that worked world-wide meant she could get those calls over with as fast as possible . . . There. She punched *Talk* and put the phone to her ear. A good thing Hugh was spinning another tale, not playing. She had an even chance of being able to hear.

Static. A phone on the other side of the world rang. An answering machine picked up. She heard Brad's voice, the bland accent, tones that were calm and correct without at all resembling Alasdair's, whose calmness and correctness concealed nuclear fires, magma pools, lightning bolts.

"Hi," she said at the beep. "It's me, Jean. I'm at Loch Ness. Roger Dempsey's here searching for the monster, but someone blew up his boat last night, and, um, the police are asking questions about submersibles and ROVs. I figured you could help. It's, um, a matter of telling the difference between the two by looking at some wreckage. Sort of. Anyway, call me back when you get the chance. Oh, and it's six hours later here. Thanks."

She punched *End*, hoping she'd given him enough information that he'd have his act together when he did call back, so that she wouldn't have to listen to the slow unspooling of his thought . . . Heck, she could have given Alasdair's number to Brad and she wouldn't have had to talk to him at all. Although she wasn't sure whether putting the two men into direct contact would be a good thing. There might be a matter and anti-matter effect.

Jamming the phone back into her bag, she stood up. Here came D.C. Gunn, reporting in from the burdensome duty of walking around the Festival. "Good evening, Miss Fairbairn."

"Good evening," she returned.

He stepped up to the door of the van just as Alasdair opened it. Gunn retreated. "Sorry, Neville," Alasdair said, and held the door for him.

So his first name was Neville, just the sort of moniker a thug like Sawyer would find diverting, although Jean supposed it was less rarefied here in the UK.

Alasdair ducked back under the canopy, the lights glinting off the water droplets collected on his hair and shoulders. Before he could speak she said, "Brad wasn't there. I left a message. I'll let you know what he says."

"Right. Thank you." Alasdair offered her a thick brown envelope. "Here you are."

"Say what?" She took the package and turned it over in her hands, but saw no distinguishing marks.

"The transcripts of Ambrose's trial for murder. I promised them to you in return for your working for me."

There was that glint in his eye, peeking out like a star from behind a cloud. No, not a star, which was an indifferent natural force. Alasdair was pretending nothing embarrassing had happened. Jean inhaled the elusive tang of whiskey once more, trying to rekindle that warm glow. "I thought we were working together."

"We are. I'm expecting you to read through this lot and tell me what's there."

"You could have had someone at your office do that."

"Wasting police time on a case from nineteen-thirty-three? This is a curiosity, is all. Although if you do go finding some relation to the day's issues, you'll be letting me know."

She managed an off-kilter grin. "Aye, aye, captain. You want me to write up an abstract for you, or will an oral report be all right?"

"That would be quite sufficient." Alasdair redirected his own awkward grin to the stage.

Jean followed his lead. Ah, Hugh was beginning his final number, the ballad "Flower of Scotland." The music tickled her vocal chords and plucked each of her muscle fibers into rhythmic contractions. This melody had the rhythm of a waltz, you could slow-dance to it — she remembered the piece Hugh had played earlier, when she thought he was making love to his violin . . . To her relief, the song ended before her glow not only re-kindled, but went nova.

"The tune's not bad," said Alasdair quietly, "but the words, now. The battle of Bannockburn was seven hundred years since. It's time to move on."

"Moving on can be like crawling out of quicksand," she replied, and, to mitigate stating the obvious, "'Flower of Scotland' is a crowd-pleaser."

"Oh aye, it is that."

Pleased, the crowd applauded vigorously. Hugh and his band bowed their way off the stage, to be replaced by two young pipers and a drummer dressed in kilts, T-shirts, and combat boots. They launched into the derisive and inspirational "Johnnie Cope." Jean tried lobbing a joke in Alasdair's direction. "Why do pipers march when they play?"

"It's harder to hit a moving target," he returned obligingly.

"I was going to say to get away from the noise. But it's not noise."

"No, it's not. Not at all."

This is the music that stirs the blood was almost the last thing he'd said to her before they parted last month. And now her blood was pounding like a snare drum. The rich scent of peat smoke hung on the air, a hint of creosote and a whiff of chocolate blended into its own unique flavor. The scent complemented the tang of the whiskey in Jean's nose and mouth, suggesting warm rooms and flickering flames. Maybe she should get it over with and . . .

And what? She didn't know what the hell she should do. It wasn't that she felt like a teenager pulling the petals off a daisy and chanting *he likes me, he likes me not.* She had pretty much conceded the answer to that. It was that she was mature enough to know the hazards of displaying her emotions for someone else to pick over and accept or reject as he wished. *He'll hurt me, he'll hurt me not. I'll hurt him.*

Hugh walked by waving his violin. "We're having a ceilidh in the hotel dining room," he announced. "Come one, come all! Music and dancing and the best of the barley!"

"Does he ever stop playing?" asked Alasdair.

"No," Jean replied. "I'm a bit envious of a job that's both work and play."

"You're not saying that about your own?"

"Not just now, no. Ask me again after a good night's sleep.

What about your job?"

He didn't answer. She looked around to see his profile against the misty lights, still and stern. Bleak, like a rocky valley scraped clean and dry by a glacier.

Last month she had wondered if he was on the verge of burning out. But he wasn't just going through the motions, not like some people did when they grew disenchanted with their jobs. No, not Alasdair. He would never just go through the motions, professionally or personally . . .

She'd done it again. Puncturing the mood the first time had been justified by circumstances. But this time she'd defaulted to her usual clumsy mix of self-defeating, self-preserving, behavior. This time there was no rekindling the glow. "I think I'll turn in."

"Good idea," he replied politely.

"Thank you for the whiskey. I should have some sort of report on the trial transcripts for you tomorrow." Jean unzipped her bag, pulled out her folding umbrella, and stuffed the envelope with the transcripts inside, next to — nothing. Her notebook was gone.

No. Oh no. Turning toward the light, Jean rooted around in the bag as though the notebook was somehow small to enough to have slipped to the bottom with her keys. It wasn't there. "Hell and damnation! My notebook's gone! It had all my notes from my interviews and what I'd been thinking about the case, everything."

In an instant Alasdair went to full alert. "When did you last see it?"

"At the hotel. I was writing in it while I had my tea. I realized earlier I left my bag open when I paid my bill. All the time I was walking around here it was hanging open. Anyone could have taken that notebook." She yanked the zipper shut, closing the barn door long after the horses had galloped down to the loch and plunged in.

"The notebook, but not your wallet?"

"A pickpocket would want the wallet, yes, but maybe he — she — just grabbed what they could get. In that case the notebook's probably lying around here somewhere, trampled underfoot." Jean peered around suspiciously, at the faces bleached out by the lights, at flags and tartans suddenly too bright, brash instead of brave.

"I'll have the lads look out for it. It's just a student copybook, is it? Spiral-bound?"

"Yes, that's it. Like the one I had last month."

"I'll walk you to the B&B," Alasdair said.

Not now, she told herself. Not like this. Not under duress. "No, thank you. Please let me go on believing that there's nothing to this, that it's just happenstance. That the notebook's lying back there in the lobby of the hotel or something."

"Jean . . ." His chin went up, but he knew better than to gainsay her. He took a step backwards. "All right then. Have yourself a good night."

"You too, get some rest." For just a moment she dared to look into his eyes, but they were shielded and told her nothing. She turned, wobbled — funny how she hadn't felt the whiskey in her knees until she stood up — and walked away not really sure just what she'd been looking for. Reassurance? Affection? Yeah, whatever.

Outside the shelter of the canopy the rain was coming down, lightly but steadily. A couple of drops dribbled down Jean's glasses and half a dozen more went down the back of her neck, extinguishing the last furtive embers of her glow. She wrestled her umbrella open and put one foot in front of the other.

Behind the clouds the sun flirted with the western horizon, but here on terra firma Scotia, mist pressed in around the lights of the Festival. Past the illuminated area the evening was so thick that the town seemed no more than a series of box-shapes spattered with the pale splotches of lights. The mountains had vanished, as though rubbed out by a giant dirty eraser.

A footprint-shaped puddle gleamed faintly before her, then another, and another, until in front of the gate the ground was a churned mess of mud and grass, like a relief map of Scotland complete with trickling streams. Jean paused, looking for a path through the mess.

The thud of steps came from behind her and she glanced back. *Alasdair?* No, yes, no . . .

It was Roger's pale face turned toward her, beard bristling like steel wool, hair matted onto his forehead. His voice was less flat than prostrate. "Oh. Jean. Hi. Going back to Pitclachie?"

"Yes." She caught a whiff of whiskey, not a warm fragrance like Alasdair's breath but something sour, evoking spoiled dreams and harsh realities.

"Allow me." He offered her his arm.

If he was stumbling drunk . . . But no, he was walking as steadily as she was. That was a mark of the alcoholic, wasn't it, to drink and drink and still appear sober? She rested her hand on his forearm — it felt brittle — and like tightrope walkers, umbrella and all, they balanced on tufts of sodden grass through the muddy area.

"Thanks," Jean said, releasing him the moment they'd achieved the sidewalk.

"No problem." Without the least attempt to share her umbrella, Roger walked on ahead, hands in his pockets, chin sunk on his chest, either lost in his own thoughts or freed from them by therapeutic booze.

The castle in the air he'd described to her yesterday had collapsed into a pile of rubble. It was possible that he himself had sapped its foundations, but if so, wouldn't he be bending her ear at this very moment with plans for new construction? Here was her chance to ask him what his plans were . . . No. No matter what evidence turned up tomorrow, either for or against him, tonight she'd take pity on him and leave him alone.

Jean glanced back at the Festival. Beneath the large tent the mass of people blended into one organic mass of movement and color, like a psychedelic amoeba. The rhythm of their clapping was lost in the patter of rain on the road and its rustle in the tall stalks of the nettles, but the skirl of the pipes came through loud and clear.

A man-shape was taking long strides across the field toward the gate. Again Jean's mind, unbidden, repeated the mantra, *Alasdair?* Then she saw the glint of metal on his shoulders and the shape of his cap. A constable, no doubt dispatched by his chief inspector to make sure a certain journalist went to ground safely.

Suddenly bright lights leaped out of the mist, making her and Roger's shadows twirl wraith-like across the asphalt. They jumped, startled. A spray of water and air wet Jean's legs and fluttered her skirt. Then the car was receding up the road to the north, its taillights swallowed by the damp and murk.

The pipe music had concealed the sound of the approaching car. Roger glanced around sharply, resentfully, then trudged on. Jean grimaced. Technically, the man — make that the gentleman — should be walking on the outside, but there was one of those old customs that had gone by the wayside ages ago. No problem. She was as much drip-dry as Roger was.

And, technically, they should be walking on the right-hand side of the road, facing the traffic, in mirror-image to the routine back home. But to do that they'd have to cross to the other side and then cross back again. Instead, Jean walked as far away from the road as she could get without brushing against the nettles. There went another car, a flash of light and a cold, damp whoosh.

The hotel's white-painted sides were illuminated by floodlights, and smears of rosy light leaked from its front door and windows. Hugh's ceilidh would be highly entertaining, but no, she was wet and cold and tired. She wanted a hot shower, a mug of chocolate, her flannel nightgown. Solitude. Safety.

She heard the crescendo of the pipes, and Miranda's voice saying, *You came here because you were tired of playing it safe* . . . A sudden roar detonated in her head. A hard rush of air spun her against Roger just as a black behemoth struck him a glancing blow.

Jean saw his face, eyes wide, mouth agape, hands flung outwards.

She heard her own voice cry out, the sound thin and weak. The umbrella launched itself from her hand and she fell, limbs flailing, fabric billowing. She landed on Roger's wiry, knobby body — arms, elbows, ribs, a surprisingly soft paunch. One of her hands was burning.

With the squeal of skidding rubber, the behemoth jounced over the curb and back into the road. Twin red eyes blinked open and vanished into the mist. Tail lights. A car. No particular shape, no particular color, seemingly as uninhabited behind the streaming windows as the ghost coach of nightmare.

Jean lay sprawled on the sidewalk, one thought looping repeatedly through her mind: *Alasdair was right. I do need to be protected.*

Nineteen

The sound of the pipes was an attenuated hum, less loud than Jean's own heartbeat leaping in a syncopated rhythm as much in her throat as her chest. Her breath was rasping. No, that was Roger's rancid breath, wheezing, cursing. Voices shouted and footsteps pounded, each one resounding in the cold, rough asphalt grating her knee.

Dazed, bewildered, suspended in that moment when something's going to hurt but it isn't hurting yet, Jean tried to struggle to her feet without adding insult to Roger's injuries. He was heaving at her, oblivious to which of her body parts his hands and knees made contact with.

She was on all fours, feeling as though she were playing a particularly gawky game of Twister, when hands plucked her upwards. Oh, the constable. And behind him came a thundering wave of humanity. Alasdair's face emerged from the murk and wet, into the light cast by the hotel floodlights, not at all rosy but ashen. One quick, raw, look passed from his eyes to hers and back — terror chased by relief, chased by the realization that all the might-have-beens had almost come home to roost. Then his face went blank and he got down to business.

Voices shouted. Bodies bustled. Jean stood swaying, tremors running along her limbs, the rain plastering her hair to her head and smearing her glasses so that the scene became increasingly impressionistic. The bright blue lights of first police cars, and then an ambulance, strobed. Jean felt as though she and Roger were surrounded by paparazzi. But then, someone probably *was* taking photos.

Roger had borne the brunt of the fall and the nettles, but was still healthy enough to stand unsupported and bellow profanities at all and sundry. Including Tracy, when she finally appeared. She stammered that she'd been having a drink with Kettering in the bar of the Drumnadrochit Hotel, she hadn't noticed anything until she'd heard the ambulance siren, what happened, someone was out to get them, she'd said so, hadn't she? And the police hadn't listened.

Kettering was close behind her, elbowing through the official cordon into the frenetic lights, his face stamped with an expression that said so clearly *Now what?* it might just as well have been tattooed on his sallow cheeks.

Then Jean found herself handed into the back of the ambulance, where she was probed and tested like a product under development. Her hand burned where it had gone into the nettles. The paramedic spread salve on it. Her knee oozed blood and mud through ripped nylon. The paramedic cut away the leg of her panty-hose, cleaned off her knee, and wrapped it in a bandage. She could have done all that herself. What she needed was a warm bath and clean clothes and a snort of sedative from one of the little phials sparkling seductively on a nearby rack.

Roger, his store of invective emptied at last, lay silently on the stretcher across from her as a second paramedic tended to various abraded, bruised, and stung body parts. Poor Roger, Jean thought. He would probably have looked just as bleary if her glasses had been clean.

The blurred ovals of faces floated disembodied in the door-way — Tracy's red lips turned down in a scowl, Kettering gabbling, Sawyer stony rather than truculent. Then the paramedics were easing her back out into the darkness. Oh, there was Alasdair again, his firm grasp on her upper arm steering her across the sidewalk and into the back of a police car. Maybe it was the same one she'd ridden in earlier that day. Last week. Whenever.

Alasdair was sitting beside her, his keen, cold face winking in and out of shadow as the car jolted past the brightly-lit island of the hotel and into the driveway leading up the hill to Pitclachie House. More lights flashed as another car, coming from the opposite direction, turned in just behind them. Lights glowed among the trees and solidified into arched windows.

The car door opened. Kirsty took one arm and Brendan the other, helping Jean onto her feet as though she were a centenarian. In the distance a couple of vaguely familiar voices, male and female, asked questions in halting French-accented English. All the dialects blended into a Tower of Babel moment — Jean didn't understand a word.

Kirsty opened the door of the Lodge. Alasdair cut Jean from the herd and ushered her through the door. Lodge, she thought. Home away from home. She took a breath so deep it made her ribs hurt and groped for the light switch. The room leaped into color and definition. Her voice was scraped a bit thin, but it worked. "I'm fine. More scared and shocked and angry and all that, you know, than hurt."

Whether or not she'd intended to dissuade him from coming inside made no difference. Grimly, Alasdair shut the door, brushed past her, and set her bag on the table. How long had he been carrying that?

Over the arm of the chair next to the fireplace appeared a small bewhiskered face and two bat-like ears. The calico cat, Mandrake, looked with a proprietary air toward the door, decided to permit the interlopers entrance, and settled back down again. He must have sneaked in when the police did their search.

With a narrow glance at the cat, Alasdair proceeded to open doors, try windows, and close curtains downstairs and up. He might be back in full inscrutable mode, but his practiced expressionlessness didn't fool Jean one bit. That quick look at the brim of disaster had shattered any remaining rationalizations about his feelings for her, or hers for him. *Oh God.*

Her knees buckled and deposited her onto the couch, wet clothes and all. She took off her glasses, vaguely surprised they were still on her face, and mopped at them with a tissue. When she put them back on she saw that the books were still in order and the dishes still gleamed in the drainer. Except for admitting the cat, the police team had come and gone invisibly. So far, only the mysterious nocturnal visitor and the ghosts had left any hints of their presence. Perhaps last night's visitor was one of the ghosts. Or perhaps he or she was only too corporeal, and had tonight been behind the wheel of a car. *Oh God, oh God.*

Alasdair descended the staircase, walked straight to the kitchen, and ran water into the tea kettle. They might be alone at last, but what he'd ask next would not be personal but professional. Had she seen anything? She collected the bits and pieces of imagery clinging like lint to her memory. No, she'd seen only the thick gray air and the tail lights of the car winking as it disappeared into the distance. Which, considering the range of visibility, wasn't all that distant.

Aha. "The lights. The car that almost hit us didn't have its headlights on. I saw the tail lights come on right after it passed."

"I'm thinking it did hit you." Alasdair spooned tea into the pot. "Driving without lights, were they? They were after hitting you, then."

"Well, no — they could have left the lighted parking lot and not realized their lights weren't on. They could have had too much to drink. In fact, that's probably the explanation, right there. It was an accident."

"Then they'd have been better off stopping and rendering aid."

"Maybe they didn't realize they, um, hit us. Maybe they did, and were scared, and weren't thinking straight. It was an accident, wasn't it?"

Alasdair committed himself to nothing more than pouring boiling water into the pot.

Jean pulled her jacket more tightly across her chest. The room was cold. She was cold, damp, chilled through and through. And not only physically. She could feel her psyche contracting into a ball, like an armadillo showing only its scales. Not that she'd seen many live armadillos, just armadillo bodies lying alongside a road, creased with tire tracks . . . It was an accident.

Alasdair's strong hands were extending a mug of tea toward her.

She took it, carefully, so it wouldn't slop into her lap. Its warmth was almost painful against her chilled fingers, but the fragrant steam wafting upward, caressing her face, and her grimace loosened.

Alasdair switched on the anachronistic but welcome electric fire. He paused by the chair to offer Mandrake a quick ear-scratch. The cat tilted his head into Alasdair's hand, smirking, then blinked in disdain when Alasdair broke off the contact and walked back to the couch and Jean.

Given a less fraught occasion, Jean would have smiled — Alasdair probably knew the secret cat passwords, he was so feline in mood and movement himself. But now, now she didn't.

He stood next to the couch, arms crossed, looming protectively. "Drink your tea."

She almost returned, *You can stop fussing over me now*, but he didn't deserve that. Obediently, she forced the cup between her teeth and drank. The hot liquid oozed downward into the fist of her stomach. Not that she was going to rekindle any glow. Third time was not the charm.

"I shouldn't have sat you down outside the police van," Alasdair said. "I shouldn't have let Uncle Tom Cobleigh and all see you talking with me."

"Why not talk to me in front of everyone? There's always been an unholy alliance of reporters and police. And our association last month is a matter of public record. Heck, I told Kirsty I was working with you, just to salve my conscience. This isn't your fault."

His face was still carefully blank. "Last time I let you work with me and you found yourself in danger."

"Last time I volunteered to work with you."

"Who came to whom doesn't matter."

Yes it does, Jean thought. The day with its exposures and denials had been long and embarrassing enough without him becoming paternalistic.

"This time," he said, "you're away to Edinburgh the morn. Away from this."

"No way."

"Jean . . ."

"I mean, yeah, I know, it wouldn't look good on your record having a colleague . . ." She bit her tongue before it said the word *die*. That came too close to the territory occupied by Sawyer's insult at the police station, reminding Alasdair of the tragic situation with his former partner. Which had earned him a promotion into this solitary responsibility, where passersby were less likely to smell the rotting albatross hanging around his neck.

He didn't reply, but snowflakes began to settle on his expression.

It wasn't all about him, the reasonable part of her mind told her. He was worried for her because he cared for her. She probably was in danger. The irrational part of her mind, the part that was still palpitating, shoved the reasonable part aside. "If someone is trying to get me because I'm helping you out, that implies I know something that could be dangerous to that someone. And I don't."

"You might not know what you're knowing, Jean. Someone nicked your notebook and an hour later you're hit by a car. You might could have been killed."

"Maybe I only misplaced the book. Maybe it was taken by a casual pickpocket." She'd tried those rationales already. They were even less likely to work now. He was right, and that just made her more stubborn. "Maybe the crazy driver was trying to get Roger, trying again to stop the expedition. I just happened to be there. What if he thought Roger was walking with Tracy? She and I are about the same size, well, without her shoes. But whoever it was couldn't have seen her shoes anyway."

"If someone was having a go at Roger, then it was no accident, was it?" Alasdair's frosty expression was taking on a crust, the crisp layer of ice atop a drift of snow.

Jean knew that at any moment she'd break through and be in it up to her neck. But she heard her voice keep on talking. "This is exactly what I was afraid would happen. What if I put myself in danger, what if I put someone else in danger, what if I . . ." She left the *met you again* twisting gently in the chill air. "Don't waste your time giving me an engraved invitation to bug out. It's too late for that. I'm here. I'm part of the case. I have to find out what the hell is going on. I'm not going to run away. I'm not . . ."

Alasdair finished her sentence for her. "Doing what I'm telling you to do. I'm that great a threat to you, am I?"

And she couldn't fool him. He graciously granted her permission to follow his orders and then admitted he knew exactly how she'd react to such noblesse oblige. Maybe that shared look hadn't meant much after all.

"I'll have a constable outside for the night, so you can have some sleep," Alasdair said, retreating toward the vestibule. At the velvet curtain he paused to send her a formal, almost stern, backwards glance. Then he was gone, the door shut so silently behind him the sleeping cat didn't twitch a whisker.

She wished he'd just gone ahead and slammed it so hard pictures fell off the walls and a rudely-awakened Mandrake shuffled off one of his lives. Gulping down the rest of her tea — it had cooled just enough in Alasdair's blizzard blast that she didn't burn her mouth — Jean stamped halfway up the stairs. At that point a vicious twinge in her knee brought her to a dead stop.

Gasping, she hung onto the banister and wondered if the pain was in her knee so much as in the foot she'd just shot. Damn Alasdair! Why hadn't he sat down on the couch beside her instead of looming? Yes, he'd intended to convey professional protectiveness. No, he hadn't intended to patronize her. Yes, he'd realized too late how she was reading his concern. No, he hadn't deserved what she'd said.

She remembered Roger and Tracy glowering at each other over their tea. A crisis was just as likely to separate a couple as bring them together. At least Roger and Tracy were a couple. She and Alasdair were simply a mutual threat, it seemed. They could so easily have taken the accident or attempt on her life or whatever the hell it was as an excuse to further their detente. But no.

Now he'd hunker down in his emotional keep and pull up his drawbridge. The next time she approached with a flag of truce, he'd pour not boiling oil but ice water through the murder holes. Damn it all anyway.

Favoring her knee, swearing less at it than at herself and Alasdair combined, Jean hobbled into the upper hall. Where the erstwhile locked door stood wide open. Odd, how the police team had left the door open when they'd been so careful to leave everything else undisturbed. Still, here was her chance.

Reaching into the shadowed room, she fumbled for, found, and flicked on the light switch, and only then realized what she'd done. If savaging Alasdair meant she would be freed from her fear of the dark, she'd just go on and be afraid of the dark, thanks anyway.

From the shadows leaped the shapes of three dilapidated cardboard boxes, a couple of framed paintings, a little table with one broken leg, and a set of dining chairs with beautifully carved backs but seat cushions in tatters. Jean was looking at exactly what Iris and then Kirsty had said was in the room, old family stuff.

The room was, however, large enough for a single bedroom. Maybe Iris was aware of the ghost and didn't want to stampede any guests. Maybe she simply needed the storage space. The room had never been renovated. Large areas of the floorboards were free of varnish and deeply scratched. The swirls of the plaster ceiling were stained as though by candle soot. The sprigged wallpaper was faded and tattered. Like the velvet in the glass case in the library revealing the shapes of vanished antiquities, slightly darker rectangles showed where pictures had once hung — the framed Nessie photos that were now downstairs, perhaps?

Jean stepped further into the room. The air was still and cold and smelled of wet dog combined with something sweet. Wrinkling her nose, she tilted the two paintings toward the light. Neither was an original Van Gogh or a stolen Rembrandt, more's the pity.

One was a portrait of a young woman. Jean recognized Eileen, although this painting was earlier than the photo in the library, before circumstances had whetted her features. Her pose was a graceful curve from her bowed head with its stylish bobbed hair to her dropped shoulder to the rosebud dangling from her listless hand. Her Art Deco earrings were interlaced silver-nubbled ribbons studded with either gems or glass. The dreamy smile on her averted face suggested she was considering some secret fancy beyond the frame of the picture.

Was that what Ambrose had seen in her, a Mona Lisa to his Leonardo, the embodiment of his romantic fantasies — over and beyond her financial expectations, that is?

The other painting was a copy of one of those turgid Victorian domestic scenes that had hit the bottom of contemporary taste so hard they were probably about to bounce back into popularity. Jean let the paintings and their dingy frames fall back into place and opened one of the cardboard boxes to reveal an ancient set of encyclopedias. Aha, here was the source of the musty smell. Gagging, she folded the top of the box back down and opened the other boxes.

One held what looked like dusty old needlework curtains or bed hangings, half eaten-away by time and mice, exuding an odor that reminded Jean of over-ripe roses . . . She sneezed. Quickly she glanced into the third box to find tissue-wrapped dishes. Not fine Chinese porcelain, just ordinary earthenware. Perhaps these were the dishes from which Ambrose and Eileen had taken their tea in the summerhouse.

Whatever, there was nothing in the room that rose to the level of personal papers. She hoped the police crew had unpacked the boxes, because the only way she was going to do it was if the Holy Grail was hidden beneath those curtains, and her particular brand of ESP didn't run to homing in on sacred relics.

Just as Jean turned toward the door, she noticed a yellowed square of cardboard lying beneath one of the chairs. She picked it up. Ah, here was another trace of the police search — the dust was just as thick beneath it as anywhere else on the floor.

She turned the cardboard over to see a faded photo of Ambrose and Eileen dressed in wedding garments, posing in front of a man wearing clerical garb. Each tea-colored photo-face was very stiff and correct, as though trying out for a dictionary illustration of the word "propriety."

Jean's first thought was to wonder what the minister had thought of Ambrose's arcane tendencies. Her second was to note that while

Ambrose and the minister were the same height, Eileen's white-veiled head didn't even reach her groom's shoulder. She must have been tiny, shorter than Jean herself, perhaps only five feet tall. Her face was so smooth and unlined, lacking the topography that years would carve, that in the glare of the photographer's lights it faded almost to invisibility. Ambrose's horse-length face, however, was so craggy that the shadows painted it starkly, making him look older than he had been — about thirty-five, if Jean remembered correctly. Eileen had not survived to be thirty-five.

Jean set the photo down on the chair, wondering why it wasn't in the house. Maybe Iris didn't know it was here? But she had to know that her mother's portrait was here.

Shutting the door to the no-longer-mysterious room, Jean grabbed her night clothes and proceeded to the bathroom. She felt bruised all over, but didn't actually find any black and blue patches except for around her knee. Not even on her upper arm, where Alasdair had grasped her like a cat a kitten, gently between bone-crunching jaws. She hated to think what Roger looked like. But envisioning Roger naked, with or without bruises, was not on her list of priorities.

She wondered what Eileen had thought on her wedding night. Although people wouldn't necessarily get naked even for that occasion, not in an era ending even as Ambrose climbed into bed with his young and winsome wife.

Jean stepped into the shower cubicle and turned on the hot water. Oh my, yes — she hadn't realized how cold she was until the hot water sluiced over her shoulders and down her back. You couldn't beat a hot shower or bath for pure sensuality.

Not that her own wedding night had been particularly sensual. She and Brad had been so young, they'd never enlisted in the sexual revolution, and so went into battle with less than basic training, book-learning only. Which was more than an upper-class girl like Eileen probably had. Ambrose, now, he'd been a soldier. And Gordon Fraser had said Ambrose was too much like Crowley when it came to women. Jean couldn't see Ambrose with groupies, but you never knew.

Even she, when she'd been young and a prisoner of her own nervous system, had found Brad's still waters appealing. Comforting, in a way. Safe. Then she'd realized his still waters not only didn't run deep, they didn't run at all. Ghosts? Monsters in the loch? *Yes, dear, if you say so. Pass the salt.*

The years in Brad's damping field had layered her nerves with insulation. During the lawsuit she'd used that insulation for survival, then realized she was looking at no more than surviving for the rest of her life. And now, thanks to fate and Alasdair Cameron, she was pressed up against the window of her own personality, watching trains going round and round, and jack-in-the-boxes leaping upward, and drums drumming and pipers piping and even that partridge sitting in a pear tree pulling its own feathers out. Be careful what you ask for.

She'd asked to find herself. Maybe "herself" included Alasdair, whose waters ran deep and fast indeed beneath his shell. . . . *Don't go there*, she told herself. And she answered, *it's too late for that, too*. She and Alasdair were destined to go there and back again, although what would happen then she couldn't imagine. Or could, rather. That was the problem. The scenario was playing out the way she — the way both of them — had both feared and anticipated.

Jean let the stream of hot water wash away any remaining mud and soothe the bruises and aches. Let it erode the rough corners of her own ego. If it wasn't about Alasdair, it wasn't about her, either. Ridiculous, that she'd find a potential lover more threatening than a letter-sending, boat-exploding, attack-driving criminal.

Suddenly she felt claustrophobic. The cubicle seemed like a coffin. Turning off the water, she stepped out, grabbed a towel, and congratulated herself for taking a shower without imitating any classic Hitchcock scenarios.

Lotion, hair-dryer, flannel nightgown, thick socks, a terry-cloth robe, and she was shocked to see the bedside clock showing ten-thirty p.m. Surely it was three or four a.m. Sunday morning. But no, Saturday went on, and on, and on. Or could have been cut as short as her life, less than two hours ago.

Once again practicing denial, Jean collected her laptop and carry-all, bundled up the duvet from the bed, and headed for the stairs. She more wired than tired. She might as well read the transcripts. That would give her an excuse to call Alasdair tomorrow and eat some crow, feathers and all . . .

She stopped dead in the center of the hall. Hadn't she closed the door to the mystery room? It was standing open, the shapes inside looking like stoop-shouldered gnomes in the darkness. She managed to reach around the armload of duvet without scraping her nettle-stung hand and pull the door shut. The latch clicked into place. Check.

Not one other sound disturbed the chilly stillness of the house. *Okay*, Jean thought, and limped on toward the stairs wondering just how many doors she'd closed recently, and if any of them were likely to open back up.

TWENTY

Between her stiff, sore knee and the duvet, she had to negotiate her way carefully down the steep staircase. Maybe Eileen had met her fate on the stairs, maybe not, but Jean didn't intend to join her in the fourth dimension and ask.

Between the soothing aura of the electric fire and the soothing aura of the sleeping cat, the living room was almost hot. Just as Jean dumped her things on the couch, her twitching ears picked up the sound of voices. She tiptoed to the window and peeked out between the closed drapes. Alasdair's constable was confronting the Ducketts. ". . . just wanted to see if she needs anything," Patti was saying.

"Glad to hear she's all right," added Dave. "Accidents can be fatal, you know."

"She's resting," the constable stated, which was more polite than *No kidding*.

Even though they apparently felt honor-bound to support a compatriot in her hour of need, the couple ceased and desisted. On their way into the house they passed the lanky figure of Martin Hall, identified by the fiery dot of a cigarette at his lips. Above them all, lights gleamed from the top of the tower. Was someone there, or were the lights on an automatic timer?

The constable was wearing a yellow slicker, which shone spectrally in the last cloud-filtered gleam of midsummer, but none of the others were using umbrellas. The rain must have stopped. Jean turned away from the window, wondering if she'd ever see her own umbrella again. It had probably been trampled or run over or both. Well, better it than her.

She poured herself another cup of tea, sponged off her muddy bag, and turned off the electric fire. On the coffee table she arranged all her journalistic implements — her laptop, the photo of the Pitclachie Stone, copies of passages from books and newspapers, Internet print-outs, the books on Nessie and on Crowley, Roger's press release and the Omnium brochures. And, last but not least, the envelope with the transcripts. Most of the notes in her notebook had been saved on her laptop — all she'd lost was another layer of insulation from her nerves. But Alasdair or no Alasdair, she wasn't going to assume the vanishment and the not-an-accident were cause and effect. Not yet, anyway.

Jean settled down on the couch, tucked the duvet snugly around her, and picked up the new addition to her bag of tricks, the old copy of *Loch Ness: the Realm of the Beast*. She fanned the yellow-rimmed pages and her nostrils puckered.

At Fraser's table in the open air, all she'd detected was a whiff of mildew and something sweet. Now, after the book had spent several hours in a plastic shopping bag in her wardrobe, that whiff had intensified to a charnel house stench. The book had been steeped too long in this damp climate, in a storage shed or barn, perhaps. The librarian with the beautiful Thai name would be appalled.

Holding the book gingerly, at arm's length, Jean inspected the flyleaf with its faded autograph: *To my dear E., remembering the good times, Ambrose Mackintosh.* Then she turned to the copyright page. This book hadn't been published by Mandrake, defunct in 1930, but by another obscure if perhaps less controversial press in 1932, the year before Eileen's exit and Nessie's entrance.

Jean leafed through the book carefully enough to ascertain that it was identical to her paperback edition. Then, with an unladylike snort to clear her nasal passages, she set it on the coffee table and fished out her cheat-sheet on Ambrose. Born 1886, the Crowley years and WWI, married 1922. He was a gentleman scientist, an enthusiastic amateur like Schliemann at Troy, except his archaeological work met Indiana Jones' definition of the word — "smash and grab."

Roger, too, had evoked Schliemann, and by inference, Jones. If not as far out on the pseudo-science limb as Ambrose had been, still Roger was a similar character. Jean thought suddenly that the prime mover of events was not Roger and his expedition, but Ambrose and his adventures along that uncertain shore where myth and fact overlapped, a coastline she herself knew only too well.

The Water-Horse of Loch Ness was published in 1934, following Ambrose's spate of articles about Nessie-sightings. *Pictish Antiquities*, his last effort at validation by an increasingly professional archaeological establishment, was published in 1939, just as another war drove the final nail into his way of life. He'd lingered until 1970, servants long gone, the house falling into disrepair, but there was no record of him doing more than brooding here in his ivory tower, his fortress of solitu . . .de

The cat leaped onto Jean's feet. She jerked, then laughed and patted the animal's sleek head. He kneaded the duvet, a cat attractor if ever there was one, and lay down beside her. At least he hadn't landed on her sore knee. Nothing like being so preoccupied she'd missed him jumping down from the chair.

She looked around the room — no, she hadn't missed anything else. The less-than-brilliant overhead light reflected off the glossy photo of the Stone, so that it looked as though it were radiating energy. Some inanimate objects did have auras, Jean had heard, and the Stone seemed as likely a candidate for one as any. She wondered yet again just why Ambrose had never set the Stone up. But that was about number fifteen on her list of questions, number one being: *Why had Jonathan Paisley been killed?*

The transcripts. She owed it to Alasdair to do her assignment conscientiously. She opened a new file on her computer and dumped a short stack of paper out of the envelope, copies of typewritten pages. A post-it note obscured the cover sheet. "Jean. Here you are. Thanks for helping out. A." The handwriting was solid, the strokes as precise, as controlled, as letters carved onto a stone monument. But his capitals hinted at frustration, the "J" of her own name slashing downward . . . Good grief! Here she was analyzing the man's handwriting! Next she'd be drawing little hearts with his initials in them in the margins of the papers. She began to read.

According to the police reports and interviews, the only physical evidence in the case of Mrs. Mackintosh's disappearance was a freshly-scrubbed floor at the foot of the stairs in Ambrose's study and a bloodstained scarf identified as Eileen's that was found caught in a shrub. The police had established that the blood on the scarf was human, but that was the forensic limit in 1933.

The trial transcripts repeated the interviews in the voices of the participants. Jean began typing notes, occasionally smiling at the archaic language of both the era and the court.

The servants — Eileen's maid, a cook, a butler/valet and several gardeners — and members of the local community all agreed that Eileen and Ambrose were not on good terms, but that Iris's birth had gratified them both and given them hope for the future. Eileen had last been seen by her maid on the morning of March 29. Then the servants had departed and left Eileen, baby Iris, Ambrose, and a companion alone.

Jean sat up, earning an eyelid shiver from Mandrake. A companion? Oh. The woman hadn't been a servant, a petty but relevant point in the days when social status had been meticulously graded. She had been a *companion*, and not even a paid one, apparently, just a woman who had lived at Pitclachie since the previous fall, fetching and carrying for Eileen during her pregnancy and then for baby Iris.

She, too, disappeared on March 29. And her name, Jean saw with a micro-thrill, was Edith Fraser. From Foyers, which was near Crowley's Boleskine estate. But that didn't mean Edith was connected to Crowley, let alone Gordon Fraser the bookseller, who disapproved so strongly of The Beast from Boleskine. Inverness-shire was Fraser territory. Still, Alasdair would be interested in this bit of synchronicity. Jean typed Edith's name, added an exclamation point, and hurried ahead to Ambrose's own testimony.

The prosecution said, probably with a sniff, "It is suggested here by the Crown that on March twenty-ninth, nineteen-thirty-three, you killed your wife, Eileen Fleming Mackintosh."

Ambrose replied, probably with an indignant bridle, "That is absolute bunkum with a capital B, if I may say it. Why should I kill my wife?"

"Mr. Mackintosh seems to have great difficulty recognizing bunkum, whether capitalized or not," retorted the prosecutor, no doubt referring to Ambrose's admiration for Crowley and implying that murdering one's wife was the logical outcome of such admiration.

The defense had contented itself with a stiff, "The Mackintosh family has always borne the stamp of respectability and truthfulness."

Ambrose had conducted himself accordingly, displaying his credentials as landed gentleman and benign scholar. No, he and his wife had sadly not been getting on well. As for the day she disappeared, its quiet had been broken only by a cup of coffee spilled at the foot of the staircase in his study. He had emerged from his sanctum late in the afternoon to find both Mrs. Mackintosh and her companion Miss Fraser gone and the infant Iris wailing in her cradle, her condition of hunger and dampness indicating that she had been unattended for quite some time. He could not explain the bloodied scarf.

What had happened to his wife? The tribulations of childbirth and motherhood had proved too much for her delicate constitution and she had thrown herself into the loch. Dreadful business, a great tragedy.

What had happened to Miss Fraser? Perhaps the terrible event had unhinged her mind. Or, fearful of attracting blame, however unjustified, she had not stayed to give notice but had run away. She was above the age of consent. He was not her keeper. She was a destitute young woman from the area, who, out of the goodness of his heart and his desire to see his wife catered to during her very difficult — blush — confinement, he had taken in.

The defense inferred that Edith killed Eileen and fled, but could not come up with a motive other than a vague suggestion of missing jewelry. Out of respect for the Fleming family's sensibilities, though, no one had inventoried Eileen's belongings. When the maid said she was under the impression nothing was gone, that was that.

Edith's destitution might explain why her family was absent from the transcripts and presumably the trial. It did explain why no one seemed more than perfunctorily concerned about where she'd gone. She had been something between a parasite and a slave, neither part of the servant's hall nor known to the friends Eileen had liked to entertain before her "confinement" had confined her within the walls of Pitclachie, alone except for Ambrose and a skeleton crew — *hah*, Jean told herself — of servants.

Edith. Was it just coincidence that "Edith" also started with an "E"? *My dear E, remembering the good times.* What? Had there been some sort of love triangle? That could explain a lot, up to and including Edith's abrupt departure. As for the Lodge's ghost-video . . .

Jean swiveled, but the staircase was silent and empty, and beyond the fringes of the rug the stone flags of the floor revealed no lingering stains, of coffee, blood, or anything else. Had her ghost-sensing been confirmed by outside evidence? If so, that was both encouraging and creepy.

Jean hitched the duvet further up over her chest, rested her head against the back of the couch, and massaged her eyes. The original uneven and slightly smeared typewritten lines would have been hard enough to read, let alone the copies.

The room was growing colder and colder, as much from the iceberg whose tip was barely revealed in the transcripts as from the chill night outside. The ticking of the kitchen clock sounded like the plunking of raindrops onto stone — well, okay, she was hearing the occasional plop of a raindrop falling from the roof onto the court-yard. The malodorous air of the old book seemed to be coagulating in her throat like slime. She was going to have to put it, as well as the cat, out for the night.

Yawning, Jean told herself that if she went upstairs and lay down, she could get to sleep before any paranormal activities started up. Maybe. But she had only a few more pages to go.

The prosecution offered only the merest hints of occult activities, either sparing the sensibilities of the court and the Crown or else assuming that those activities were so well known in Inverness-shire they went without saying. If the defense had ever considered a change of venue, to, say, Timbuktu, it was not recorded.

Aleister Crowley had last visited Pitclachie when he sold Boles-kine in 1919. The proprietor of the local hotel, the building that was now the Official Exhibition with the floating Nessie, reported white-robed figures carrying flaming torches on the hillside behind Pitclachie House. Ambrose pooh-poohed the idea of secret rituals and the like, wisely cutting himself off before launching into a defense of Crowley's not-so-secret and less-than-savory activities. That, Jean supposed, had come indirectly, in his theories about ceremonial magic in *Pictish Antiquities.*

While many locals had not been gladdened by this business of digging up graves, let alone associating with wizards, digging at the castle was seen as a legitimate endeavor. As for Ambrose's collection of bronze and silver artifacts, Jean deduced that it served as a character reference. And Nessie? Well, every landed gentleman was allowed his eccentricities, especially one who had suffered such a terrible tragedy. Jean reminded herself that at the time of the trial, in late 1933, the Nessie tsunami was no more than a wavelet on the loch.

Manners and morals had changed so drastically in seventy years that trying to understand those of an even earlier period — why the Picts carved and erected their stones, for example — was the philosophical equivalent of landing on Mars. Impatient, she skimmed ahead to the verdict and the formal discharge of the prisoner. The court had probably greeted "Not Proven" with an air of bemused futility, no joy but no sorrow for either defense or prosecution. So Ambrose's life had gone on, and Iris's life had begun, under a cloud.

Jean stacked the pages and tucked them away in the envelope, thinking that if not for Ambrose's slightly sinister reputation, the jury would have found him Not Guilty and had done with it. Trust the Scots, with their streak of grim practicality, to invent a verdict that split the difference between Guilty and Not Guilty. Not Proven was draped in shades of gray that hung over you like your own personal overcast the rest of your life — and after. People who had actually done the deed deserved that. People who were simply in the wrong place at the wrong time did not. But it wasn't Jean's responsibility to pass judgment, tempted as she often was.

Mandrake lifted his head and looked past her, toward the stairs. The fur along his back rose into a serrated edge. His eyes were chips of amber, unblinking. If she leaned over and looked into those eyes, she'd see what he was seeing. But she didn't need to. The back of her neck puckered. The frigid air pressed her down into the couch, a cement overcoat.

Jean, too, looked toward the stairs, but saw nothing. Mandrake's head, though, lowered and turned, tracing the path of the ghost as it walked down the steps and across the floor to the vestibule. The velvet curtain twitched. One edge curved outward, grasped by an unseen hand. It moved slowly across its rod and with a flutter fell back into place.

Was she hearing faint voices, male and female intermingled? Or were the microscopic hairs in her ears waving like sea anemones to otherwise undetectable currents in the air? Ah, there was that coffee smell again, and tobacco, and something else — the reek of the old book, probably, cutting through the extrasensory odors.

Mandrake's pink nose expanded and contracted. And then, with an audible sigh, his eyes closed, his fur smoothed, and his chin dropped onto the duvet. Jean wished it were that easy. She sat there, skin prickling, waiting for the oppression to lift, for what seemed like an hour but was probably only a minute. Exhale, inhale, exhale, and her own fur settled. The tick of the clock filled the silence. That, and . . . Well of course there would be footsteps outside, the constable was walking his beat.

Maybe that ghostly display had been the exhibition for tonight. Maybe it was only the prelude to something more vivid. She wasn't going to wait around. It was almost midnight, time to finally call Saturday a done deal. Midsummer's Day, the longest day of the year. No joke.

Yawning again, and resisting the urge to scrub at the grit in her eyes, she saved her file and shut down the computer. If nothing else — and there was plenty else — the transcript gave her an excuse to call Alasdair tomorrow. To talk to him, face to face. He'd be polite, professional, distant. He'd look like an ice sculpture. If she wanted to start him thawing again she'd have to . . .

The trilling notes of Mozart sounded abruptly from the kitchen.

TWENTY-ONE

Jean broke her own record at the sitting high jump. The duvet went one way and, in a scramble of paws, the cat went another. Pressing her heart back into her chest, Jean stumbled to her bag, still sitting beside the sink, and pulled out her cell phone. *Alasdair?*

It was Brad, his voice bland as mashed potatoes. "Hi. I got your message. What's going on?"

She leaned against the counter, catching her breath and waggling her knee. She'd told him what was going on. She'd told him . . . "Brad, it's midnight here."

"Yeah. Six hours later — I knew that, you didn't have to tell me. But you said it was a police matter, so I thought I'd better call. You can get pretty impatient."

She shouldn't fault him for those remarks. Trying not to do so, Jean walked over to the table, pulled some notepaper and a pen out of the drawer, and established the order of business: "Someone blew up Roger Dempsey's boat."

"What for?" Brad asked.

"That's what the police want to know, especially since a man was killed."

"Whoa. That's not good."

She didn't need to explain the entire case to him. He'd probably object if she tried. "Roger's here showing off all his equipment and searching for the Loch Ness monster."

"Sounds like the sort of thing he'd go for. He was telling me all about some treasure galleon sunk off a Scottish island — you'd know all about that."

"What do you mean, he was telling you? You've never met him."

"Sure I have. I was sitting at the bar at that convention in Williamsburg — you remember, the one about layers of wallpaper and blocked-up doorways and stuff."

"The archaeology of standing buildings. Yeah, that's where I met Roger, but I didn't . . ."

"I told you I talked to him."

She winced. He probably had. But they'd started tuning each other out a long time ago, more shame to them both.

"Anyway, I was sitting in the bar and he was sitting in the bar and we started visiting, you know, the way you do when you're just having a drink. He asked me if I was at the conference and I said I was only there to carry my wife's luggage."

He didn't mean that as a jab, Jean told herself, just fact.

"We got along great. He was working on a submersible, even called me up a few months after the conference to ask about the mechanics of ballast tanks and watertight seals and stuff. I didn't mention it to you, you never understood that sort of thing."

She felt her jaw tightening. "What about tanks and seals?"

"The problem with using water for ballast in your submersible is that you need pumps and valves to blow it out when you want to get back to the surface. That means more parts that can malfunction. And watertight seals, well, that's obvious."

Yes, it was. Jean noted those interesting factoids, then drew loop-the-loops not unlike the interlaced tail of Ambrose's signature. From the phone emanated faint voices, rising and falling, similar to the intimation of ghostly voices she'd heard earlier. She imagined Brad sitting in his favorite old recliner, TV remote in one hand, phone in the other. "The police want to know whether Roger had a submersible on board his boat when it blew up," she prodded. "He's implying that all he had were remote-operating vehicles, but someone else saw a sub. Was he building one, then?"

"Oh yeah. He got it to the beta-testing phase before it went down off the Gulf Coast somewhere, Tallahassee, maybe."

Jean didn't think Tallahassee was on the coast, but that hardly mattered. "Roger's sub went down? You mean, when it wasn't supposed to go down? When did this happen?"

"I heard about it last year, maybe year before last now."

"And it sank because the pumps and valves didn't work?"

"Oh no, no, it was the hatch that didn't work. Or the latches and seals on the hatch, probably. It leaked, the sub filled up with water, and it sank like a rock. The pilot drowned, but fortunately he was the only one on board."

A metal coffin sinking into the water . . . Jean shuddered. So Jonathan was the second man who'd been killed on Roger's watch? *Oh boy.* Her pen raced across the paper. "Not so fortunate for the pilot's family. Did they manage to retrieve the sub and the man's body?"

"Eventually, yeah. Roger gave up on the submersible and went into ROV research. I think he's working on an AOV, too, a vehicle that doesn't need to be tied to the boat but can pilot itself. That would work better in the loch there, when the boat's going back and forth and tangling up its cables. An ROV should work just fine for that treasure galleon."

Treasure galleon . . . "You mean the Armada galleon that sank in Tobermory Bay off Mull? Funny, I saw something about that today. Yesterday. I thought it was right up Roger's alley."

"Yeah, he was really excited, said there was Spanish gold on board that ship."

"There's a long shot for you, although I suppose there's a better chance of him finding gold in Tobermory than Nessie here. He's looking for her on land now."

"If I was him I'd climb out on land, too, cover my butt. Sounds like he might be in line for a second lawsuit, depending on how your explosion thing plays out, I guess."

"Lawsuit?" Jean enunciated, pen poised. "What lawsuit?"

"The guy's family, like you said. His wife was threatening to file a suit against Omnium. Wrongful death or negligence or something. Saying that the sub was faulty so Omnium should pay to support the kids. I bet Omnium is saying the guy just didn't close the hatch properly."

"But no lawsuit's actually been filed?"

"I don't think so, but I got to working on that project for NASA and lost track. Omnium probably settled out of court. Way out of court, to keep the story from leaking."

Leaking like the sub . . . Jean caught a movement from the corner of her eye. Oh. Mandrake was pussyfooting along the kitchen counter, sniffing at the plastic bag of bread. "Can you find out the name of the man who was killed?" she asked Brad.

"Why do you want to know?"

"What don't I want to know?"

"No shit, Sherlock."

"What?"

"I read about that murder case you were involved in on the Internet, in *The Scotsman* headlines. Way to go, Jean. Curiosity killed the cat, you know."

Mandrake was alive and well, Jean thought huffily. And so was she. Barely . . . Beyond the faint hum of the airwaves she heard an announcer's voice say, "A swing and a miss!" Ah yes. A summer Saturday. Baseball, hot dogs, apple pie. "Brad, can you just find me the name of the man, please?"

"Okay, okay, I'll ask around on Monday. I don't know why you think it has anything to do with anything, though."

Alasdair wouldn't have wasted his breath with that comment. As far as he was concerned, everything had something to do with . . . A suspicion swelled in the back of Jean's mind like a thunderhead on the horizon. "You told Roger your name. He knew you were my husband."

"What?" Brad asked, dumped off the back of the truck as her thought accelerated. "Oh. Of course I told him my name. Geez. And after you told him off, I bet he remembered yours. Yours as it was then."

Inglis isn't all that common. Neither is Fairbairn, but you were born with that."

She confined herself to, "Yes," and went quickly on, "So can you tell the difference between a submersible and an ROV from the wreckage?"

"Sure. If you've got people inside, you've got to have a tough environment. In fact, I doubt if you could blow one up without actually putting explosives inside it. You could damage the heck out of it, sure. Look for a pressure hull lined with glass foam or the equivalent. Tell the cops to e-mail me some photos." The announcer in the background exclaimed over the swelling cries of a crowd, ". . . and it's a home run!"

"I'll tell them," Jean said loudly. "If you hear anything else about Roger or the lawsuit or the submersible accident, let me know, okay?"

"Sure," he repeated. "Wow, can you believe those Red Sox?"

A woman's voice answered Brad's question before Jean could. Oh. He had someone there with him. Only Brad would call his ex-wife with his — girlfriend? — in the room. Not that him having a new female friend was surprising. He was subsiding into middle age, less gracefully than helplessly, but still, to some women he'd be a good catch, a safe port. A home run.

"Thanks," Jean said, ended the call, and carried the notepaper over to her collection of reference material. She could hardly walk, her knee was so stiff and her feet were so cold. Her hands and arms were cold. Her nose was cold. She stood where Alasdair had stood, telling herself that it was time to go to bed . . . The tiny screen on the cell phone indicated that she had a message.

Quickly she pressed the keys. Ah, Michael had called while she was in the shower. His voice, its accent seeming all the livelier after Brad's, filled her ear. "Jean, Rebecca and I are just off to the Royal Infirmary. Linda's thinking she'll not wait for the Fourth of July but come a bit early. Not to worry, the doctor says she's well within tolerances. What's worrisome is Dougie's Nessie toy. He and Riccio tore it open, and there's a bittie electronic gadget inside. Rebecca and me, we're guessing it's a listening device. A bug."

Jean's chin and eyebrows took off in separate directions. A bug? In the Nessie toy that Roger included with his press kit? Alasdair had said that none of the other reporters mentioned a toy.

Michael's voice concluded, "I'll hand it in to the police soon as I get the chance. Take care."

"Yeah, y'all too," Jean said into the ether. She remembered vigils by the phone, waiting for word from her brothers about their wives, comforted by knowing they were in a hospital, with the best of care.

Eileen, on the other hand, had probably labored alone here at Pit-clachie.

But that was old news. This was a fresh headline, big type, black block letters. Roger had planted a bug on her! The bloody nerve of the man! That was just the sort of thing a two-fisted gadgeteer like him would think was clever.

Jean slammed her phone shut and pressed her hand to her head, trying to squeeze out the sequence of events. The press kit had arrived at her office late Tuesday. She'd taken it home. Hopefully, Roger had been amused listening to the TV news and her music and her inane one-sided conversations with Dougie. Until Michael and Rebecca came to visit on Thursday, when she sang the same old song about Brad, Dempsey, and the conference, that she'd sung to Miranda, too. They'd taken the toy away. Soon after that Roger had called to set up the interview. To keep his enemy close.

Her thunderhead of suspicion crackled with lightning. Both Dempseys kept asking about Brad because they thought he'd told her about the submersible. They thought she'd go public with it, the way she'd gone public with the scandal at the university, the way she'd waded into police work last month. But the sub accident hadn't touched her personally — until now.

Oh God. She and Alasdair had been speculating whether Roger had a motive to kill Jonathan. He'd been motivated to plant a bug on Jean, and maybe to search the Lodge and take her notebook — what if he'd been motivated to try and kill *her*? For a long moment Jean cowered against the back of the couch, seeing bearded, baseball-capped assailants coming out of the woodwork.

But no. She'd been walking with Roger. They'd both been side-swiped by that car. Unless . . . Jean remembered Tracy's anger both at the hotel and at the Festival, and Roger almost taking a swing at her, right there in front of God and Alasdair and the Ducketts. Had Tracy decided that Roger, like Jean, was more of a liability than an asset?

Tracy had been having a drink with Kettering. She hadn't been driving a car without its headlights down the fog and dusk-darkened highway. Or had she? What if Kettering was in on the whole thing, thinking there was no such thing as bad publicity. What if . . . Well, there was an appalling number of what-ifs.

Jean gazed longingly at her phone. She needed to info-dump on Alasdair. She needed to hear his calm voice, to touch the still surface above his unplumbed depths and watch the ripples of his thought spreading outward. But no. What he needed was his sleep. Assuming he was sleeping, when his mind was as much a perpetual motion machine as hers.

Jean hadn't realized her face was wrinkled up like last year's Halloween pumpkin until the thought of Alasdair — and his nearby constable — relaxed it into a rueful smile. She pried her icy fingers off the phone and switched it off. Its little trill of farewell made Mandrake, still on the counter, look around sharply. First thing tomorrow morning she'd talk to Alasdair. Tonight she'd recharge the phone and herself as well. It was time to go to bed. Really, really, time to go to bed.

She piled everything back into her carryall except for the old book. She couldn't just put it outside . . . Aha, the plastic bread bag. She dumped the rest of the bread into the breadbox, tucked the book into the bag, and closed it with a twist-tie. Mandrake observed the proceedings, nose twitching, then leaped onto the floor. After a valedictory twine around Jean's legs he trotted toward the velvet curtain and slipped past its edge.

The curtain was hanging perfectly still, the folds of its fabric like sculpture. Jean tiptoed toward it, then pounced, throwing it aside. Mandrake sat in front of the door, tail swishing, waiting for his servant to let down the drawbridge. *Okay, then.* Jean unlocked the door and opened it. The damp chill of the night gathered around her like a shroud.

Shivering, she laid the book on a bit of decorative stonework just outside the door, where it would be protected from all water short of an earthquake dropping the entire hillside into the loch. The air was thick with mizzle, drizzle not heavy enough to fall to the ground. The main house and the tower loomed against the fragile glow of the clouds, a huge angular ink blot, the occasional lighted window seeming no more substantial than a streak of paint. Someone moved in the window to the right of the front door — ah, the private office. That lissome silhouette had to be Kirsty's. She was up late.

Jean inhaled the fresh air scented lightly with smoke, clearing the smell of the book from her lungs. The constable had disappeared. If she'd been him, she'd have nipped into the kitchen for a cuppa, too.

The distant sound of music and singing hung eerily on the air. If Alasdair was staying at the hotel, he was sleeping with a pillow over his head. Hugh in full spate wouldn't have awakened Brad, but Alasdair wasn't Brad. And she wasn't the Jean she'd been for Brad, either. Encouraged by that thought, she turned back into the Lodge.

A scream sliced suddenly, urgently, through the night, and was cut off by a thudding splat. The ghosts? No. The noise came from behind her.

All five of her normal senses flaring with adrenalin, Jean spun around, looking up, looking down. Was that a shadow flicking along the row of murder holes as someone ran through the tower room? That was most certainly a human form crumpled on the terrace, one that hadn't been there a moment before. A shape as pale and indistinct as though seen through water. *Drowned Ophelia* . . .

She forced herself to walk toward it, her hands curled into fists at her sides, her socks and slippers swishing through the icy water gathered on the stone.

There, in a nimbus of reflected light, lay a body, limbs splayed loosely as a rag doll's. An ashen face was turned upward, eyes staring past the tower, past the clouds, seeing nothing. A dark crimson stream oozed across the rain-slick terrace and pooled in the carved symbol of the gripping beast, Roger's water horse.

Oh my God. Jean's mind leaped and skidded. Her ears buzzed. She realized her hands were pressed to her face — she could smell the odor of bread and of the rotting book on her own fingertips. *Oh my God.*

The front door of the house opened with a crash and a clatter of the knocker. "What is it?" shouted a male voice. And just behind him came a woman's, "What's happened?"

Jean couldn't speak. She couldn't move. It was all she could do simply to stand, there beside Tracy Dempsey's dead body.

TWENTY-TWO

If the scene by the roadside earlier that night had seemed like an impressionist picture, now Jean felt as though she'd fallen into a non-representational painting, something by Pollock, perhaps, all splatters and smears . . . There was an unfortunate image.

The constable was talking into his small radio unit. No matter that he'd been inside. He could have been standing right here, and he could have done nothing to stop Tracy from falling.

Falling? Jean's gaze darted upward. She had seen movement in the tower room. Whoever it was should have been rushing down to the terrace — assuming Tracy had fallen, assuming she hadn't been pushed, because if she'd been pushed . . .

If Tracy had been pushed, then there was no debating whether her death was an accident. Maybe Jonathan's death was an accident. Maybe the sideswipe by the car was an accident. This, though, this was murder.

The shiver rising from Jean's cold feet met the shiver flowing outward from the splash of that word in her mind. Wrapping her arms tightly around her chest, trying to quell her trembling, she shrank away from Tracy's broken body — one step, two steps, three.

Kirsty appeared through the mirk and mist, wearing slippers and a robe over loose pajamas. The color drained from her face, leaving her complexion fish-belly white. Even her lips, the lower one caught between her teeth, were gray.

"Have you got a blanket, Miss?" the constable asked her.

She didn't react.

"A blanket, Miss?" repeated the constable.

Kirsty's stare moved from Tracy's empty face to his intent one. She whispered, "Oh. Aye." She plodded into the house and several long moments later returned with a red and blue knitted afghan that might have been one of Iris's cottage industry samples. The constable shook it out and laid it over Tracy's body, over her sweatshirt and jeans and athletic shoes, like a flag draped over a coffin.

The blanket helped give her mortality a little dignity, a little privacy. But the image of Tracy's blank staring eyes was printed on Jean's retina. The scream, outraged, terrified, scraped her senses like fingernails against a chalkboard. Murder. It had come to murder at last.

There was Martin Hall, wearing only a pair of jeans, his shoulders bony and his chest concave. His face was a mask, eyes wide, mouth flapping open and shut again. Faintly he said, "Tracy? Tracy, what, how . . ." With a sharp glance at the constable and then at Jean, he tightened his lips into a slit.

The lights went on in an upper room, and the curtains flew back, and Dave and Patti's ample shapes jostled each other in the window. Jean wondered where the rest of audience was — no sign of the Bouchards, and the cat was probably halfway to Edinburgh by now.

If she'd listened to Alasdair, she'd be halfway to Edinburgh . . . No. Doubly no, now.

A police car turned into the driveway, its pulsing blue lights sending waves of sickly sheen over the watching faces. Doors slammed. Footsteps raced. "Miss Fairbairn. Miss Wotherspoon."

She looked around. She recognized that youthful, puzzled face. Gunn.

"What happened? What did you see?"

"I was standing here," Jean said. "She fell. There was someone in the upper room."

"She was lying here," said Kirsty.

Martin said nothing.

Gunn waited, but Jean had nothing else to offer and the others looked as though they couldn't have spelled their own names. At last he said, "You'd better be getting yourself inside. The lot of you."

Oh yes. Please. Thank you. Jean turned toward the Lodge. Only then did she realize her feet were so cold and numb they felt like ice-filled galoshes. Her knee twinged and she lurched. Gunn seized her forearm. His hand seemed small, his grip tentative next to Alasdair's. Feeling older than a centenarian now, like a set of bones echo-located by one of Roger's sensors, Jean allowed Gunn to walk her toward the Lodge.

Another car roared up the drive, and another. Alasdair's strong arm around her shoulders pulled her away from Gunn and pressed her so tightly against his side that his deep intake of breath reverberated through her own body. He was wearing blue jeans. And a sweatshirt. Beneath a yellow police jacket. She'd only ever seen him in a suit and tie. And in a kilt, getting in touch with his inner peacock. Now he'd look as though he was getting in touch with his inner punk if his face hadn't been set in such stern lines she could have chiseled stone with it: On Duty.

Alasdair placed her inside the Lodge. The tiled entry seemed warm to her feet, and the lights, modest as they were, seemed garish. When he removed his arm from her shoulders and turned back toward the courtyard, she felt fragile and transparent, not like fine crystal but like cheap plastic. "Alasdair?" she asked.

He stopped, silhouetted against the glow of lights. "Jean?"

"I was standing there when she fell. Someone was in the upper room. I don't know who it was. They ran away, but I didn't see anyone come out the tower door."

"There's a second door, into the house. You're saying she was pushed?"

"She had to . . . someone had to . . . yes." Jean waved her hands, groping after the right words. "Listen, I know this isn't a good time, I just . . . I'm sorry about what I said earlier, and there's some stuff in the transcripts you need to know, and about the submersible and Roger, and that toy Nessie in the press kit, there was a bug in it . . ."

A cacophony of voices rose from the courtyard. Multiple yellow jackets swirled like autumn leaves.

Alasdair's eyes flashed, but all he said was, "Lock your doors. We'll have us a blether the morn." And he was gone, off to the wars, leaving her with only that swift compression and breath to hint at the riptides swirling beneath his professional armor.

Jean locked the door. Alasdair, she thought, would make tea. He'd search the Lodge. He wouldn't loom over her, not this time, even though a good masculine loom would actually have been comforting, now.

Her stomach gagged at the thought of tea. Her brain gagged at searching the Lodge — it had been searched already, by an expert . . . She'd stood there in the courtyard, her back turned to the open door, plenty long enough for someone to sneak inside. Although, if the evildoer was in the tower pushing Tracy, he or she would have had to move fast to get down the stairs and through the second door, wherever it was, and around the back of the house into the Lodge.

But why? She didn't want an answer to that, but one came to her anyway. Dressed down, in the dark, Tracy would look like Jean. If the driver of the attack car thought it was Tracy walking with Roger earlier, then the opposite could be just as true. Whoever pushed Tracy out of the window might have thought they were pushing Jean. And yet it was Roger and Tracy who had the motive, wasn't it?

To snoop on her, yes. To kill her? Well, the explosion had been drastic. Pushing Tracy out of the tower had been drastic.

Jean checked the doors and windows. Upstairs, the door to the storage room stood wide open. She slammed it shut. She had no time for paranormal hocus pocus right now, thank you very much.

She laid her wet footwear out in the bathroom, warmed her feet with the hair dryer until she could feel her toes again, and put on dry socks. Then, making two careful trips, she retrieved the duvet and her books and papers from downstairs. Each time, the damnable door stood open. Finally she just left it that way, scurrying past its dark, gaping maw and into the bedroom.

Jean locked the door and jammed a chair beneath the knob for good measure. Pulling the dressing table bench close to the window, she sat down and watched as the crime scene investigators went to work. Their raw white lights cast a shimmer on the mist, making the night outside their range even darker. Each figure appeared as abruptly as though from the wings of a theater, made its ritualistic gestures, and exited the scene. Softer lights rose and fell in the windows of the house and tower, flash bulbs winked, and headlights flared and died in the distance. Like fireworks, she thought.

She identified Alasdair from his stance, alert and contained, taking up more space than his compact stature required, and from his gestures, like those of a conductor before his orchestra, made with efficient economy rather than with flourishes.

Gunn was taller but thinner, looser of limb. He came and went, his notebook at point. And here came the ape-like form of Sawyer, ushering a shambling, limping man who had to be Roger. Alasdair conducted him to the chrysalis-like shape around which the activity accreted, lifted one end of the blanket, grasped his arm as he reeled. His voice rose. Alasdair's met it and brought it down again. Roger staggered away again, assisted by a shapelier male figure that had to be Brendan.

At last the lights went out in the courtyard and the house, and the actors departed with Tracy's now plastic-bagged body. Alasdair's pale face turned up to toward Jean's window. He raised his hand in a motion that was neither a regal wave and nor a traffic cop's *Stop right there*. She wasn't surprised he knew she was watching. If anyone had eyes in the back of his head, it was Alasdair.

Two constables stayed behind. If there was another murder, Jean wondered, would Alasdair then leave four? She hauled herself to her feet just as a couple more human figures appeared in time for the curtain call. Ah, the Bouchards, leaning together as close as honeymooners. Or conspirators. They exchanged nods with the constables but didn't stop to ask questions. The news had spread.

Imagining Peter Kettering banging his head against a wall, Jean trudged to the bed and did not look at the clock. The day and then the night had stretched out like Macbeth's tomorrows, until the last syllable of recorded time.

Alasdair had asked if Tracy was playing Lady Macbeth. He'd said that the other reporters hadn't mentioned getting toy Nessies. He was too perceptive by half. By three-quarters, even.

Jean crawled beneath the duvet, assumed the fetal position, and played with the concept of a strong, compact body snugged to her back and a whiskey-scented breath on her cheek . . .

In the hallway a door shut. Footsteps made each floorboard creak in turn. Ah, Ambrose's nightly show. The wet-blanket sixth sensation flowed over her and weighted her down. A sweet scent of what was either flowers past their prime or a heavy perfume teased her nostrils. Pipe tobacco. Coffee. Ambrose had testified that he'd spilled a cup of coffee at the foot of the staircase. And there was the mutter of voices, a man's and a woman's.

She was expecting the scream, and yet when it came it was so penetrating a repetition of Tracy's real-time shriek, short and sharp, that she gasped. Her body spasmed to the slightly different timbre of each thud as Eileen's body ricocheted off the treads and the balusters and came to rest on the floor below. This time Jean heard the shaking male voice, saying quite clearly, "Oh God, no, no, God, no," although if he referred to the usual capital-G God or some lower-case entity, she had no way of knowing.

Holding her breath, she waited, but heard nothing more than the pacing steps of the constables outside her window. The heaviness in the air dissipated, and she realized she was curled into so tight a ball her shoulders were cramping. Inhale, exhale, inhale, and she relaxed, as much as a taut rubber band could relax. She could still see Tracy's broken body. She could imagine Eileen's.

If she kept thinking about it, trying to work it all out, she'd lie awake the rest of the night and be utterly useless in the morning. Instead, she deliberately slackened each muscle fiber and cleared her mind — she was a calm pool, unruffled, smooth. She was driving a submersible the same way she'd drive her car, and it was dropping through the water too fast, and she kept pumping on the brake pedal but nothing happened. Until the hatch popped open and peat-dark water flooded in.

She saw her own face, wet, eyes staring, pulled from the water by Alasdair's capable hands.

TWENTY-THREE

A sudden noise jerked Jean out of her dream. She blinked upward at daylight tinting the ceiling amber, the same color as the curtains. Oh. She'd slept after all. What had that noise been? It sounded like the clanking clatter of garbage men heaving around metal trash cans. But they'd hardly be doing that on a Sunday morning. Maybe the chill of the bed indicated that the ghost — *ghosts* — had added something else to their repertory. Once they reached their last act, she wondered, then what?

Jean crawled out of the bed and discovered that her knee, while stiff, functioned properly. The clock read nine a.m., hours after sunrise. She opened the curtains to see the sun shining through a mist thin as chiffon, casting tenuous shadows over courtyard, terrace, and garden, but illuminating no signs of life. No signs of death, for that matter, only blue-and-white police tape across the door set into the angle where the tower abutted the main house. People used to mark plague houses with charcoaled crosses, Jean thought as she headed toward the bathroom. The tape worked just as well.

Across from her bedroom, the door to the storeroom was now shut. *Fine. Be that way.* Quickly Jean washed and threw on jeans and a sweater, gathered up her things, and headed downstairs. She felt headachy and nauseated, but if that indicated a hangover, it wasn't from the one glass of whiskey. She was hungry, that was all. Hunger had to be a good sign.

The velvet curtain was pulled across the vestibule. Behind it the tiles were littered with squashed yellow broom petals, tracked in the night before. She went outside, locked the door, and reached for the old book she'd left on a stone gewgaw last night. It wasn't there. It wasn't anywhere, neither on the pavement nor in the shrubbery, knocked aside by some distracted police person. She could ask the constable now standing by the base of the tower, but decided she didn't care.

Averting her eyes from the water horse logo carved into the dew-dampened stone flags, Jean went into the main house and followed her nose — coffee, toast, bacon! — past the library and down the hall into the dining room. Its arched windows and French doors echoed the neo-gothic extravagance of the rest of the house, but its furnishings were less fussy. Four small tables in assorted styles, less antique than simply pre-owned, were scattered across the polished planks of the floor. A sideboard displayed not the family silver but assorted cereal boxes, fruit bowls, and pitchers. The drinks cart sat to one side, its array of bottles looking sad and neglected. And still lacking a corkscrew, Jean assumed. Had Martin palmed it, so he could loudly announce its absence?

The other two Halls, Noreen and Elvis, were sitting by the window. She was staring into her teacup — foretelling a meeting with a handsome stranger, perhaps — while the child ate a soft-boiled egg with strips of toast, utterly focused. Multi-tasking came along with adulthood and the worries thereof. Jean seated herself at one of the two tables still set.

Kirsty pushed her way through the swinging door from the kitchen, a pot of coffee in one hand, a pot of tea in the other. Her face was almost as ashen as it had been the night before, and yet, on her, pallor was attractive, romantic as a drooping rose. Jean's own face in the mirror had resembled an albino cactus. She held out her cup. "Coffee, please."

Kirsty filled the cup expertly, without spilling a drop. "Help yourself to juice and the like. I've got bacon, eggs, and tomato on the cooker."

"Thank you." Jean poured milk in her coffee and took a healthy swig. *Oh my. Oh yes.* She swallowed again, then headed for the sideboard.

"We only booked the room 'til today," Noreen said to Kirsty, as though resuming a conversation interrupted by a kitchen timer. "If the police want us to stay on, then they can pay the tariff."

"I'm sure we can work something out," Kirsty replied. "Is Mr. Hall coming down for breakfast?"

"Don't know. Couldn't be bothered to say." Even Noreen's scowl seemed anemic. "This isn't a safe place for the child, is it now? He's never a suspect. But no, that prat Cameron, he's saying we're obliged to stay on."

Alasdair was no prat, Jean harrumphed silently. Keeping your suspects corralled was standard procedure, child or no child. And she wasn't surprised he was already out and about, delivering directives and no doubt asking questions.

"Me, I'm obliged to ring the folk with rooms booked the night and cancel," Kirsty muttered darkly as she hurried back to the kitchen. "Iris won't be half . . ."

Upset, Jean finished, and starting spooning bran flakes and fruit salad into her mouth.

"Mummy," said Elvis. His ensuing soliloquy was muffled by Noreen's wiping his face with a napkin. She grasped his hand and pulled him out of the dining room, acknowledging Jean's presence by turning up one side of her upper lip. Elvis's voice disappeared down the hall and up the stairs. "Nessies climb out of the water, don't they? Daddy says they climb out of the water. And he says the arky — arkylogies — will find their bones buried like treasure."

Jean chewed. So that's what Daddy — er, Martin — was saying about Roger's archaeological plans, was it? Bones like treasure. Or maybe bones and treasure. Is that what Martin and Tracy had talked about during the boat tour, leaving Noreen to chase after Elvis? It had probably been Martin in Tracy's hotel room, after all, plotting . . . Well, plotting something. He'd looked horrified last night, but then, they'd all looked horrified last night.

Kirsty reappeared, holding a plate of runny eggs, charred bacon, and a tomato half, a dishtowel serving as hot pad. She set the plate and a rack of toast on the table. "Sorry, we've got no sausage or beans. Most times Aunt Iris is off to the shops of a Saturday, but she's . . . Well, you know where she was. Your pal Cameron, he's saying she'll be back home the day."

"Good," said Jean, and swallowed the "your pal Cameron" with a bit too audible a gulp.

Kirsty clattered the Halls' dirty dishes into a stack and started for the kitchen.

"Did you hear anything last night?" Jean asked. "Before Tracy — you know."

"I heard people walking about. I'm always hearing people walking about. Then she screamed."

"Do you ever hear ghosts walking about?"

Kirsty stopped in the doorway, bracing the door open with her elbow. Her face was hidden but her voice was sharp as a paring knife. "Ghosts? Why are you wanting to know that?"

"I like ghost stories. A lot of these old places have gray ladies and blood spots, that sort of thing. It's not all that unusual for people to sense, well, presences." When Kirsty didn't reply, Jean said, "Did you hear a metallic crash about twenty minutes ago?"

"I was cooking toast for the Americans then. They wanted coffee and toast is all. Hard to credit, them not wanting the full breakfast, but that's all they ate yesterday morning as well."

"Maybe they were upset about Tracy. And yesterday about the boat explosion."

"They were that, aye, pulling long faces and talking about what a tragedy it was and all, and how things happen that you don't intend."

Amen to that. "So you didn't hear a crash?"

"Brendan's saying they'll be digging the day. You heard him and Roger. Dr. Dempsey. Digging for monster bones when his wife's been murdered." Kirsty vanished through the swinging door, leaving it to creak to and fro a couple of times and then quiet. Her Glasgow accent gave each sentence a sarcastic tail, but Jean bet the sarcasm ran deeper than her voice.

In lonely splendor — a state that was less compelling now than it had been several months ago — Jean finished her cereal, ate her eggs, and considered the different skeins of evidence. Ambrose and Eileen. Roger and Tracy. Aleister Crowley, the Picts, Nessie. Iris.

Then she stacked up her dishes and started toward the kitchen, planning to offer her assistance . . . Who was she kidding? She'd help clean up, yes, but she was hoping that in the process Kirsty would render up a clue, one that would not only satisfy some of Jean's curiosity but earn her points with Alasdair.

Her shoulder was against the door when she heard voices. Brendan was saying, "You've got to give it to the police."

"Don't you go telling me what needs doing," Kirsty replied. Dishes jangled and water ran.

"Listen, if that book's important enough for Iris to call and tell you to hide it, then it's got to be important enough to give to the police."

"It's one of Uncle Ambrose's books. It's got nothing to do with the police, with your boat, with Tracy, with Roger, with anything."

"Then why hide it? Roger already has copies of all of Ambrose's books. Big deal."

"So that's it, is it? Roger. And here's me, thinking you wanted me for myself. No, it's you who's the spy, I reckon, not Jonathan. You and your boss, coming here, digging things up, it's all your fault."

"Our fault? We've had two people killed!"

"There's work to be getting on with. Yours and mine both. You'd best be away now."

"Kirsty, I . . ."

A businesslike clatter of pots and pans drowned out the rest of the sentence and also, probably, the sound of Brendan's crest falling. A door slammed, and a moment later he strode past the dining room windows. He bore a shovel and that universal masculine pout meaning, *Women! Can't live with 'em, can't live without 'em!*

Repelling male boarders seemed to be the thing just now, Jean thought with a grimace. Kirsty might have more justification for that than Jean had, though . . . From the kitchen came the sound of china smashing, followed by a choice four-letter word.

Charles and Sophie walked into the dining room. When they saw Jean standing beside the door and holding her dishes, they exchanged a cautious glance, probably wondering whether this was some custom of the country they should know about. With a bland smile in return, Jean put the dishes back on her table and strolled leisurely out of the room and down the hall. Behind her she heard the scrape of chairs, the kitchen door opening, and Kirsty's taut voice. "Tea is it? Coffee?"

So, if she were Kirsty hiding a book, where would she put it? In her room? Jean didn't know where Kirsty's room was. In the office off the foyer?

Kirsty's voice still emanated from the dining room. Picking up her pace, Jean went straight for the door marked *Private*. It was locked.

A rustling noise behind her made her spin toward the brochures on the table — looking at them was an innocent enough activity. But no one was sneaking up behind her. The rustling noise, followed by a thud, came from the library.

Martin? One of the Ducketts? Ghosties and ghoulies? Jean walked as casually as she could into the library. The ranks of books, the mantelpiece, the display cases with their ancient ornaments, Kirsty's knitting piled on the wingback chair, all were inert. Mandrake, though, crouched on the floor by the roll top desk, guarding his victim, a rectangular shape in a bread bag. He was sniffing so intently that his head was inside the bag.

Well, Jean thought, look what the cat dragged in. Or off the desk, most likely — the sliding top of the desk wasn't quite shut, leaving plenty of room for an inquisitive paw to grope around and an efficient claw to snag the plastic. Maybe Kirsty thought the book would be suitably hidden in the desk, maybe she tucked it away until she had a chance to put it somewhere else. Or give it to Iris.

Knowing the folly of coming between a hunter and his prey, Jean slowly pulled the package away from Mandrake. At last the cat withdrew, his eyes crossed and his whiskers lopsided, as though the sweet, moldy odor was heady as catnip. Maybe it evoked rancid mouse.

To Jean and her full stomach, the odor was even more nauseating than it had been. Depending on when Kirsty took the book, it could have spent hours outside in the damp. Way to go, she told herself. She should have put it in the lumber room with the mildewed curtains.

Her morning caffeine suddenly cut in. *Wait a minute.* How could Iris have told Kirsty to hide this book? Iris didn't know Jean even had it, let alone where it was. All Jean had overheard was a suggestive reference to hiding one of Ambrose's books. She could have misinterpreted the entire conversation, poetic justice for eavesdropping.

Still, Kirsty had taken the book and hadn't asked about it. Jean stood up, holding the book and the bag at arm's length. What to do now? Put it back in the desk? If she didn't, someone would miss it, whether Kirsty sooner or Iris later. Or save it to show Alasdair? In the desk it wouldn't smell up the Lodge, and maybe Alasdair's steel-trap mind could discern its significance. Even Jean's steel-sieve imagination couldn't devise a connection between Tracy's murder and Aleister Crowley's life story.

Mandrake leaped onto the chair, snuggled up next to Kirsty's knitting, and began licking the odor into, or out of, his multi-colored fur. Wrapping the bag back around the book, Jean raised the lid of the desk a bit further. It squealed, not too loudly, but loudly enough. Quickly, she leaned over and thrust the book into what felt and sounded like a pile of papers. Her nostrils flared. A cloying scent, stirred up by her movement, was either that of flowers past their prime or a heavy perfume, or perhaps even aromatic tobacco . . .

The smell was that of the nightly apparition in the Lodge.

She straightened up, pushing the lid back down to where it had been, slowly, so the squeal was as thin as her nerves. Well, the desk had been Ambrose's desk, and the book his book, and the curtains in the lumber room had probably been his, too. He haunted Pitclachie on several different levels. He and Eileen's tiny sepia-toned eyes were even watching her from the photo atop the desk.

Abandoning Mandrake to his ablutions, Jean fled into the open air. Outside, the sun was shining brightly, drawing wraiths of mist up from the green fields and the glistening surface of the loch to dissipate against the blue bowl of the sky. So much for Thursday's forecast of torrential rain. Although any number of Thursday's assumptions had been exploded by now, and too many had been confirmed.

The sound of bells rippled down the cool breeze. Jean was tempted to go sit in a church and think thoughts of peace and justice, poetic or otherwise. She settled for breathing deeply of the fresh air, which loosened the tight muscles in her chest and shoulders so effectively she inhaled again. This time she caught a whiff of cigarette smoke and looked around.

Martin Hall was standing where Tracy's body had lain, his long, thin neck cocked back as he peered up at the tower. He looked like a stork swallowing a fish.

"Good morning," said Jean.

Martin took a deep drag of his cigarette, as though in defiance of the fresh air, then inspected either his feet or the carved flagstone they stood on.

"Noreen says y'all are staying on for a few days, during the police investigation." Not that Noreen had said that to her, but Jean wasn't going to let an inconvenient explanation get in her way.

"You know that we've been told to stay on. You're working with the police, aren't you now?" The *teacher's pet* was implicit in his half-growling, half jeering tone.

"You have a problem with that?" Jean asked, but the sharp angle of his shoulder turned toward her and he didn't reply.

Could he act any more like he had a guilty conscience? Which probably meant he'd never so much as gotten a traffic ticket. Jean glanced at the constable standing watch beside the tower, but his face remained impassive beneath the bill of his cap, perhaps contemplating the righteousness of toast and tea. Life is brief. Comfort food is eternal.

She walked into the Lodge and up the stairs. The door of the lumber room was standing open — nothing like an architectural feature with contrarian tendencies . . . Her phone rang. She fished it out of her bag and flipped it open too quickly to look at the I.D. *Alasdair?* "Hello?"

"Jean," said Hugh's voice. "I'm just now hearing about your night, the stramash with the car, Tracy Dempsey and all. Are you all right?"

"Sure. Scared, frustrated, curious — in both senses of the word. The usual. How are you?"

"Flattered and fed and right well lubricated. Starr PLC is making sure the lads and I are in good form for the festivities."

"How was the ceilidh last night?"

"Ah, the room was hot and heaving. Thought my lord Kettering would have to go unbuttoning his jacket. But he kept popping out to massage his mobile phone."

Hmm, Jean thought. If Kettering was at the ceilidh, he wasn't pushing Tracy out of the tower. Him killing one of his guests of honor was hardly likely, although Jean wasn't sure what was.

"Then there was a French couple," said Hugh, "who stripped off so far I was thinking we'd be hosing them down. They're stopping at your B&B, are they? They're well and truly fans of the water of life, it seems. Not quite under the table but crawling fast in that direction."

"They were drunk? Well, they'd already had a fancy dinner. Most of those multi-course dinners come with so much wine you need to be rolled out on the serving cart. Or I do, at least." Jean eyed the boxes in the darkened room. Here, too, the odor of mildew was moderated by the sweetish smell of the curtains, as though a wet dog had bathed in perfume.

"I'm away to the Festival," Hugh said. "We're playing a set at half past eleven. There's another ceilidh tonight, after the Festival closes down, if you've got a moment amidst your sleuthing."

"Isn't there something tomorrow night, too?"

"Oh aye, Starr's hired a boat for a farewell cruise, just for the punters, I'm thinking. We're the entertainment — Hugh and the lads, unplugged, unbowed, and un-sober, likely enough. You'll be there, won't you now?"

The thought of a boating trip had lost just a bit of its appeal. Nevertheless . . . "Oh yeah, that's on my marching orders."

"I'll expect to see you dancing, then," said Hugh. "Cheers."

"Bye," she returned, without commenting on her lack of resemblance to Ginger Rogers. Jean brushed her teeth, applied lip-gloss, and checked to make sure her laptop was locked in the wardrobe. She couldn't remember putting it there, but there it was. She'd been on automatic pilot last night.

Next to her canvas carryall sat the plastic bag with the stuffed toys for her younger relatives and for baby Linda . . . Oh my goodness. The wee Scottish-American bairnie had probably made her appearance by now. Jean hoped everyone was all right. Things could go wrong, as the Ducketts kept pointing out like corn-fed versions of a Greek chorus.

The Ducketts, buying bags of gifts for their grandchildren. What had Patti said, something about them losing their father? That phrasing implied death, not divorce. In Florida, where Roger's submersible had gone down.

Come on now. She was just as likely to have misunderstood Patti as Kirsty. Lots of people lived in Florida. Lots of them had accidents. Jean knew she had a tendency to build supposition upon conjecture into a structure so flimsy it made a house of cards look sturdy as Edinburgh Castle — just because everyone else seemed to have ulterior motives didn't mean the Ducketts did, too . . .

The warble of the phone interrupted whatever clever deduction she'd been formulating. *Alasdair?* she thought again, and told herself to stop acting like a teenager with a crush. This time she checked the I.D. "What ho, Miranda."

"Up to your neck again," her partner's voice said. "Good job you've survived. So far."

"It's not my fault," Jean insisted, then launched into the tale of the listening device in the Nessie and story of the sinking submersible, which proved that some of the epic, if not her fault, could at least be considered a flaming paper bag left on her doorstep.

Miranda responded with murmurs augmented by the discreet peal of fine china. She must be having her breakfast. "Well, well, well," she said at last, "no surprise, then, that I'm hearing Dempsey's been asked to resign from the Omnium board of directors. They're putting it about that he's after pursuing his own researches and will still have an advisory role and whatnot. But . . ."

"They haven't exactly scheduled a farewell banquet and the presentation of an engraved gold watch. Roger hasn't breathed a word of this. He's implying Omnium is his own personal fiefdom."

"Of course he is. He's under something of a cloud. No one's

saying just how thick that cloud is, but if it's to do with that lawsuit, that's enough for a wee rain shower, wouldn't you say?"

"I would," said Jean. The door of the lumber room was closed again. She opened it halfway, as an experiment, and went on down the stairs.

"Could be the lawsuit's been settled on the sly."

"Or that they're piling on as much red tape as possible, to hide it. Neither Omnium nor Roger want any publicity over it, that's for sure. Are they still paying him anything, a pension or whatever?"

"Haven't a clue. As for Tracy, for what it's worth now, mind, my friends at the *Chicago Sun-Times* are telling me she built herself one of those faux-European mansions and filled it with antiques and collectibles."

Collectibles, Jean thought. A synonym for *junque*. "What sort of antiques?"

"Objets d'art and French furniture."

"Ah, that spindly gilded stuff."

"Not all French furniture is Marie Antoinette tushery. Though Tracy's taste might have run to such. All show and no comfort."

"Like high-heeled shoes?" asked Jean.

"Shoes are another topic entirely," Miranda replied demurely.

Not really. Tracy had worn high-heeled shoes to make herself taller. To rise in the estimation of the people she dealt with. She'd died wearing athletic shoes. It didn't seem quite fair. "Speaking of French antiques, do you know a shop called La Bagatelle d'Or in Paris?"

"I've heard tell of it, aye. Rare books and antiquities, genuine and faux. No furniture, but small things, easily carried through customs, shall we say."

"So they have a reputation for not being entirely conscientious about the niceties of the antiquities trade such as import-export licenses, signed expertises, attested provenances?"

"If the rumors have any truth to them. It's possible to have smoke but no fire, as you know yourself. Why are you asking?"

"The owners of La Bagatelle, the Bouchards, are staying here at the B&B." Jean looked around the living room of the Lodge and decided nothing had been either moved or removed. Even the gallery of old Nessie photos hung blandly in their frames. "I'm thinking antiquities like the artifacts Ambrose uncovered. Iris has sold off a few, and I bet she's sold off some rare books, too . . ."

"Oh aye, she's done that, I've got a chum who's a dealer."

"And Roger's looking for Nessie on land."

Miranda laughed. "Is he now?"

"I'm wondering if he's after artifacts himself, with the Bouchards standing by as receivers, and the whole monster thing is just a smokescreen. If he has money problems, it could be."

"He and Tracy looked to be heading toward a divorce, although how recently the cracks appeared is hard to say. So is whether Tracy had a pre-nup."

"Pre-nuptial agreements weren't in style twenty-five years ago. She probably thought that investing in Roger was enough . . ." Jean opened the door of the Lodge. Alasdair was standing on the threshold, his hand raised to knock.

TWENTY-FOUR

Jean jerked back into the house with an annoyingly loud gasp. Alasdair recoiled.

"Jean?" Miranda asked.

"I'm okay, no problem," Jean lied. "I need to go. Talk to you later."

"Take care then. Ta ta."

Jean spent longer than was necessary switching off the phone and tucking it away. When she finally stepped outside, locked her door, and turned to face Alasdair, he was, of course, waiting as patiently as a cat outside a mouse hole.

Even though he was wearing his uniform of dark suit and white shirt, enhanced by a tie patterned in a flowing gray and red design, he looked as though he'd been dragged through a barbed wire fence backwards — to use the vernacular of her state of origin. His skin was pallid, his cheekbones sharp, his eyes hard, the curve of his lips flattened into a rigid line. How much longer was he going to endure the pressures of his job, she wondered, before he collapsed in on himself like a black hole?

Without demonstrating any Einsteinian physics just yet, Alasdair said, "Sorry to startle you," and held out something small and flat.

It was her notebook, the pages curled with damp and a muddy footprint embossed on the cover. She took it and flipped through it. The moisture had made the ruled lines bleed blue, and the pencil tracks of her notes were almost illegible. She popped it into her bag. "Where did you find it?"

"One of the lads turned it up in the nettles beside the road. I'd be thinking it fell from your bag when the car hit you, but you'd already found it missing."

Found it missing. She liked that. "So did someone take advantage of the, er . . ." No point in wasting her breath with the word "accident," not any more. "Of the car, or were they working with the driver of the car?"

"Good question. We've got loads of good questions, haven't we?"

"Is that an editorial we, Alasdair?"

He looked at her, unblinking, unmoving, impenetrable.

"You could have sent Gunn or someone with the notebook. You didn't have to bring it yourself."

"I told you we'd have us a blether the morn." He took several deliberate paces to where Martin had been standing earlier but was now, thankfully, not. Beyond the edge of the terrace the roses and the broom rustled to the breeze. Against the breeze.

Jean's skin prickled to the touch of invisible cobwebs and her shoulders puckered beneath the chill weight of another reality as she walked slowly to Alasdair's side. He was watching the invisible shape move through the leaves. Except now it wasn't invisible. The branches and the flowers bowed and parted as the transparent shape of a woman ran past them. Ran through them, the red and yellow petals becoming part of the flowered skirt she wore beneath an oversized cardigan, blending with the silk scarf that trailed from her hand. Her face was little more than eyes and mouth agape with alarm, turned toward the Lodge. A small hand, a diamond flashing from the fourth finger, swept up and covered the mouth, and a cry of dismay mingled with the wind. Then she was gone. The plants waved innocently, no longer reacting to an uncanny memory-movement but to an ordinary breeze scented with the raw, chill odor of the loch.

Jean closed her eyes and opened them again. Beside her Alasdair said matter-of-factly, "The ghost was walking in the shrubbery all the while we were working last night, but I never saw her, not the once. "

"I have the awful feeling that the two of us together make some sort of critical mass," Jean replied. "It did last month, when we saw the ghost walking down the hall."

Alasdair didn't follow up on that one. "This ghost's Eileen, is it?"

"Oh yeah. There's both a painting and a picture of her in the Lodge. I wonder what she . . . why she . . . I mean, her ghost is in two places at once. Although I guess if Anne Boleyn's ghost turns up all over England, why not Eileen twice here?"

"Loads of questions," he repeated, this time without the evocative *we*, "and bloody few answers. Do you fancy a tour of the tower room?"

"Yes, please," she said, and walked across the terrace an arm's length from his side.

Was that offer an olive branch? Or was he rewinding the tape, pretending those too-revealing moments the night before had never happened? Yesterday his manner had come perilously close to flirtatious, but now — thanks to her own sharp tongue — he was locked in his emotional tower, buttressed by duty. She was overdue for a meal of crow, yes, but now wasn't the time to serve it up. Not if she didn't want him to retire beneath a layer of frost like an old-fashioned freezer.

The constable on guard might have wondered why Alasdair and Jean had been staring into the underbrush. Now he acknowledged his superior's nod by dutifully stepping aside and lifting the tape. Alasdair drew a key from his pocket and opened the wooden slab of a door.

Jean ducked under the tape, feeling as though she were being ushered past the bouncer into an exclusive nightclub. But the room inside the door was blank and bare except for blocks of sunlight cut by the curving shadows of the mullions in the east windows and was several times taller than it was square, like the inside of a bell tower. "Kirsty said that Iris keeps the tower locked up. Was this door locked last night?"

"By the time we arrived it was." Alasdair led the way onto the staircase that angled up the interior walls. Its wrought-iron banister was a neo-Gothic fantasy, but the stark stone treads seemed suitably medieval, if not at all hollowed by centuries of climbing feet. On the second floor landing he indicated an arched doorway. "This door now, this one was unlocked. It opens into the upper corridor."

"So the killer ran out this way?"

"Either that or he flew."

She was tempted to say that the murderer could have climbed down the wall of the tower like Dracula, but restrained herself. She followed Alasdair up the next flight, carefully, favoring her sore knee. "Are you saying 'he' for any particular reason?"

"No. Could have been 'she,' right enough."

Four stories up — Jean was grateful she wasn't acrophobic — the staircase ended at a trap door in an expanse of rafters and planks, the floor of the tower room. Alasdair threw open the trap, climbed through, and disappeared. He wasn't going to offer her his hand, then. Once bitten, twice shy.

Not that she needed a hand up. Grasping the edge of the opening to steady herself, Jean climbed up into Ambrose and Iris's eyrie and stood catching her breath.

Kirsty had said nothing was here but dust, and there was plenty of that, especially around and about the ceiling rafters. A table and a straight-backed chair sat in front of one of the windows, beside a bookshelf that held only a pair of binoculars. Perhaps the notebook Alasdair was leafing through had also come from there. The wooden planks of the floor were scuffed and dirty in the center of the room, sprinkled with forlorn yellow broom blossoms, and were clouded by sheets of dust in the corners, even the corner propped up by several rusty gardening tools.

Jean had expected the place to look like a monastic cell, perhaps even the sort of cell in which an anchorite would have him or herself walled up, the better to contemplate the mysteries of the soul. But she hadn't taken into account the view. Two windows on each side of the room opened it to the glory of the physical world — the moss-edged slates of the roof, the cascading leaves of trees, the green fields stitched with pink foxgloves, the mauve humps of the mountains, the royal blue sky above indigo water that flowed to the wind and to its own subtle rhythms, its depths concealing a mystery . . . Wasn't that one of Aleister Crowley's magical precepts, *as above, so below*?

Jean frowned. A crease in the surface of the loch showed several low undulations, darker than the already dark water . . . Oh. It was the wake of a barge that was just disappearing behind the tower of Urquhart Castle. Shaking her head — as inside, so outside — she turned toward another window.

It was closed now, but last night it had been open, and Tracy had fallen through. Jean walked over to it, noting that the sill and the floor beneath were clear of dust. The crime scene specialists had been thorough. She peered through one of the windowpanes.

There was the roof of the Lodge, and the terrace, each stone looking smooth, hard, and unforgiving. Now it was the Ducketts, their bodies oddly foreshortened from this angle, who were standing where Tracy's body had lain. They were leaning together the same way the Bouchards had been leaning together last night, for mutual support, Jean supposed. And to what end? Her suspicions about them were one more thing to dump on, er, share with Alasdair.

The glassed-in murder holes ran around the edge of the floor, two or three to each wall. She leaned over to peer through the closest one and saw a dizzying vista straight down. Something was caught on a branch of ivy — no, the glass was cracked, that was all.

She straightened. "I take it there's nothing in that notebook."

"The stubs where some pages have been torn out is all." Alasdair replaced the book on the shelf, inspected his fingertips, then brushed them off.

"What evidence did your people collect here last night?"

Leaning against the edge of the table, he crossed his arms and looked at Jean. It was the first time he'd looked at her since he'd stood on her doorstep. His face was so uncommunicative it might just as well have been covered with a visor. The visor of a plain, simple helmet, without plumes or the trailing tokens of a favored lady. "Fingerprints," he said. "Footprints. Dirt and pollen. A skein of wool and a broken knitting needle. Bread crumbs. A cigarette butt. Some bits of plastic, cloth, and threads. Nothing that shouts, 'clue here.'"

"A cigarette? Martin Hall smokes, and he was one of the first people on the scene. I think there was something going on between him and Tracy. But then, we saw Roger almost bash her one at the Festival."

"Roger's right out. He has an alibi. Sawyer flushed him out of the ceilidh."

"And was probably less than diplomatic informing him he's now a widower."

"Like as not," Alasdair agreed, desert-dry. "Even so, we're taking fingerprints, clothing samples, and the like from everyone concerned, and a few who are not."

"Did you find any evidence on Tracy's body?"

"Nothing yet." His gaze fell, as though he pictured the medical examiners going about their work. When he looked up again, she could see the cold steel of the morgue reflected in his eyes. "What was it you were telling me last night?"

Jean's breath snagged in her throat. But no. He just wanted the facts, ma'am. She told him the facts, trying not to stray into opinion any further than she had to. Ambrose's trial. Iris's instructions to Kirsty about one of his books. Roger and the submersible. The bug in the toy Nessie. She didn't spare herself Brad's role, and she didn't spare Alasdair her wilder speculations about the Ducketts and the Bouchards.

He listened, his brows lifting and tightening in turn, his eyes casting sharp glances at the stairway or the windows, as though he could look down on the suspects, the bystanders, even the dead. Like hers, his mind worked just fine as a remote sensor. "Well then," he said when Jean reached her last full stop and with a gesture ceded the floor to him. "That's a tale and no mistake. A bug in your soft toy, is it? The man's not half daft."

"Roger, you mean? Or Ambrose?"

"I'm thinking Roger, but Ambrose, now, he must have been quite a piece of work. One of his books, eh? You're right, Iris can't have known you bought one at the Festival just as we were taking her away."

"Kirsty says Iris is on her way back here, that you've let her go."

"We couldn't keep her without bringing charges, and once she told us she'd confessed to sending the letters to protect Kirsty, we had no charges to bring."

"And you don't think Kirsty sent the letters."

"I had a word with her this morning. She owned up to the incident in Glasgow and says she had nothing to do with Roger's letters, and, well, I'm believing her."

"What did you do, try trapping her with the exact wording or something?" Alasdair glanced down at his feet, an affirmative answer if Jean had ever seen one. "So she and Iris are both in the clear, for the letters and the explosion?"

"The former, aye. And the latter, I reckon. Still, Iris knows more than she's telling — and who doesn't — but . . ."

"She has a cast-iron alibi for Tracy's murder," Jean finished.

"Oh aye. Opportunity's not everything, though. Motive, there's your bottom line."

"That's what lacking in Ambrose's case. Motive."

Alasdair strolled over to one of the windows, braced his hands on both sides of it, and tilted forward, looking at something outside. "What about this Edith, then? Is she the 'E' in your book? Was there a love triangle? Or a lust triangle, come to that? Jealousy, there's a motive for you."

Trust Alasdair to call a spade a spade. Jean looked at the rusty old tools in the corner next to where he was standing and thought of the spick and span house and garden below. She hefted a small dirt-crusted shovel. "Iris wouldn't let her gardening tools get this dilapidated, would she? And why would she haul them all the way up here? I bet these are Ambrose's excavation tools."

Alasdair looked around.

The metal blade fell off the rickety handle. Jean skipped back, but it missed her feet and clanked to the floor, sending up a cloud of dust and dirt particles. "That's the sort of sound that woke me up this morning. I wondered if it was another ghost noise. Kirsty said it was Roger and Brendan going to work. I guess Roger's on automatic pilot, not that you'd let him leave anyway. Them."

"They're up the field behind the house, digging themselves a trench, right enough."

"Having excavating equipment on hand would have made it easy for Ambrose to bury a body. A lot easier than hauling one across the main road and pitching it into the loch." Jean set down the handle and inspected her fingertips for splinters. All clear. "Odd, isn't it, how we've gone from thinking Eileen committed suicide to thinking Ambrose did kill her. She fell down the stairs while she and Ambrose were arguing and smashed her head. He wrapped the wound in her scarf and buried her, then cleaned up the floor and blamed the wet patch on a coffee spill. He knew he had such a bad reputation in the neighborhood, no one would believe the truth. The only reason they brought him to trial to begin with was that same reputation."

"Ghosts aren't evidence," Alasdair pointed out, not without a hint of a smile.

She shrugged agreement.

"We'll never know the truth of the matter. And it might not make any difference, not when it comes to Jonathan and Tracy."

"You think it does, though, don't you? It's not just an intellectual exercise."

"We've got no time for intellectual exercises just now. The lads are setting up in the dining room to interview everyone here at Pitclachie, about Tracy, mostly, but we'll have another go at Jonathan's death as well, with your information and all."

"Glad I could help." Jean hoped he'd take that statement the way she meant it, straight up.

He did. There was that implication of a smile again, but still his face didn't crack. "Let's have us a look at the Pitclachie Stone and see what Roger's on about." Without waiting for her reaction, he headed for the trap door and the staircase.

All right — not only a couple of *we's* but also a *let's*. *Be careful what you ask for,* Jean reminded herself. Her knee reminded her to take the stairs slowly. Alasdair had never asked about it, had he? Well, she couldn't have it both ways.

He held the outside door for her, then locked it and made sure the police tape cut just the right diagonal across the opening.

D.C. Gunn was kneeling beside the open front door, balancing a laptop on his thigh and stroking Mandrake's helpfully arched back. Just as Alasdair and Jean approached, Andy Sawyer burst through the doorway with all the subtlety of a train exiting a tunnel. "Oh for love of . . . Get a move on, Nancy. We've got a nice bit of crumpet inside, not that you're up for it, are you now?"

His face going flat white, Gunn leaped to his feet, computer in hand, and disappeared into the house. The cat showed great discernment, if not excellent taste, by sprinting across the courtyard into the shrubbery.

Sawyer's bull neck swiveled just enough to see Alasdair gazing at him as gimlet-eyed as a gunner taking aim. Sawyer gave off a sound between a snort and a cough and followed Gunn into the house. Alasdair took off into the garden so fast, Jean could hardly keep up with him.

Each one of his steps hit the path so hard, the gravel crunched like a shot. It was probably just as well she could see only the back of his head. His ears were cherry-red. In another moment smoke would be trailing from them. And she'd thought earlier he was under pressure. Sawyer's toxic smog was coming close to melting Alasdair's ice cap.

He pushed through the gate and on up into the pasture, toward where Brendan was digging while Roger stood by. A long trench, extending perpendicularly from the fence encircling the pine glade, was marked out by pegs connected with string. So the remote-sensing equipment had detected something, then. Or Roger believed it had. He stood very still, the bill of his cap low over his face, holding a rock in his hands in the same pose as Hamlet contemplating the skull of Yorick.

Two days ago he'd been brash but charming. Yesterday he'd

seemed flabby, somehow, like a balloon that had lost most of its helium. And now? Jean couldn't see his face and wasn't sure how to read his stance — tense, certainly. And not only because parts of his body had been chopped and pureed by the hit-and-run. Two major emotional blows in as many days must have taken their toll, and yet he was keeping on keeping on. Jean had to admire the man for that.

Alasdair stalked past Roger and Brendan as though they were so many sheep and burst through the gate in the deer fence. Jean followed, on tiptoe, into the shadow of the glade, where she found Alasdair standing before the Stone like a pilgrim before a shrine, head lowered.

The Stone was standing as it had the day before, aloof but not lonely, a riddle of lost time. Several of the tumbled rocks at its base seemed darker and grayer than Jean remembered, showing not the bright whorls of lichen but damp root tendrils . . . Oh no. Someone had turned more than a few rocks over. The Bouchards, perhaps, treasure-hunting? She'd seen them coming out of the enclosure yesterday afternoon. Or Martin? He seemed to be on Roger's wavelength. Or Tracy's.

Well, no real harm had been done — the rocks been disturbed several times, most recently by Ambrose's excavations and by Iris when she had the Stone set up. Still, Jean was as indignant on the rocks' behalf as she was on Alasdair's.

Edging around him, she stepped onto the cairn and again traced the carvings on the Stone, delicately, with her fingertips. The line incised beneath the horse's head seemed not only shallower than the others, but also not patinated — not showing the brownish film of age but instead gleaming gray, like the top of the Stone where it had been cut. The hole, though, was old. It wasn't as though some recent iconoclast had recreated an ancient ritual by ritually "killing" the Stone. But then, the gradations of color were hard to see beneath the rills of shadow cast by the pines.

Alasdair asked, in his usual quiet but intense voice, "Where's the rest of it?"

"Another good question. Ambrose found it, but never said it was complete. It was broken fairly recently, although 'recently' is open to definition."

"Has someone been digging about in these stones, do you think? That rather supports your treasure-hunting hypothesis."

"I do think, yes." She turned around, relieved to see his expression back to its usual still coolness.

"Roger's pressing on, I see, in spite of it all."

"He was saying yesterday that Jonathan would have wanted him to keep on. I don't know why he lost it for awhile there, but I guess now he's thinking that Tracy would want him to go on, too."

"Oh aye, that she would."

"She may have tried to play the dutiful stand-by-your-man role, but I bet she was half the brains and guts of the operation, wanting to protect her investment . . ." Jean's thought somersaulted. "You know, I was wondering several days ago if Roger had sent himself the letters. What if the Dempseys themselves blew up the boat? You were hinting at that with your insurance scam, weren't you?"

"Oh aye," Alasdair returned with a knowing nod. "You finally twigged it."

She'd finally put it into words was all, but she let it go. "Tracy made a big deal out of the propane stove, but not the gasoline smell. And Roger has never said he had a submersible here."

"He was after destroying his prototype."

"So no one could prove that the hatch was defective and use it against him in the lawsuit. He would have lost, and lost big . . ."

"American juries being notorious for handing down huge settlements. Money's aye a grand motive." Alasdair stepped forward and caressed the stone, his right hand cupping its edge and sliding down lightly, curiously.

He was grounding himself, Jean thought. Literally. His stance was alert as always, but no longer armed and dangerous. "So if Roger and Tracy blew up the boat, did they intend to frame Iris for it? I wonder what it is that came between them."

"Iris might could have heard of the submersible accident."

"Yeah. It keeps coming back to Roger. So how about revenge as a motive? What if Roger and Tracy have been the target all along, and Jonathan was just collateral damage?"

"And the driver of the car thought you were Tracy, oh aye. Two birds with one — stone." His thumb brushed the gritty surface. "The Ducketts, by the by, were at the Festival at the time of the hit-and-run. Having a blether with D.C. Gunn, as luck would have it."

"Or as good planning would have it?" She couldn't see Dave and Patti committing mayhem on anything larger than a scone, but then, she was just as likely to see what she wanted to see as everyone else. "And then there's Roger planting a bug on me to see whether I was going to blow the news up — if you'll pardon the expression. What a jerk."

"Oh aye, a right pillock, but that doesn't mean he was after killing you."

"No," Jean admitted. "But maybe whoever pushed Tracy out of the tower last night thought they were pushing me." She hoped that didn't come across quite as pitiful as it sounded to her. Or as critical. What if Tracy had demanded police protection? What if Alasdair had thought to offer her any? He'd no doubt thought about it since last night . . .

"You, Jean," he said even more quietly, "are having police protection." His hand flattened itself against the face of the Stone. In the dappled sunlight his blue eyes glowed and gold touched his hair, as though he were a sentry at the gate of Faerie.

By "protection" he didn't mean the constable downstairs. He meant himself. She opened her mouth to respond, but couldn't think of anything to say that he might not misinterpret.

He didn't wait for a response. "I was saying I'd prefer the killer to be determined rather than careless, then he'd be predictable. I don't think I'm getting what I wanted."

"What you've got is either someone who's careless, or two people working at cross purposes. Or with the same purpose, just with different means of getting there."

"And thinking their ends justify their means."

That brought them back around to Sawyer's omelet, but Jean wasn't going to go there.

Alasdair stepped off the cairn and offered her his hand. His chin was set, she saw. So was his will. *Take it or leave it.* Taking his large, warm, dry, steady hand, she let him balance her onto clear ground, then quickly subtracted her hand from his before she was tempted to cling to it. "Thanks."

The answering spark in his eye was so subtle Jean wasn't sure she'd actually seen it.

Voices outside the grove broke the silence within. Sophie Bouchard said something about digging holes in the ground. Roger replied with a twenty-words-or-less explanation of archaeological technique. A shovel clanged, against rock, perhaps. Alasdair started off toward the gate.

At his elbow this time, Jean said, "The Bouchards were at the ceilidh last night, too. I don't know where Brendan was."

"He and the Bouchards need to be giving their statements at the house, not hanging about with Roger and his windmills."

Tilting at windmills. Yep, that was Roger.

"As for Roger," Alasdair continued, "I'm thinking that asking him outright about the submersible and all would be counter-productive just now. Same for the Ducketts. Fishing's only worth the while when you know what sort of fish you're after and are ready with the proper bait."

"If you'd like to send photos of the debris to Brad, I can give you his e-mail."

"No need, thank you just the same." Alasdair didn't turn a hair at the name. "We've looked out an expert. He's got the photos now."

That was a relief. Alasdair opened the gate and held it for Jean. She stepped through and then aside into the bracken while he turned back to make sure the latch caught properly.

In the pasture, Brendan was up to his thighs in the brown soil, his not insignificant chest rising and falling attractively beneath his Water Horse T-shirt. All Jean could see of Roger was his baseball cap and his shoulders, bobbing up and down as he fussed about in the hole which had not yet become a trench. Sophie stood alone and spouseless to one side, her hands in her pockets, her head tilted like a bird's, her blonde hair fluttering.

Alasdair turned around just in time to see Roger vanish into the earth as abruptly as though he'd been beamed away into inner space.

TWENTY-FIVE

Jean was, for once, rendered speechless. All she could do was run with Alasdair down the path and into the field, where they joined Sophie in craning over the lip of the excavation.

Brendan was down on his knees beside a table-sized and -shaped boulder that filled the hole horizontally, disappearing into its dirt wall on one side and resting on a flat upright stone on the other. A fresh gray scrape on the muddy upright had no doubt been produced by his shovel or by Roger with a trowel. An irregular layer of small water-worn rocks, like the rocks in the cairn beneath the Stone, were half-obscured in the dirt above the boulder and down the sides of the trench.

A pair of work boots extended from beneath the flat stone like the wicked witch's shoes from beneath Dorothy's house, and for a second Jean thought it had fallen on top of Roger. But no. It was immobilized. He had uncovered an opening beneath it and with typical go-for-broke bravado had dived right in. Better him than her, Jean thought with a shudder.

"What's he on about?" Alasdair demanded.

"It's a passage grave," explained Brendan. "The big stones and the empty chamber showed up on the survey."

"Pictish?" asked Sophie.

"These sorts of tombs are ages older than the Picts," Jean said. "But the Picts supposedly re-used them." *And Ambrose wrote about them*, she added to herself.

The boots disappeared. A muted wink of light came from the dark cavity. So Roger had provided himself with a flashlight. Nothing like being prepared. "Bones," he shouted, his voice muffled. "Big bones. The bones of the Loch Ness monster. The Picts probably worshiped them."

"Oxen?" Alasdair asked under his breath. "Deer?"

"The Museum needs to know about this," said Jean, and as Alasdair glanced at her, "I'm not telling you your job, I'm doing mine."

Brendan reeled back. With a wriggle and a slither, Roger popped out of the hole. He hardly set foot in the trench but leaped straight out of it. He was bedaubed with mud, like a color-blind Pict painting himself brown instead of blue, but his grin was all white teeth framed by the gray-streaked beard. "I've found it. I've found the bones," he said, speaking so fast Jean thought he was going to hyper-ventilate. "Nessie bones. Well, there are a lot of other ones down there, too, and small stones and dirt , and some artifacts, I think — we need to get things cleared out, it's in great shape — Brendan, let's widen the trench, get the entrance passage dug out, and set up a protocol."

"Very amusing" said Sophie, her tone just a bit edged.

Roger stared at her a moment and then held out his hand. On his palm lay a bottle-cap-sized dirt clod. Sophie's nostrils flared in distaste, as though he'd offered her a dry turd.

Jean caught the quick glint of reflected light from one side of the lump — the same thing that had no doubt attracted Roger's attention. She took the clod from his hand, dug a tissue from her bag, and began wiping the damp dirt away from what appeared to be interlaced black twigs.

Roger said, "This makes it all worth while, you know, it really . . . Oh, hello there, Chief Inspector."

"Hello, Dr Dempsey," Alasdair said, clearly intrigued if far from amused. "Makes all what worth while? The boat explosion? Jonathan Paisley's death? The hit-and-run? Your wife's murder?"

Roger's grin wobbled, and for a moment Jean could see his old self as in a fun-house mirror. Then the grin contracted to a grimace. "She worked hard for this. She wouldn't want me to stop, not now, not right when I've found the bones."

And the artifacts, Jean finished for him. Ah, the black twigs were tarnished silver, encrusted with tiny whitish knobs. The larger lumps were faceted glass or even semi-precious gems. This was not the sort of object she'd expect to find in a Neolithic tomb, whether re-used by the Picts or not. "I'm impressed, Roger. You went right to the entrance of a passage grave. How long were you digging, Brendan, an hour and a half?"

"Seemed like three." Brendan brushed dirt from his hands and inspected several red patches that held every promise of turning into blisters. "I'm a diver, not a digger."

"Of course we went right to it," said Roger. "I was using Omnium remote-sensing devices."

Alasdair smiled, thinly and humorlessly, and picked up on his cue. "You were right lucky then, that you began using your devices at just the part of Pitclachie Farm covering the grave, eh?"

"I think I deserve a bit of luck, Chief Inspector, with everything else that's happened."

Luck had very little to do with it, Jean thought. Ambrose now, Ambrose and his occult Pictish ceremonies and his unrecorded digging and . . . The last flakes of dirt fell away and light flared from the object in her hand. It was a modern earring with a clip back. And it reminded her of something, something very immediate. "Look at this."

"Diamonds? That's why it's so well-preserved?" hazarded Brendan.

"No," Sophie said, in a quick intake of breath. "The Pictish have no diamonds."

"I think it's badly-tarnished silver," Jean said, "set with marcasite, which is some sort of stone — I'd have to look it up. And these square gems are probably Czech glass. It's Art Deco design. It's only been here since nineteen-thirty-three."

Alasdair kept his outward composure — she would have expected no less — but she bet his inner child was turning cartwheels. "I hope you noted where you found this," he said to Roger, and extended his hand. Jean dropped the earring into it.

The ruddy glow in Roger's face drained away and his grimace contracted even further, so that he looked like a moss-bearded gargoyle. He stepped back, and would have fallen into the pit if Brendan hadn't grabbed his arm. "It was lying on some bones. You don't mean . . ."

"You might could have found some animal bones," Alasdair told him, "but I reckon this was lying on human bones. I'll have the torch now, please."

Brendan was looking from face to face, his noble brow furrowed in puzzlement. "Human bones? Nineteen thirty-three? What the . . ?"

"I know that earring," said a clipped voice.

Like an ungainly chorus line, everyone spun around to see Iris, tall and stark as a standing stone. If her tanned face held any expression at all, it was of stunned recognition. The portrait in the Lodge lumber room, Jean realized with a frisson that started at her nape and ran all the way to her toes. Eileen was wearing those earrings in that portrait.

Alasdair thrust the earring into his jacket pocket. "Good morning, Miss Mackintosh."

"It's gone noon," she replied. "When I phoned Kirsty at eight a.m. she told me you were digging in my pasture."

Roger bridled. "You gave me your permission, Iris."

"May you have joy of your findings, then," she said in tones that made Alasdair's iciest voice sound positively tropical. She turned on her heel and marched back down the path. With perfect timing, a strain of pipe music swelled in the Festival field and rolled up the hillside.

"Iris, I never meant to find . . . I didn't know this was where . . ." Roger began, then darted quick glances to the faces around him. Jean could imagine what he saw, Brendan bewildered, Sophie critical, Alasdair authoritative, and Jean curious. And none of them on his need-to-know list.

Alasdair took the flashlight from Roger's hand and turned toward the excavation. Jean heard her own voice saying, "Here. Let me. You've got your suit on."

He stopped in mid-stride, looked her up and down, and with a spark that was anything but subtle, handed over the flashlight. "If Dr. Dempsey survived the trip, then I reckon you will do as well."

"Thanks." So what was she trying to prove? Jean asked herself. She wasn't concerned about his suit. It was her riposte to his *take it or leave it*.

She stepped down into the mucky depth of the trench. The opening to the entrance passage was almost blocked by dirt. Roger hadn't waited for Brendan to clear it all away before he'd plunged in. Not that the passage itself, lined by flat rocks, would be very big. She just hoped it wasn't very long. Number two on her phobia list, after darkness, was enclosed spaces. Bones now, were just that, bones. Structural members. Of course, during her physical anthropology course the bones had been laid out in trays, on lab tables, all dried and tidy and remote.

Reassuring herself that this tomb appeared relatively low and squat, which might indicate a smaller circumference, and that she didn't have to go all the way in, anyway, Jean knelt down and faced the yawning darkness of the opening. And decided she knew how Anne Boleyn felt on the scaffold, waiting for the kiss of the headsman's sword on the back of her neck.

What she felt were the multiple gazes of her audience, especially Alasdair's. The damp soil against her sore knee. The flashlight in her hand — oh, she might consider switching it on. Cold air scented with earth oozed over her, and she broke out in gooseflesh and sweat at the same time. Spirits of the dead? No. Spirits of her own nervous system.

Go for it. She forced herself to crawl forward, between the sill of dirt and the lintel-stone and on into the passage. The beam of the flashlight bounced around, off the slabs beside and above, off the water-worn cobbles below. She might have been able to stand up here, although even as small as she was, she'd have to walk with knees bent and back horizontal. Safer to crawl, sore knee or no sore knee.

Blackness gaped before her and she stopped. In the moving ray of light all she could see at first was an empty space perhaps ten feet across, a primitive corbelled roof tapering to a top sealed with one massive stone. The walls were edged by upright stones, the floor was all brown undulations, the still, cold air was thick with the moldy odor of undisturbed time. There were Roger's footprints in the dirt — jeez, what had the man done, wallowed? Protocol indeed!

Was something written on one of the flat curbstones, or was that just a natural crease or smudge on the rock? Jean squinted, trying to hold the light steady. Yes, those were words, English words. *Do what thou wilt.* Kilroy might not have been here, but Ambrose, and perhaps Crowley, had.

To one side lay a set of antlers, Alasdair's deer, probably. To the other rose a pile of lumps that had to be an animal's bones — those spiky pieces extended in a gentle curve looked like vertebrae, and the elongated skull could be a horse's. Funny, the assemblage *did* sort of look like a Nessie-head on its long neck. It sure wasn't likely to be a giraffe.

But there — oh yes. Jean's neck would have prickled if she'd had any prickle left in her. Two femurs, an upturned pelvis like an empty dish, ribs in their ordered rows, a skull. Jaws separated into a silent scream, each tooth a chip of marble. Eye sockets looking up into nothingness, like Tracy's empty eyes had done last night.

Archaeology, Michael had said, murders its witnesses. Jean backed away, blindly, with no room to turn around in the passage and no strength to go on into the chamber. Her feet hit the dirt sill. She maneuvered backward over it and into the blessed bright light of day, remembering at the last second to grasp the hem of her sweater so it didn't end up over her head. So she was coming out rump-first, she'd never claimed either grace or glamour.

Regaining her feet, she clambered quickly up and out of the hole, Alasdair pulling one arm and Brendan the other. Roger was shifting impatiently, his fingers opening and shutting beside the seams of his sagging jeans. Behind him Sophie stood huddled in her canvas jacket, every one of its pockets as tightly shut as her face.

Alasdair took the flashlight and switched it off. "Well?"

Jean expelled the thick odor from her lungs and rubbed her arms — beneath her sweater her skin must look like that of a plucked chicken. "There's a human skeleton there, all right."

"And the creature?" asked Roger.

"There's some sort of animal, too."

Roger's mouth set with determination. He grabbed the flashlight. "Brendan, my trowel . . ."

"Hang on," Alasdair said. He produced his cell phone from an inside pocket, punched a couple of buttons and informed whoever answered, "We've got another body at Pitclachie. No, this one's a bit older. Set up a perimeter and call in the forensic boffins."

"This is my dig!" Roger protested. "I did the research, I provided the sensors. The bones of the Loch Ness monster, they're my discovery!"

"Just now this is a crime scene." Alasdair snapped his phone shut like John Wayne re-holstering his gun. "Just now you're away to the house to make a statement. You as well, Mr. Gilstrap. Madame Bouchard. I'll stop here until my people arrive."

"You don't understand, Inspector, I have to do this, I have to vindicate . . ."

Brendan took Roger's arm and pulled him away and down the path, saying, "You can't fight city hall."

Sophie took off past them, her hair flying out behind her, bearing the news to her better half, Jean supposed. She dragged her shoes sideways along the grass, cleaning them off. Her hands were filthy. So were her jeans. Whatever. She turned to Alasdair.

He was actually smiling. "Well done."

"I'd say I aim to please, except it's pretty obvious that I don't."

"Ah no, you made a good point about Roger and his dig, here. He's swotted up on Ambrose's writings."

"Sure he has. But I've read all of Ambrose's books, and nowhere does he say he found a passage grave, let alone where it was. He wouldn't, not if he was getting up to fun and games there. Crowley's 'do what thou wilt' is written on an upright."

"Ambrose's excavating did make it easy to hide a body, then."

"But Roger didn't expect that, did he? It's like he was apologizing to Iris."

"Eh?" Alasdair said encouragingly.

Encouraged, Jean said, "Those papers of Ambrose's that Iris was talking about. What if Roger read them? What if Ambrose not only gave the location of the passage grave but also said Nessie bones were there? Maybe some old bones were why Ambrose came up with the Nessie story to begin with. Vast mythologies have been based on less. Especially with people like Roger filling the pulpits."

"Oh aye."

"I wonder . . ." Jean looked down the hill toward the loch. A tourist boat was heading out of the bay and around the Castle. In the Festival field the pipes and drums played on. Somewhere a horn honked. One of her brain cells clicked over, like a domino falling against its neighbor. "Roger was afraid I was going to expose his past. Maybe the only reason he went out on that limb — and a damned shaky one it is, too — is because he was already out there, blackmailing Iris by threatening to expose Ambrose's past. I mean, most of Ambrose's seamy side's been exposed already, sort of. But the entire Edith and Eileen thing . . . well, if Iris knew her mother's bones were in that grave, she'd never have given him permission to dig there."

Alasdair looked a bit giddy. Leaping after her thoughts took the agility of a mountain goat. He was with her, though, and started to speak, then went to attention.

Jean looked around. Two constables were walking up through the garden. "Duty calls, I see."

"And yours as well."

"I need to stop at the house and make a statement. Yes, I'll take care of it, soon as I clean up."

"I'll come round the Lodge after dinner. You might as well let me in, as I'll be squatting on the step in any event."

She searched his eyes and saw only concern informed by courtesy, nothing to pin either her hopes or fears on. "Come for dinner. I'll throw something together. Sevenish. Whenever you're free."

His minions were tramping up the path. "Aye then. As you wish," he said, and went to meet them.

This had nothing to do with what she wished. And everything. Jean passed the three men, already deep in technical consideration, and headed down the hill.

TWENTY-SIX

Jean stood in the courtyard watching as Alasdair's forensics technicians trooped away, bearing boxes and bags of evidence. The working day was over, then. She glanced at her watch, warily. Seven-thirty p.m.

The official delegation left a temporary fence of orange netting surrounding the excavation and probably scaring the sheep. It shone like a beacon — *there's something interesting up here!* But so far, any attempt by the reporters keeping vigil at the end of the drive to penetrate the fastness of Pitclachie had been repulsed by a flying squad of constables, the same constables who had admitted the various witnesses to the house and ushered them out again after they'd given statements about Tracy's death.

Jean had said her piece without provoking any reaction from Sawyer, who showed as much personality as mud from his post at the windows of the dining room. Did he realize he'd royally teed off his boss? He had to. He was an obnoxious overbearing ego on two legs. He wasn't stupid.

Now the last of the car doors slammed and silence fell over the house and the hillside, broken only by the occasional burst of amplified voices or music from the Festival field. The closing ceremonies, with or without Roger Dempsey at the helm, were under way. The Sunday night ceilidh was still to come, and the cruise tomorrow, but the Midsummer Monster Madness Festival and its unanticipated criminal sideshows were almost over.

Even the constable who'd been standing by the tower door had taken off for parts unknown, Jean noted. Feeling as though she were the last person left on planet Fairbairn, not one of the solar system's more scenic destinations, she went into the Lodge and moved her canvas carryall, laptop, and notebook from the dining table to the coffee table. Yeah, she'd gotten a lot done today. Every time she'd sat down to work on an article, any article, all she could see in the screen was Jonathan's beetling brow, Tracy's carefully outlined lips, the empty eye sockets of the skull. She no longer doubted it was all part of the same intricate pattern, right down to that small dropped stitch that was herself. But she couldn't see the entire design to save her life — and she certainly hoped she wouldn't have to.

Now she set the table with silverware, plates, glasses, and bottles of whiskey and water. The whiskey might help wash down her serving of crow. It might not. Crow wings. Stir-fried crow. Crow and cornbread dressing. Whether Alasdair would listen to her apology, whether he would think her trying to discuss their relationship wildly inappropriate, considering, whether he, too, felt matters had come to a head, murder cases or no murder cases . . . Why were relationships so damned difficult, she wailed silently, and galloped up the stairs, ignoring her sore knee.

The door of the lumber room was still ajar. Every time she'd passed it that afternoon, it had been ajar. She was onto something.

Jean went into the bedroom and changed clothes yet again, from the *Great Scot* T-shirt she'd worn to splash food on, back to the blouse she'd worn with her khaki pants for her day's formal appearances, errands, and reportorial duties . . . What the heck? She caught a glimpse of her bare back in the mirror above the dressing table. A tiny black bump was stuck to her skin just above her waist.

She craned around with her hand mirror and then shuddered in revulsion. She'd picked up a deer tick from the bracken fronds. It had been crawling up her leg and digging in beneath the waistband of her jeans just as she had been crawling into and out of the tomb.

Grabbing a pair of tweezers and leaving her blouse un-tucked, Jean hurried back downstairs and toward the door. She'd go across to the main house and get Kirsty, Iris, Noreen — whichever female she fell over first — to get the blood-sucking beastie off of her.

Her hand was on the doorknob when she heard the voices. Alasdair and Sawyer. She diverted to the front window, where she peeked out from behind the curtain to see the two men standing in the courtyard, their shadows long parallel streaks on the flagstones. Sawyer was holding the laptop beneath his arm. Alasdair was holding Sawyer's attention. His shoulders were back, his chin up, and his forefinger pointed into Sawyer's chest might just as well have been a dirk.

". . . back to Inverness," Alasdair was saying. "You're off the case."

"Here," protested Sawyer, "you can't be giving me the sack over that little pervert Neville . . ."

"D.C. Gunn's no more than a side issue. You had your reasons along with your warning yesterday, and now you're away."

Sawyer's face took on the smirk of a stuffed toad. "While you stay on with your bit of Yank . . ."

"Go on, say it, and you'll find yourself collecting litter bins in Stornoway so fast you'll not have time to pack that bloody great chip on your shoulder."

Sawyer shrank back a step. "I'll file a complaint."

"Be my guest. And hand that laptop in at the local station while you're about it." Alasdair turned away and paced toward the Lodge.

"Boss," Sawyer called after him. His thick features worked, but produced nothing except a squirm of his moustache.

"You've had your second chance," Alasdair shot over his shoulder. "There's no third."

Jean heard Sawyer's ponderous steps thudding away and Alasdair's light steps tapping swiftly nearer. His knock was brisk and businesslike, like his confrontation with Sawyer. She opened the door to see him a bit white around the cheekbones and set around the jaw, but composed. Once he made a decision, then the decision was made. She could do that, too. "Come on in. Ah, I overheard . . ."

"Sorry for having it out below your window."

"I'm just glad there's some justice left in the world." She stepped back so Alasdair could cross the threshold. "I agree Gunn isn't the entire issue, but still — Sawyer calling him 'Nancy' this morning should have tipped me off. What happened? Did Gunn come out of the closet? That took courage."

"Not a bit of it. One of Sawyer's mates saw him coming out of a gay club in Glasgow is all. Like as not the lad's just curious, working things out. But that's his business and none of mine."

"Isn't that the truth?" Jean said. "I saw him talking to Brendan and Kirsty last night. Sawyer said something nasty to him — I can imagine what — but Gunn was doing a great imitation of you."

"Eh?" Alasdair asked.

Great. He was barely in the door and she'd already inserted her foot into her mouth. "You know, ah, coolheaded."

"With a shell, you're meaning." So he, too, remembered his parting shot last month. *Don't go breaking my shell, woman, you might not like what's inside.*

She ducked his scrutiny, suddenly aware she hadn't yet combed her hair or applied lipstick, even more aware of her own awareness. They stood, heads bowed in a moment of silence, but not for the departed Sawyer.

At last Alasdair walked on into the living room. "Are you planning to close the door at all?"

"Oh." Jean waved her tweezers. "That bracken's a launching pad for ticks. One got me. I was going over to the house. I figured Kirsty or Iris was used to dealing with them."

"No one's there. They're all away to their dinners or the Festival. Andy and I were the last rats off the ship. I can phone for a W.P.C. if you like."

"Oh no, there's no reason to drag one of your people up here."

"I'll get it for you, then. Come into the light."

Slowly she shut the door. What did she expect, that he'd let the insect go on injecting God knew what bacteria into her body? No need to let her pendulum swing to the touchy subject of his protecting her. No need to let it swing the opposite way, either, to girly flusterment.

She walked into the glare of the kitchen light and hitched up her blouse. "A policeman's work is never done," she said, and promptly kicked herself for betraying her nervousness with a stupid joke.

Alasdair didn't offer her a dunce cap. He took the tweezers and went down on one knee behind her. "Ah, there's the wee bugger."

His left hand cupped her waist the same way his right hand had cupped the edge of the Stone, gently, almost inquisitively, the smooth cool flesh of his palm against the smooth warm flesh of her torso. His breath on her back made an exquisite tickle. She felt heat mounting into her face and told herself that if ever there was a time to be businesslike, this was it.

The tweezers poked and tugged delicately, surgically. "There you are." Alasdair went outside, ground his foot against the paving stones, and wiped his shoe on the mat. When he came back into the house, he closed and locked the door behind him.

Jean realized she was still holding her blouse bunched up beneath her breasts. Quickly she smoothed it down around her hips. "I've never been so embarrassed in my life."

"Then you've not been trying, have you now?" he returned, but his face was hidden by the shadow of the vestibule and she couldn't see what variety of deadpan he was displaying. "I'd better be washing my hands."

"Just drop the tweezers in the bag by the sink. And while you're up there, take a look at the earrings in Eileen's portrait in the lumber room."

His steps went up the stairs and down the hall. Water ran. No, she thought, she hadn't been trying. Well, she'd been a trial to Brad, she supposed. She was certainly being one to Alasdair.

The footsteps returned down the hall and entered the lumber room. Jean contemplated the cool virtues of salad, wondering if a tomato slice down the back of her neck would help. Maybe she should mourn the summarily executed tick — talk about an ice breaker! She expected to see icebergs bobbing along in Alasdair's wake as he descended the stairs, the sort of innocuous icebergs that had sunk the *Titanic*, and yes, he was his usual self-possessed self. Even though he was now carrying his jacket and his tie over his arm, the top button of his shirt unbuttoned and his sleeves rolled up, exposing a plain, efficient watch wrapping his wrist and a toothbrush emerging from his pocket.

"Nice tie," she said, diverting her gaze from the pale vulnerability of his exposed throat. "Rennie Mackintosh design?"

"Oh aye. Not so's anyone at the cop shop has noticed, mind. Philistines, one and all. Here's a bit antiseptic for the tick bite." He handed over a damp cotton swab, then threw his jacket and tie over the back of a chair.

So he'd dug through her cosmetics bag to find the cotton and anti-septic. Well, it wasn't as though she kept any secrets there. Jean dragged the cotton across her back until the sting told her she'd hit the spot. Wincing, she turned to see Alasdair eyeing the bottle of whiskey.

"A drop of the creature, is it? May I?" At her gesture of assent he poured dollops, added water, offered her a glass, and lifted his. Behind the rim his eyes were aloof. Businesslike. "Here's to us."

"Who's like us?" she responded appropriately.

"Damn few, and they're all . . ." His mouth formed the word "dead" but made no noise except an long exhalation that she had no idea how to interpret.

With a sip that was more fire and air in her mouth than liquid, Jean busied herself getting the food on the table. She never quite looked at Alasdair. She didn't need to. Every one of her nerve endings was aware of him standing at the window, a riddle wrapped in an enigma wrapped in flesh. *Alone at last*, she told herself. It was her move. He didn't give third chances.

One hand was knotted in his pocket. The glass in his other hand glowed amber in the diffused sunlight. His keen face was still as that of the Stone. He said, "'The day has gone down in the west, behind the hills into shadow.'"

She blanked on the next line of Tolkien's poem, but saw her chance. "The shorter versions of all three *Lord of the Rings* movies are on the shelf, there. We could watch one after dinner."

"Oh aye," he returned.

"Sit down. Eat."

With a polite smile that didn't crinkle one corner of his eyes, Alasdair sat down at the demilitarized zone of the table and began to eat.

Jean rearranged her mashed potatoes rather than trying to force them past the knot in her throat "Full disclosure. I didn't make the shepherd's pie. I bought it. I'm sure it's nothing like . . ." She stopped before she said, *your mother used to make*. She didn't want to compare herself to any of the women in his life.

Equally, he piled food onto the back of his fork. "How was your day?"

"I cleaned up, missing the tick, and I checked back with Miranda, so that she wouldn't think I'd been abducted by aliens, and I did the statement thing. I went down to the Festival and hung out with Hugh, and reconfirmed with Kettering that I'm on the list for the cruise tomorrow night."

Alasdair nodded knowingly. "Oh aye, we'll be there as well."

This time "we" meant various official presences. "Then I went shopping. When I got back Roger was wandering around like a stray dog looking for a handout. You could almost count his psychic ribs. How have the mighty fallen. It's sad."

"He'll be allowed back to his dig tomorrow. We've removed all the human bones."

"Is the body Eileen's, do you think?"

Alasdair chewed thoughtfully on a bite of bread, his gaze focused unblinking on Jean's face. Trying to decide how much to tell her, probably. He swallowed and said, "Like as not it is her body, with the evidence of the earring and all, though we found only the one. Other associated artifacts indicate a modern burial as well. The bones appear to be a woman's. Just one thing. I had a good look at the photo in the library, and the one on the chair upstairs, and the only place you're seeing Eileen's left hand is in the portrait."

"Well, yes, she's holding a rose."

"The left forefinger of the skeleton in the passage grave is missing its two end joints. And no, the bones didn't go astray in the tomb. The wound was healed up well before death. Clean cut, the medicos are saying. With a meat cleaver or the like."

Ouch! Jean made a face. "It must have happened after she had the portrait painted. Unless the artist painted her fingertip back in."

"That sort of distinguishing mark's right helpful in identifying a body. DNA tests take weeks. I tried to get onto Iris to ask her — not that she ever knew her mum, mind — but she's away again, to Fort Augustus, Kirsty's saying."

"You need to ask, yes — and if Iris doesn't know, my friend Michael Campbell-Reid's grandmother probably would."

With a nod, Alasdair filed that bit of information in his mental rolodex.

"But why would Eileen be whacking at a joint of meat?" Jean went on. "She was born a princess and married as the lady of the manor. Butcher or cook wasn't in her job description."

"Oh aye, there is that." Alasdair's eye sparked. Okay, Jean wondered, what bright idea was he about to produce, like a rabbit out of hat? "I had a squint at your book as well — aye, it was still in the desk in the library. It has a bit of a pong, doesn't it? Same smell's in the box upstairs, something both sweet and rotten. And the inscription, to 'E,' that's a bit suggestive, eh?"

So that's what he was thinking. Jean gestured with her fork, spearing the rabbit on the upswing. "The woman who was killed and buried could have been Edith, not Eileen. All the earring proves is that Eileen's maid didn't know what she was talking about when she said no jewelry was missing."

His features cracked into a grin, all the more dazzling for being brief. "Got it in one. There's your reason for Eileen running through the shrubbery and also screaming down the stairs."

"Because it's not her screaming down the stairs." In unison, they looked toward the staircase, where each tread mounted innocently and emptily upwards into shadow, and then turned back to each other. "But how can we prove that, Alasdair? For one thing, if Edith is the skeleton, where the heck is Eileen? Did Ambrose kill both of them?"

"Perhaps these papers of his tell the story."

"Roger sure seems to have those papers. Or some of them. Maybe that's what my mysterious prowler was looking for, more papers. The lumber room would be the first place to look. Maybe it wasn't about me at all, and my notebook really did just happen to fall out of my bag."

"The same way Roger just happened to give you a toy complete with a bug?"

"Oh. Well."

"Still, Roger could well have been the prowler. Or Tracy."

Jean looked down at her plate. Once they'd defaulted to discussing the case she'd inhaled her food with good appetite. Without tasting it, particularly, but with good appetite. She thought of the Dempseys arguing over their tea, and wondered if Tracy had tasted anything of what had been her last supper. "Have you learned anything from her body?"

"She died from the fall, no surprise there. She'd taken a drink or two, though not enough to make her drunk. You're sure you saw someone in the tower room with her?"

"Yes, I am. I can see where she might have fallen by accident, but then, wouldn't whoever was there have come running down to see about her?"

"Unless he or she didn't want it known they'd been together."

"Which makes me think of Martin. Does he have an alibi? I think I saw him with Tracy in her hotel room yesterday." Standing up, Jean stacked the plates and carried them to the kitchen sink.

Alasdair appeared at her elbow with the salad bowl and bread basket. "His wife's saying he was with her and the lad. They were awoken by Tracy's scream and he ran to see what happened."

"Can we believe Noreen, though? She's pretty well brow-beaten. In my opinion, of course."

Alasdair inclined his head, admitting her opinion into evidence, and reached for the dishtowel. "The Bouchards were at the ceilidh, aye, and Roger, and the Ducketts were here asleep. Said they were awoken by people shouting and the scream, and they heard someone running down the hall. Which leaves them without a proper alibi, mind."

Jean minded — they seemed like such babes in the woods — but . . .

"Young Brendan was in the bar at the hotel — the barmaid took special notice — and came away here with Roger and Sawyer. You saw Kirsty in the window and the constable on duty saw her in the entrance hall." Alasdair stacked the last plate on the shelf.

Nothing like sharing a domestic task to be companionable. Alasdair had thawed from ice-rimed to merely refrigerated. His drawbridge might be closed, but somebody was home. She could see the movement through his arrow slits and murder holes. "There's a notebook in the tower room with the pages torn out," she said, "That couldn't have been Ambrose's book, could it?"

"It could hardly have been there for seventy years."

"No, no, I mean what if Ambrose's mythical, mystical papers were really a notebook where he kept his field notes or whatever. Maybe that's what Iris wanted Kirsty to hide. Although I don't know what else there could be in those papers — Roger went right to that passage grave. I bet he thinks that's where Ambrose found the treasure, you know, Picts using it as a handy storage dump or something."

Another grin was threatening to smooth the arch of Alasdair's lips, and his expression was askew with bemusement and amusement both. Yeah, she was babbling. Whiskey and nerves.

He didn't babble. He said, "Maybe so, Jean," and spread the towel over the handle of the oven. Without asking her, he refilled their glasses with whiskey and water.

A wee doch and dorris for the road ahead? she asked herself. For the next item on the agenda? The whiskey had already loosened her tongue. Now if she could just avoid tripping over it.

Twenty-seven

Jean retrieved a platter of fruit and cheese from the refrigerator and dumped a few digestive biscuits onto it. "Coffee?"

"No thank you," Alasdair said, strolling across to the TV and DVD player. "I'm thinking it'll be difficult enough sleeping on your couch the night."

"I'm just as likely to be in danger during the day, you know." Jean scooted her books and papers to one end of the coffee table and set the plate down.

Alasdair fed a DVD to the player. "That's as may be, but criminals are a bit like cockroaches, seen off by the light."

"Are you really all that sure I'm in danger?"

"Are you sure you're not in danger? Except from me, that is."

There was a provocative statement. His back was turned to her as he wielded the different remotes, but she tried to read his shoulders, and deduced only that he was neither braced nor relaxed. She should respond with something eloquent and profound about the proximity of danger, death, and destruction, and the benefits of detente . . . Instead, the words spilled out: "Alasdair, I'm sorry, I shouldn't have said what I said last night. It was rude. It was wrong."

"No matter," he replied.

Baloney with mustard. It did matter. Big time. But he wasn't going to make it easy for her. Wiping black feathers from her mouth, Jean switched off the kitchen light and closed the curtains against the long, lingering evening light. The light was on in the upstairs hall — that was enough. The room was enveloped in the tender shadow of dusk, bright enough to tell an apple from a grape, dark enough to blur awkward expressions.

Cate Blanchett's resonant voice sounded from the television. Logically enough, Alasdair was playing the first of the three segments of *The Lord of the Rings.* Jean sat down, not at the opposite end of the couch but not right next to him, either. "Fruit? Cheese?"

"Thank you." He chose a biscuit and a morsel of Orkney cheddar.

They watched the movie from their own individual islands of space — no woman is an island, Jean thought, nor is any man . . . Then she didn't think much of anything, but only felt. The music, the words, the imagery, sent delicious shivers trickling down her limbs — well, that was the fiery fragrance of the whiskey, too, and the sweetness of the fruit, and the saltiness of the cheese, and the crunch of the cookies. And Alasdair's presence, his flesh too solid upon his bones and his energy field licking her like a cat's tongue.

If they spoke at all, it was to comment on individual scenes and debate the adaptation, amiably enough. If they moved it was to offer each other the platter and set down their empty glasses. And yet as the movie reached its climax Jean realized they were sitting close, angled toward each other. When the first arrow hit Boromir, they flinched as one.

Oh no, there she went, her jaw aching and her eyes swimming. The emotions tangled not in her esophagus but in her gut. They whispered of danger and desire, not necessarily danger from anything physical nor desire for it, and yet the physical was there. And it could be snuffed out at any moment, by an arrow, by an explosion, by a fall. "This is ridiculous," she said, and of course her voice wobbled embarrassingly.

"Eh?" asked Alasdair, no doubt thinking she was talking about the movie, where Sam was now floundering in the river, risking his life to reach out in love and hope.

Her eyes still facing front, she said, "We can sit on our own little desert islands, or in our castles with the icicles dripping off the battlements — choose your image — trying to out-stubborn each other. Trying to out-neurosis each other, for that matter. But it's not going to work."

"Ah," he replied, his voice more of a purr than a growl.

"You made it pretty clear last month that I was the danger to you."

"You are that. Although I'm thinking now I was wrong to give you the elbow then."

Wait a minute. She turned her head to see his blue eyes gazing at her steadily but no longer coolly, less ice than melt water, and his mouth set in its ogee curve, carved not in stone but in something more pliable. He was goading her. Moderating the tart words that first came to her, she said, "You didn't break up with me last month. There was nothing to break up."

"You asked me to dinner. I took that as an overture."

"I just wanted to get to know you better."

"You're knowing me better. And I'm knowing you."

She looked around the room for inspiration and saw Aragorn strapping on Boromir's gauntlets, dedicating himself to the task ahead.

You didn't get the cool armor-plated guys until the next movie, the actors who looked so much smaller without the layers of protective gear. If she stripped away Alasdair's armor, broke his shell, chipped him free of ice, dragged his drawbridge open, what would she find? Not something small. Something rich and strange. As for whether she'd like it . . . That was what didn't matter. She could trust him. She might not always like him, but she could trust him. Just as he could trust her.

Jean waited until the credits began to roll, angelic voices singing of love and loss. Then she said, "I've pretty well proved I'm not much good at relationships."

"You've got a better record than I've got. At least you're talking to your ex."

Taking a deep breath that had a slight ragged sound to it, like a stifled sob, Jean said, "Never mind who we were in the past, with other people. This is you and me. Now."

He didn't reply. He didn't move.

She looked around at his grave, still face, now gazing past her, past the television, past the walls of the cottage. Her heart bungeed down into her knotted abdomen, then bounced up into her throat. "Alasdair?"

He didn't turn toward her brandishing a crucifix, or his warrant card, for that matter, reminding her that he was a cop on a case and she was no more than an associated artifact. He smiled, his lips wry, his eyes rueful. "We've been setting out the rules of engagement, I'm thinking, and the provisions of the treaty. Could we make the running together?"

"It's worth a try."

"Oh aye, I reckon it is that." His hand landed gently on her shoulder and moved up so that his thumb traced her jaw and his fingertips brushed the back of her neck, the spot activated by her sixth sense. Now her usual senses detonated — rock-steady flesh, the aura of sun-warmed grain, the catch in his own breath. A thrill fizzed through her body as though her blood had carbonated. *Oh my . . .* "Mind," he went on, "it's not the done thing to seal this sort of agreement with a handshake."

"I should hope not." She took off her glasses and set them aside, and laid her palms flat on his chest so that his heartbeat reverberated up her arms and matched her own. She leaned toward him as he leaned toward her, like pilots searching for a safe port in the fog — although which was the pilot, and which the rocks she couldn't say and didn't care.

Their lips met, tentatively. Her thought evaporated like whiskey in her throat. *Oh my, oh yes, oh . . .* Tentative became firm became mutually invasive, a delicate teasing and twining, then a full-bodied exploration, then delicate again, so that sparks danced behind Jean's eyes and tremors ran delightfully up and down her limbs and her chest burned — okay, it was probably oxygen deprivation, so what. She hadn't expected, anticipated, dreaded a quick chaste peck, but this was . . . *Oh my.*

At last she found her arms wrapped around Alasdair's torso, his arms locked around her, her cheek squashed against his collar, seemingly swapping the same breath back and forth. His chest was rising and falling as though he'd run a race. His face was pressed against her hair and she could feel his lips moving somewhere around her temple. *Please don't get regretful,* she pleaded silently. *Please don't make it all seem foolish. Just hold me, now, for the moment.*

He didn't say anything. He held her. She'd never thought his taut body could actually yield, surrender to such an embrace, but there he was, and there she was . . . Somewhere behind the piping of her blood in her ears, the drumming of his heart in his chest, and the music still flowing from the DVD, she heard another rhythm. Footsteps, walking down the upper hallway.

Slowly Jean extracted herself from Alasdair as he extracted himself from her. They exchanged a careful, questioning look footnoted with exasperation, and turned toward the staircase just as the voices began to speak.

The woman said, each word clear as a whiskey glass etched with thistles and heather, "You've got no heart, Ambrose, and no stomach either. You're playing the laird, with right of pit and gallows and all, and I'm no more than a sheep to you."

The man's voice, like his daughter's, was trained in proper English. "How impertinent! I'm caring for you, as is my duty, and you throw my family name in my face."

"Ah, this for your family name! And your duty as well. You dinna care, not for her, not for me, only for him, the Devil take him and good luck to them both!"

Alasdair's shoulder against Jean's stiffened as she tensed against him. She didn't need her glasses to see the shadows of two people extending along the staircase, their feet thumping quickly down the steps to the landing. She was in the lead — thick-heeled shoes, a sack-like dress, long reddish-gold hair frilling over her shoulders, a square face. She turned back to the lantern-jawed man in his three-piece suit, who stopped on the step behind and above her. "A divorce, I'm thinking, there's grounds right enough."

"How dare you?" he retorted, and lifted his hand as though to strike her.

She dodged, and lost her balance on the narrow step. For a long breathless moment she seemed to hang in mid-air, resisting gravity, both her expression and his changing with exaggerated slowness from anger to surprise to terror. Ambrose grabbed for her hand, too late.

She screamed, a short sharp outraged shriek that made both

Alasdair and Jean jerk back. She fell. Her body crashed from step to step and against the balusters, limbs jerking every which way, and landed at the foot of the staircase in a heap, a very still heap, like a puzzle of clothing and body parts disassembled by some giant hand. Blood trickled from beneath the bright hair and over the flagstones of the floor, past the splayed left hand with its shortened forefinger.

"Oh God, no, no, God, no!" Ambrose howled, and ran down the stairs.

The front door flew open and the velvet curtain whisked aside — or the shadows of the door and curtain, rather, like shapes in smoke against the actual objects. And a second woman stood there, her flowered skirts settling around her dainty form, a scarf clutched in her petite hand, her bobbed dark hair framing a sharp face struck with horror. Her gaze moved from the broken body to Ambrose's trembling form. And her expression segued from horrified to something sly and fox-like.

They were gone, all three of them. The velvet curtain stood open, the door was shut and locked, and the staircase gaped like an empty gullet. The aroma of perfume, of coffee and smoke, of blood, of age and mortality, filled the room and then dissipated.

With a cough, Jean exhaled both the odor and the breath she just now realized she'd been holding. She subsided against Alasdair. "You were right. Edith is the one who died. Eileen was outside, in the summerhouse, maybe, heard her fall and came rushing in to see what had happened."

"Oh aye." Alasdair's body was stiff, withdrawn into itself, no longer yielding to her touch. His arm wrapping Jean's shoulders seemed affectionate and yet perfunctory.

"I should have noticed the first time I heard the rhythm of their voices. It was like hearing Jonathan and Brendan talking. I could tell their accents were different without hearing the actual words. Ambrose spoke Oxford English. Eileen was American. Edith was a Scot."

"You were hearing what you expected to hear. Like seeing Nessie."

"But ghosts can't give testimony. They're not evidence."

"Edith's body needs identifying, right enough. Proof she, not Eileen, was missing a finger."

"And some reason why she was wearing Eileen's earrings."

"Earring. One"

"Whatever. Damn it, every time we get an answer to one question, we get five other ones. Like who's the 'he' Edith was throwing in Ambrose's face. Crowley? And what happened to Eileen?"

"She gave up on a bad marriage." Alasdair's hand grasped Jean's shoulder almost too tightly for comfort. The crease between his brows indicated deep thought, and not, she bet, thought entirely about the case.

Loosening his grip, Jean tucked her hand inside his. Her lips felt bruised from the urgency of their kiss. That was a *fait accompli* — a faint accompli, whew — a commitment, even if the unearthly echo of Edith's voice had re-introduced issues of caring, condescension, and marriage gone sour.

The television screen went blank and the speakers fell silent. Outside, a breeze rustled the leaves on the trees. Distant laughter stirred the eternal twilight. "Alasdair," Jean said, "part of the deal here is that we have to talk to each other."

With a ghost of a smile, evoking things past, things present, things yet to come, he laid his cheek on the top of her head. "And part of the bargain is that we're obliged to listen, is that it?"

"That's it," she said, and settled down in the security of his arms.

TWENTY-EIGHT

Once again the sound of footsteps stirred Jean's sleep. She opened her eyes and stared at the ceiling. She'd had the strangest dream . . . It wasn't a dream, she realized with a rush of adrenalin that made her cheeks burn. She and Alasdair really had — what was the pop-culture expression? Taken their relationship to a higher level?

Just admitting they had a relationship, let alone exchanging a passionate kiss and some frank conversation to prove it, had taken them to nose-bleed heights. Playing tortoises rather than hares, ants rather than grasshoppers, suited their emotional phobias. In six months or so they might actually work their way to erogenous zones below the shoulders.

Smiling, Jean climbed out of the bed and opened the drapes. A gauzy curtain of mist flirted with the surface of the loch. Whether those billows beyond it were clouds or mountains she couldn't say — they looked like the same substance, neither earth nor air. "The Misty Mountains of Home" was one of those evocative old songs she'd always liked. Home was more than a building, wasn't it? Home was where the heart was, and right now her heart, for better or worse, was downstairs asleep on the couch.

No, she corrected as she heard the sounds from the kitchen, he was making coffee, bless the man for having domestic skills. It was his quiet steps past her door, to the bathroom and back, that had awakened her.

Padding into the hall, she noticed that the door of the lumber room was now wide open. Alasdair must have shut it after he'd checked on the pictures last night. When she'd finally gone to bed, long after midnight, she wouldn't have noticed that door if it had flung itself off its hinges and onto her feet. Her senses had still been humming from Alasdair's touch, her ears still satiated by his voice. Their exchanges about seeing ghosts, their childhoods, their work—-but not their marriages—-had proved that the physical was only half of intimacy.

It had been time well-spent, she thought, and peered at herself in the bathroom mirror. Still, she could tell by the dark circles cushioning her glassy eyes that she'd stayed up way too late for two nights in a row. Make-up? Well, just a bit of mascara. If Alasdair was frightened away by her bed-headed face, then he was made of weaker stuff than she thought.

Jean walked downstairs, wondering how to greet him. If she threw herself into his arms, would he disclaim all knowledge of last night's alliance and offer her only his name, rank, and serial number?

He was leaning on the cabinet with a resigned air, probably telling himself that a watched toaster oven never toasts. At her step he looked around, considered her awkward smile, and finally returned a lopsided smile of his own, the crease in one cheek deeper than the other. *What a revealing development this is.* With that mutual smile, his drawbridge squealed open by several more rusty links, and the Gordian knot of her nerves broke a few more strands.

"So far so good," Jean said.

"We've survived a whole nine hours or so together," agreed Alasdair, and glanced at the toast. Since he'd turned his back on it, it was starting to char. They bumped elbows retrieving it, and between them managed to get the toast, butter, jam, and coffee onto the table.

"Did you sleep well? I thought I heard the footsteps a time or two." Jean nodded toward the velvet curtain, now pulled across the vestibule.

"You did that. They were up and down all the night long. But policemen are like doctors, they learn to sleep when they can."

"No one living tried to get in, anyway, although I suppose that doesn't prove anything."

"Not a thing." Alasdair crunched his toast, to the accompaniment of Mozart . . .

Oh. After a brief scramble, Jean found her bag beneath the coffee table and fished out her phone. The tiny screen was illuminated with the legend "Michael Campbell-Reid."

"Michael! How are you? How's Rebecca?"

It was Rebecca's voice that replied. "I'm just fine, thank you. Sitting up in an uncomfortable hospital bed and wishing they'd hurry up and let me take Linda home."

"That's where it gets really fun, I hear." Jean spared one second's thought for her own very brief pregnancy, back in the distant deeps of time. It hadn't lasted long enough for her to start seriously researching issues of childbirth, let alone baby homecomings.

"You should see her, Jean. Eight pounds, a little Amazon."

"I can't wait. I guess she's got all her fingers and toes and everything?" From the corner of her eye Jean saw Alasdair look up sharply. *Policemen!* she thought. "How's Michael?"

"Standing here teeming with information. He's been to work and back already this morning, just to amaze and gratify you with his research. Here he is."

Michael's voice said, "Good morning, Jean. I saw the headlines about Mrs. Dempsey. Dreadful, that. I hope you're watching your back."

"It's being watched," Jean said.

"I handed the bug from the Nessie in to the police here yesterday, and they've sent it up to your D.C.I. Cameron in Drumnadrochit. Bit of luck, him being on the case again, eh?"

"I prefer to think of it as fate."

"You wanted the name of the mason who uncovered the Pit-clachie Stone whilst working for Ambrose," Michael went on. "Turns out to be a chap named Gordon Fraser."

"Gordon Fraser found the Stone?" That took the wind out of Jean's sails. She ran aground on the couch. Alasdair, brows on full alert, stopped pretending not to listen and sat down beside her. She tilted the phone so he could hear.

"What's right interesting," Michael went on, "is that according to the report, the Stone wasna broken when he found it. There's a drawing of it on file — above that double disc was a gripping beast crossed by a Z-shaped line, a Z-rod. The hole was there already, why, no one knows."

So Roger was right about the missing pictograph being a gripping beast. Pretty damn good guess, that. "But you have nothing about it being dropped when they moved it or anything?"

"Not a word. As for the silver chain the Museum was offered last year, a dealer in Paris was trying to get up an auction for it, but we couldn't compete. He claimed the chain was from the Great Glen, then admitted he'd bought a job lot of goods at an estate sale in London and there it was, Pictish and genuine, but no provenance at all."

Feeling as though fate was playing the old shell game with her, Jean repeated, "A dealer in Paris? His name is Charles Bouchard, isn't it?"

"Oh aye, that it is. Friend of yours?"

"He and his wife are here, probably hoping to grab up whatever Pictish artifacts Roger Dempsey uncovers."

"Dempsey's gone from searching for the monster to searching for artifacts, has he?"

"Yes and no. What he's done is uncover a passage grave, just up the hill behind the house. So far, all he's found there are bones, some of them human. We think . . ." Alasdair's elbow landed sharply in her ribs. "We think the police will identify who it is fairly soon now."

"Surely it's Eileen," said Michael.

"Well," Jean replied, her own elbow nudging Alasdair back again, "did your granny ever say anything about Eileen missing part of her left forefinger?"

"Not that I can recall, no. You're not meaning . . ." He was interrupted by the delicate piping cry of a newborn baby. Rebecca's voice crooned a response. Michael said to Jean, "You'll be telling us all about it soon. We're holding Dougie hostage 'til you do, right enough. Must run."

"Hug the baby for me," Jean said, and clicked off the phone.

Beside her Alasdair was sitting to attention. "Gordon Fraser found the Stone?"

"That's the name of the mason who uncovered it when Ambrose had the Lodge moved up here from the road. It can't be the book dealer, he's elderly, but he sure wasn't an adult in the nineteen-twenties."

"Even so, the name Fraser keeps turning up, doesn't it now? The mason. The dealer. Edith. Did your Fraser say anything that might could connect him to Edith?"

"No, but he was saying that Ambrose was too much like Crowley when it came to women, and I'm thinking now he didn't mean as a babe magnet. Maybe he meant when it came to women meeting premature and nasty ends. But he wouldn't know about Edith. Or Eileen."

Or would he? Alasdair's eyebrows asked.

"He was telling me some lurid stories about Crowley, his butcher severed an artery and — oh my."

"There's someone with a meat cleaver for you."

"We're onto something." She was getting mighty free and easy with that "we," Jean told herself, but if Alasdair had a problem with that, he'd let her know. She dug through her bag. "Here you go, Fraser's card. He's in Fort Augustus. Kirsty was telling me that Fraser had no use for Iris, but . . ."

"Damn and blast! Why weren't you telling me this yesterday, Jean?"

"What?"

"Iris was away to Fort Augustus last night. If I could have had a word with them separately! By now they've compared their stories, synchronized their watches, and sung the same chorus of 'Will Ye No Come Back Again!'" He stood up, lunged toward his jacket draped over the chair, and yanked his own phone from an inside pocket.

"You don't know Iris went to see Fraser," Jean retorted, and added indignantly, "What did you expect me to do, foretell the future?"

"Hello? Is that D.C. Gunn? Get on to Fort Augustus. I want Gordon Fraser, the book dealer, collected and brought here." Alasdair extended his hand. Like a nurse assisting at an operation, Jean placed the card in it. "Highland Books and Maps. Aye, that's it. Good man."

She assumed Gunn was the good man, not Fraser, whose reputation was open to discussion at the moment.

Alasdair thrust his phone into his pocket and his arms into his jacket. He started toward the door, then whirled back around, suddenly recalled to a different duty. "Jean, sorry about that . . ."

This is a test, she told herself. *It's only a test.* Besides, he was probably right about Iris and Fraser, circumstances making strange bedfellows and everything. "It's all right. Go on, I'll hang around here. Maybe I'll find that little hank of yarn that connects all of this into one story."

"We're getting to it," he told her, and with a swift kiss that missed her lips to land on her cheek, he pushed past the curtain and slammed through the door.

She stood listening to his receding steps, then shook her head. Yep, this was going to be interesting, and she didn't mean only the resolution of the case. She pitched the dishes into the sink, then gathered up her computer and papers. Taking them upstairs, she stowed them in her wardrobe. A quick pit-stop for toothpaste and lipstick, and to check that the site of the tick incursion was healing properly, and she was ready to go — do what? Make waves, she supposed.

The door to the lumber room was now shut. Inside, something was making a scratching sound. A mouse? Warily, Jean opened the door and peeked into the shadowed room. A sudden movement at the window made her leap as though she'd been shocked, then laugh. She could see the shape of the bird perched on the outside sill through the gap between the shutters. Poe's raven, no doubt, coming home to roost.

Her nostrils dilated. What was the smell in that room, anyway, over and beyond the scent of mildew? It was the same cloying sweet smell that clung to the book, and to the objects in the desk in the library. The smell of perfume that had accompanied the ghostly re-enactment of Edith's fall?

She should ask Miranda what posh perfume had been dabbled behind wealthy ears in 1933. Roses, she thought with another sniff. Distilled roses, spilled and then spoiled. But there was something spicy, too, like the first whiff of a National Trust shop with its pot-pourri, or even a New Age shop with its . . . "Incense," she said aloud. That's what she'd been smelling all along, not pipe tobacco. Incense.

Jean's gaze moved from Eileen's painted, impassive face to the plaster ceiling with its smudges of what had to be smoke. Candle smoke. Incense smoke. What had Ambrose been doing, staging occult ceremonies? Or simply burning incense as inspiration for his wilder theories, like an earlier generation would have drunk absinthe or smoked opium?

Was that the door opening downstairs? The ghosts must be at it again, in broad daylight this time. Talk about her and Alasdair making a critical mass!

Jean walked downstairs. She was glancing guiltily at the dishes piled in the sink as she reached out to shove the curtain back on its rod. Still holding a handful of thick velvet, she turned toward the door and saw that she wasn't alone.

By sheer force of will, Jean stopped herself from leaping backwards yet again. She stood with her hand on her chest, cramming her heart back behind her ribs, looking down at the small boy and the cat. "Elvis," she managed to say. "How did you get in?"

Oblivious to the sensation he'd caused, Elvis kept on stroking Mandrake's sleek back. "The moggie pushed the door open. Listen, he's making a funny sound."

"Yeah, he's purring up a storm." The cat was smirking so smugly he'd probably orchestrated the entire episode. Not only had Alasdair not locked the door, he hadn't even left it properly shut. She could flatter herself that he'd decided she could take care of herself, but she suspected the paragon of protocol had simply made a mistake. She wouldn't be mentioning it to him.

"Let's go on outside," she said, shooing both child and cat onto the terrace and making sure this time the door was locked.

The mist was starting to burn off. Wraith-like tendrils wafted upward from loch and land, toward a sky veiled with silver that would soon, Jean estimated, turn blue. And hot. Not one breath of wind stirred the flowers and the trees. The humid air pressed close around her, seeming to muffle the voices of Elvis's parents.

Noreen and Martin were standing at the edge of the terrace, he hulking over her, she crouched defensively. They weren't so much talking as hissing to each other. Jean recognized those tones, the spat that couldn't wait for a private venue.

". . . and me no more than a bit on the side?" Noreen was saying.

"That's not how it was. It was for all of us," Martin replied. "She could have gotten me a fellowship. Do you want to work in a motorway café the rest of your life?"

"A fellowship, is it? Last year it was a teaching post. The year before that . . ."

Elvis tried to pick up the cat. Mandrake slithered through his hands like a ferret and ran for the shrubbery, Elvis on his tail.

Martin's long arm swept Noreen aside and seized the back of the boy's *I'm a Wee Monster from Loch Ness* T-shirt. "Let's walk up to the dig, lad, have us a look at the Nessie bones. Mummy's not feeling well. Mummy's going to have a lie-down." And, as he turned and saw Jean standing outside the door of the Lodge, "Mummy should have been looking after you."

"I was watching him," Noreen said. "He only stepped inside for a bleeding minute. She's right friendly with that detective, isn't she? He came out the door not half an hour ago. It didn't hurt nothing letting the boy go inside there. It's a safer place than the house for him."

Martin gave Noreen a look of pity and contempt mingled. Jean expected him to use Ambrose's "impertinent!" but he merely took Elvis's hand and started off toward the garden, his manner changing to patient indulgence as quickly as a traffic light changed from red to green.

Noreen looked toward Jean, shamefaced but stubborn. "Tell your policeman that me and the boy, we need to get away from this place. We need to go home. I'll lose my job, Martin will . . ." She blundered toward the house.

No point in saying that Alasdair wasn't *her* policeman. They weren't exactly making a public spectacle of themselves, but the clues were there for anyone to see. As for Noreen . . . "He knows you want to go home," Jean called after her. "He can't let you go until he finds out who blew up the boat and who pushed Tracy Dempsey out of the tower."

Noreen's steps faltered. She looked back. Some impulse seemed to swell in her face and then die, and wordlessly she went on into the house.

She could have gotten me a fellowship. Tracy had promised Martin some sort of pie in the sky job in return for helping her — do what? Cover up the submersible disaster? Send the threatening letters? The Halls had stayed at Pitclachie in April. Martin could have picked up the notepaper. And the old corkscrew, for that matter, assuming the Dempseys themselves blew up the boat.

Jean didn't believe for a minute Tracy had any personal interest in Martin. Still, there was another triangle, like Ambrose, Edith, and Eileen's. Would it be better to have a man not do his duty by you if by doing it he felt entitled to treat you like a mentally defective rat? And what duty did Ambrose owe to Edith, anyway? Was she his mistress, or simply a feisty employee who helped herself to the lady of the manor's earrings?

As though evoked by Jean thinking those names, Iris paced around the corner like a sentry at the changing of the guard. She was carrying a basket containing a pair of knitting needles and some balls of off-white wool yarn, the color and texture of the cardigan she was wearing. "Good morning," she said. If her words had been any more formal, they would have been wearing little black ties.

"Good morning." Jean fell oh-so-casually into step beside her. "Do you have a moment, Miss Mackintosh? I'd like to ask a few more questions for my article about you and your father's interests."

"I'm sure you would, Miss Fairbairn. Especially in the light of recent events. However, you'll please excuse me if I say . . ." she stopped in front of the tower door, pulled a key from her pocket, unlocked the door, and stepped inside "No comment." The door shut in Jean's face and the tumblers of the lock turned.

Well, she couldn't blame the woman for that. She could be irritated and impatient, but she couldn't blame. Jean craned her neck, the same way Martin had done. Iris's tall, neo-classical shape appeared in the window from which Tracy had fallen. A quick double flash was the metal tips of her knitting needles catching the light. She hadn't stationed herself looking out over the loch but up the hill. Jean wondered not whether but when Alasdair would turn up present-dimensional evidence proving that that the body in the tomb wasn't Iris's mother after all.

Not that that would mitigate the situation. Technically speaking, Ambrose hadn't gotten away with murder, but with manslaughter. Jonathan's death would probably come under the heading of manslaughter, too. As for Tracy's death, well . . . Jean walked through the garden and up the hillside, thinking that it was too much to either hope or fear the perpetrator had already fled the area. No, among her acquaintances here at Pitclachie was someone — or several someones — capable of killing.

Martin and Elvis were kibitzing as Brendan toiled inside the orange-netted boundary zone. A couple of royal blue tarps had been added to the color scheme. The austere Scots pines in the glade just beyond the excavation seemed to be pulling their skirt-branches away in disdain.

As Jean drew closer, she saw twenty or so angular brown lumps, the animal vertebrae from the tomb chamber, spread out on one of the tarps in a line longer than she was tall. At its end rested a small skull like that of a greyhound. Several other brownish chunks, along with a camera and other bits of electronic equipment, lay on the second tarp. Charles and Sophie sat nearby, wiping, assessing, and placing the occasional item into a plastic bag or cardboard box. They were the seagulls following the archaeological plow and picking over the remains.

Brendan sat on the side of the trench, mopping his pink-suffused face with a bandanna. He, no doubt, had removed the sill of dirt half-blocking the entrance passageway. Roger came crawling out of its dark maw, dragging a plastic bag behind him, blithely ignoring the finer points of archaeological procedure. Ambrose had had an excuse for his vandalism, Jean thought. Roger didn't.

Roger flailed a bit, then with a groan managed to climb out of the hole. His Water Horse T-shirt was grimy and sweat-stained, and the bandages on his arms were gray rather than hospital white, clashing with the red scratches and pink splashes of lotion on his nettle stings. He had definitely gotten the worst of the hit-and-run.

But as he turned toward Jean, she could see a glint in his eyes indicating flint in his soul. *This makes it all worth while*, he'd said yesterday, with a touch of his old devil-may-care spirit. Now he looked devil-possessed. "Hi, Jean," he said, baring his fangs in a smile.

"Hi. How's it going? Any breaking news?"

Roger made an expansive gesture over his array of bones, a priest blessing his congregation. "Kettering's sending a photographer. I told him I'll make the announcement during tonight's cruise. I can't promise you an exclusive, Jean, I mean, Starr's been very helpful with funding and all, but look at those vertebrae, they're the classic Nessie profile with the long prehensile neck and the small skull — horsy, isn't it? And we're picking up the bone fragments that have to be fins. This will be the story of the century. The bones of the Loch Ness monster, proving that the stories are true. You'll be in on it from the get-go."

In exchange for being in on it, Roger would expect her to follow his script. Jean cast her gaze right and left, from Sophie and Charles's disdainful sniffs to Brendan's dubious shrug. Martin's mouth hung open. Elvis clung to his father's hand, eyes huge. There had to be some logical explanation for those bones, but no one was raining on Roger's parade with it. Yet.

"They worshiped them," Roger went on. "The Picts, that is, they worshiped the Nessie population. That's what the whole story of St. Columba is about, driving away the old pagan Nessie religion. That old guy from Foyers, whose grandmother warned him about the loch, that just goes to show you how long memories last here. The Nessie cult must have been active for centuries. See, there are some little plaque things. Offerings." He pointed toward Sophie, who was holding a small and scabrous metal plaque between thumb and forefinger, like a worm.

"Thanks." Jean was about to start asking some rather pointed questions about Roger's sources of information and inspiration when her cell phone rang. She fished it out of her bag. *Whoa! Alasdair!* She retreated down the path, out of earshot. "Hello again."

"Come down by the station, Jean, Gordon Fraser's just arriving."

"That was fast."

"The lads stopped by his shop as he was opening up."

"I'm on my way." Stuffing the phone back into her bag, Jean shot one last dubious glance at Roger and another at the camera-laden figure just emerging from the garden path. Up the garden path was where Roger was leading them all. It had to be.

The mist evaporated into a clean-washed blue sky. The loch shone blue in the sunlight, each slow swell viscous as Jell-O. A large boat — or small ship, nautical nomenclature not being Jean's area of expertise — was gliding into Urquhart Bay. Strings of colored flags rippled lazily fore and aft. Ah, yes, the evening cruise. Alasdair would have everything up to and including a SWAT team inspecting that boat for combustibles. Pity the steward who tried to flambé a dessert.

The sunlight intensified the humidity and, in just the few hundred yards between the excavation and the house, Jean started to ooze sweat. Even in the tree-shaded parking area the air was so heavy with the scent of mud and vegetation she expected to see serpents dripping from the trees. Instead, a cloud of midges descended upon her like micro-miniature vampire bats and she launched into the midgie jig, a version of St. Vitus's dance.

Roger's van was squeezed up against her car. She couldn't begin to open the driver's side door wide enough to climb in, so she went around to the other side, next to the Bouchard's Renault. Its pale gold coat had been dulled by rain and run-off to nickel.

Just as she opened her passenger door, Dave and Patti Duckett burst around the side of the house and jogged toward their own car. Dave was unlocking its doors by the time Jean called, "Hello!"

"Oh!" Patti almost stumbled. "Oh, hello."

Jean winced. Yeah, we're all nervy. And the midges didn't make for a leisurely chat. "Sorry to startle you. Off for a drive?"

"Mailing some things home," said Dave. "Overweight baggage fees, you know." He took a bulging shopping bag from Patti's hand and threw it in the back seat, where it spilled clothing and small objects, including a toothbrush.

"See you later." Patti barely got her door shut before Dave started the car and peeled off down the drive, scattering gravel like buckshot. He would have run down a reporter lurking by the road if one of the constables stationed there hadn't dragged him away. The car turned north, toward Inverness. Surely the closest post office would be in Drumnadrochit . . .

A toothbrush. Funny how indicative toothbrushes could be. And mailing a shopping bag? Yeah, right. The Ducketts were doing a midnight — er, midday — flit. Running away. Like Martin, they couldn't look any guiltier if they tried.

Apparently the constable agreed. He was already talking into his radio by the time Jean drove by, taking a dozen or so midges on a brisk ride to the police station.

TWENTY-NINE

Jean burst through the doorway of the little police office. Alasdair half rose from his barricade behind the desk and tucked his phone into his shoulder. "The Ducketts are away," he told her.

"Yeah, I saw. Their car is something dark green and bigger than my Focus, and there's a five in the license number."

"Very helpful," he told her, and put his phone back to his ear. "North on the A82, aye. No, don't go chasing them down, stop them at an intersection."

It would have been entertaining to get a jump on Alasdair, but she had to admit that getting a jump on the Ducketts was more important. At least she'd called his attention to them to begin with. Jean seated herself on a plastic chair out of the line of fire, next to D.C. Gunn and his notebook. He was already in his shirtsleeves, ready for action and almost suppressing his grin — Sawyer was exhilaratingly conspicuous by his absence. Alasdair would be shocked if she and Gunn high-fived each other, though, so Jean offered him a friendly smile.

From the incident room next door came a low hum of activity, almost drowned out by the hum of activity from Alasdair's brain. Somehow he'd found time since he left the Lodge to shave and put on a clean shirt, plus a different tie, this one with little figures on it that looked suspiciously like dragons. He seemed less drawn and pale than he had yesterday morning, due perhaps to his progress on fronts both public and personal.

He switched off his phone and lifted a plastic bag containing a small metallic object, like half a ballpoint pen, from the desk. "Here's your listening device. Your bug. No Omnium trademark, more's the pity. I'll be having a word with Roger directly."

Jean's smile evaporated. "Yeah, you and me both. The nerve of the man. I wasn't any threat to him."

"Right," Alasdair said, with no more than a hint of skepticism. He set the bag down and closed the cover of a file folder lying in front of him. "Crime scene reports. We've got a couple of items from the tower room that look to be interesting, a scrap of plastic and a knitting needle. The trace evidence reports haven't come along yet."

The outer door opened and a constable ushered in Gordon Fraser. His glance around the room missed nothing. His gray eyebrows were so thick and heavy they were set in a perpetual frown, which deepened when he registered Jean's presence. His granite-domed head, square granite jaw, and sharp granite shoulders reminded her of an ambulatory Easter Island statue.

Alasdair stood up and extended his hand. "Chief Inspector Cameron, Mr. Fraser. I'm in charge of investigating the recent deaths here in Drumnadrochit. Please, sit down."

Fraser shook hands, his huge hand engulfing Alasdair's merely large one, and sat down in the straight-backed wooden chair. It squeaked a protest. "My shop needs seeing to, Chief Inspector. I gave my assistant a day out, with him working all the weekend whilst I was at the Festival."

"We'll be taking you back to your shop soon as you help us with our inquiries."

"I wish I could help, but I've got nothing for you."

"That's for me to decide, Mr. Fraser," Alasdair said in his menacing yet mild manner. "You were born and raised in this area, were you?"

Gunn began to write. Jean leaned forward, the better to listen, to observe, to counsel and comment when the time came.

"That I was," Fraser answered. "In Foyers."

"Near Aleister Crowley's house at Boleskine, then."

"He was long gone from the area by the time I was born, and good riddance to him."

"You were telling Miss Fairbairn here that Crowley raised demons. That people went mad and suffered accidents when he was about. But you say you weren't seeing any of this for yourself?"

"My mother and her mother, they raised me up to fear God and walk righteously. They warned me off folk like Crowley and those telling tales of the loch as well."

Jean half rose from the chair and sat herself back down. Roger's old guy from Foyers. She was looking at him.

Alasdair caught her reaction, even though he had no way short of ESP — which she wouldn't put past him — of knowing what had produced it. "By 'those telling tales of the loch' do you mean Ambrose Mackintosh?"

"He was right daft. Not wicked, not like Crowley, but daft."

"You knew him, then?"

Fraser shifted his weight, the chair creaking piteously. Gunn turned a page. Jean held her breath. At last the man said, "He was a bit of a kenspeckle figure in the district, known by all."

"But not liked by all?"

"You're known by the company you keep, Chief Inspector. You're known by the fruit of your work. Ambrose was a fine scholar, a decent man in some ways, but well off his head in others."

Alasdair lifted and then let fall the cover of the file folder. "Your father was a stone mason who worked for Ambrose."

"Aye, he was that," Fraser replied without surprise — he didn't know Alasdair hadn't had time to actually check him out. "I worked with him for some years, then on my own, conservation and restoration work, mostly."

"Your father turned up the Pitclachie Stone."

"Oh aye. A pagan stone, he said. Just the thing for a pagan like Ambrose."

Most people, Jean reflected, would have asked what the heck the Pitclachie Stone had to do with the recent deaths. But no. Fraser had been warned.

"Was your father the only member of your family to have dealings with Ambrose?"

Fraser hadn't exactly been slumping, but at that he sat up a little straighter. Jean couldn't see his face, but from the clenching of his shoulders she deduced an internal struggle. Alasdair waited, his hands folded on the desk in front of him, not looking away, not even blinking.

Fraser said, "No. My aunt, my father's sister, worked at Pitclachie."

"Edith."

"How do you . . . Ah. You've read up on Ambrose's trial, have you?"

"Your aunt disappeared just as surely as Mrs. Mackintosh did do, but no one inquired after her," Alasdair went on. "Why not?"

Fraser didn't reply. His shoulders rose toward his ears and his massive hands clenched into clubs on his lap. The room was so quiet that Jean could hear Gunn breathing, and the voices and footsteps of people on the sidewalk outside, and the low rumble and cough of a passing bus. She was starting to sweat against the plastic chair — two small windows did nothing to keep the room from being still and close and hot. Alasdair, though, was wrapped in his cool professional shell.

Fraser was beginning to sweat, too. At last his shoulders relaxed, and his hands opened and his gnarled fingers spread out on his thighs. Decision made, Jean thought, and sat back with a glance at Gunn. His pencil was poised.

"You're known by the company you keep," Fraser said, his voice as deep a rumble as that of the bus, dragged out of his depths. "Mind, I never knew Edith, save as a cautionary tale whispered about the fire on a Sunday evening. She was first at Pitclachie in nineteen-nineteen, as scullery maid. Respectable work that, no shame in it. Then Crowley came to visit. He had an eye for the ladies, he did, and promised her clothes and jewels and adventure. Away she went with him, to the Continent and to God in his heaven knows what sorts of evil doings. And that after maiming her for life."

"Maiming her?" Alasdair asked, with a glance at Jean.

"Another so-called accident. She was cutting a joint of venison and struck off her forefinger. My father said 'twas God's judgment for her impure thoughts, but I'm thinking 'twas Crowley."

"And your family disowned her when she went away with him?"

"She fell into sin, forsaking her proper upbringing to follow the Beast."

"But your father went to work for Ambrose even so."

"He was feeding six bairns — I'm the seventh — and the two grannies as well, then. When Ambrose made his apologies fair enough, asked that bygones be bygones, and offered a steady wage, well . . . Edith was dead to the family. As a lad I was thinking she was genuinely dead and in the ground, be it sanctified ground or no."

"But she came back to the area in nineteen thirty-two and Ambrose took her in."

"Felt guilty, like as not, more credit to him."

Alasdair's gaze darted to Jean and back again to Fraser. She knew he was hearing Ambrose's ghostly voice saying, *I'm caring for you, as is my duty.*

"He was daft, right enough, but not so wicked as Crowley," Fraser insisted. "Crowley, he raised demons, and I reckon one took Edith. My father did his best with the pagan stone and all, but there was no help for her."

Alasdair was inhaling for the next question. Jean made a cramped time-out signal in her lap. Gunn looked over curiously, which reminded her that unless Alasdair was a closet fan of American football, he wouldn't know what she meant. But her gesture attracted his cool blue gaze. She mouthed the word *stone*, and made a breaking motion with her hands.

With a nod considerably more subtle than her gesture, and with a telltale curl at the corner of his mouth — *historians!* — he asked, "What did you father do with the pagan stone, Mr. Fraser?"

"He cut it in half, so Crowley widna be getting his hands on it and using it to raise more demons. I mind we're thinking now there's no harm in such stones, and maybe not, but when the Beast himself is squatting on your doorstep, you do what you can to defend yourself."

Jean buried her face in her hand. Her first impulse when she'd seen the photo of the Stone had been almost right. Unfortunately. She tried telepathy: *Ask him where the other half is.*

But Alasdair was after more immediate answers. "What happened to Edith, then, Mr. Fraser?"

He gestured, stiffly, looking right and left with a sort of desperation. "No one knew, so far as I can tell. I most certainly didna know.

'Til just last year."

"What happened last year?"

"After Mrs. Mackintosh, Eileen, disappeared — driven to suicide, I'm thinking, may God have mercy on her soul — Edith went off to America. She was in the family way with Ambrose's child. Truly, once you step off the straight and narrow path, 'tis a long way down."

Jean felt her eyes fly open so far dust settled on them. Edith being pregnant she could buy, even though Ambrose's charms escaped her personally. But Edith fleeing to America? Crowley's so-called magic or not, she couldn't have been in two places at once, both dead and alive.

"And how were you finding this out?" Alasdair asked, his eyes showing no reaction at all.

Fraser's hands worked on his thighs, flexing and loosing, digging out an entrance passage to the past. "No harm in saying, now that the woman's dead. 'Twas Mrs. Dempsey told me the tale."

Aha! Jean thought, so clearly that she almost clapped her hand over her mouth. But no, she hadn't spoken aloud. Finally the story got back around to Roger and Tracy.

"Mrs. Dempsey," Alasdair enunciated clearly. Again he shot a quick glance at Jean, a glance that if it didn't say *aha* at least said *hmm*.

Fraser sighed so heavily Jean could see Alasdair's hair wave in the breeze. "She and her husband came to me a year or so past, whilst organizing their expedition. Looking out a creature in the loch, the man's got more silver than sense. I was telling him how my granny talked of water horses and the like, her putting superstition behind her like the braw, virtuous lady she was, meaning to put him off, but he took it all the other way round."

If believing is hearing, Jean thought, then hearing is believing.

"Mrs. Dempsey visited again in April this year — a handsome fair-spoken woman, for a Sassenach wed to a Yank . . ." Fraser's eyes turned toward Jean. "Meaning no insult, Madam."

"None taken," Jean told him.

Alasdair cut to the chase. "Why did the Dempseys come to you?"

"They were asking me whether my father had uncovered a pagan tomb at Pitclachie."

"How did they know about that?"

Fraser's face twisted, so that its seams deepened into fissures. "Mrs. Dempsey was telling me her husband was Edith's grandson. Ambrose's grandson. She was telling me we're cousins."

Jean's mouth dropped open. *What?* Gunn's hand jerked so that he had to cross out what he'd already written and try again. Even Alasdair reacted to that, his eyes narrowing.

"She gave me a book that Ambrose had given to Edith, by way of proving their claim," Fraser said, calmly, carefully. "The same one you bought, Madam. Twould be better for a burning, it has got an unhealthy air about it, and no mistake."

Jean's disapproval of book-burning matched Fraser's disapproval of Crowley, although she agreed that that particular book did tempt the business end of a match. But the book itself didn't prove a thing. If it weren't for the testimony of the ghosts — she knew she shouldn't be counting that, but she did — and the testimony of the skeleton, which she knew Alasdair was very much counting, Fraser's story would make sense. But it didn't.

"Let me guess," said Alasdair. "Iris is denying Roger Dempsey his birthright, some part of Pitclachie."

"She's embarrassed to acknowledge the man. Here he is, looking to be the spit of Ambrose, a right loony, and here's Iris, gey respectable, a fine sensible woman and all."

Which wasn't exactly what Fraser had been saying Saturday, Jean noted.

"So sensible she stopped in last night, by way of talking all this over with you?" asked Alasdair.

By this time Fraser had accepted Alasdair's prescience, and responded with nothing more than a nod. "She was after owning the truth, aye. And me, I apologized for having been sharpish with her, soon after I first heard the story."

"Right," said Alasdair, almost whispering.

Jean mopped surreptitiously at the moisture dewing her forehead. *Wait for it.* Gunn flexed his fingers and re-installed his pen. Fraser looked down at his monumental and empty hands. The back of his neck and the top of his head, between thin strands of hair, glowed pink and damp.

"Did you know of the passage grave at Pitclachie, then?" Alasdair asked.

"Oh aye. My father, he helped build up the entrance way. Was still pointing the location out to me in his last years. Nothing wrong with it as an archaeological exercise, he was saying, but Ambrose didna want it only for that. Cursed ground, it was, even after it went back to the elements."

The hotel owner had testified at Ambrose's trial about white-robed figures carrying flaming torches. Jean herself had seen the graffiti on the curbstone. Ambrose had been playing his occult games there as well as in the upper room of the Lodge. What a handy dandy place to dump a body! All Ambrose had to do was fill in the entry way and the area just outside it, and let the rain and the heather do their work. The Dempseys had clearly been reading Ambrose's papers, ones that had inspired their — it was a scam, wasn't it?

"Was that what Iris was telling you last night, that Dr. Dempsey's uncovered the grave?" Alasdair asked.

Fraser said nothing.

"There's a human skeleton inside. We've got reason to think it was placed there in nineteen-thirty-three, the year both Edith and Eileen disappeared. It's the skeleton of a woman five foot ten inches in height who's missing her left forefinger, amputated well before death."

Still Fraser didn't react.

Alasdair tried stating the obvious. "We're thinking it's your aunt, Edith Fraser."

Again the room fell silent. This time, along with the traffic and pedestrian noise from outside, Jean detected the scent of frying potatoes and grilling meat. Her stomach growled. Man did not live by testimony alone, no matter how interesting. And contradictory.

Gunn stirred in his chair and tapped his pencil against his notebook. Alasdair sat unmoving, not staring at Fraser so much as watching him. Waiting. Even he seemed to be developing just a bit of a sweat-sheen along his hairline. Unless it was his brain leaking lubrication fluid.

At last the old man stirred, limbs creaking, chair squeaking. "My mother and father, they taught me my aunt was dead, and I honored them as I should do. They taught me she had fallen from grace, and I honored them. Even so, after all these years I'm thinking that she deserved a second chance. Ambrose was giving her a second chance. He wisna pointing out the mote in her eye when he was feeling the beam in his own. Scripture tells us that if we're not forgiving others, then our Father in heaven will not be forgiving us."

Alasdair rewarded Fraser's laudable sentiments with a thin smile.

"And now, Chief Inspector Cameron, my shop needs seeing to. If you canna see your way clear to driving me home, there's a bus . . ."

"No need, Mr. Fraser." Alasdair rose from his inquisitor's throne, shook Fraser's hand, and ushered him out the door. Jean heard his voice giving instructions.

Gunn closed his notebook and mopped at his temples. "The world lost a grand gambler when the Chief Inspector turned to police work."

Laughing, Jean stood up and shook out her skirt and blouse. *Whoa. Air.* "He's also a scientist. You know, testing hypotheses and reproducing results."

Car doors slammed. An engine started up and was absorbed in the general traffic noise.

Alasdair walked back into the office and shut the door with an emphatic click. After a long moment of dazed silence, he said, "I've never before been stonewalled with such class."

"He was really helpful for a while there," Jean said. "All that about Edith's early life and Crowley and everything fits what we already know."

"Dr. Dempsey might could be Edith's grandson," suggested Gunn, "if she had a child before she died, and it was him taken to America."

Jean shook her head. "But that's not what he said. Or rather, that's not what he said Tracy said. He shut down when you disproved her story. There's more to that, and to what Iris said to him last night, but he doesn't want to tell. Can't tell, because telling violates his principles."

"Got it in one," Alasdair said, brows knit.

Jean's own eyebrows were knitting and purling. "I bet my book spent a long time in that mildewed box in the lumber room of the Lodge. Maybe not seventy years, though. Thirty years? Ever since Ambrose died and Iris came back to Pitclachie with her new broom?"

"I'm believing Tracy gave Fraser the book in April, all right, that bit he saw for himself . . ."

"Oh!" Jean exclaimed. "Martin Hall! I overheard him talking to Noreen, something about 'she' making promises about getting him a fellowship. Tracy. She who must be obeyed."

"She seems to have been our organizing principle," said Alasdair.

Gunn flipped open his notebook again and began to write.

"Oh yeah. If she and Roger sent themselves the letters — if they blew up the boat themselves, for that matter — then she could have had Martin pick up the notepaper and the corkscrew in April. And the book, if she had him searching for those personal papers. They had to have had at least some of them already, to get them started."

"They blew up the boat themselves," Gunn repeated doggedly. "They planted the corkscrew. They sent the letters."

"Time to have a word with Martin Hall," said Alasdair. "Jean, your car's outside?"

"Just up the way in the Tourist Information Center parking lot."

"Good. We'll have us a lunch, first. Neville, stay here 'til P.C. Milton returns, then come by Pitclachie. Oh, and have yourself a meal as well."

"Yes, sir." Gunn shut his notebook and walked purposefully over to the desk. Alasdair opened the door for Jean, offering her a softer smile than the one he'd offered Fraser.

She responded in kind and stepped out into the sultry — afternoon, she saw with a glance at her watch. The day was burning away like the fuse connected to a bomb.

THIRTY

In the sunlight, the Gothic extravagance of Pitclachie House seemed more whimsical than sinister. The castellated battlements of the tower looked like a gap-toothed grin, Jean thought as she drove up the driveway, and the arched windows like eyebrows raised perhaps less in humor than astonishment at how deceptive appearances could be. A case in point being the business-suited, tie-knotted detective sitting next to her and casting a cold eye on passersby. The same detective who had turned out to be a great kisser with a gratifyingly ticklish spot just behind his right ear lobe.

She and Alasdair had scarfed down salmon salads in one of the restaurants beside the village green. They had not talked about the case, but had confined themselves to meaningful glances and the occasional monosyllable. Still, the reporters buzzing around like overgrown midges no doubt noted that the mildest-mannered of their number, the one from *Great Scot*, had the inside track. That she had no desire to write about the case, merely to survive it, was probably beyond their ken.

Now Jean reclaimed her spot beside the Renault, noting that while the Water Horse van was gone, the Halls' nondescript car was still there. She stepped out onto the gravel with a wary look around. Swallows skimmed through the cloud of midges, scooping up beak full after beak full and driving the ragged remnants into the dark branches above, where each leaf hung heavy and motionless. On the Festival field, tents were coming down and trash coming up. Police cars were parked on the road leading to Temple Pier, their fluorescent stripes washed out by the damp sunlight. A smoke-like haze was gathering over the mountains to the east, blotting rock and rill into a blur.

Alasdair wasn't scanning the scene but the front of the Renault. He reached into his pocket, pulled out his handkerchief, and gingerly removed a couple of leaves that were caught in the curling end of the bumper. "Nettles. And look here, a bit of a scrape and dent on the finish."

"Nettles?" Jean walked around her car and peered at the soggy shriveled leaves. "Like the nettles along the sidewalk where Roger and I . . . Oh boy. You can see where I brushed up against the car not two hours ago, there, where the dirt is smudged, but I never looked at the bumper."

"Who owns this car, then?"

"Charles and Sophie Bouchard."

"Where were they on the Saturday night?"

"They said they were going to eat dinner at the Glengarry Castle Hotel and headed off south. They got back right after the, er, accident . . ." A metaphorical light bulb illuminated a dark corner of Jean's memory. "But then they came from the north, not the south. Whoa — what if they hit Roger and me as they drove by, then kept on going past Pitclachie, to Abriachan, maybe, and turned around and came back? That's a left-hand drive car. Whoever was driving was right on top of us."

"There you are." With a half-smile that she chose not to interpret as *Gotcha*, Alasdair tucked the folded handkerchief into his pocket, produced his phone, and called for both crime scene investigation and back-up.

"But their motive," Jean said, reminding herself this was not a competition. "They have no reason to try and kill me. Even if they thought I was Tracy walking along with Roger, wouldn't they want to keep the Dempseys alive and producing artifacts for sale? And they didn't exactly come back for Tracy later on, did they? They were at the ceilidh when she was killed. Maybe it was an accident, after all."

"I'm thinking a word with them as well wouldn't go amiss." Just as he tucked his phone away, it rang again. Hauling it back out, he answered, "Cameron."

Jean walked on toward the house, casting her gaze heavenward. Iris was still sitting beside the now-open tower window, her hands webbed with white yarn, knitting away so efficiently the needles flashed like dueling sabers. She looked down on Jean with god-like disapproval. Jean did not genuflect.

Alasdair ranged up beside her, tucking the phone away yet again, and followed the direction of her gaze. "No need for her to be playing hard to get. The letters are a moot point by now, and she's got the best possible alibi for the time of Tracy's murder."

"We thought Roger might be blackmailing Iris. Now it looks like he's adding scam to blackmail by claiming to be her nephew. She thinks the body in the grave is Eileen's and that he's telling her the truth. A truth she doesn't want to go public."

"Roger's hoist himself with his own petard, then, finding Edith's body. As for Eileen . . ."

Jean couldn't complete his sentence. She looked up again, then spun toward Alasdair. "What were you saying back at the police station about a knitting needle?"

"The crime scene boffins found a broken plastic needle. Looks to be blood on its tip. Could be there was a struggle, Tracy found it ready to hand, and she stabbed her killer with it."

"You could do a DNA test."

"Easier and quicker to have a suspect strip off. But then, having just one suspect for the letters, the explosion, the hit-and-run, and the murder would be easier and quicker as well. I doubt you're right. We've got at least two people each working his own dodge and compounding each other's crimes as they go."

"I could live with being wrong every now and then," Jean told him, and received a hollow laugh in return.

The Water Horse van crunched into the parking area and stopped. Brendan leaped out, carrying a couple of grease-stained paper bags, whose pungent odor identified them as fish lunches for the excavator-cum-tomb robbers. With a friendly, guilt-free smile at Alasdair and Jean's cynical faces, he loped past the house and up the hillside.

Jean and Alasdair strolled far enough into the garden that they could see the dig and Brendan doling out the food. Roger sat down beside his bones, close enough to occasionally reach over and pat one — they were real, yes, precious, indeed they were. Brendan sat with his back turned to Roger, facing toward the house, probably watching for the fair if fickle Kirsty. Charles and Sophie, mopping their brows, retreated to the shade of the pines and made pained faces over their fried fish and vinegar-doused chips. Jean wished them ticks, and then rapped her wish over its knuckles.

Alasdair considered the pattern made by the bones. "That's never Nessie."

"Then what is it?"

"Just now, none of my concern. As for what is my concern, I'll not be interviewing Roger in front of the Bouchards. Or the other way round. Soon as the lads have done their car, I'll have them taken in and questioned through a translator."

The thuds of slamming doors reverberated from the parking area. A constable materialized from the garden — oh, he'd been sitting on a bucket behind the boxwood hedge, surveilling the group on the hillside. Another strolled around the far corner of the house and took up a position at the end of the terrace. Alasdair was keeping his suspects covered. And in play. Turning toward the front door, he said, "Now for Martin Hall, and his wife as well. We've talked to them one at a time already. Let's see if a mutual interview gets better results. Gunn's not yet here, do you have your notebook?"

"Sure." Jean said, following close behind. "At least little Elvis isn't on your short list of suspects. Brendan's okay, and Kirsty, too. Iris sure didn't kill Tracy, not that she's giving you the whole truth and nothing but. And just because the Ducketts might be connected to the submersible doesn't mean they're up to no good, although running away this morning doesn't look . . ."

Alasdair stopped so suddenly she collided with him. For appearance's sake, with the constables in view and all, she took a step backward. "That was the second phone call just now," he said, walking again. "You mind how Jonathan told his family he was working for someone else besides Roger? The manager of his bank is saying he received two sizeable checks written on a bank in Illinois, USA."

"Omnium's headquartered in Illinois, of course he'd be getting . . . Wait a minute." Jean fixed Alasdair with a triumphant gaze. "The Ducketts are from Moline, Illinois!"

"Oh aye. Amateur villains that they are, they paid him from their own account, name, address, and telephone printed on checks with twee photos of otters and seals."

"So Brendan was right, Jonathan was a spy. He was checking out the submersible for the Ducketts. Do you think they blew up the boat to avenge their son-in-law's death? Or Jonathan did it for them, and was accidentally caught in the explosion?"

"No, not a bit of it. They'd have wanted to keep the submersible in good shape, as evidence in their wrongful-death suit, wouldn't they now? I reckon Jonathan was sneaking back on board to take photos of the sub for them when the boat went up."

"Yeah, that's the best explanation. Roger and Tracy themselves as the mad bombers. Oh what a tangled web and all that." Jean gritted her teeth and went on, "The Ducketts have both the motive and the opportunity to kill Tracy, don't they?"

"Oh aye," said Alasdair, untroubled by the personal appeal of the genial couple.

Opening the door, Jean eyed the dragon knocker. It reminded her of Roger's mysterious skeleton, a long sinuous body except with little wings instead of flippers. And the knocker had feet, too. Back in the mists of the twentieth century some jokester had used a hippopotamus-foot umbrella holder to make Nessie tracks along the shore of the loch.

Alasdair tapped the knocker. "Wings and four legs. Odd how so many fantasy beasties are hexapods." His hand on her back urged her on into the house.

For a moment the darkness of the entrance hall made the air inside seem cool. Then Jean felt the warmth close in like syrup. Houses in this part of the world were made to keep heat in, not out. From the library came Elvis's high-pitched, perfectly rounded voice. "But Mummy, that big boat's going out on the loch. I want to go out on the loch."

Alasdair seized Jean's arm, pulling her to a stop. He might have a scientific bent, but eavesdropping was more of an art, akin to stalking a stag on the hillside.

"I'm sorry," said Noreen. "The cruise is only for the Festival folk."

"You're always so quick to give over, aren't you?" Martin said, and, his tone going from scornful to softly cajoling, "I'll have a word with the man at the pier, Elvis. Slip him a tenner, like. Maybe a twenty. We'll get ourselves on that boat."

"A twenty?" protested Noreen. "You can't go on spending our money like that, Martin, this place here's bad enough, we'll be skint . . ."

"We never paid for this place here, you stupid cow."

The door of the private office opened and Kirsty stepped out. When she saw Jean and Alasdair standing in the entrance hall, she quailed. So did they. She had abandoned all pretext at mature sobriety and defaulted to short shorts and a snug cropped T-shirt that left little to the imagination, and, accordingly, fueled the fantasy. Her hair was swirled gracefully atop her head. "Can I help you?"

"The Halls need interviewing," Alasdair told her, focusing only on her face. "Could you look after the lad? We may be some time."

Kirsty thought that over. "Aye, I'll mind him, if it means moving his folk on the sooner." She started down the hall, her plastic sandals slapping on the floor, her white shorts tracing a pattern in the gloom like an animated version of the Stone's double disc symbol.

Jean looked at Alasdair. "Kids today!" he hissed from the corner of his mouth, and with a satiric quirk of his brow followed Kirsty into the library. At his heels, Jean smothered her grin.

The large casement windows, open to their limits, admitted a wheeze or two of damp air that did nothing to dispel the aura of mold from the oldest books and the breath of incense, as Jean now realized it was, from the desk. Martin was slumped in one of the windows, eyeing the excavation in progress like a Little Leaguer watching the Red Sox. Noreen huddled in a chair, her sundress crumpled around her. Kirsty's and then Jean's entrance provoked only a dull upward glance, but when she saw Alasdair, she squeaked in alarm. Martin whirled around and petrified, every limb at an awkward angle.

It must be hard on Alasdair, Jean thought, for people to greet his entrance with fear and loathing. But the moment he stepped through the door he'd buckled on his armor, closed his visor, and raised his shield.

Elvis was trying to entice Mandrake with a scrap of paper. The cat, lying stretched out like a fur stole on the cool stone of the hearth, was snubbing him as only a cat could snub. Pulling a long, flat, colorful box off a lower shelf, Kirsty said brightly to the child, "Fancy a game of Snakes and Ladders? We'll set up on the kitchen table, and the winner gets an ice cream."

"May I?" Elvis asked his parents, bouncing to his feet.

Noreen managed a stiff wave, Martin a stiffer nod. Kirsty took Elvis's hand and led him away. No one moved until his voice, going on about ice cream and snakes and Nessie, disappeared behind the swing of the kitchen door.

Then, with slow deliberation, Alasdair took off his jacket, draped it over the desk chair — his gaze strayed to the photo of Ambrose and Eileen — and loosened his tie. To help him keep cool, Jean knew, but he was also playing off his threatening aspect, signaling it was time to get down to brass tacks. "Miss Fairbairn," he said calmly, "would you be so kind as to take notes?"

She almost replied, *Of course, Chief Inspector Cameron*, but decided that would be laying it on too thick. From her bag she pulled her decrepit notebook and a pen.

"Shit," Noreen said, shrinking down even further. "They've found it."

Martin snapped at her. "Shut up."

"I told you, Marty, I told you you'd get yourself banged up if you wasn't careful, and what about us, then?" Tears welled in Noreen's eyes.

Jean stood holding her notebook. Oh. Alasdair had wanted to see if they'd recognize it. The man had a streak of low cunning, no doubt about it. And economy — he really did need someone to take notes. Sitting down in the closest chair, a high-backed overstuffed antique, she poised her pen over a blank page. Sweat prickled along her back and beneath her thighs.

"Mrs. Hall," Alasdair said, "you are not obliged to testify against your husband, but if you choose to do so, whatever you say will be used against him."

Noreen's face seemed to implode. She buried it in her hands, her shoulders shaking. Instead of walking across the room to render aid and comfort, Martin glared at her and repeated *stupid cow* under his breath. He glanced around as though considering whether to leap through the unscreened window, but a constable — by no chance at all — was strolling past. His legs folded and deposited him on the windowsill, where he bent double in the universal posture of woe.

The front door opened and closed. Swift, light footsteps came down the hall, and like Jeeves bringing a tray of drinks, Gunn glided into the room. Nodding to Alasdair and then to Jean, he sat down and produced his own notebook, ready to go. With relief, she turned hers into a fan.

Alasdair said quietly, to the balding top of Martin's head, "I might could charge you with the murder of Tracy Dempsey, Mr.

Hall, unless you're giving me good reasons not to. Where did you first meet the woman?"

"At the Bristol University," said Martin, voice flat. Noreen looked up with a sniffle, her eyes red and swollen. "Roger was lecturing. I thought he could help me move up in my field, but when I went to talk to him I got to talking to her, and after a bit she said he needed a second research assistant for work at Loch Ness. I applied straight-away — what a leg-up that would be, part of the expedition that actually finds the creature. But Roger chose himself another Yank, didn't he, that Brendan chap. Still, Tracy said she liked my work experience and my attitude, said she could get me a fellowship if I helped her and Roger with a small problem. Said she'd pay my expenses and bonuses as well, for work well done. Just as long as I did what she said and didn't ask too many questions."

His attitude being eager to please and desperate for money and position, Jean footnoted. Susceptible to Tracy's wiles.

"What work were you doing here in April?" asked Alasdair.

"April? You know about . . ." Martin looked up, assessed the glacier thickening along Alasdair's jaw, and slumped even further. "I collected some notepaper for her. And she said she wanted something that could be identified with the house, so I lifted an old corkscrew from the desk there. Pretty clever, eh? Nothing so big they'd call out the plods, but seen to be from Pitclachie."

Unimpressed, Alasdair asked, "What else?"

"She wanted an old book as well. One written by Ambrose Mackintosh."

Alasdair's gaze flicked like the snap of a whip toward Jean. "A book? Not loose notes?"

"No, a bound book. *My Life, by Ambrose Mackintosh of Pitclachie.* Autobiography, sounds like."

Jean let her head fall back against the scratchy velvet of her chair. So that was it. Ambrose's autobiography. He had written it and had it printed and bound — once a publisher, always a publisher, perhaps. A truthful autobiography, not a puff piece, would be sensational, the location of the passage grave the least of the revelations that Iris would be dead set on keeping private. But if Tracy and Roger already had a copy, wherever it came from, why did they want another one?

"You found the book, then, Mr. Hall?" Alasdair was asking.

"I looked at every book in this bleeding house, even the ones in the trout's office. I turned up one buried in a filthy old box in the lumber room of the Lodge, *The Realm of the Beast*, and thought maybe Tracy'd make do with that. And she took it, right enough, said thank you kindly, very useful, but not the one she wanted. If Iris has a copy of *My Life*, she's walled it up in her tower."

But if it was that well-hidden, Jean told herself, why would Iris call Kirsty and ask her to hide it? Martin just hadn't looked carefully enough.

Alasdair said, "You were stopping at the Lodge in April."

"Ever so much more room," said Noreen through her teeth. "I could cook the meals, save a few pence — you never told me, Marty, you never told me she was paying the tariff for us!"

"Was the lumber room unlocked then?" Alasdair's cool voice cut Noreen's sweaty mumble.

"I pinched the key from the office," answered Martin. "Had it copied, put it back. The trout, she never knew, did she?"

Jean saw that her exploratory efforts had been hampered by honesty.

"I knew." Noreen sniffed, a sound like a drain clearing, and sat up straighter. "I knew. I told you that woman would leave you banged up, and I was right!"

Alasdair's stern expression neither contradicted nor agreed with her. "You returned to Pitclachie in June, for the Water Horse Expedition."

"The frogs, they got the Lodge, then moved out, then you . . ." Martin's glance at Jean would have been hostile if it wasn't so lifeless, like his pale face, drained of blood as though by some deep internal injury. "I used my key and searched again, Friday night, just so the trout hadn't changed things round from April. No joy."

Jean wasn't sure whether to be relieved or insulted that she hadn't been the object of the night crawler.

"The key, the copy, it's in my sponge bag upstairs," said Noreen. "He thought no one would go looking for it, there, with my things."

Alasdair tilted his head toward Gunn. Gunn tilted his head toward Alasdair. *Check.* "Please go on, Mr. Hall," Alasdair said.

"She told me to hide the corkscrew from the drinks table on the Friday, and I did — it's in the shrubbery. She told me to lift your notebook . . ." His chin jutted toward Jean. "Your bag was hanging open there at the Festival, didn't even have to go back into the Lodge to get it."

If he survived this, Martin had a future in pickpocketing, Jean thought. She'd never felt a thing.

"What did Mrs. Dempsey do with Miss Fairbairn's notebook?" asked Alasdair.

"Glanced through it, then told me to throw it down somewheres, so she'd think she lost it."

"Why did Mrs. Dempsey want Miss Fairbairn's notebook?" A subtle difference, but a vital one.

"Cause she, Fairburn . . ." Martin wasn't the first person to skew

Jean's name. Still she frowned. "She's a reporter, isn't she? She had something on Roger, Tracy never said what. She had something on him and was going to make trouble, and if she did, then Roger wouldn't be able to fund a fellowship for me. She was asking too many questions, Tracy said."

Asking questions was her job, damn it! Jean tried to meet Martin's eye with a hostile glare of her own, but he ducked, wrapping his long arms around his narrow chest and folding back on the windowsill. So Tracy had read through her notebook for the same reason Roger had bugged the toy. To see what she knew about the submersible disaster. To see if she was going to publicize it. There was privacy, and there was secrecy . . .

Alasdair walked to the empty fireplace and looked down at the cat, who was dozing peacefully, his calico sides rising and falling. Not that Alasdair was interested in the cat. He was deploying one of his significant silences, letting the Halls sweat. Letting Jean sweat, too, but not because she was on the hot seat. "Were you working just for Tracy," he asked in that prickly velvet voice of his, "or for Roger as well?"

"I never talked with him at all. Why should I? She was a strong woman, she was, dressed right smart, had a good head on her shoulders. She knew what she was about."

Noreen wiped her nose on the back of her hand and sat up even straighter. Her face was pink, and not only from the heat, Jean estimated. She was getting mad.

"And the boat explosion?"

Martin took off his glasses, mopped them across his shirt, put them back on. Through them he peered molishly up at Alasdair. "I don't know anything about the boat explosion. I was as surprised as everyone else. I'm sorry that chap Jonathan was killed. I had nothing to do with it."

"And Mrs. Dempsey's death?"

"I didn't do it. I swear. I was with Noreen and the boy. We were asleep."

"We weren't asleep," snapped Noreen. "I was after talking to you, and you was snoring like an outboard engine. Pretending to be asleep, so you wouldn't have to talk to the likes of me."

"Noreen," Martin protested, "not now . . ."

"Then when, Marty? You didn't kill Tracy, I was with you, I'll tell any policeman who asks that I was with you. Because that's the truth. You can ponce about, putting on airs, sniffing around that woman — she's dead, I'm sorry, but that bitch had no right using you and you had no right letting her use you. If you can't act like an honest man for the child, then when can you?"

"I did it for the boy, I wanted a better life for him. I did it for us."

Noreen came straight up out of the chair, her quivering forefinger leveled at an impassive Alasdair. But she wasn't looking at him. Her red face was turned to Martin, who by now was cowering on the windowsill like a crab next to a boiling pot of water. "He'll do you for murder, he will, and where's us, then, where's us?"

Better off, Jean answered, playing judge and jury. Martin might be only a sneak-thief and toady, not a murderer, but by showing Elvis the wrong way to treat a spouse he was as guilty of child-abuse as of wife-abuse.

In the sudden silence, Gunn's pencil hitting the page in an emphatic dot — the period at the end of Noreen's tirade — sounded like a gunshot. Alasdair pointed toward the door. In one move, Gunn was up and down the hall.

Noreen spun around to Alasdair. "What are you doing with us?"

"We'll be taking Mr. Hall to Inverness for the night, so he can make his statement. He'll stay overnight in the cells, but I've not yet decided whether to charge him with anything. You'll need to be making as statement as well. I'll have a W.P.C. drive you to the station here in Drumnadrochit and bring you back again. Pop down the hall and have a word with Miss Wotherspoon, if you like."

"I don't know what I like, not now," Noreen replied, but with an effort that made her entire body quiver, she pulled herself together and popped down the hall.

Alasdair watched Martin, arms folded. Martin watched his hands opening and shutting in his lap. Jean pushed her notebook through the air like an oar through water, but produced only a tentative zephyr on her warm face.

Just as Noreen reappeared, so did Gunn, two constables, one male, one female, trooping at his heels. Efficiently they gathered up their respective wards and walked them away. Martin sidled along as though his ankles were manacled. Noreen stepped out, chin jutting, ignoring her husband. The front door slammed, leaving Jean, Alasdair, and the comatose Mandrake in control of the field.

THIRTY-ONE

Alasdair wiped his forehead on his sleeve and rotated his shoulders as though he'd been doing hard labor. Which he had, Jean told herself. He might feel as though he was shoveling out the Augean stables, but the case was well on its way to a solution. Wasn't it?

The heavy chair seemed to be sucking her down. She peeled herself out of it and turned her back to the window. Her damp blouse feel clammy against her skin. "Now what?"

"They'll stop in at the infirmary and have a look for scratch or puncture wounds from the broken needle. But I reckon Martin's innocent. And Noreen as well, before you go asking me about her."

Jean smiled. *Who, me?*

"It's not worth the time and energy trying him for stealing notepaper and the like. He'll find himself with a probationary sentence, and her with the phone number of social services. There's just one problem."

"Our list of suspects is getting short. We're down to the Ducketts or some mysterious master criminal or passing tramp, unsuspected by all, who just happened to be hanging out in the top room of the tower. Or else someone's got a false alibi."

The crinkle of deep thought tightening his eyebrows, Alasdair strolled over to the window. Jean noticed the slight creak and catch in his posture as he loosened his armor and leaned on his sword. She could offer to massage his shoulders . . . No. He wouldn't want that, not here, not now.

She stepped up beside him, to see that he was looking at Roger and Brendan, back at work on the hillside, sorting their bones. And sorting the Bouchard's *objets de* dirt, too, because Charles and Sophie themselves were being conducted toward the parking area by three constables.

Their voices drifted down the heavy air, a duet of protests in both French and English. Jean caught something about consulates and embassies and the European Union. Like that was going to do them any good. If nothing else, they'd find themselves on the fast track back to France and their shop . . . Their shop. Their job lot of goods from a London estate sale, that just happened to include a Pictish silver chain. Their inventory of antiquities and old books.

"I bet Tracy bought a copy of Ambrose's autobiography from the Bouchards. That's how they got involved in all of this — they wanted first dibs on any more Pictish treasure, especially since they have a certain lack of concern when it comes to provenance. Or so Miranda says."

Alasdair glanced around, the crinkle giving way to a glint of silver in his eyes. "We were thinking the Dempseys were our organizing principle, but . . ."

"It all goes back to Ambrose, with his antiquities and his books and his mania for the occult and Nessie." Jean whirled around so fast she almost lost her balance. Alasdair grabbed her arm but she hardly felt his grasp, shaking it off and rushing toward the dark corner of the shelving. She knelt down and with her fingertip traced along the rank of books until she came to the ones she remembered. "Look — there were three books from Crowley and Ambrose's Mandrake Press here on Saturday. Now there are only two, Crowley's book and the Lawrence. But the Boccaccio is gone."

Alasdair leaned over her shoulder, so close she could feel the warmth of his body, venting now that he'd set his cool persona aside. "Eh?"

She eased the two books from the shelf and then apart — the heat made their bindings almost sticky — and leafed through them. They were as advertised. "What if the Boccaccio, the *Decameron* . . ."

"The what?"

Oh. She laughed. "It's a book of one hundred medieval Italian stories, lots of fighting, sex, and magic, the sort of thing that wouldn't have gone over well in the thirties. Like these." She shoved the Lawrence and the Crowley back onto the shelf, making sure they were aligned properly. "The name's from the Latin root for ten, you know, like decimal or Decalogue. Nothing to do with your family. Just an alphabetical coincidence, if a pretty good one."

"The Camerons have done as much fighting and all over the years as any medieval Italians," said Alasdair, not apologetically. "You're thinking that's the book Iris told Kirsty to hide?"

"She couldn't speak plainly in front of your people, so she just said the book Ambrose wrote. And Kirsty saw the book from the lumber room sitting outside the Lodge and thought that was it. I mean, it was mine, it was under threat, right?"

"Right. But Ambrose didn't write . . . Ah, that's what you're on about. You can't judge a book by its cover."

"No way. Just because it says Boccaccio on the spine doesn't mean the *Decameron*'s inside the binding." Jean stood up, trying to brush the dust from her hands but making little pills of it instead. "When Iris came back from Inverness, she squirreled the real book away somewhere. No more of this purloined letter, hide-in-plain-sight business."

"Like as not Martin was just reading the titles. If he'd pulled every single book from the shelf, he'd be working yet."

"Exactly."

Alasdair walked across the room to the desk and rolled up the cover. There was *Realm of the Beast* in its tacky plastic bag. "And this bittie red herring is still here."

Mandrake's nose wrinkled. He stirred, stood up, stretched, and trotted toward the enticing odor.

"Smells like corpse of herring with a funeral wreath." Jean trotted to the desk, too, and rescued Kirsty's knitting project from the chair just as Mandrake leaped up onto it. "This book was never hidden. It was discarded along with a bunch of other useless items."

Alasdair picked up his jacket and eased it on, smoothed his lapels and snugged his tie against his throat. "Useless items? Yon photo of Ambrose and Eileen is here on the desk, but their wedding photo and Eileen's portrait are both in the lumber room."

"Yeah." There was something about that . . . Jean wrapped the half-finished scarf around the ball of yarn and the needles, set it inside the maw of the desk, and closed the lid. Kirsty, the beginner, was knitting the scarf in a basic garter stitch, the building block of more complex patterns. But even an old pro like Jean herself could miscount a complex pattern. Accidentally moving the sequence of stitches over by just one place would leave a fault line cutting across the design. *Moving your assumptions over just one place* . . . She looked up, meeting the eyes of her colleague, another old pro.

"What now?" he asked.

"The ghosts on the staircase last night. Even when she was standing on the step below Ambrose, the top of Edith's head came to Ambrose's nose. She was almost as tall as he was."

"Never mind the ghosts, her skeleton measured a good five foot ten. No surprise that Gordon Fraser's well over six foot."

"How tall is Iris, would you say?"

"Two inches taller than I am myself, five foot ten as well. . ." Comprehension swept over his face, his eyebrows shooting up to his hairline, his lips pursing in a reverent, "Bloody hell."

"Everyone's been assuming that Ambrose killed Eileen. Even when we found out that it was Edith he killed — we know it was an accident, but we'll never be able to prove that — we were still assuming that Eileen was Iris's mother. But she couldn't have been more than five feet tall."

Alasdair's forefinger indicated caution. "That's circumstantial evidence. Eileen's family might could have been tall. And how . . ."

"Women wore loose dresses in those days, not like that outfit Kirsty's wearing. And most births were still at home. How many people would know it was Edith who had the baby, not Eileen? Not if they were all in it together, and bought off the maid and everything.

We've been assuming there was a rivalry between the women. What if they were working together? What if Edith was wearing Eileen's earrings because Eileen gave them to her? Maybe it was Eileen who fled, to America, down the road, I don't know where she went. The point is, either she died, too, or she ran away. And if she ran away, why didn't she take her baby? Because the baby wasn't hers, that's why." Jean threw her hands out to her sides. *Ta da!*

Alasdair tilted his head, trying to roll all those little ball bearings of words into the proper holes. "Wouldn't be the first time the wife adopted the mistress's child."

"Iris must know the truth is in the autobiography, or she wouldn't be hiding it. And she wouldn't have given in to Roger's demands if he hadn't approached her with the truth — she'd have given him some equivalent of publish and be damned. But if Roger and Tracy knew Edith was dead, why risk telling Fraser she wasn't? And why did Tracy have Martin looking for another copy of the book?"

"It might be that Roger's copy of the autobiography is missing out some pages. They based the blackmail and Fraser's scam on the incomplete story, and were looking out another copy because they're still searching for where Ambrose found his treasure."

"But Iris thinks Roger's copy is complete! Bingo!"

As if punctuating her words — *we have a winner, folks!* — Alasdair's phone rang. His face still a little askew, he answered and listened intently to the voice emanating from the tiny speaker.

Mandrake settled down on the chair and yawned. Jean scratched his ears, his fur soft and warm beneath her hand. Funny, her theory about Edith and Iris had sounded perfectly reasonable while she was articulating it, but now . . . Well, Alasdair was probably right about the Dempseys basing their scheme on an incomplete book. And if the phone hadn't rung, he'd have pointed out that like Nessie, Iris's parentage was none of his concern. Or was his concern only peripherally, in that it provided motive and machination.

"Bring one of them round the terrace overlooking the loch," he said, and switched off his phone. "We've got the Ducketts back again. Fancy another spin on the Pitclachie carousel?"

"You're not kicking me off the merry-go-round now." Jean followed Alasdair out onto the terrace and around to the shady side of the house, where the air seemed somewhat thinner and fresher.

He kept on walking, pacing up and down. Jean sat and then lay back on a chaise lounge, breathing in the scents of asphalt and roses, listening to Kirsty's voice and Elvis's laugh through the kitchen window. From here she had seen the boat explode, not three days ago. Now another, larger boat rode the turbid waves of the Bay. The reddish stone tower of Urquhart Castle stood up against the gray-green smudge of the far shore. The sky was no longer bright blue, but bleached by the haze.

Oh for a glass of iced tea, she thought. But she had as much chance of getting that as she had of going water-skiing with Nessie.

Two police cars came up the driveway and Jean sat up, trying to look like an alert and competent participant in the case. A moment later Gunn appeared, guiding Dave Duckett with a hand under his elbow. Dave was rolling from side to side, not drunk but traumatized. Self-traumatized, the worst kind. His color was terrible, a pasty white, and his plump cheeks sagged. He made the Pillsbury doughboy look like the model of health.

"Please sit down, Mr. Duckett," Alasdair said, back in knight-justiciar pose.

Dave didn't so much sit down on a lawn chair as collapse. "We didn't know all this was going to happen. I feel like it's our fault, even though we never, we didn't . . ."

Gunn sat down on the terrace wall, notebook at the ready. Alasdair loomed. "Go on."

"Our son-in-law, Chris Peretti, was testing a submersible off Florida. The hatch was defective, it wouldn't shut properly. The sub sank. He drowned. It was a terrible, terrible . . ." Dave's voice broke.

"Take your time," Alasdair told him.

Shaking his head, Dave plunged on. "Melissa, our daughter, the three little ones, if it wasn't for us they'd have been living on the streets. Chris couldn't get insurance for a reasonable price, his work was so dangerous. We knew his work was dangerous, but heck, you're in danger just crossing the street, aren't you?"

Denial, Jean thought, was a very useful skill.

"He was contracted to Omnium because Roger Dempsey had developed the sub, but Omnium wouldn't pay anything, said they weren't liable, Dempsey wasn't working for them any more. We tried contacting Dempsey, but he sent a message through some slick-willy lawyer saying he didn't sweat the details of these things, that Chris must not have shut the hatch properly and, basically, tough luck." Dave's jaw firmed with indignation. "We found a lawyer of our own. He said we could sue, but that we'd only have a strong case if we could prove the hatch was defective. But the sub disappeared into a warehouse somewhere. Kind of like the Lost Ark, I guess."

Jean turned her smile into a crinkle of sympathy.

"You hired Jonathan Paisley to get the proof for you," Alasdair said quietly.

"Yeah. We found out about the Water Horse Expedition and who was on it and that Dempsey was shipping a bunch of water-exploration stuff over here. We thought maybe he'd try to use the sub again. Jon had the right technical expertise, so we made a deal with him. Brendan came along later. Maybe we chose the wrong guy, I don't know — Jon seemed to think that putting one over the boss was a good joke. He found our evidence, though. He said the sub was on board, but it had been partially disassembled, and Dempsey never said anything about using it. Jon himself thought the hatch looked dodgy. We gave him a camera, asked him to get photos. So he sneaked back onto the boat Friday night."

"And it exploded."

Dave subsided into a puddle of horror and remorse, his head sunk in his hands. With a sigh, Jean looked past him toward the water. The cold, uncompromising water. A shimmer was gathering above it, a mirage caused by the warm air against the chill surface of the loch. Good monster-spotting weather. Starr had chosen the right evening for their cruise.

"We just wanted to get the evidence, Inspector. Chief Inspector, isn't it? We wanted to get what was coming to our kids. Is that so wrong? But the Dempseys blew up the sub rather than face us in court fair and square."

"Do you know that for a fact, that they themselves blew up the boat and the sub?"

"Well, no." Dave looked up, eyes pleading. "But the newspaper said you'd found evidence that the explosion was deliberate. What other explanation is there? They wanted to damage the hatch so badly we couldn't use it as evidence. I don't think they intended for Jon to die. As for the rest of it . . ."

"Tracy Dempsey's death?"

Dave stared, mouth opening and shutting as though he was gathering bugs. At last he croaked, "Saturday night, Patti and I had some drinks at the Cameron Arms. Brendan was there, but he didn't say anything that could help us and we didn't dare ask him outright. We came back here and we were asleep, really deep asleep, you know? It took us a few minutes to come around and realize we were hearing people shouting. Even when she screamed and we heard someone running down the hall, from that door into the tower, I guess it was, we weren't too quick on the uptake. That's what we told your people when we made our statements yesterday. We've never lied to your people or to anyone here. We just never told the whole truth."

There was a lot of that going around, Jean thought.

Alasdair met Dave's stare evenly, his impassivity a question.

"We didn't push her out of the window. What good would that

do us? Revenge? How's revenge going to bring Chris back and send our grandkids to college? We wanted justice, and we didn't get that. We're not going to get it, now. Roger Dempsey screwed up, and Omnium screwed up, and now we're screwed." He groaned. "Running away today, that was stupid."

Alasdair did not disagree. He met Gunn's eye and nodded. Gunn stood up, tucking his notebook into his pocket. "Come along please, Mr. Duckett."

Dave had to try twice to heave himself to his feet. He trudged off, Gunn at his elbow, Alasdair just behind with Jean at his elbow. She looked at him, rolled her eyes toward Dave, looked back. Alasdair shook his head, an infinitesimal movement, but a negative one, nonetheless.

Slumped in the back seat of the police car, a policewoman beside her although presumably not handcuffed to her, Patti was in full meltdown. She wasn't even trying to wipe away the tears that flowed down her face. Jean's heart wrenched with compassion.

Patti reached through the open window. "Dave, hon, we're going to jail."

Taking her hand, Dave turned back to Alasdair and drew himself up with one last grasp at dignity. "Are you sending us to jail, Chief Inspector? We should have come to you right after the explosion, and we shouldn't have left when you told us to stay put. We're sorry we caused you and your people problems. But I don't see where we've actually broken any laws."

"We're hoping you'll continue helping us with our inquiries for a wee while yet," Alasdair replied, and taking Gunn aside, "Take them to the station, brew up a pot of tea, get her calmed down a bit. Have a blether about the grandchildren. I'll stop in directly."

Gunn, the model of efficiency — he was probably enjoying his impromptu promotion — organized the Ducketts and assorted police people into the cars and away.

Even after they had negotiated the telecommunications siege engines at the foot of the drive and disappeared toward town, Alasdair stood cogitating, almost but not quite expressionlessly. Jean could trace the thoughts moving across his face the way physicists traced neutrons passing through the earth, with great difficulty . . . Suddenly he made a frustrated gesture, turned around, and saw Jean biding her time just behind him. "Ah, there you are."

"I'm not anywhere else," she replied, and as he started around the side of the house she fell into step beside him. His helpmeet. His cheering section. His gadfly. So much for her vaunted independence.

Iris was still knitting in the upper window, like Madame Defarge knitting beside the guillotine. She had to be hoping the blade would fall before any awkward truths came out about her parentage.

"You're going to talk to Patti, see if her story matches Dave's?" Jean asked.

Alasdair's smile was thin as a blade. "I reckon it will."

"That's my gut feeling, but then, I'm not an experienced detective. And we're still faced with one question."

"If the Ducketts didn't kill Tracy, then who did do?" Looking like Napoleon scanning a map of Europe, Alasdair stopped at the end of the garden path to scan the hillside, Brendan, and Roger. "Let's have ourselves that word with Dr. Dempsey."

Roger, Jean thought. Ambrose might be the prime mover, but Roger was sure his prophet.

THIRTY-TWO

Every flower petal, every leaf and twig, hung limp in the still moist warmth of the afternoon. In his black and white uniform, the constable standing by the hedge seemed as out of place amid the flowers as a penguin in a drift of confetti. Alasdair, Jean thought, must have conscripted police personnel from the farthest reaches of Northern Constabulary territory. This would be a good time to rob a bank in Orkney.

He held the gate open for her. Just as she stepped through, Brendan shouted, "Hey! Look at this!"

Roger glanced up from his array of boxes and bags, each now holding a bone or some other bit of excavated loot, like a time-traveling crime scene. "What?"

"It's a carved stone, just down from the entrance. Put there really recently."

"How can you tell?"

"By the bottle cap behind it."

Stone? Jean sprinted up the hill, Alasdair at her heels for once, and came to a stop beside the trench, lathered in sweat and expectation. "Stone?"

"Here." Brendan handed her a dirt-encrusted bottle cap. "It was wedged in right there, between the edge of the stone and the rocks behind it. I bet that'll give you a good date."

Jean already had a good date. 1933, when the entrance to the tomb was filled in — a task not done by Gordon Fraser, she bet. She handed the cap to Alasdair, who inspected it, popped it into a plastic bag he liberated from Roger's stash, and stowed it in a pocket.

Brendan was right. The stone that was emerging from the dirt wall of trench did seem to have been propped up against the smaller stones that formed the main body of the passage grave. But it wasn't the same shape and size as the other curbstones. It was larger, perhaps four feet tall, and tapered upward from a stubby base like a giant stone canine tooth. Brendan scraped delicately at the very bottom of the stone, revealing a dirt-filled pictograph — a gripping beast crossed by an ornately-decorated Z-rod.

Roger clambered to his feet. "Is it the other half of the Pitclachie Stone?"

"Looks like it," Jean said. "It fits the description."

"There's a description?" asked Brendan. "You knew it was here?"

Alasdair said, "Quite startling what you'll turn up in a criminal investigation."

"Oh? I'd like to hear about that." Roger didn't specify whether he meant the disposition of the Stone or the investigation. He chose a camera from his collection of electronic paraphernalia and started taking photos. "And I was about to tell you to give that up and help me pack, Brendan. Good going! Nessie's bones and her image carved on the sacred Stone, too. Absolute proof!"

Alasdair plucked the paparazzo back, just as the rim of the trench was crumbling beneath his oversized athletic shoes. "All in good time. Just now, Dr. Dempsey, I've got some questions that need answering."

"Sure. Yeah. No problem." Lowering the camera, Roger blinked around him as though wondering why no one stepped forward with a press release. "Brendan . . ."

"Mr. Gilstrap," Alasdair directed, "go down by the house, please, and help Miss Wotherspoon look after the Hall lad."

"Kirsty? Sure." Brendan leaped from the trench and bounded down the hillside like a buck scenting a doe. Some men, Jean reflected, would have just looked dirty. Brendan seemed all the manlier for his coating of grime. Put him together with Kirsty and her skimpy outfit and they'd be ready for a photo spread in *Maxim* or some other men's magazine. So had they gotten back together last night, when — something sensual — had been in the air?

Roger just looked grubby. "I'm sure he'd be glad to help and everything, but I really need him to be up here working. We've got to get the bones packed up and into a safe place. Locked up." As though illustrating his point he lowered himself down onto his tarp and went back to packing bones, not without the occasional possessive glance toward the trench and the Stone inside.

Alasdair loosened his tie and removed his jacket and sat down across from Roger, his pose as casual as though they were having a picnic, the flicker of light and shadow and thought in his eyes not casual at all. Jean arranged herself on a flat rock to one side and pulled out her notebook. She couldn't make notes like Gunn, but she could get something down.

Her gaze drifted to the landscape behind Alasdair, the mountains that seemed made of paper, not stone, the banks and braes plunging into the loch, the water glistening gunmetal blue-gray in the diffused sunlight. When he asked, "And then what?" she jumped.

Roger didn't. "What?"

"After you get the bones to a safe place and locked up. What then?"

"Why, I'll study them. I'll invite scientists from all over the world, and news teams, and I'll apply for funding for a Museum. Jean," Roger called to the side, "you can have a lifetime ticket."

"Thanks," she said, and wrote *baloney* on her blank page.

"Documentaries, books — this is a big story, Cameron. I'll have to retire after this one. No more worlds to conquer."

"So that's why you felt justified in planting a bug on Miss Fairbairn here?"

Roger's hands stopped dead. He looked from Jean to Alasdair and back, warily as an animal from the cover of his cap and his beard. "Ah. Well. That was Tracy's idea. Sorry about that, Jean. She got a little carried away. Very supportive, you know. I'll name the Museum after her."

"Did she send the threatening letters, too?" Alasdair asked.

After a long pause, Roger answered, "I told you. She got carried away. She was always getting carried away. That was just her personality. She was very clever, you know, arranged for the boat hire company in Inverness to send the letters thinking they were just self-addressed receipts. I didn't know about it, I didn't know a damn thing about what she was up to, not until . . ." His hands closed protectively around the bone they were holding, a vertebra that looked somewhat like a chalky caltrop. His head bowed over it so that the bill of his cap hid his face from Alasdair. But Jean could see Roger's expression, very still, very calm, as though he was thinking that by playing dead he could fool the predator into going away.

He didn't know Alasdair. "Until the boat exploded?"

"Yeah. Until the boat exploded. Then she told me everything."

"Everything? Meaning what?"

"Like I said, she was really clever, picked up a lot of electronics know-how from hanging around me. The bug, the timing mechanism on the petrol bombs, she really did a good job."

"Why did she do it?" Alasdair asked.

Again Roger looked from face to face, and then from the top of the Stone to the grove of trees. The faint breeze spilling desultorily down the hillside seemed cool, as though it were an exhalation from the pine glade, a sigh of recognition from the cold depths of time.

"There was an accident with a submersible," he said at last. "It was a rotten shame. All my fault, I'll take full responsibility — I wasn't supervising the mechanical people well enough — not my thing, the mechanics, more into electronics, you know, although my degree's in business."

But he was into the mechanics enough to pick Brad's brain, thought Jean. Alasdair said, "You were that concerned about the mechanical systems to question Miss Fairbairn's former husband about them. And then to stalk Miss Fairbairn herself."

"I saw her — your — name on Tracy's promotion list," Roger said, with an ungainly little bow in Jean's direction. "Your editor set up an interview with you about two minutes after we announced the expedition. I said to Tracy, I wonder what the deal is, if Jean wants to do some sort of expose about the sub. I mean, you showed me up at the conference that time."

Thanks, Miranda, Jean thought caustically. So in Roger's book there was publicity, and then there was publicity.

"Tracy said, oh, I'll take care of it. I thought she'd send you another press release or something, you know, spin. I didn't know she'd included a bugged toy in your press kit. Geez. What you must have thought when you found that."

Since she'd been asked, Jean said, "Among other less repeatable things, I thought that you didn't know I was divorced."

"Well, no, not until Tracy said you were talking about Brad in the past tense. She was really good about picking up on things like that."

That explained Tracy's look at Roger when she'd met Jean on the boat. *I told you so.*

Alasdair said, very quietly, "You were thinking Miss Fairbairn was a threat to you."

"I didn't. I mean, freedom of the press and all that. If Jean wanted to pick holes in my theories, fine. It was Tracy who was worried. Jonathan was poking around in places he didn't need to be poking, and she thought he was doing some sort of industrial espionage — me, I figured he was just impressed by my stuff, you know? But then Tracy saw Jean give Jonathan a note before she came on board . . ."

"That was a business card." Jean turned another page in her notebook.

Roger waved — easy come, easy go. "Sure it was. I told you, the woman was paranoid. She tells that idiot from Bristol, Martin — he was eating out of her hand, like he was going to get anything out of her — she tells him to keep an eye on you, Jean. I'm sorry about that, really. He sees you talking to the other Americans, and then he hears them talking about some secret deal they've got going with Jonathan. Except they called him Jon, and he thought they were saying Jean, and . . ."

Jean dropped her face into her hand. She'd moan *why me?* except why her was irrelevant, now.

"Hey, that American couple, they're connected to the guy who drowned in the submersible, right? I'm really sorry about that, I wish I could do something for them, but my hands are tied — things happen, space shuttles fall apart, it's the march of science and everything and well, it's a mess."

"It's a right mess," Alasdair agreed. "Especially since Jonathan was killed."

"Tracy was very upset about that, you know, very upset. That's when she came to me. Should have done that ages ago, but then, that's twenty-twenty hindsight. I bet it was the Ducketts who tried to run us down Saturday night, Jean. They thought you were Tracy, and they were out for revenge — you can't blame them, can you? They got Trace later on that same evening. I'll never forgive myself for having a good time at the ceilidh while she was — in danger." Roger stared off across the glen, every line and crease in his face turning downwards like economic trends during a depression.

Alasdair gave Roger a few moments with that thought, even though his steely eyes didn't leave the top of the grungy Omnium cap that shaded Roger's face. Alasdair's face was looking a bit pink, even though he was turned away from the sun. Jean felt her own skin, pale as his, starting to sizzle in the steamy sunlight. Another breath of air spilled down the hillside and teased the roots of her hair.

Roger was doing it again, she thought, playing his audience like a stand-up comedian. That was his personality. She shouldn't read anything into it.

"What's your position with Omnium now?" asked Alasdair.

"I'm afraid we're on the outs. We're having — what do the Hollywood types say, creative differences?"

"Usually when Hollywood's saying that, they're meaning a disagreement over money."

"Well, there's that." Roger leaned toward Alasdair confidingly, a twitch of his beard including Jean in the cozy little group. "That's why I'm so excited over the Nessie bones. And now the Stone, too! What a coup for Omnium and their equipment!"

"You were telling me yesterday it was luck that had you using Omnium's equipment just here."

"Hey, you've heard the expression, the harder I work the luckier I get?"

Alasdair didn't react.

"Well, it's been a lot of hard work, but it was luck to start with. Tracy was shopping at a boutique in Paris and found an old book, a privately-printed autobiography of Ambrose Mackintosh. We already knew Iris from her environmental work — what a gal, huh? — so Tracy bought the book."

"This was the shop owned by Charles and Sophie Bouchard?"

"Oh yeah, he's an old acquaintance, shouldn't be forgot, or however the song goes. She was his clerk and now they're married, just like a romance novel. Charles bought some stuff that had belonged to Aleister Crowley — now there's a nut case for you. Can you imagine people used to be afraid of him?"

"Was there a Pictish silver chain in that same collection?" asked Jean, flexing her writing hand.

Roger glanced around at her, his bushy eyebrows twitching upward. "Yeah, there was, Charles got a small fortune for it. You're good, Jean you're really good!"

Baloney, she wrote again, and added the note that probably both the book and the chain had been given to Crowley by Ambrose. Alasdair was still looking at Roger, unblinking. "And the book?"

"Once I got through all the verbiage, it was a real eye-opener, all that stuff about Crowley and Ambrose taking in his old mistress Edith Fraser, and there was her brother finding the Stone and everything. And yes, I already knew there was a gripping beast on the broken half, and about old Gordon chiseling it in half, saving his family from the boogeyman."

This being something Roger hadn't bothered to tell Brendan, Jean thought, the better to amaze him in case the Stone turned up. But then, the Stone had become a secondary, maybe even tertiary, quest.

"And even better," Roger went on, "Ambrose described the passage grave and — okay, can't keep any secrets here, can I? He said he found the bones of the monster there."

Ah, thought Jean. *All right*. Alasdair went so far as to nod.

"He didn't give its location," Roger continued, "but I was able to triangulate by using the pine grove, the tower of the house, and the tower of the Castle down by the loch."

"But Iris didn't want you go excavating here," Alasdair pointed out.

"Well, no. She was smart enough to be an early investor in Omnium, but after the sub accident she pulled out." Again he gestured dismissively. "Stubborn old woman. Just doesn't have any imagination, can't rise above her own petty . . ."

Into his pause Alasdair dropped the word, "Principles?"

Roger shot him a suspicious look. He had to know what was coming. Jean stirred, the rock she was sitting on becoming very hard. Funny though, how cool it had also become, as though the sun had only warmed the first millimeter, and the chill of a thousand fog-shrouded winters still lingered in its depths.

Judging by the sheen on his brow, Alasdair was warming up physically, but his manner was as cold-tempered as always. "You blackmailed her with information you got from Ambrose's autobiography. And you tracked down and gulled Gordon Fraser into helping you find the tomb. It was his description that helped you triangulate the location."

"Just applying a little leverage for the greater good. Imagination, right?" Roger held out the bone. "I mean, here's Nessie! What a deal! And thanks to Ambrose's book, I solved the old mystery about Eileen Mackintosh too. Here she is! You think Iris would be grateful I found her mother's body."

"I doubt she's grateful to you for fitting her up for the letters and the boat explosion as well."

Nice use of the ambiguities of the word "doubt," Jean thought.

Roger *tsked* beneath his breath. "Tracy framed her, not me. Either Tracy thought she should be punished for refusing to help, or was just hoping to get her out of the way. Tracy went overboard, got carried away, trying to protect me, you know."

Alasdair had heard that verse before. "I don't suppose your book tells where Ambrose found his hoard of Pictish treasure."

"Nah. The last chapter's torn out."

Alasdair half-winked in Jean's direction. *Gotcha.* She wrinkled her nose at him.

"Not a frigging word," Roger went on. "The area could be riddled with tombs and hoards and monsters, and if he said anything about it at all, it's in that last few pages. I tell you, Inspector Cameron, what's a man to do?" Roger grinned and shrugged.

Jean expected Alasdair to reply, *A man could stop playing silly beggars with the police*, and yet, was Roger playing them for fools? What Alasdair asked was, "You're working with the Bouchards then, hoping to recover more treasure?"

"Sure. No harm in that. I need them back up here, too, when you're done — with them." He was about to say "harassing" or the equivalent, but thought better of it. Again he looked from face to face, exuding helpfulness. "The book's at the hotel, you can have it if you need it for evidence or something. I found what I came here for. I'll be back on the fast track before you know it!"

"Are you saying 'I' because your wife's dead, or because you were always after following that track on your own? Sounds to have been a bit of a rift between you, with her planting bugs and bombs and the like, and never telling you."

Roger looked pained, as though Alasdair had just hit him below the belt. "Every marriage has its ups and downs. You know what I mean, I bet you're a married man, Inspector Cameron."

Jean would have winced, but she wanted to keep her eyes open for the expression on Alasdair's face.

It was something between a sniff and snarl. "No, Dr. Dempsey, I'm not a married man."

"Hello!" shouted a voice from below. Jean looked around to see Peter Kettering trudging up the hill, his suit jacket slung over his shoulder, his vest gaping open, fashionable sunglasses looking like a bandit's mask across his face.

THIRTY-THREE

Alasdair stood up and brushed off his trousers, then gave Jean a hand up. His expression was set, but she could swear she caught a sigh of decompression. Maybe he was glad Kettering had broken up the cheery little gathering before Alasdair told Roger just what he could do with his bones, the ones that made everything worthwhile.

Roger scrambled to his feet. "Hey, Peter, look, I found the rest of the Pitclachie Stone! There's still time to get photos of it into the press release."

"Well then, better and better!" Kettering stumbled to a halt, out of breath, face polished cherry-red. He glanced at Roger's osteological booty, stared, then knelt down and probed the skull with a forefinger. "The photographs came out quite well, but I wanted to see for myself — these look to be . . ."

"Authentic?" Roger asked with a chortle of glee. "They'll stand up to any test you want to throw at them, Peter. What a day for science!"

"I wasn't meaning to suggest," Peter hemmed and hawed, although he clearly was meaning to suggest, and was taking the precaution of checking out the situation himself. "Very impressive. Amazing story."

Jean met Alasdair's jaundiced eye. All the instrumentation in the world, but there's a difference in actually seeing for yourself. The problem was, even seeing for yourself proved nothing.

Kettering stood up, his insectoid sunglasses still turned toward the bones. "The boat sails at half past seven. If you could come a bit early to assist with the display?"

"My reputation for getting lost in my work and running late precedes me, I see. No worries, Peter, I wouldn't miss this for anything. My life's work, vindicated! Soon as Inspector Cameron here gives the word, Brendan and I will get everything boxed up here and clean up for the cruise." Suddenly Roger's face pleated into his beard. "Geez, Tracy would have gotten such a charge out of this. She worked by my side all these years, contributed so much . . ."

Jean wondered what Jonathan would have thought, and decided it was better not to know. As far as Kettering was concerned, the upside of a Big Discovery trumped the downside of two Unfortunate Deaths, publicity-wise. She glanced at Alasdair.

All he said was, "Mr. Kettering, could you see your way clear to including a wee boy and his mum in the evening's events? The lad's a fan of Nessie. A future consumer."

"Of course, Chief Inspector. Plenty of room. We've only invited sixty people — including Iris Mackintosh, of course, if we can lure her down from her ivory tower." He brayed at his own joke, the glare off his teeth almost casting a shadow. "Miss Fairbairn, we'll see you there with the other members of the fourth estate. And Chief Inspector, I know a fair number of your people will be there in their official capacities, but if you would care to be Starr's honored guest — we're having Hugh Munro and his band on the lounge deck, playing their own unique blend of traditional and modern tunes."

"Thank you," said Alasdair.

"You won't mind my mentioning that the event is formal dress," Kettering went on. "I'll be dressed in the style of the country, myself. My first experience as a kilted Highlander, but I won't be indulging in the same sort of undergarments that a proper Scotsman would be wearing. Or not wearing." He bleated again.

Alasdair's eyes were starting to cross. Jean kept her face hidden by continuing to make notes.

Roger shifted his vertebra from hand to hand like a gambler shaking luck into his dice. Unlike Alasdair, whose gambling consisted of counting the fall of the cards and playing the odds, Roger was the type who would risk everything on one throw. "Tracy would have loved Hugh. Great band. Heard them at the ceilidh Saturday night and enjoyed them so much I went back on Sunday for more. Takes your mind off, well, takes your mind off."

"Yes, yes, of course, very brave of you to persevere. Most admirable," said Kettering. "I'm afraid I made a bit of a fool of myself Saturday night, dancing and all — you just can't keep your feet on the floor, now can you, when Hugh is playing?"

Yeah, Jean remembered, Hugh had said something about Kettering prancing around when he wasn't ducking out to take a call.

"No way," said Roger. "You remember that sequence of songs he did — oh, it must have been around midnight. The pop tunes, 'Bad Moon Rising' and 'In-a-Gadda-da-Vida,' and the jigs and stuff in between. If you weren't drunk when he started, you were drunk . . ."

An electronic trill made all three men go for their pockets. Kettering won the jackpot. "Starr Beverages promotion! Ah yes, I'll be there straightaway." And, slipping the phone back into his dangling jacket, "Must see to the catering. Good job for me, eh, catering, Kettering?" Exuding ghastly jollity, he cantered back down the path.

"See you tonight, Peter! You too, Jean. Inspector. Champagne's on me!" Roger gathered up a camera, and what was probably a GPS unit, and what could just as well have been Captain Kirk's tricorder, and descended into the trench, there to lavish his affections on the top half of the Pitclachie Stone.

Alasdair jerked his head toward Pitclachie House. Jean walked beside him in silence until they were past the first gate and into the moist shade of the garden, where they were bushwhacked by a cloud of midges. They hurried the rest of the way into the courtyard of the house. Only then did Alasdair stop, and after a searching look up, down, and sideways had ascertained no one was watching — even Iris's window was now vacant — he closed his eyes and let his shoulders sag.

Jean felt as though she'd been dragged through two barbed-wire fences, and she hadn't been doing half the work he had. She applied her right hand to his left shoulder and allowed herself to both massage and appreciate the firm musculature concealed beneath his shirt. "Bonus points for remembering Elvis. How about one of those nice cups of tea for yourself?"

For five seconds he leaned into her touch, then opened his eyes and withdrew. With a nod of thanks, he said, "A wee dram wouldn't come amiss, but I'll not be getting that 'til after the cruise. If then. We've gone through our list of suspects, and we've come to a dead end."

"But you have your eye on Roger."

"When a wife is killed, your first suspicion falls on the husband. And the other way round. He wasn't half angry with her Saturday night. I reckon she cut him off at the knees right and proper when she told him she'd destroyed the boat."

"He was mad, all right. Angry. However . . ."

"He was at the ceilidh while Tracy was being pushed out the window. A fact he took a right bit of care pointing out just now."

"No kidding. He sure did give you the charm offensive. The well-meaning but slightly goofy inventor going happy-go-luckily about his business, while his wife machiavellies behind his back."

"Owned up to quite a bit, he did, though you'll never convince me he didn't know that submersible was on board, partially disassembled or not."

"I bet he was going to dump it in the deepest part of the loch. Which would have been a lot better than Tracy's blowing it up, but like he said, Tracy was over the top."

"And wanted to show him up, I reckon. Feeling unappreciated and all." Alasdair wiped his forehead. "In any event, he shopped Tracy and Martin good and proper, and suggested the Ducketts murdered Tracy. Everyone's guilty but him."

"And the Bouchards. They were working with him while Martin worked with Tracy. I'm surprised they didn't all collide in the hallway outside my door — well," Jean amended, "the Bouchards had the Lodge all to themselves for several days. I thought somebody had picked the lock of the lumber room. And here I was thinking they'd moved into the house because they'd sensed the ghosts."

"No, they've not got the personality to sense ghosts."

Ghost-sensors tending to be nervous and intense. "I wouldn't think they have the personality to run people down with their car, either, but . . . Funny how Roger went off to the ceilidh that night when he was hurt worse than I was, and I was aching all over. No way could I have gone dancing. Maybe he couldn't stand being in the same hotel room with — no, Tracy wasn't there."

"She was sneaking about Pitclachie, looking out a complete copy of that book, using the keys Martin copied for her."

"Yeah, she was wearing sneakers when she died because she was sneaking. And since she was a sneaky person, she thought I was, too. If it weren't such a tragedy it would be a farce."

"These things usually are," said Alasdair, so blandly Jean suspected he was covering bleakness.

She looked discreetly away. There was the garden constable pacing along the path. He must be using bug repellent for aftershave. And Mandrake the cat was ambling across the terrace, his coat of many colors flicking in and out of shadow like a jaguar on the prowl. "Roger would probably turn the Bouchards in, if he could. As for vice versa, I know Hugh saw them at the ceilidh, but did the Bouchards ever say in so many words they saw Roger?"

Alasdair scowled so fiercely his eyebrows met at the bridge of his nose. "No matter — Andy Sawyer saw him there."

"Oh. Yeah. He did." The egregious Sawyer, whose work Alasdair now had to do along with his own.

"I'll get onto him, get the details," he said, discarding his scowl as useless distraction. "We might be obliged to interview all the people who were there, work out a timetable or the like."

"Hugh said the place was heaving. I bet the bar was packed, too. It would take a long time to find everyone, let along talk to them. And meanwhile Roger's congratulating himself for pulling everything, including Nessie, out of the fire. Or the water, as the case may be."

"Oh aye. Best I can do now is go back to the station and have a look at everyone's statements and the trace evidence reports, perhaps I've missed something."

If he had had a warhorse, he'd be getting Jean to winch him back onto it. "Do you need me to drive you back?" she asked.

"I'll cadge a ride from the constable at the end of the drive, thank you kindly."

"Okay then. I'll go put on my glad rags for tonight. Of course, with all the men in kilts, no one's going to notice me."

"I'd not be so sure of that." One corner of his mouth thawed enough to crimp into a wry half-smile.

"You don't have time to get your own kilt from Inverness, though."

"I'll borrow Hamish's, we're much the same size. The runts of the Cameron litter, I'm thinking, though I doubt our ancestors were the giants among men that legend paints them."

"Who is?" she replied with a smile, not so much at the joke as at Alasdair being able to make one at this fraught moment, and tore the relevant pages from her notebook. "Here you go."

He folded her notes into his pocket. The other corner of his mouth melted, drawing his lips up into a full smile. "Half past seven, then."

"See you later," she called to his retreating back.

With a smooth pirouette, he turned around, blew her a kiss, and went on his way — toward Noreen Hall, who was climbing out of a police car in the parking area like someone climbing out of a sickbed. With a hold-that-bus gesture to the car, Alasdair spoke to Noreen. Her desolate expression cracked and flowed away, revealing an actual smile. "Thank you, thank you. Elvis, I'll tell Elvis, shall I . . ." She ran across the courtyard and into the house.

Smiling and digging in her bag for the key — it was at the bottom, of course — Jean started toward the door of the Lodge. Just as she put the key in the lock, her cell phone rang, sending her back into the bag. "Hello?"

"Hiya," said a male voice. "Here I am."

Her brain spun without traction. She knew who it was, who was . . . Oh. Brad. "Hi. Where are you supposed to be?"

"You asked me to call you back," he said with exaggerated patience. "Nancy Drew and the case of the sinking submersible, right?"

"Oh yeah. Sorry. Things have been happening here."

"No shit. Tracy Dempsey bit the dust. Has Dudley Do-Right caught the killer yet?"

Jean gritted her teeth and resisted drop-kicking the phone. "About the submersible . . ."

"The guy who was killed was named Christopher Peretti. His wife was Melissa Duckett — must be her maiden name, huh? — — and they had three kids. Does that help?"

"Yes it does."

"I wrote it down, so I'd remember. Bet you thought I'd forget. Anything else I can do to — what do they say there, assist the police in their inquiries?"

It could have been worse. He could have called while she and Alasdair . . . She had to be mature about this. "I'll let you know. Thanks for checking it out for me. Gotta run now. Bye."

"Bye," said his voice from the speaker as she squashed *end*. Independent, disinterested confirmation of the Ducketts' story *was* a help. It was her own prejudice that made Brad seem to be a day late and a dollar short. Or a pound short.

Speaking of pounds, eight infant pounds to be exact, she walked into the stuffy Lodge and called the Campbell-Reid's flat. She got the voice mail, and duly left her message. "Hi, it's Jean. I wanted to let you know that Roger's assistant uncovered the rest of the Pitclachie Stone. Thanks to your I.D. of the mason, we've got the full story and are making progress on the case . . ." From her lips to the ears of Justice, she added silently, never mind that intrepid *we*. "I'm cruising the loch tonight, so I'll call y'all back tomorrow. Give my love to the baby."

She closed the phone and noticed the time on its face. Five-thirty. Time flies when you're shoulder-to-shoulder with Sisyphus, rolling a boulder up a mountain. But Miranda should still be in the office.

She was, and answered the phone herself. "Ah, Jean. You've not been abducted the day, then."

"Not by aliens, anyway." By a certain detective chief inspector, but she'd save that until Miranda wormed it out of her with a third degree beyond even Alasdair's capabilities.

"Getting forwarder on the case, are you?"

"More or less. Roger's assistant turned up the missing half of the Pitclachie Stone, so at least the Museum's going to come out ahead. How are things at the office?"

"Hardly had time to look over this month's print run, the phone's been going all day long with folk asking for advice."

"You should hang out a second shingle — Dear Aunt Miranda."

"Not that sort of advice. Names for boards of directors and the like. Protect and Survive is looking out a security chief for overseeing historical properties, the National Portrait Gallery is looking out a curator for sharing an exhibition with the Met in New York . . . There goes my other line. Sorry, Jean. We'll have us a good blether when you get back, all right?"

"All right. Take care." Jean switched off again and thought, get back? Could she ever get back? And she didn't mean to her flat in Edinburgh and her office above the Royal Mile.

She looked out through the open doorway of the Lodge to see Mandrake poised on the terrace wall. Was he watching Eileen's ghost? No, the hair wasn't standing up on his back. And even when

Jean herself stepped to the door, she sensed nothing except the warm humid air, like Alasdair's breath on her cheek teasing her with possibilities.

A bird erupted from the shrubbery and the cat sat back with a shrug. *Just sightseeing. Nothing serious.*

Would there in time be another ghost walking at Pitclachie? Jean wondered. She went to her kitchen, got a paring knife, then cut a bouquet of red roses from the garden. Mandrake watched curiously as she laid them on the flagstone carved with the symbol of the water horse.

Will all great Neptune's ocean wash this blood Clean from my hand? No, this my hand will rather The multitudinous seas incarnadine, Making the green one red. But if Tracy had ever felt Lady Macbeth's remorse, Jean had no way of knowing. What she did know was that Tracy's killer was coming close to getting away with murder.

THIRTY-FOUR

Jean had brought along the appropriate garb to uphold *Great Scot's* — and Miranda's — image, a bugle-beaded top and flowing rayon skirt in a teal blue that flattered her fair skin, brown hair and browner eyes. It would clash with Alasdair's red and green tartan kilt, but then, she hadn't known she'd be color-coordinating.

Now she strolled away from Pitclachie, down the length of the drive, and, with a spurt of speed across the main road, further down to the pier. Strolling being advisable not only because of the heat but of her shoes, beaded sandals with low heels that looked good but in practical terms could only be said to leave her less handicapped than stilettos.

Dark water lapped languidly at the dirt and gravel shore. Reporters with mini-cams and other equipment drifted hither and thither, their garb not upholding any images. Just above the water line, a pair of beady-eyed constables stood guard over a pile of debris demarcated by police tape. The remains of Roger's boat, no doubt, including a man-sized cylinder that had to be the body of the submersible.

Jean joined the sequined and tartaned throng waiting at the gangplank. She contributed a knowing smile to the murmur of anticipation — a cabaret and a crime scene, what better way to spend a warm summer evening? — and was duly admitted to the boat. She walked past the wooden benches lining the back deck and paused beside a life preserver hanging on a bulkhead to catch her breath and settle her nerves, not that either was going to cooperate.

What had Tracy intended to wear tonight? If Roger had come across the no doubt stylish garment back at the hotel while he was dressing, had he felt any qualms? More importantly, was Alasdair going to succeed either at breaking Roger's alibi or finding another suspect? If neither, the case would trail off into inconsequence, taking Alasdair's reputation with it. And how would that affect their nascent relationship, inconsequential as that might be in the greater scheme of life, the universe, and everything?

Jean lifted up her eyes to the hills, whence the shadows of evening were flowing down to the loch. An upside-down image of the castle was reflected in the bay, an image that wavered as the ripples from a passing inflatable creased the surface tension but didn't break it. The skreel of bagpipes echoed thinly across the water. The piper was probably making a fortune — tourists were jammed atop the tower like commuters at rush hour.

Lowering her eyes, but not her expectations, she worked her way around the main deck. Two uniformed constables stood in the bow of the boat like twin figureheads.

Elvis was clinging to a railing, his solemn gaze fixed on the water. His hair was slicked back and his short pants ironed to cellophane crispness. Beside him stood Noreen, almost lost in the flowered fabric of her peasant skirt and loose blouse. Her hair was tacked up on her head in an imitation of Kirsty's swirl, so that all the ends stuck out like antennae. Noreen was a work in progress, more power to her, Jean thought, and returned her shy smile with a grin.

Aha! Gunn was standing by the stairway leading to an upper observation deck, his kilt just a bit too long and his calves spindly in their tall white socks. But his stance was suitably official and his face mimicked Alasdair's expressionlessness. Jean returned his greeting with a question. "Where's D.C.I. Cameron?"

"Reading reports, Miss Fairbairn."

"You've both had a busy day."

"Oh aye. We've processed Mr. and Mrs. Duckett and released them — nothing to charge them with, the boss is saying."

Good for the boss. "And Martin Hall?"

"In a cell in Inverness just now, but like as not he'll be released the morn."

Jean glanced at Elvis and Noreen, their heads close together as the boy pointed out a couple of diving birds. "What about the Bouchards?"

"They're our guests for the night as well, and perhaps a bit longer. They've finally admitted they hit you and Dr. Dempsey, but are saying it was on accident, Charles having taken a bit too much to drink."

"And they drove all the way from Invergarry without lights? Yeah, right." Jean snorted. "I guess they're also saying they didn't stop because they were afraid they'd be deported, and they wanted to keep on working with Roger. Otherwise known as searching for a complete copy of the book and picking over his archaeological leavings."

"Right." Gunn's thin smile would have copied Alasdair's except for a slight softness at the corners.

"Did they see Roger at the ceilidh?"

"They're not so certain of that, said the room was crowded, and they'd taken more drink, and perhaps he was there, perhaps not."

"But Sawyer saw Roger there when Tracy was killed."

"Oh aye. That he did."

"But," Jean asked, grasping at every possible straw, "was Sawyer in the dining room, at the ceilidh, himself? Or did he just go there, looking for Roger, after he got the call? And how long between the time the constable at Pitclachie radioed for help, and everyone in the chain of command was notified?"

"The boss asked the exact same ques . . ." Gunn's mouth stopped in mid-word.

A pair of long bare legs came down the steps, followed by a short beaded dress, followed by Kirsty's long hair flowing around her face and shoulders. She moved like a spring coiled with tension, ready to fly up like a jack-in-the-box. Jean sympathized with that.

Just behind her walked her squire. Brendan was wearing a simple suit and tie and a hunted look that only intensified when Jean pounced. "You were at the bar in the hotel when Tracy was killed, weren't you? Was Roger there, too?"

Darting a glance at Gunn — was this an official query? — Brendan replied, "Yes and no, in that order."

"Who else was there?"

"Half the population of Scotland. And the other half was up the hall in the dining room."

"The barmaid was chatting you up," Kirsty said stiffly, "and there's me, doing the accounts back at Pitclachie."

"Hey, I told you about that. It was funny. Your guy, Sawyer — "Gunn did not correct Brendan's misapprehension. "— he was hitting on the barmaid and she was hitting on me. Sort of a chain reaction."

"So Sawyer was in the bar," Jean repeated. "When did he leave?"

"He got a phone call and puffed up like an old bullfrog, and he said to me, 'come along lad, there's been a right turn-up, your boss's wife's been killed.' I was horrified, duh, and went with him upstairs to Roger's room."

"But he wasn't there."

"No. So then Sawyer says, let's have a look at the ceilidh."

Gunn picked up on that. "And there's when you saw Dr. Dempsey?"

"Yeah, he was standing in a corner jiggling up and down, out of breath. He's not much of a dancer. He was wiping his face off, like everyone was, but I took his arm when Sawyer told him the bad news and he wasn't hot at all, just really chilly. The shock, I guess. He was white as a ghost."

Well, well, Jean thought, and met Gunn's questioning gaze evenly. In other words, Roger could have run through the cool, damp night and reached the hotel moments before Sawyer came looking for him. Even with the sergeant seeing events from his own Sawyer-centric universe, he wasn't fudging a thing. But just because Roger could have killed Tracy after all didn't mean that he had.

"They're casting off the lines. We're away," said Kirsty, and led Brendan to the railing.

Jean looked pointedly at Gunn. Where was Alasdair? He couldn't miss the boat, on either a physical or a metaphorical level.

Gunn, another great mind at work, pulled out his phone and bounded up the stairway.

From far below, the engines coughed and then thrummed. The flags strung from stem to stern trembled. The deck reverberated beneath Jean's feet. She seized a handy pole. Temple Pier and the land slipped backward, and a fresh cool breeze dissipated the scent of diesel. Breathe, she told herself. Just keep breathing.

In moments the boat was out of the bay and onto the main body of the loch, rolling gently to a slow swell. The heat haze brushed the sky with an opalescent shimmer. The mountains lining the loch marched away down the Great Glen, each rank becoming an ever more tenuous shade of blue-gray, until on the southern horizon they opened out like the hands of earth cupped pleadingly to heaven.

Close by, the water glistened a dark steely blue, in the distance it flashed and writhed with mirages like imperfections in an antique mirror. A looking glass, Jean thought, the better to see yourself in.

A few of her fellow passengers were pointing out the black reflection of the opposite bank, or the ruined walls of Urquhart Castle, or the tower and trees of Pitclachie House. But the majority of the attendees had gathered in the lounge, waiting for the show. So was Jean, if for a slightly different sort of show.

She stepped over the metal threshold into the long low room. Large windows looked out on the passing scene. In the back, against a Starr Beverages banner, Hugh and the lads were tuning their instruments and checking out a few small amplifiers, "unplugged" being relative. A bar to one side glistened with bottles and glasses. Two young women poured and served, and two young men passed through the gathering throng, offering trays of food. To the other side, a display of posters and photos were propped on easels and covered with tartan cloth, ready for the Great Revelation.

Roger stood nearby, clean but hardly sober — the empty glass in his hand was replaced by a waiter even as Jean watched. His tuxedo hung on his wiry body as though it was still hanging in a closet. It was Peter Kettering, however, who was the sight that made eyes sore.

As he had threatened, he was dressed in the full wretched excess of Hollywood-Highland garb, high-laced shoes, tartan socks and kilt, fur sporran, tartan plaid draped over a gold-buttoned double-breasted jacket. The spill of lace at his throat made him look as though he'd forgotten to remove his napkin after a messy lunch. His teeth, exposed in a maniacal grin, resembled a solid sheet of porcelain. His gaze bounced around the room, his ear tilted toward Roger. Between the squeaks and trills of the band, Jean caught the words "Tobermory" and "gold." So much for Roger promising to retire.

A choking noise came from the riser that was the bandstand. Hugh? His T-shirted and suspender-framed belly was quivering, and his cheeks had gone beyond pink to crimson. He was trying not to laugh at Kettering — no biting the Starr hand that fed him — but his glee kept escaping like puffs of steam from a boiling pot.

Jean sidled toward him. "He looks like the bastard child of Queen Victoria and Walter Scott."

That set Hugh off again, until at last he wiped his face with a handkerchief the size of a pillowcase and said, "Thank goodness Dempsey's wearing an ordinary monkey suit. Two of them and my head would explode."

"You said you saw Kettering at the ceilidh Saturday night. I don't guess you saw Roger there."

"Ah, no, the place was heaving. I only saw the people just beside the stage. Or passed out beneath it."

In the corner Billy's bagpipes honked and squealed. He adjusted his drones, tried again with the first few notes of "Bad Moon Rising," and then played a measure of "The Rights of Man," his fingers dancing on the chanter.

"That's the pipes for you," said Hugh, "like squeezing a pig under one arm and knitting at the same time."

Jean grinned. "I love it when y'all play off-the-wall pieces. You'll have to do 'In-a-Gadda-da-Vida' tonight, like you did Saturday."

"That was Sunday," Hugh amended. "And it was our Billy's doing, a punter bet him twenty pound he couldn't play it. Man was away with the fairies, most likely, our Billy can play anything."

Jean stiffened like a bird dog spotting a grouse. "So you haven't added 'In-a-Gadda-da-Vida' to that medley of pop and trad? You only did it on Sunday?"

"Oh aye. Bit of a stunt really, but then . . ."

But then, Roger had lied. Jean grabbed Hugh's arm, exclaimed, "Thank you!" and whirled toward the door.

She was just in time to see Brendan and Kirsty walk into the room, and behind them Alasdair. *Yes, yes, yes!* His dark jacket with its epaulettes, his heather-colored tie and white socks, his red and green kilt swinging provocatively above those braw Cameron calves — there was a class act. As for his less than gigantic stature, well, tall was as tall did, and right now he needed to do.

He was scanning the room. His gaze landed on Jean and brightened like headlights going from low-beam to high. He started toward her as she started toward him. The crowd swirled and thickened from individual bodies to a barricade as Kettering stepped forward. "Ladies and gentlemen!"

Roger set down his glass and stood poised, his dogs groomed, his ponies curried, and his water monsters bedecked with tartan bow ties. Maybe he was swaying because of the drinks, maybe because of the slow rise and fall of the boat. Maybe he was swaying because he stood at the top of a precipice and was ready to jump.

"Ladies and gentlemen," Kettering proclaimed. "I present to you Roger Dempsey, the discoverer of the Loch Ness monster!"

Roger whisked away the cloth covering the easels. With various gasps and exclamations, everyone pressed forward, kilts sweeping, bosoms heaving, cameras whirring. Even the waiters and barmaids and musicians leaned toward the exhibit.

Jean stopped working her way around the back of the crowd and gaped. Poster-sized photos of the bones from the tomb, artfully arranged, were accompanied by drawings of various concepts of Nessie, some more zoologically possible than others. Another poster showed the Pitclachie stone, with 8x10s of the newly-revealed upper half pinned to its edge. Roger pulled a marking pen from an inside pocket and sketched in the gripping beast, just to make sure everyone appreciated it for what it was. Kettering babbled about museums, openings, sponsorships, advertising campaigns.

Alasdair ranged up beside Jean, seized her arm with his strong right hand, and pulled her into the back corner. "Gunn's saying you've knocked a bittie chip out of Roger's alibi."

"Yeah, and Hugh just blew it to pieces — one of the tunes Roger said he heard the band play on Saturday they only played on Sunday, and it was a one-off then."

"Well then. No surprise the trace evidence . . ."

"Rubbish!" shouted a deep but unmistakably female voice. Jean's and Alasdair's and every other face in the room swung toward the door.

Iris Mackintosh stood there, tall, straight, and regal. Her high-collared jacket and loose trousers shimmered silkily, her iron-gray hair swept back from her forehead. She cut a path through the onlookers like Moses through the Red Sea.

Roger stood his ground, beard out-thrust belligerently. Kettering smiled, gracious to a fault. "Miss Mackintosh! So glad you can join us for this wonderful moment, the vindication of your father's writings . . ."

"Rubbish," she said again. "If Dr. Dempsey had bothered to consult a proper scientist, he'd have discovered right smartly that what he has discovered are the calcified remains of a basking shark."

"A what?" asked Kettering.

The color drained from Roger's face. Iris grabbed the pen from his limp hand and began drawing on the largest poster. "Here is the shark's tail, and here its head, and here its mouth . . ." she sketched in a huge, gaping maw, drooping down from the skull like a debutante's crinoline skirt. "They feed on zooplankton. Once the flesh and less-calcified bits of cartilage rot away, and the other perishable parts of the animal are no longer extant, you are left with the spine and skull. What you've interpreted as flippers are no doubt bones of some other creature. You're not the first person to jump to the wrong conclusions, Roger, but you're by far the biggest fool amongst them."

The room was so quiet that Jean could hear the swish of water around the bows of the boat, an undertone to the thrum of the engines. From just outside the door came Elvis's, "I want to see the pictures, Mummy," and Noreen's, "Not just now."

Jean leaned toward Alasdair as he leaned toward her. "It was never Nessie," he whispered.

"Basking sharks have unusually well-calcified skeletons," Iris went on. "Plus, this specimen was quite large and probably very old, which is why its remains are heavy and dense as bones. It's remarkably well-preserved, even so. Perhaps the shark was originally found on the shores of the sea and brought here by the Picts as a totem, to protect their borderland. Perhaps it had somehow found its way into the loch. In any event, it was buried long ago, and forgotten until my father Ambrose discovered it, and from it constructed his myth. I will not apologize for that. Each of us is free to believe anything we wish, but that does not mean that believing something makes it true." She handed the pen to Kettering, who stared at it as though it were a grenade.

"Iris," Roger said, his usual rumble strained and thin.

"Roger," said Kettering, in a slightly stronger voice.

Bedlam broke out in the room, people chattering to each other and shouting questions at Kettering and Roger and Iris and calling for more alcohol to wash down the headline news.

Smiling like a cherub on steroids, Hugh put his fiddle to his shoulder and started to play "MacPherson's Rant," supposedly composed by the titular MacPherson just before he was hanged. If Hugh had realized the full implications of the moment, he'd never have chosen that piece. Did anyone else recognize it? Her hand over her mouth, holding in something between hysterical laughter and a scream, Jean turned to Alasdair.

"The forensics reports," he said, his breath tickling her ear. "The trace evidence. The clothes Roger was wearing the night Tracy was killed. Bits of dust and pollen match those in the tower room. So do microscopic bits of wool, from Iris's knitting, most likely. A scrap of plastic from the floor of the tower, just below the window, is a bandage from a paramedic's kit. I'll be asking the medicos to examine Roger for a scratch or stab wound from the knitting needle."

Jean, chilled, could see it all. Roger and Tracy, already at odds, in over their heads, their ship sinking. They thought the hit-and-run meant their enemies were closing in. They doubled their efforts to find the complete book — a treasure would rectify everything. But they also doubled their resentments. One word from a tense, edgy person to another. Shouts. The shove . . . It had truly been a crime of passion. "We might have looked right at that wound. He had bandages and scratches on his arms anyway."

"Oh aye." Alasdair's gaze transferred itself to Roger.

Above the beard Roger's tanned skin was pale as beeswax, sagging like a candle burned too long. He lurched back against the wall. Jean thought he was going to slide down it and melt into a puddle on the deck. But no. Suddenly his body solidified. He thrust Iris against Kettering, sending them both against one of the easels, which in turn fell over with a clatter.

Roger shoved his way through the crowd, batting away microphones, ignoring grins, and strode out onto the forward deck. Hugh segued into a jig. The other instruments joined in.

Alasdair's mouth set itself in a grim line. "Let's finish it, shall we?" He started toward the door, not waiting to see if Jean was with him. That had been a rhetorical question.

But she wasn't going to shrink away now. Now that she'd done everything she could to bring down Roger's castle in the air, including feeling pity for the man.

Alasdair burst out of the door, sweeping away a cameraman in his path, Jean right behind him. She saw Gunn standing by the railing next to Noreen and Elvis. She saw Roger come to a halt in the middle of the deck, arms crossed, half-crouched as though in pain. She saw high on the green bank of the loch, above a huge metal boat-house so incongruous it seemed alien, the row of white houses that was Foyers. She couldn't see Crowley's Boleskine House. It lurked in the trees, wrapped in darkness and despair.

Alasdair jerked his head at Gunn and with a gesture summoned the constables. He took Roger's shoulder and turned him around, not roughly but firmly. He met Roger's shocked, furious, desperate stare with a flinty stare of his own. "Roger Dempsey, I arrest you in connection with the murder of Tracy Dempsey. You are not obliged to say anything, but anything you do say will be taken down and may be given in . . ."

"Roger!" Brendan, Kirsty at his side, popped out onto the deck. "Roger, I'm sorry, I thought those bones might be a whale of some kind, but the head wasn't right — vertebrates aren't my field — I didn't think there'd be any harm . . ."

"Mummy," said Elvis, "it isn't Nessie, is it? The man lied."

In one convulsive movement Roger wrenched away from Alasdair, pushed Gunn sprawling onto the deck, evaded a constable's tackle, and sprinted for the side of the boat. He grabbed the little boy and set him up on the railing so that his feet dangled over the water. "You're going to get this boat turned around, Cameron. You're going to turn it around and get me back to shore."

Noreen's scream was anything but short. It was Edith's cry, it was Tracy's — disbelief and rage mingled. She lunged for Roger. Alasdair diverted her towards Jean. Jean handed her off to Kirsty. Jean was vaguely aware of Gunn clambering to his feet, of people spilling out of the lounge and down the stairway, of the music ending abruptly, of cameras clicking. All she could see was Elvis in Roger's hands, suspended above the cold water of the loch.

"Mummy?" he asked, not yet frightened but wondering why his mother had screamed. He wriggled. In another minute his bottom would slip off the railing and only the strength in Roger's arms would keep him from falling. And Roger was trembling, his pallor taking on a shade of green. Great, Jean told herself, he was going to faint and drop the child anyway.

"Sit still, lad," Alasdair said, and taking a step closer to Roger, "Don't be stupid. You're adding charges on top of charges, and this time you've got witnesses aplenty."

"It's all over," Roger mumbled. "I gave it my best shot. Tracy, she meant well."

"You've done remarkable work. Omnium's a going concern. You found the upper half of the Stone. That's quite genuine." Alasdair took another step.

Behind Jean's back, she heard Gunn whispering, "Put the inflatable into the water, now." Footsteps slowly retreated, then broke into a run. The sound of the engines changed timbre, throttling back.

Elvis sat still, staring out at the expanse of water between the boat and the shore. Maybe he thought this was some sort of thrill ride. Maybe he was just stunned. Noreen was sobbing in Kirsty's arms. Brendan was flanking Alasdair, and two uniformed constables were standing ready — to do what? They couldn't shoot Roger. They could try lassoing him, Jean supposed.

She felt utterly helpless, utterly useless, cursing Roger, cursing herself — all she'd done was challenge Roger's assumptions and ask questions, it wasn't her fault that his suspicions of her had fueled his and Tracy's plots . . .

Roger inhaled, shuddering. For just a second his head fell forward and his grip on Elvis' torso loosened. In that second Alasdair leaped. He seized Elvis's small shoulders and yanked him free of Roger's grasp, then pirouetted and threw the child into the arms of the constable who had followed his leap.

"No!" Roger snapped erect and scrambled up onto the railing, first rung, second, and teetered at the top. In a flurry of tartan, Alasdair leaped up beside him and wrapped his right arm around Roger's chest. They struggled, Roger straining toward the water, Alasdair pulling him back, tilting further and further. And were gone.

Brendan and the second constable lunged into the railing and leaned over it, grabbing at air. A deep-throated splash resounded from the water.

Alasdair! Jean didn't go for the railing. She didn't even go for conscious thought. Kicking off her shoes, she dashed for the doughnut-shaped life preserver hanging on the bulkhead — red and white, it wouldn't clash with Alasdair's tartan. The life preserver seemed to bound off its hook and into her hands. Spinning around, she clambered up onto the railing — trajectories, the speed of the boat, the hump of its wake moving across the water surface, the patch of roil and froth there, limbs splashing like dark snakes, going under. She jumped.

Somewhere about half way down, and it was a long way down, her brain kicked back in. What the hell was she doing, protecting her investment in a certain policeman? Refusing to go on without him? She hit the surface of the water. It was hard, breaking beneath her weight, sending a shock wave through her body. The dark water closed over her head. Her breath shattered into pellets of hail, so cold they burned her throat and chest.

Fight! Fight! Hooking her left arm around the life ring, she didn't only let it pull her to the surface, she pushed it upward. Her skirt wrapped her legs and she kicked and flailed. Something touched her thigh, a trailing bit of weed or a tentacle or a bit of fabric. Blindly she grabbed and came up with a handful of stiff cloth — a collar, she realized, connected to a heavy body. *Please, please, let it be Alasdair.*

Like breaching a membrane, she broke the surface of the water. Prisms danced in her eyes — her glasses, they were gone, like she cared. The black wall of the boat rose out of the black water several yards away. Clinging desperately to the buoyant ring, she pulled the collar upwards with every micron of strength she had and some she didn't know she had, and Alasdair's head popped into the air beside her, streaming water.

He gasped, gulped, and coughed, and started to sink back. The wet wool of the kilt was dragging him down. A tremendous splash doused her face with ice water and Brendan was swimming toward them, arms stroking powerfully. He pulled Alasdair back up and toward the life ring. And here came the inflatable, bouncing over the swells toward them, a sailor and a constable already leaning over the sides.

Jean's hand was frozen onto Alasdair's collar. Even when he wrapped an arm around the life preserver and looked up with wide eyes reflecting the multicolored light, still she hung onto him. She couldn't feel her feet. Shivers were wracking her body.

His icy fingers fumbled for hers, and closed around them, and held on.

THIRTY-FIVE

From her table on the terrace of the Visitor Center, Jean gazed down over Urquhart Castle and the loch beyond it, trying to think serene thoughts. A Scottish flag rose from the highest rampart, fluttering in the brisk, cool wind, its colors repeating the blue of the sky and the white of the occasional meringue-like cloud. The afternoon sun picked out the shape of each battered red stone, the swell of each pewter-blue wave, the bright paint of the boats that were transporting cargo, and carrying tourists, and searching for Roger Dempsey's body.

Her thoughts were more dazed than calm. She felt the bone-chilling cold of the water, the brush against her leg, the men dragging her into the inflatable. She felt the warm blankets and the hot tea that had tingled in her fingertips and toes. She saw the ambulance, maybe the same one she'd seen Saturday night. This time Alasdair was sitting across from her, his face white, strained, closed, and Brendan was standing by the door wearing a blanket like a toga, Kirsty pressed against his side. She heard the worried voices, Hugh, Gunn, Iris, Noreen.

She saw her clothes making a teal puddle on the floor of the bathroom in the Lodge. And she saw herself tossing and turning all night without hearing a single ghostly noise. Perhaps Ambrose, Edith, and Eileen's confession, teased from them by the critical mass of two watchers, had been good for their souls.

Jean saw the dawn creep across the loch, and heard her phone ringing again and again — Michael and Rebecca and Miranda, was she all right, was Alasdair all right? "Well then," said Miranda, "if you throw yourself into Loch Ness of ill repute to save the man's life, I'm thinking the pair of you, you're an item."

Jean did not disagree.

"Mind you, Peter Kettering is by way of making lemonade from the lemons you handed him — he's auctioning off the rights to his eye-witness account of the entire weekend, let alone the stramash on the boat. *Great Scot* isn't bidding."

Jean heard her own voice saying, "Thank you." And she saw the newspapers, her own body in black and white, looking like a drowned rat. But of the four people who had gone into the water last night, only one had drowned. Loch Ness had given up Jonathan Paisley's body, but Jean doubted it would ever relinquish Roger Dempsey's.

Breaking the surface of her own thoughts, she inhaled the fresh air, licked the crumbs of scone and jam from her lips, and drank deep of the rich, sweet, milky tea. Her backup pair of glasses steamed up.

When they cleared, she could see Alasdair seated next to her, and Iris across the table. It was all over but the shouting, and neither of them was likely to shout.

Iris was caught in her own reverie, her knitting motionless in her gnarled hands, her weathered face turned to the far hills, still as a plaster death mask.

Alasdair gazed down at the castle his ancestors had sacked. His face may have blushed in Monday's heat and light, but today his complexion was pallid, stretched tautly across the austerity of his cheekbones, and his eyes were the bleached blue of yesterday's sky. He'd been up most of the night, and to Inverness and back today. What wasn't over was the paperwork.

"Did you get everyone taken care of?" Jean asked.

"For the time being." He shook himself very slightly, as though shrugging off cold water droplets. "We've sent Martin on his way with Noreen and Elvis. The lad, he's saying he saw Nessie's head and humps in the water while Roger was holding him up on the railing. That's why he sat so still. I'm thinking he saw the wake of the boat."

"One often sees strange wave effects on the loch," said Iris, half to herself.

Jean felt the dark water closing over her head, and the black depths of the abyss beneath her, and again swam up through her own mind.

Alasdair's gaze lingered on Jean for a long moment, curious and cautious at once. If his eyes were the mirror of his soul, then he was doing some heavy-duty soul-searching. "The Bouchards now," he said, "they've finally owned that hitting you and Roger was less than an accident. Seems Roger was that horrified to learn Tracy blew up the boat, he let it slip to his collaborators, Charles and Sophie."

Jean would say something about a fraternity of thieves, but there was no point. "They got to talking about it during their boozy dinner, and when they saw me walking with Roger, they thought I was Tracy and tried to frighten her into leaving. Or even take her out."

"They meant no harm to Roger himself — he was looking out antiquities for them. But Tracy, she'd become a loose cannon. When she was killed later on that same night, they reckoned Roger to be the guilty party and tried to protect him without digging themselves any further into his hole."

"All this being the sort of thing that seems logical when you're drunk." Jean refilled Alasdair's cup, and her own, and offered the teapot to Iris.

"Thank you, no," she said, and leaned forward slightly, peering down over the terrace railing.

Jean followed the direction of her gaze. Ah, Kirsty and Brendan came strolling out of the castle and stopped on the drawbridge to embrace and nuzzle. Kids today, she thought. Or any day. Damn the emotional torpedoes, full steam ahead. But then, Brendan was the sole survivor of the Water Horse Expedition. He deserved a little consolation. And he was going to have go home to the U.S. At least she and Alasdair lived in the same country, separated by only one hundred fifty miles of motorway. They could meet for tea at some halfway point.

Meeting halfway. They were already working on that. Distance could fan a large flame or extinguish a small one.

Briskly Iris turned her sweater-in-progress around and started another row. "Have you sent Jonathan's and Tracy's bodies on to their families? I assume Tracy has family beyond — Roger."

"Jonathan's gone back to his people in England, aye. Tracy will be another day or so, the mills of the judiciary grinding right slowly."

"The Ducketts stopped in at Pitclachie to get their things," Iris said. "They're away home."

"Maybe the publicity will wring some money out of Omnium for their grandkids," Jean suggested. "A one-time settlement or something. I just hope they're not blaming themselves for Jonathan's death."

"I expect they will do. That path paved with good intentions and all. Even so, they're not as culpable in Jonathan's death as I am in Roger's. I overestimated his hold on sanity. I pushed him over the edge. Literally, in your case, Chief Inspector."

"You can't be blamed for telling the truth," Alasdair told her.

"I didn't tell the truth, not in time." Iris turned to him, her voice astringent, her eyes like steel. "He was blackmailing me, you know that. You know about my father's autobiography."

Jean nodded. So did Alasdair.

"I finally decided that Roger should not be allowed to go on, no matter the cost to me. So I denounced him. And, selfishly, I hoped that if he turned about and denounced me, the witnesses would believe his denunciation came from the same source as his identification of the bones."

"But his copy of the book . . ." Jean began.

"Was incomplete. So Kirsty told me, this morning, Brendan having told her." Iris looked down again at the young couple.

Jean saw no need to tell Iris that she and Alasdair could have told her the same thing, yesterday, if only she'd come down from her tower. It wouldn't have made any difference in the end. "Brendan never knew what Roger's hold over you was."

"His hold over you being Edith Fraser," added Alasdair.

"In part, yes." Iris secured her knitting, then reached for her basket. She pulled out the old biography of Crowley, now wrapped in a clear plastic book bag, and handed it to Jean. "This is yours."

"No, it's not. It was stolen from your cottage."

"No matter. It's no more than a curiosity, a confirmation of poor Edith's existence. Of my mother's existence, but I suppose you've twigged that as well." Her keen eyes looked from face to face with more challenge than embarrassment.

"The bones in the passage grave," Alasdair said, "they're . . ."

"Edith's. Yes. I knew once Roger exposed the tomb, he'd turn them up. And yet there were other secrets that needed protecting — or so I thought. But in the end, it's like this book. If I'd only kept it out in the open air all this time, it would never have taken on such a bad smell."

Jean tucked the book into her bag and met Alasdair's eye. *Here it comes.*

From her basket Iris drew out two more objects, a tiny velvet jeweler's box and a leather-bound book. *The Decameron*, by Boccaccio, Mandrake Press edition.

She opened it. Inside nested a simple cardboard-bound book, smaller and thinner than its protective covering. *My Life, by Ambrose Mackintosh of Pitclachie.* Entire and complete. "He wrote his — confession, if you will — in nineteen-forty-six, and had two copies printed by a printer he had patronized during his association with Mandrake Press. One was for me when I came of age in nineteen-fifty-four. The other was for Aleister Crowley. Crowley must have torn out the last chapter of his book. Perhaps his monstrous ego couldn't bear, at the end of his life, to have his disciple at last condemn his behavior. All the occult folderol, and what finally drew Ambrose's censure was Crowley's treatment of his women and his children. My father was in so many ways a traditional old gentleman."

Iris stroked the book, as though by touching it she could stroke Ambrose's hand, no matter how stained. "When Crowley died in nineteen-forty-seven, his possessions, including one of Ambrose's Pictish silver chains, were dispersed."

"It's Crowley's copy that Roger and Tracy bought from the Bouchards," said Jean. "And Charles had the chain, too."

"That's the way of it, yes." Iris opened the jeweler's box. The polished silver, marcasite, and Czech glass of the earring inside flashed like a beacon. "Eileen gave these earrings to Edith. When she died so terribly and suddenly, Eileen helped Ambrose to dispose of her — she was never properly buried, was she? Edith had long hair. They didn't realize she was wearing the earrings until they found one on the floor of the study, dislodged by her fall."

"They concealed the death for you, did they?" asked Alasdair.

"Yes. They had put it about that Eileen was expecting, that Edith was there only as a companion. No one was in attendance when I was born save the maid and the local doctor, who was a temporary locum and had never met Mrs. Mackintosh. They made a gamble, but it succeeded. And then fell to pieces with Edith's death soon after."

"They weren't able to have a child themselves," said Jean.

The corners of Iris's pale lips turned up in something that wasn't quite humor. "Ambrose never explicitly said so. Just as he never explicitly defined his relationship with Crowley. Even when he spoke of it to me, on his deathbed, he employed circumlocutions that would be laughable in today's rather overly frank world."

Not all of us, Jean thought with a glance at Alasdair, think strewing your guts in public is a good thing.

"I believe," Iris went on, "that Crowley was the love of his life. If that was the love that dare not speak its name, so be it. When Ambrose felt obliged to marry, he agreed to what was virtually an arranged match. The years passed, and Ambrose and Eileen led increasingly separate lives, quarreling over money and friends. Then Crowley cast off yet another mistress, a local woman, the sister of the mason working to restore the cottage. Edith Fraser. She was pregnant. Eileen wanted a child and Ambrose needed an heir. The three of them struck a bargain."

"Hang on," said Alasdair. "Edith was pregnant when she came to Pitclachie?"

Iris looked into his face, then into Jean's, sparing herself nothing. "Ambrose was my father. He cared for me. We were estranged for a time, after I came of age and read his book, but . . . Well. We made our peace before his death. And yes, Miss Fairbairn, Chief Inspector Cameron, it's not only the truth about Edith's death that is in last chapter of the book, but of her life. The truth that I thought needed concealing. The identity of my genetic father, Aleister Crowley."

Whoa, Jean thought, and caught the flicker in Alasdair's eye. So much for biological determinism. "What happened to Eileen?" she asked softly.

"Edith's death convinced her to cut her losses and start over. She was still a young woman, mind. She returned to the United States and obtained a divorce on grounds of non-consummation — whether truthfully or not, I can't say. She re-married, and died surrounded by her children and grandchildren in nineteen-eighty-five."

Jean knew Alasdair was hearing Edith's ghostly voice: You dinna care, not for her, not for me, only for him, the Devil take him and good luck to them both! And, A divorce, I'm thinking, there's grounds right enough.

"You've met Eileen, then?" he asked.

"Yes. She told me that after Edith's death she'd had enough. But she and Ambrose knew that a public divorce would have brought out my true parentage. Therefore, they arranged for her to simply disappear, an assumed suicide. They never suspected he would be charged with her murder. But the scarf she had wrapped about Edith's poor wounded head blew away in the wind, and was found. Eileen would have reappeared to save Ambrose from the hangman, but, in the event, that was not necessary." Iris looked down at her hands, folded in her lap. "The maid, by the by, accepted a considerable settlement for her silence and emigrated to Australia. We exchanged letters before her death."

Kirsty and Brendan were ambling up the sidewalk toward them, Jean saw. They lived in a different world than Ambrose's. The only thing constant in life was change, yes, and yet the more things changed . . .

"My father, Ambrose," said Iris, "was at heart an intelligent, imaginative man who wanted something beyond the life he had been given. And yet he risked everything to protect me, to provide for me. He took care to have a will written that left Pitclachie to me. Full stop. That I am not biologically related to him makes no matter."

No, Jean thought, it doesn't.

"He was a bit cracked, yes. When he saw the remains of the shark, he thought they came from the loch, and then, half-crazed with guilt after the events of nineteen-thirty-three, he imagined he saw the creature still living there. Even after he lost his faith in Crowley as a man, still he believed in him as a mage. It comforted my father to think that there is another side of life, one that we cannot see but is there for us nevertheless. He turned to the occult. I, on the other hand, turned to science."

"And Gordon Fraser?" asked Alasdair.

"The Dempseys had no call involving him. It's as well they did, though, as it spurred me to visit him and own the truth. I hope that in time Edith's bones will be released as well, Chief Inspector, so that her family can take her back, and see her through to the other side of their own beliefs."

How carefully, Jean thought, had Fraser phrased his answers, so as not to betray his cousin Iris.

"The greatest irony of all is that nowhere in my father's book did he reveal where he discovered his hoard of Pictish treasure. Nor did he ever tell me. The treasures of this earth, they weren't important to him. They were only a means to an end." Iris picked up her knitting, finished the row, rolled up the half-completed sweater and stowed it in her basket.

Jean remembered the oversized cardigan Eileen's ghost was wearing. Perhaps Edith had knitted it for herself and then given it to her friend and protector. Did Iris know the Lodge was — had been — haunted by Ambrose's memories, and by his guilt? If she did, fine. If she didn't, well then, that didn't matter either.

Iris set the basket on her arm and rose from her chair. "Do what you wish with what I've told you, Chief Inspector."

Alasdair stood up as well. "It's none of my business, Miss Mackintosh. None at all."

Her narrow lips curved up in a smile.

"Thank you for the tea," Jean said, getting to her feet. "And for paying our admissions to the Visitor Center."

"I know when I am confronted with a fait accompli," said Iris, with the slightest of twinkles in her eye. "Making my peace with Hysterical Scotland seems minor enough, considering."

"Considering," said Alasdair.

"Well then, I must be getting on. The bookings for the week are in complete disarray, and my niece has had to do more than her share of the work."

"So I have," said Kirsty, walking up the steps onto the terrace with Brendan close beside her. Her determined grimace took in Jean and Alasdair both. "I'm sorry about the aggro with the letters, the, ah, poltergeist story and all. I should have spoken up. But I'm that tired of people teasing me for being a bit — spooky."

"That's quite understandable." One corner of Alasdair's mouth tucked in a very private smile.

Everything was understandable, added Jean. Not always excusable, but understandable. She turned to Iris. "You'll be hearing from the Museum of Scotland about the passage grave and the top half of the Stone."

"Yes, now that the multitudes have trodden over it, it's past time to have the archaeologists in for a proper excavation. Brendan, if you'd fancy participating . . ."

Brendan, yet another of Iris's faits accompli, shook his head. "Thank you, but I'm a diver. I think Roger only hired me for protective coloring. It's really, well . . ." His voice died away.

Everyone stood for a long moment with faces averted. But if Roger Dempsey left a ghost, it wasn't walking here.

At last Iris pulled herself to attention and shooed Kirsty and Brendan toward the exit. "Miss Fairbairn, if you'd still fancy an interview, feel free to ring me. Until then, good-bye."

"Good-bye," Jean called to them all, and looked at Alasdair.

He was watching her. She might once have thought that his expression was cool and correct, but now she saw it for what it was, a mask. Thick as a glacier, but still a mask. She said, "Let's walk down to the castle."

Silently they walked down to the castle and through the entrance tunnel, along with tourists for whom modern Scotland was little more than a theme park built on the calcified remains of history. How many of them, Jean wondered, had the knowledge and the will to thread the labyrinth of myth? And yet they still wanted to see for themselves. Mankind needed mystery to blunt the edges of reality and demonstrate its limits. Like Ambrose and his passion for Crowley, and the upper room where he had enacted his self-conscious, self-created rites. Like Jean herself, taking up residence at the intersection of fantasy and reality.

At a low wall overlooking the loch, Jean and Alasdair stopped and stood at ease. Below them the water rippled and frothed and heaved with mighty secrets. At last Alasdair said, voice rasping, "My jumping on him, it might could have made Roger drop the lad. They could be looking out his body in the loch. They could be looking out yours."

So that was it. He was doubting his vocation. Again. And she'd thought he might be doubting the relationship that left them hostages to fortune. "Roger would have dropped him anyway. You did what you had to do. And you tried to save Roger."

"All the way down to the water, he was shouting, sorry, sorry, sorry. Not so much to me, I'm thinking, as to everyone. To the Ducketts' son-in-law, and Jonathan, and Tracy. I reckon he never intended to survive. Suicide by loch."

Jean shuddered. "He never intended to kill anyone. Tracy never intended to kill anyone. One thing led to another and to another, and there they were."

"You're not blaming yourself, are you now?" Alasdair asked, with a sideways glance sharp as a scalpel.

"Everything I was afraid of happening, happened. And yet, here we are, you and me. Maybe it's one of those strong in the broken places things. Maybe it's just selfish."

"Maybe it is that, aye." He looked out over the water, his profile slicing the distant mountains.

She'd go back home and have nightmares and second and triple-guess herself, Jean thought. She'd continue to jump at every noise. But she did feel stronger. Or resigned to her fate, which might be the same thing. Alasdair, though, had a strong shell to begin with. How many wedges were now prying apart its fissures?

From the tower of the castle came the skreel of the pipes. Not the twee tourist standards but something livelier, an age-old war cry or a modern rant in the ancient tradition, in-your-face, up-your-spine. The music flowed across the loch, its echo off the opposite bank a ghostly undertone. Far below, a tourist boat presented its stern to the castle so the passengers could take photos. Jean waved.

She turned to Alasdair with a determined smile. "It was an unexpected treat seeing you in a kilt again."

"I'm owing Hamish for a new one, I reckon." And he, too, chose to smile.

"Maybe you can bring your own to Edinburgh. There's a restaurant called The Witchery just up from my flat. It's not cheap, but then, a posh dinner would do us good." Jean didn't ask herself just what she had in mind for afters.

Alasdair's brows registered but passed on the same question. "It's my shout, then. You saved my life."

"We made a deal. I wasn't going to let you get out of it that easily." And she had to ask the deal-breaking question, "You're not upset, are you, that you were rescued by a girl?"

"Don't go any dafter than you are already," he retorted, and then, miraculously, he laughed. The frown lines in his face eased and his eyes glinted like the sky peeking through storm clouds. "You're away to Edinburgh just now?"

"I'm all packed and ready to go. I can stop off in Inverness, though . . ."

Alasdair's phone rang. With an apologetic shrug, he answered it. "Cameron. Oh. Yes, sir."

Sir? The next rung of command was calling to congratulate Alasdair on another case well-solved.

His lips tightened, freezing out their smile. Every line in his face deepened. Frost crept down from his hairline. "Yes, sir. I'll be there directly."

"What is it?" asked Jean, her heart sinking.

"Andy Sawyer was transcribing Gunn's notes, and found the ones you made. Gunn admitted you were sitting in on the interviews — and so he should have done, it's no secret. But now Sawyer's filed a report with the Chief Constable saying I've violated procedures." Alasdair thrust his phone into his pocket so sharply Jean was surprised it didn't rip right through the cloth. "I'd not have solved the case without you. And it was my decision to let you in, in any event."

"So the Chief Constable's called you on the carpet?"

"It's not as bad as all that. I'll sort it. And I'll sort Andy while I'm at it. But that means going, now." He lunged away from the wall and down the sidewalk, Jean hurrying along behind.

In the darkness of the entrance passage, below the vaulted roof no longer hidden by a ceiling pierced by murder holes, he stopped and spun around. Jean changed course so quickly she stumbled. Alasdair caught her and pulled her close. "Here I am rushing off again, without properly taking my leave."

"I'm out of practice with this relationship stuff, too," she returned, wrapping her arms around his chest so snugly she felt the phone in his pocket pressing into her breast. And she heard herself say, as she had once before, "Have you ever considered quitting the police force?"

"What should I do with myself, then?" This time the question was less a challenge than a plea.

"Miranda was saying something the other day — I don't remember — she'll find you something."

"Right."

Light gleamed behind them, and light before them, but for just this moment they were alone in the shadows. Their lips met, gently, firmly, and they touched foreheads, drinking in each others' breaths, each others' electricity. He murmured something, something she swore was *Bonny Jean*, but he had already released her and walked away. "I'll be phoning you," he called over his shoulder.

Jean stood where the long-vanished portcullis had once closed off the castle, watching him stride up the walk and into the doorway of the Visitor Center. The sound of the pipes mimicked the thrumming of the blood in her veins.

"Right!" she called after Alasdair, and began her own trek home.

ABOUT THE AUTHOR

Lillian Stewart Carl has published multiple novels and multiple short stories in multiple genres. Her work blends mystery, romance, and fantasy, has plots based on history and archaeology, and often features paranormal themes. She enjoys exploring the way the past lingers on into the present, especially in the British Isles, where she's visited many times.

The Murder Hole is her thirteenth novel, book two in the Jean Fairbairn/Alasdair Cameron series: *The Secret Portrait*; *The Murder Hole*, *The Burning Glass*, *The Charm Stone* and *The Blue Hackle*.

Three of her twenty-five published short stories have been reprinted in *World's Finest Crime and Mystery Stories* anthologies. Eleven have been collected in *Along the Rim of Time* and thirteen more in *The Muse and Other Stories of History, Mystery, and Myth*.

Lillian is the co-editor, with John Helfers, of *The Vorkosigan Companion*, a collection of essays and other material on the science fiction work of Lois McMaster Bujold.

All of her work is available in electronic form from www.fictionwise.com and other venues.

Her web site is www.lillianstewartcarl.com

Made in the USA
San Bernardino, CA
28 October 2012